'A quirky tale of love, work and the meaning of life'
Company

'A smart, witty love story'
Observer

'Full of laugh-out-loud observations . . .
utterly unputdownable'
Woman

'Gorgeous location, dancing dialogue and
characters you'll fall in love with. Irresistible!'
Jill Mansell

'Cheery and heart-warming'
Sunday Mirror

'A Colgan novel is like listening to your best pal,
souped up on vino, spilling the latest gossip –
entertaining, dramatic and frequently hilarious'
Daily Record

'An entertaining read'
Sunday Express

By Jenny Colgan

Mure

The Summer Seaside Kitchen
A Very Distant Shore
(novella)
The Endless Beach
An Island Christmas
Christmas at the Island Hotel
An Island Wedding

Kirrinfief

The Little Shop of
Happy Ever After
The Bookshop on the Shore
Five Hundred Miles from You

Little Beach Street Bakery

Little Beach Street Bakery
Summer at
Little Beach Street Bakery
Christmas at
Little Beach Street Bakery
Sunrise by the Sea

Cupcake Café

Meet Me at the Cupcake Café
Christmas at the Cupcake Café

Sweetshop of Dreams

Welcome to Rosie Hopkins'
Sweetshop of Dreams
Christmas at
Rosie Hopkins' Sweetshop
The Christmas Surprise

The Little School by the Sea

Class
Rules
Lessons

West End Girls
Operation Sunshine
Diamonds Are a
Girl's Best Friend
The Good, the Bad
and the Dumped
The Loveliest
Chocolate Shop in Paris
Amanda's Wedding
Talking to Addison
Looking for Andrew McCarthy
Working Wonders
Do You Remember
the First Time?
Where Have All the Boys Gone?
The Christmas Bookshop

By Jenny T. Colgan

Resistance Is Futile   Spandex and the City

Jenny Colgan is the author of numerous bestselling novels, including *The Little Shop of Happy Ever After* and *Summer at Little Beach Street Bakery*, which are also published by Sphere. *Meet Me at the Cupcake Café* won the 2012 Melissa Nathan Award for Comedy Romance and was a *Sunday Times* top ten bestseller, as was *Welcome to Rosie Hopkins' Sweetshop of Dreams*, which won the RNA Romantic Novel of the Year Award 2013. Jenny lives in Scotland. She can be found on Twitter at @jennycolgan and on Instagram at @jennycolganbooks.

JENNY COLGAN

An Island Wedding

SPHERE

SPHERE

First published in Great Britain in 2022 by Sphere

1 3 5 7 9 10 8 6 4 2

Copyright © 2022 by Jenny Colgan

'Another Day', music and lyrics by Roy Harper, quotation appears
by kind permission of Roy Harper and District 6 Music

Map copyright © 2017 by The Flying Fish Studios

The moral right of the author has been asserted.

A CIP catalogue record for this book
is available from the British Library.

HB ISBN 978-0-7515-8036-5
C format 978-0-7515-8037-2

Typeset in Caslon by M Rules
Printed and bound in Great Britain by Clays Ltd, Elcograf, S.p.A.

Papers used by Sphere are from well-managed forests
and other responsible sources.

Sphere
An imprint of
Little, Brown Book Group
Carmelite House
50 Victoria Embankment
London EC4Y 0DZ

An Hachette UK Company
www.hachette.co.uk

www.littlebrown.co.uk

To Andrea MacDonald, whose commitment to keeping an affordable Highland dance school open and running for the children of Fife, both throughout the pandemic and beyond, is an absolute inspiration

Introduction

Hello there!

And welcome to the island of Mure. It is, I will tell you, writing this, a blustery spring day, and the sun keeps popping its head in and out of the clouds and then changing its mind. I wanted to write a few quick words if you're new, or actually even if you've read other Mure books: we're all so busy and have a lot going on.

So! Here is a quick reprise just so you are up to date. (I find it particularly tricky reading on download if I have to check who somebody is and it's hard just to flick back a few pages.) Also, I am not crazy about books that do it all in exposition – you know the kind of thing I mean:

'Hey, Peter! How's your sister Jane?'

'Jane, my younger sister of age twenty-eight, you mean? Who just lost both legs in a terrible traffic accident in Minsk?'

'Yes, that's the one. The one whose wedding we – by which I mean you and me plus your brother John, thirty – are all here to celebrate.'

So I am going to get you up to speed, whether you've just joined us (welcome!) or whether you have just finished reading all the others.

Okay, Flora MacKenzie moved back to the tiny island of Mure, off the north-eastern coast of Scotland, where she grew up, after her mother died. Her father and three brothers still run the family farm there. She opened the Seaside Kitchen, a small café, and has now taken over the fancy Rock hotel following the death of its proprietor, Colton.

She is also engaged to be married to Joel, her complicated American boss from London, who was raised in a series of foster homes and has found settling down something of a challenge. They have a baby called Douglas who is now almost one.

Lorna MacLeod is the primary school headmistress, who is having a secret relationship with Saif Hassan, the local GP, who is a refugee from Syria. They are nuts about each other. His two sons are on the island (and attend Lorna's school). His wife was lost in the war in Syria; Saif has recently seen a photograph in which she appears to be not only remarried, but pregnant.

Of Flora's brothers, the widowed Fintan is very relieved he doesn't have to run the Rock any more; Innes is giving his marriage another shot while trying to raise his daughter Agot; and Hamish is just being Hamish. He doesn't change very much.

And okay, I think we are all caught up!

Normally I like writing books, but if I had the chance to make films, now you would definitely see one of those little breezes, just a little one, that comes out of nowhere, and it would flap the pages a tiny bit . . . and there would be a salty tang to the air, and suddenly I would have one of those soaring camera shots – you know the ones I mean, that go really fast over the sea, faster and faster, zooming towards a tiny dot in the distance, that becomes bigger and bigger on the horizon, a cool breeze blowing even under sunny morning skies, a great long stretch of golden sand appearing that reveals itself to be the Endless Beach, followed by a lighthouse and then the Rock, right at the top, and on the other south side of the beach, you can make out a jumble of little friendly buildings in different colours – red, yellow, pink – and the slightly faded black and white of the old Harbour's Rest hotel. And now you are slowing, just gently dipping over the top of the fishermen's clattering masts with their jolly flags, and now you are being deposited gently on the grey cobbled wharf, just in front of where the Caledonian MacBrayne ferry is puttering up on its first run of the day, with papers and parcels ready to be unloaded from the mainland, with the captain looking out on the wharf, manoeuvring carefully. Bramble the dog is padding past with the paper in his mouth, heading back to Eck, Flora's dad, at MacKenzie farm, and the door of the pink building – the Seaside Kitchen – is already open, and you can already hear BBC nan Gàidheal playing some fiddle music inside, and smell good coffee and fresh cheese scones, so you may as well come in and sit down for a while, next to the Fair Isle knitting group, take a little break for yourself and watch the comings and goings at the harbour – welcome back to Mure.

Love,

Jenny

x x x x x

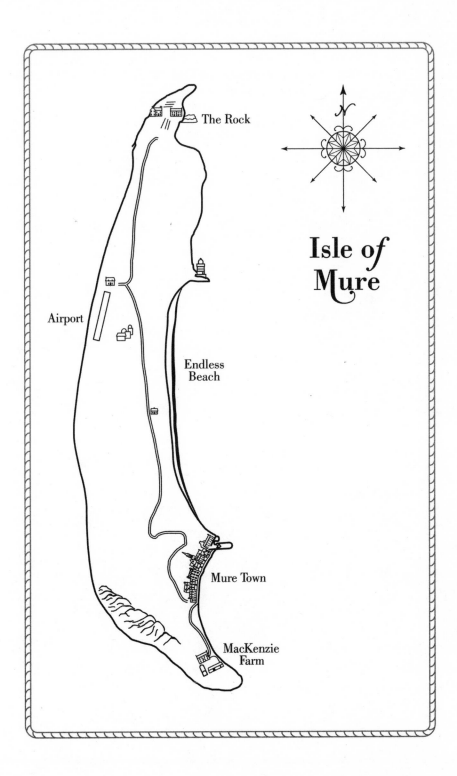

The Rock

Airport

Endless
Beach

Mure Town

MacKenzie
Farm

Isle of
Mure

'I loved you a long time ago, you know
Where the wind's own forget-me-nots
    blow, you know'

'Another Day', Roy Harper

Chapter One

It was the tail-end of March, and the Rock hotel on Mure was booked absolutely solid. The visitors had got lucky too: the end of the Atlantic storms had brought snow and ice well into the third month of the year, but for the last week the sun had shone bright every day.

As long as you had a decent coat and some stout shoes (the hotel would of course lend you some wellingtons), the island looked glorious: the sand on the Endless Beach was so pale it was practically white, the water lapping turquoise and clear, the sky huge and blue as a child's painting. The little brightly painted houses lopsidedly leaning against each other in the harbour were jolly and gay, and the fishing boats were freshly painted and eager to take to the waves.

'It is absolutely. Sodding. Freezing,' said Flora, stepping out into the bright sunshine, going round to check the gardens around the back of the house, where the daffodils were in full bloom.

Her fiancé Joel, on the other end of the phone, let out a barking laugh.

'It's because you heat that hotel so much you've got soft.'

Flora sighed. This was almost certainly true. In the MacKenzie farmhouse, where she'd grown up, the windows were single-paned and draughty and you had to hurtle to the damped-down peat kitchen fire every morning, your feet freezing on the icy stone, to stir it up again, then heat your chilled fingers around a warm, strong cup of tea.

The Rock, on the other hand, a huge old grey stone building, had been converted into a hotel by a rich Texan who couldn't bear discomfort of any kind. The traditional-style windows were triple-glazed; a heat pump had been installed, giving out vast amounts of cheap energy; and every bathroom had underfloor heating. There were thick rugs and cosy blankets everywhere, as well as deep carpets in the library and sitting rooms. Colton, Flora's brother Fintan's late husband, had basically compared living at the very northern tip of the British Isles to living in a ski resort, and built accordingly. Except, as a newcomer to Scotland, he had gone for what he thought would be a design to blend in with the locals, and as a result there was tartan carpet of deep greens and blues and stags' heads everywhere. At first, Flora had thought it was naff and ridiculous. Now, she rather loved it. It reminded her of Colton every time she strolled the long corridors or opened the door to the restaurant (then quickly shut it again, if Gaspard the temperamental chef was shouting at someone in the kitchen).

She found her way round to the side of the hotel which faced the water; there was a little dock there, and many people arrived by boat. The gardens by the wall hosted a suntrap the wind could not reach, and they had benches for people to sit and watch the big boats go by in the distance, on their long journeys up and over to the fjords. In the direct sun, it was incredibly pleasant. She sat down for two seconds' break from the endless demands of running a hotel and a café – nobody could see her from here, but it wasn't hiding exactly – and she continued her conversation with Joel.

'How's it going?'

Joel sighed in a way that indicated he didn't think he'd be back soon. He administered Colton's trust fund, which had contributed to the development of a global vaccination programme. It had made him busier than they had ever thought possible, particularly after he'd moved to Mure for a quiet life.

'That well?' said Flora, glancing at her watch. It was 6 a.m. where he was, in Mexico City.

'It is going well,' said Joel. 'This is a problem. They think it might be down to me.'

'Because it is,' said Flora. Joel was the best and smartest man she'd ever met, in her opinion. The rest of the world catching up to this fact didn't surprise her in the slightest.

Joel harrumphed. 'I think several thousands of actual scientists might have something to say about that. Anyway. I am desperate to get home.'

Flora looked out at the sea. It was habit, scanning the horizon for whales. There was a pod due, she felt it in her bones, though the horizon was choppy but clear. Everyone on the island knew the MacKenzie women were descended from selkies, the seal people. It was clear as day in their pale hair and translucent eyes; creatures who came from the sea, who might one day return. Of course it was absolute nonsense, Flora would harrumph. Nonetheless, there was no denying she did have a connection with the wild creatures around the shores of

3

the island. She did feel a kinship, particularly with the whales. But surely every islander felt that way, she told herself.

'Come back before the whales come,' she said. 'Then the whole of summer will be ahead of us.'

'Okay, my selkie girl,' said Joel, smiling to himself. He liked thinking of Flora as a sea spirit sometimes. Joel himself, although he had used to be a keen lap swimmer, did not like the deep seawater at all. He kept this from everyone but Flora, and was trying to get over it by joining the RNLI.

'I'd better get back to it.'

'Be careful,' said Flora frowning. 'Is it dangerous where you are?'

She could hear the smile in Joel's voice.

'Everywhere is dangerous compared to Mure,' he said. 'It's not rational, what you think is dangerous.'

That was true. Ewan Clark, the local policeman, worked pretty much full time on his farm, was only occasionally called to an altercation outside the Harbour's Rest hotel late on market day, or to sort out some optimistic parking by tourists who didn't quite understand that the strong discouragement to bring cars over on the ferry also applied to them. Children roamed free most of the year, and everyone knew everyone else, more or less.

'How's Douglas? Walking yet?'

'Stop pressuring Douglas!'

All the MacKenzies had been, apparently, 'nine-month walk-ers' and, now that Douglas was almost one, the pressure was on.

'No, I don't want him to walk! I want to be there!'

'Oh well. In that case, he's pretty much still all drool and snot.'

'Good, good,' said Joel, who as someone who had never known much parenting himself had nonetheless turned into the most devoted father imaginable. 'Also, we need to talk about ... Oh, it can wait.'

'What?' said Flora, sitting up straighter. Nothing good ever came from the phrase 'we need to talk' in her experience. 'What do we have to talk about? What?'

'Oh, nothing, honestly; wait till I'm back.'

'That's not for days! And now I will panic and think it's something bad.'

'It's nothing bad,' said Joel. 'At least I don't think so.'

'What? Oh my God oh my God oh my God *what*?'

'Nothing! Honestly!'

'TELL ME!'

'When I'm home . . . Can we talk about the wedding?'

'*Our* wedding?'

'No,' said Joel, 'all those other weddings I take a deep and abiding interest in. Probably a Kardashian one.'

Flora headed into her office after the phone call, wondering what he meant exactly – presumably he didn't mean 'cancel' the wedding if he was making jokes about the Kardashians, but even so. He'd proposed at Christmas, and it had just been wonderful and gorgeous and there seemed no reason to delay having it this summer – but he had been rather cagey about discussing actual wedding details and the like. Flora would have been perfectly happy if he had said 'do what you like' given she had a hotel, a chef and a lot of good pastry at her disposal, but he hadn't said that either. And if they did want to do it this summer, they had better get moving . . .

She looked out at the north end of the Endless Beach. Tourists had taken up residence in wildly optimistic swimsuits and more realistic windbreakers. Every so often someone would dare go up and touch the water, pale blue as a Caribbean shore, lapping gently up to the perfect white sands – then jump back in absolute horror as they felt the temperature. Flora smiled. It didn't really matter how hot the sun shone: it was still the North Atlantic. They had lots of so-called wild swimmers who turned up all winter with lots of expensive kit and huge dry robes talking about how wild swimming was amazing and had completely changed their lives and how fantastic it was, before running in and out for five minutes. On Mure, they just called it swimming.

The phone rang in the office the second she opened the door, and Flora looked out of the window as she picked it up. Oh, there they were – she thought she'd run into them on her way to the garden. Eck, her dad, and Hamish, one of her three brothers, were trying to persuade Douglas into a standing position. Agot, the daughter of Flora's brother Innes, who had followed her in, looked out and sniffed dismissively.

'That Baby is RUBBISH at walking. *Tha e gòrach.*' Agot was learning Gaelic at school and liked to mutter in it, particularly remarks too cheeky to say aloud.

Flora's funny, serious-looking baby, the spit of his dad, was sitting in the grass, toggled up in the nine layers of knitted wool considered essential by Mure knitters, i.e., most of the population, and eyeing them suspiciously. It was a look Flora knew well from his father, and it said 'whatever you think you're talking about, I'm going to do exactly what I think is right in my own good time'. It was what made Joel an excellent lawyer and an occasionally frustrating partner.

Still, they made a pretty sight, three generations of MacKenzie boys – plus Bramble of course, who was looking

6

for the muddiest patch of the flower beds to roll in, and avoiding the enthusiastic attentions of Bjårk Bjårkensson, the huge and rambunctious kitchen dog. They really shouldn't have a kitchen dog, Flora thought, for the nine thousandth time, as she answered the phone.

'Hello? The Rock hotel.'

'Yah, hello?'

The voice was calm and flat. It was, from the first syllable, a voice that sounded used to getting its own way.

'Am I speaking to the proprietor of the Rock hotel?'

Flora's heart sank. Whatever they were selling, she didn't want to buy it and couldn't afford it anyway.

'Yes, hello, this is Flora, but we're not really in the—'

'Jan MacArthur gave me your number.'

Ah. Jan MacArthur née Mathison Jan was a local woman who ran camping and survival courses and had an entirely inexplicable dislike of Flora, who had got off with her husband years ago. Way before they were married, in fact, but somehow this didn't seem to let Flora off the hook.

'Oh, great!' Flora said brightly.

'Actually, she tried to discourage me, but I'd seen your article ...'

A journalist had come to the hotel last Christmas to sneer, but had ended up thoroughly enjoying herself and had written a massive rave.

'Anyway. I want to talk to you about weddings.'

Flora was ready for this.

'I'm sorry, we don't do weddings,' she said apologetically.

The plan was that soon they absolutely would do weddings; they got called all the time about them, and a more photogenic spot could barely be imagined. Once Flora was confident that the hotel, which had only been open for three months, could handle it, that Gaspard wouldn't have a meltdown, that guests wouldn't throw up in the flowerbeds, that they could serve a hundred people at the same time, then she was definitely going to start running it as a wedding venue. She and Joel were going to get married first – well, at least, that was the plan – as a test run, and after that they'd go for it.

But there was a little more to it than that: she couldn't forget Colton and Fintan's wedding. It had been the most glorious day, the most perfectly planned occasion, wonderful in every way – weather, food, guests, toasts, speeches, everything a dream under a bright blue sky – and it hadn't saved him from the cancer that had spent the following year eating him from the inside out, breaking Fintan's heart in the process. It had made everyone a little superstitious.

'Jan said you would make an exception for us? My name is Jacinth; I'm calling on behalf of her sister?'

Flora's eyes went wide.

'*Olivia?*'

'Yah!'

Chapter Two

'Oh my God, Olivia Mathieson!' said Flora, heading into the farmhouse to return Agot, who absolutely was not meant to go to the hotel after school, but was supposed to go straight back to the farmhouse. Unfortunately, she was a great favourite in the hotel kitchens, where Gaspard was trying to develop her palate and would make her try olives, anchovies, ducks' hearts, raw garlic and whatever else was in season. She would then return and try to get her uncle Fintan to make his cheese stinkier, to everyone's annoyance apart from Bramble's.

Flora's oldest brother Innes, the day's work done, was lying stretched out on the sofa and Flora perched Douglas on top of him, where he immediately started pulling at his uncle's buttons. The cold sunlight streamed through the windows, making the room, with its shabby rugs, old family photos, piles of back copies of *Farmers Weekly* and chipped earthenware on the Welsh dresser, look pleasant and inviting.

'Your baby's an idiot, sis,' said Innes without getting up,

but caressing Douglas's face fondly nonetheless. 'He still can't walk. Every MacKenzie baby is a nine-month walker. Every single one!'

'He'll walk when he wants to walk!'

'Maybe he could crawl around with brushes strapped to him and clean out the high barn.'

'Shut up,' said Flora as Douglas held up his chubby arms again for his mother, although, as Flora always thought, with a slightly disappointed air that she wasn't his beloved father. Between Eck, Joel and Flora's three brothers, Douglas had a very man-heavy existence. It would have been nice to get his cousin Agot involved, but Agot hated him with a deadly and unrelenting commitment.

'I think That Baby has done some poo,' she said now, wrinkling her tiny nose. 'I can't believe we have something in this house that does poo. Bramble doesn't even do poo in the house, and he's a *dog*.'

'Stop talking about poo,' said Innes lazily.

'Poo poo poo,' said Agot instantly. 'Poo poo poo poo poo.'

'I'll change Douglas,' said Flora, picking him up.

'Hang on,' said Innes. 'Did you say Olivia Mathieson?'

He sat up suddenly.

'Um yes,' said Flora over her shoulder, carrying Douglas to the bathroom. Innes got up and followed her.

'Wow!' he said. 'I haven't seen Olivia for ... God. Since school.'

'Jan never even mentions her. I thought she was a myth ... You know you are allowed to change my baby,' said Flora, looking at the bomb disposal site that was Douglas's nappy. Innes bid a hasty retreat.

Agot was still singing the poo song when Flora came back in with a sweetly scented baby to find Innes rapidly scrolling on the farmhouse's ancient laptop.

'She's not on Facebook,' he said, a slightly dreamy look on his face.

'I never knew her; she'd left for boarding before I got to big class. But she was famous even then,' mused Flora.

'Olivia Mathieson,' said Innes again in a slightly reverential tone, then looked around guiltily. His wife, Eilidh, was out having a drink with Inge-Britt at the Harbour's Rest.

'What's she like? Why does Jan not talk about her? I don't think I really connected them until just now. I didn't know Jan then either. No loss.'

Innes smiled to himself. 'Oh, it wasn't ever easy for Jan, having a sister like Olivia.'

'Why not?' said Flora, intrigued.

'Prettiest girl on the island,' said Innes. 'For miles around, I mean. High school too.'

Flora bristled.

'Yes, but is she *nice*?'

Innes shrugged.

'Dunno.'

'Did you ever go out with her?'

Innes had been quite the island lothario in his day. He shook his head sadly.

'Nope. I always thought I might have a chance, but she was very clear she wasn't interested in island boys. Hardly ever here. And you know Malcy: he's got money, you know.'

Indeed, the Mathiesons were the richest family on the island. Or at least they had been, till some awkward development with Bitcoin nobody quite understood. Flora had had quite the run-in with Malcy, the patriarch, the previous Christmas when he had tried to have the island statue pulled down.

But time had worn them down: if you didn't patronise the

Rock for your birthday lunch or the Seaside Kitchen for your sandwiches and pastries, you were going to be on fairly thin pickings as far as eating on Mure was concerned, and with a great deal of huffing and puffing, Malcy and the rest of the family had gradually sidled back in, making a great show of criticising the drinks, Flora always noticed, if they could find something without enough ice in it. They never complained about the food as a) there was very rarely anything to complain about and b) they were terrified of Gaspard.

'What kind of a famous lothario are you?' said Flora, as Innes immediately threw a cushion at her.

'Shut up!' He smiled. 'So anyway, what's she up to?'

'She wants to get married at the Rock.'

'Who does?' said Fintan, wandering in from the dairy and washing his hands down in the big old butler's sink. 'Hey, Douglas! Hey, Agot!'

'Poo!'

Fintan glanced at Innes, who held his hands up innocently.

'Agot, how old are you?' said Fintan gravely. 'Are you a big girl of six or are you a tiny baby who says silly words all the time?'

'I am poo years old,' said Agot, and Fintan gave up.

'Who is getting married at the Rock?' he asked again.

'Olivia Mathieson.'

Fintan burst out laughing and clutched his hands to his chest in a faux swoon.

'Ooooh, not Olivia Mathieson, loveliest little lady in the whole damn island!'

'I swear to God I never saw her around,' said Flora.

'That's because she vanished the second she could. Got the hell out of Dodge. And so did you, if I recall.'

Flora harrumphed.

'Didn't she go off to be a fashion model or something? She never ever comes back.'

'That's a shame.'

'Neither did you!' said Fintan, until Flora hushed him with a look.

'I bet she's not marrying anyone local,' said Innes, opening two beers and handing one to Fintan, who took it gratefully.

'Where's my beer?' said Flora.

'Oh, aren't you breastfeeding?'

'Not for, like, *four months*!' said Flora, wishing not for the first time that there were a few more females in her family. Fintan fetched her a beer, which Flora didn't really want, but she didn't like being left out.

'Who is she marrying then?'

'I didn't ask,' said Flora. 'In the scheme of weddings, grooms aren't actually that important.'

'I didn't find that,' said Fintan, and a look passed over his face that was so sad. It hadn't even been two years since Colton had died; it would be this summer that their wedding day had dawned, so glorious in the sunset in the grounds of his own home.

'Sorry, bro,' said Flora softly.

Fintan shrugged.

'Aye well, it is what it is.'

Innes was staring at his laptop and scowling.

'I can't believe Mure finally gets enough internet to run Facebook and everyone immediately leaves Facebook.'

'It'll be Instagram,' said Flora, trying to manoeuvre Douglas, her beer and her phone all at the same time.

Innes made a face.

'Instagram has been very good to us,' reminded Flora. Iona,

who ran the Seaside Kitchen, spent a lot of time posting beautiful pictures of cakes interspersed with the harbour, the pretty houses and the wonderful landscapes. She might possibly also have taken most of the photographs on sunny days, thus leading to something of a false sense of security in people showing up with bikinis for their holidays.

Flora scrolled and finally found Olivia Mathieson from who Jan followed. Jan posted a lot of pictures of her round-faced baby, Christabel, and them dressed up in identical outfits. But . . .

'There she is,' said Innes immediately. 'Cor. She hasn't changed a bit.'

'She has,' said Fintan, peering over his shoulder. 'She's got better-looking.'

Olivia's 'Gram was something else. Innes whistled through his teeth. Olivia was tall and willowy, with high rounded breasts shown off to some advantage in a succession of extraordinary bikinis and swimsuits with cut-outs. Here she was getting onto what looked like a private plane. Here she was, pouting a suspiciously large mouth on the prow of a white boat. Here she was in a very expensive shop waiting as someone wrapped her up a handbag. They were almost all of her, and she was making the same pouty face or broad, evenly white grin in all of them. But there was no doubt she was swishing around the world doing some pretty amazing things – there were infinity pools and skyscrapers and LA and Hong Kong and Singapore and the hashtags #lovingmylife #blessed #beyourself.

Innes looked with some regret at the bikini shots; Fintan and Flora pointed out the expensive bags to one another. In one of the final shots, there was a picture of a ring and two hands clasped. The diamond in the ring was the size of a Lego brick.

It looked like it would break Olivia's delicate hand. The two hands – the person who had given it to her wasn't in shot at all – appeared to be clasped over the back of a yacht at sunset. It had thousands of likes.

'Bloody hell,' said Fintan.

'Oh lordy,' said Flora. 'And she wants to get married at our place.'

Flora lay awake half the night, wondering what on earth a rich Instagram influencer would expect from them, and whether or not she ought to do it. She could just say no, of course. But then, if Olivia was from the island, and wanted to come back to her roots – well, who was she to tell her she couldn't?

And if she didn't book the Rock, she might book the only other place suitable on Mure, the Harbour's Rest, and that would not be nice. It was a homey place, the Harbour's Rest, the big black and white hotel and bar on the harbour front, but run very sloppily and half falling down. Flora didn't think she could bear it. They were going to start sometime, weren't they? To be honest, they needed the money. Staffing costs were high: Gaspard in the kitchen was brilliant, but he demanded top quality produce.

And she wanted to hear the rooms of the Rock echo with laughter, with toasts and happy feelings and dressed-up people. If Olivia's friends were as beautiful as she was too, that would be something to see . . .

Half convinced, Flora dropped off, sending a goodnight kiss to Joel and mentally adding thinking about the wedding to her extremely long list of things to do the next day after baby clinic. To anyone who asked, she would say baby clinic was a waste of time as Douglas was so obviously healthy and thriving.

But secretly, like many new mothers, she rather loved any excuse to discuss her baby with anyone, even someone paid to ask her dry medical questions about him. And given how busy she was, going to baby clinic counted as a good time these days.

Chapter Three

Neda Okonjo always enjoyed arriving on Mure, particularly on sunny freezing days like this one, as the morning ferry chuntered back and forth to a stop. Normally based in Glasgow, she was in charge of refugee resettlement, and some cases went better than others.

Dr Saif Hassan's was one of their great success stories: he had taken over from the doddery old island doctor and proved a great hit in the community with his slow, patient manner, his thoroughness and gentleness. Now, as well as doing a quick check-in on his two sons, who lived with him, she was finally bringing some excellent news.

She made her way up through the little harbour streets; daffodils – already over, further south in Glasgow – were waving in full bloom from every bank. She smiled wryly at the huge angel statue someone had plonked in the middle of town, which was becoming quite the tourist attraction. It was certainly striking, the sun's rays hitting it full on, the great wings rising behind it. Mure was such a lovely place, she thought. If her job wasn't in Glasgow, and Mhairi wasn't so committed to her library job and all the restaurants and bars of the West End ... No. It was a pipe dream for them. But still. She could see its appeal.

She knew Saif's schedule well enough: he stopped work at three to pick up the boys, even though Ib pointed out that he was a Primary 7 now (he'd been held back a year as he adjusted to his new life) and absolutely didn't need to be picked up like a tiny baby, then did his house calls once they were settled with a peanut butter sandwich and *Horrible Histories* or, on days like today, the football out in the back garden while Mrs Laird kept an eye on them.

Right now, Saif had morning surgery, which was just as well because Neda had notes to write up, which she would happily do in the Seaside Kitchen with a cheese scone warm and fragrant from the oven – nowhere did a cheese scone as good – and a large mug of coffee, and her good news could wait. Then she could pop in on those lovely boys. As workdays went, this one was shaping up to be excellent.

Normally on the mainland, nurses would run baby clinic, but here on the distant and small island of Mure, they didn't have the staff, so Saif did it.

He normally enjoyed it: healthy patients were always a bonus, and he marvelled at how quickly the pregnant women turned into mothers, the bouncing bairns got their MMRs, then the next minute they were nearly ready for school. Realising how quickly the children grew up made him slightly panicky from time to time. He remembered how his wife Amena had gone to the large, noisy clinic near their home, even though he had been able to keep an eye on the boys' progress perfectly well. She had liked it, she explained, because she could see how obviously superior and more beautiful their boys were to the other babies there, and Saif had said didn't she think the other mums would be thinking the same thing and she had looked pityingly at him and said yes, it was such a shame they were so deluded and wrong.

First off, Flora MacKenzie charged in with Douglas, coming up on a year old and so like Joel with his dark curly hair and intense gaze.

Flora grinned as Saif put the baby on the scales and tested his reflexes.

'My brothers say he's an idiot because he can't walk or do very much,' she said.

'Can he sit?' said Saif, testing the hypothesis. Douglas sat up carefully, surveying the clinic like a little pasha. He stuck a little hand out for the toy giraffe Saif kept on his desk.

'He can but he can barely crawl! He just scoots along on his bum! Innes says he's a moron and is going to end up in prison.'

'This is Agot's father you speak of?' said Saif, with a slight twitch of his mouth. Agot was his son Ash's sworn best friend and defender against the world.

'Exactly! So I said, "Better a drooling moron than an evil psychopath going to take over the world." And instead of disagreeing he said, "She'll remember that when she takes over the world."'

Saif smiled, tracing his pencil in the air and watching Douglas's eyes follow it wherever it went, both pointing in the same direction. He then put headphones on the baby which was so comical Flora wanted to take a picture but was gently dissuaded

'But he's *so cute*!'

'Don't distract him please,' said Saif, testing the baby's hearing with a set of buttons. Douglas responded in the right direction.

'What words and sounds is he using?'

'*None!* Oh my God, is Innes right? Joel says just ignore him, there's nothing wrong with Douglas.'

'There is, to the best of my knowledge, nothing wrong with Douglas,' said Saif, listening to his heart, then putting a measuring tape round his head. He hid the giraffe behind his back and watched as the baby pointed towards where he thought it was.

'Good boy,' he said. 'You have nothing to worry about.'

'Except . . .'

Saif smiled and went to collect the syringe.

'I promise it's very quick,' he said.

'I know,' said Flora. 'But I hate it. Like, nothing bad has ever happened to this baby. Except when the person who loves him most in the world, the person he trusts completely, holds him down while you hurt him. I feel this is like the beginning of the end of his innocence.'

'It is also,' said Saif, tapping the syringe, 'the beginning and the end of his measles.'

Douglas looked shocked as the needle slid into his chubby thigh, but recovered after a quick yelp and a huge cuddle.

'All done,' said Saif. He looked up at Flora.

'And you,' he said, 'in yourself. How are you?'

'What do you mean, how do *I* feel?'

He shrugged. It could be a tricky question. 'How is motherhood treating you?'

'Oh!' said Flora, understanding his meaning. She grinned at Douglas, who grinned back at her, showing his five teeth.

'Well, it's exhausting, terrible, I will never ever get my hips back in my old jeans, I am weirdly grubby all the time, Joel and I never get to the end of a sentence without one of us having to get the baby or falling asleep, and I basically stopped breastfeeding like four months ago but sometimes he still likes some before he goes to sleep and I haven't the heart to refuse him – don't tell anyone – which means I will be a terrible soft parent who never gives any discipline and will raise an absolute brat and I can't focus on my relationship, my work, my friends, my home and my baby all at once so I do an absolutely terrible job at most of them.'

She smiled again.

'I absolutely love it.'

Saif nodded and made a note.

'That is all very normal.'

'Thank you, doctor,' said Flora with a grin. 'I brought you a Bakewell slice.'

'That is kind,' said Saif. There were few women on the island who didn't think he needed feeding up, but Flora's offerings were by some way the best. 'What are you up to today?'

'I am going to work, then I am going to phone Joel and then we are going to put out a joint conference call to my stupid brothers to tell them that my baby is perfect. Can I have a certificate of some kind? Perhaps a badge or a gold star to say my baby is the best?'

Saif smiled.

'That is a good idea. I should definitely give all the babies on the island grades. I think that would work very well.'

'Lorna says you're very sarcastic,' said Flora, referring to her best friend and Saif's secret girlfriend. 'But I am choosing to take you literally. See you later.'

And she walked out, holding a placated Douglas, beaming.

In the waiting room, Jan was trying to get Christabel to stop yelling and remove her from her buggy, where she was bucking and squirming and bright pink in the face. Jan had, up until twenty-four hours ago, also been feeling happy to be going to baby clinic. Christabel was gifted, and she needed Saif to see that.

Since yesterday, however, the worst had happened.

It wasn't the worst, she knew. In the scheme of things, there were almost certainly other people who would be really happy for their rich, beautiful, talented sister, whom everybody loved, to be getting married to a millionaire and coming home to rub it in everyone's faces.

They hadn't had to live with her.

One of Jan's earliest memories was an old lady coming up to Senga, her mother, pointing at Olivia and saying, 'But that one! That one is *beautiful*!' as if completely amazed. Stolid, near-sighted Jan had stood there, innocently waiting for her own compliment, which had never come.

As they had grown up, it didn't matter how well Jan did at school or how efficiently she ate her vegetables. Olivia was graceful, beautiful and sweet as pie – to everyone who wasn't Jan. As soon as the adults' backs were turned, she would pinch her big sister hard on Jan's beefy legs, then as soon as Jan complained, make her beautiful green eyes wide and brimming with tears and insist it was an accident. If Jan retaliated, things got very bad for her very fast.

Jan had learned to ignore her little sister, but as they grew that made things worse; Olivia was unendingly popular. Everyone was dying to be friends with the girl who looked like Snow White, who lived in the big house with the hot tub (so far the first and only hot tub on Mure; it had been and remained quite the sensation). Which meant that her weird, plain older sister got more and more ostracised and Olivia more and more triumphant. Finally, Jan gave up on girls all together, having more or less decided they were all evil, and found her purpose working with little boys on the Outward Adventures courses for special schools, and never mentioned her sister (her mother knew better than to mention Olivia in her presence too).

Olivia had left their tiny, parochial island as soon as she could. She had moved to London, modelled for a bit, found a nebulous kind of job in travel PR which involved her jetting off expensively to fabulous places, posting them on Instagram – and now she was engaged to someone clearly very, very wealthy, if the vast rock on her finger was anything to go by.

And suddenly she was coming back! Storming in with some presumably super-rich, super-hot lover, stomping all over Jan's turf, and it was going to be school all over again. Olivia hadn't even bothered to come to Jan's wedding, pretending to be too busy in Hong Kong, and had sent a set of Louis Vuitton luggage, incredibly expensive and something she must have known Jan, who never went anywhere, couldn't possibly use. Now Jan was in for a solid year of people wanging on about how amazing Olivia was again. Great.

'Hello,' said Flora to her in the waiting room as she left, trying to be nice and thinking, well, as usual she was not getting much back for her efforts. 'We're all done! Good luck!'

Jan looked at Douglas suspiciously, as if expecting to see something terribly wrong with him. Jeannie the receptionist glanced over.

'Okay, Miss Christabel MacArthur, you're up!'

Christabel, bright red in the face, screamed louder than ever as Jan fumbled with the straps.

'Good luck,' Flora said again, as Jan shot her a filthy look that made Flora feel slightly guilty.

'I think,' said Jan, 'she's very gifted.' Christabel hadn't stopped screaming from the moment she got into Saif's consulting room. 'She can speak and baby-sign.'

'That is very good,' said Saif, warming his stethoscope. He was intrinsically rather suspicious of baby sign, and even now Christabel was frantically waving her arms in the air and hitting out in a bit of baby sign that very clearly meant, 'GET AWAY FROM ME RIGHT NOW, STRANGE MAN!'

'Hello, little baby, do not worry,' he said softly in his gentle accent.

'She's very advanced for her age,' went on Jan stolidly. Christabel bit Saif on the finger.

'Okay,' said Saif, disengaging himself as carefully as possible and handing her back. 'Would you like to hold her facing me while I check a few things?'

He looked at Jan. Normally so in control and bossy running the camping group – his boys had taken her courses and had

had an absolutely wonderful time – she looked drab and down-trodden today. The practical short-cut grey hair looked messy rather than neat; her glasses were smeared, and her mouth was in a downward line.

She took the baby with bad grace, almost roughly, and Christabel hollered even more. Saif frowned. The contrast between Flora's harassed but easy acceptance – shared by most new mothers – was rather noticeable.

He examined the infant but kept talking to Jan.

'So, in yourself, how are you?'

There was a short pause.

'I'm fine,' snapped Jan. 'Why wouldn't I be?'

Saif frowned.

'Some people find having babies quite an … emotional experience. And can find things difficult.'

'Not me,' said Jan immediately. 'I look after children all the time. And I'm good at it too. I looked after your boys.'

'I know,' smiled Saif, keeping his voice very soft and gentle, 'and I am so grateful. They loved spending time with you.'

Jan almost told him about Olivia. There was something about the tall, thin doctor, with his huge, dark puppy-dog eyes, his palpable sense of sadness, of loneliness, that made you think he would understand. He was so gentle and careful and quiet. She very nearly did. Then Christabel let out a huge yell and she was distracted, shushing her and too tired to talk any more. She saw his concerned face and could not bear it, so ended up saying, 'I'm fine!' as he finished up testing Christabel's tracking and hearing.

'Good,' said Saif, marking quite the opposite on her notes. Just in case. 'Now she is ready for her vaccine.'

Once more, as Jan heaved a screeching Christabel back into

her arms, she wanted to tell him – to tell someone, who she knew would be kind and sympathetic – but it was pointless. In fact, worse than pointless. Now Olivia had grown up and hadn't, as Jan had hoped, betrayed her early promise and turned out to be disappointingly unattractive or suffer from untreatable boils, she didn't just have to deal with women wanting to be her friend, but also with men turning into slavering idiots with their tongues on the floor.

'Bye,' she said gruffly, as if she'd done Saif a massive favour coming into the surgery.

'Goodbye,' said Saif, genuinely worried about her.

It was, as ever, a busy morning. After three more babies in baby clinic, which was a pleasing population increase for the island in recent years, there were his regular patients.

'So.' Saif was squinting at his notes. 'You have "languishing syndrome"?'

Mattie McGuiness nodded doughtily.

'Aye, right enough.'

Saif blinked and rubbed his beard thoughtfully. He normally didn't mind people looking up symptoms on Google: it could be very useful once he'd persuaded them they almost certainly didn't have dengue fever. Other times, however, he was stumped.

'And the symptoms are . . .'

'No' really fussed to get out of bed, like? And feeling it's all a wee bit pointless, ken?'

Saif ran through the official depression and anxiety

assessment, but as far as he could tell Mattie wasn't suffering at all. In fact, in his private opinion, Mattie was suffering from a case of 'mildly fed up' but of course he wouldn't say that.

'Has anything changed in your home life?' he asked in his slow, mild way.

Mattie shrugged.

'Lambing. Little buggers. Get you up all night they do too.'

Saif smiled apologetically. He knew a little about being woken at odd hours of the night.

'I don't know how I could write you a sick note for the lambs,' he said, but Mattie was still talking, going on about how they bounded away from you so you couldn't catch them, how some of the mothers just ignored their offspring and no other mother would have them, so the abandoned lambs tore around, increasingly frantic, looking for milk and you had to either find a ewe who'd lost her lamb, slice fur off the lamb who had died and tie it on the new lamb so they caught the smell, which was impossible, or take the lamb back and hand-rear it in the house, which was worse because then they wanted to live in the house all the time and they wound up all the other animals, like the dogs, who weren't allowed in the house.

Saif realised belatedly that all unmarried Mattie needed, in fact, was a listening ear, so he kept an eye on his appointment timer and let it run down, making sympathetic nods at appropriate moments. He knew farming was a business but, like so many others, he couldn't help but be cheered when the lambs turned up, sometimes born to the cold, wild storms of the stinging tail-end of winter, but sometimes, like this week, arriving in a soft golden morning, mists rising above the meadows as he drove down to surgery from the draughty manse house where he lived. There was a bog at the bottom of Mattie's field and the braver young lambs liked to congregate there and take turns daring each other to jump over it. Ash, his youngest, thought it was the funniest thing he'd ever seen in his life.

'Aye,' said Mattie finally, finishing up.

Saif nodded.

'I ... Anything I could prescribe you would just make you feel worse,' he said. 'Like life was just passing you by. My best prescription would be a holiday, but there aren't a lot of those on the NHS.'

'Oh, I don't know,' said Mattie. 'I went to the mainland to get my knee replaced and it was like being in a hotel. Do you know they bring your meals round? And there's a TV? Four days I was in there. They said I could go home earlier, but I said, no you're all right, doll, this is heaven.'

Saif tried to figure out what was the right expression for someone whose life was so unrelenting that a stay in hospital was the best fun they'd had in years, but he didn't quite know what it was.

'I have this leaflet,' he said. Unfortunately, the leaflet – as was common to much of the centralised NHS advice – had a lot to say on the benefit of exercise. There was absolutely nothing you could tell a Mure sheep farmer about exercise. They all lived to 106.

Mattie looked over to behind Saif's computer. There was the tell-tale recycled brown cardboard box with 'Seaside Kitchen' printed on it which Flora had left.

'What's in the box, like?'

'That is not a medical question,' said Saif.

'Is it a Bakewell slice, is it?'

Silence fell. The Seaside Kitchen was a sensational local

bakery, with the lightest of pastries and pies. Everything there was a treat.

'Why are you asking?' said Saif, feeling as if this consultation was slipping away from him somewhat.

'I just ... I was thinking,' said Mattie, who had in fact thoroughly enjoyed his morning, coming into the village from his farm on the other side of the MacKenzies', popping in to see everyone, planning on finishing up at lunchtime with a pint and perhaps a game of dominoes at the Harbour's Rest, 'that do you know what I bet would see me right?'

Saif looked at him.

'A Bakewell slice?'

'Well, it's psychological, isn't it? Looking to put the zest back into life?'

'With my Bakewell slice?'

'It *is* a Bakewell slice! I knew it!'

Silence fell as the phone buzzed for Jeannie the receptionist to let him know his next scheduled meeting was here.

'You think I can cure you by giving you my Bakewell slice?'

'Worth a shot,' said Mattie.

'I didn't know you let people eat during consultations,' said Neda, breezing in in a dark business suit, her flat-top as sharp as ever, her make-up perfect, throwing everyone else in their fleeces and wellies into sharp relief. She glanced backwards at Mattie McGuiness happily munching his way down the hallway.

'Don't ask,' said Saif, his farewell smile to cunning Mattie vanishing from his face, which became guarded and wary.

Mure, the small island with its changing weather but stead-fast inhabitants, had proven the perfect place to escape the stress of war, of being a refugee, of a world that had cracked in his hands. Neda was his link to that world, and they were both aware of it. His heart started beating so quickly that he gave a sharp, betraying glance to his stethoscope coiled up in its black case on his desk.

'How are the boys?' said Neda.

'They are well ... I do not know how much Ib is looking forward to boarding.'

Mure children had to weekly board on the mainland when they reached secondary age; the Monday morning and the Friday afternoon ferries were both absolutely raucous affairs. With very few exceptions, the island children (the Faroes and the outer-island children also boarded) were fiercely loyal, tight-knit groups, who loved their time away.

Neda nodded.

'I'll speak to him about it. He's twelve though, rising thir-teen – he'll have to separate at some point.'

Saif nodded.

'I know, I know.'

Already, Ib had the ghost of a moustache on his top lip, and the occasional pimple. His glower, though, had always been with him and could not be put down to becoming to a teenager.

'Anyway,' said Neda with a smile, putting down a file on the desk, 'for once, I have good news!'

She realised her error almost immediately. What would he think? They had tracked down a picture of his wife, although not a location. She had been getting married, and was visibly pregnant. She'd looked, to Saif's eyes, happy. And she would not contact him, would not answer messages. She was, in many ways, no longer even his wife at all. The pain cut deep. He could not even think of telling the boys. How could he? She had moved on with her life, and he would not hurt his sons with that information.

'. . . Not like that,' she added quickly. 'Sorry, sweetie.'

Saif nodded shortly.

'No, it's this.' She pulled out a sheaf of papers. 'You've officially been here nearly five years . . . Now you can apply for legal residency.'

Saif blinked.

'Become a Scottish person?'

'Well, not yet, but it's a step towards citizenship. And it's British person. At the moment.' She smiled privately to herself. 'You're integrating too much.'

Saif blinked.

'And the boys . . . ?'

'So. First, you'll get your leave to stay for another five years; I think that's pretty clear. I think your usefulness is beyond question, and I'll be your sponsor. That will go straight through this summer. And at the end of that, you'll get your citizenship. Assuming you don't, you know, launch a major crime ring in the interim.'

She leaned forward.

'And you know, then the boys would have British passports – Ib will still be a dependent in five years. It's happening, Saif.'

He stared at her, taking it all in.

'They'd be safe,' she said softly.

Saif felt something shift inside him. He wasn't quite sure what it was and suddenly didn't quite trust himself to speak.

To be safe. The boys too. To have a nationality that would grant them access to the world – British people, he felt but never said, had no idea how lucky they were to be born in a rich country. They moaned and complained about the government; they never dreamed of turning on a light switch not knowing if there was electricity, or worried about being turned away from a hospital or not being able to get on a plane and go wherever they damn well pleased.

To be western Europeans, from the worst of starts – what an extraordinary hand his children would be dealt, their passport a golden ticket millions would risk their lives for. Did, every single day.

He looked at Neda directly.

'What else?' he said mildly. But he knew what was coming. He shouldn't really have to think about this now. There had to be a reason for the urgency.

'You have to do it now,' she said. One thing he liked about Neda, she never tried to pretend things were different, never lied to him. He nodded.

'You know, they are saying Damascus is safe,' said Saif. 'Have you seen the pictures? It is not even rubble. It is what comes after the rubble is blasted. It is dust.'

Neda nodded.

'How could anyone raise a family in that?'

'Nonetheless,' said Neda, 'you were granted refuge here while your country was at war. They are saying your country is no longer at war.'

'Only because there is nothing left to fight over,' said Saif bitterly. 'Bleached bones and burning tyres.'

'I agree with you. Unfortunately, I have to tell you, we are expecting some political pressure. At some point in the future. I think this is going to become important. Maybe very important, if there's an election in London. Obviously, you're a doctor in a

32

region with a shortage. Which helps you. But even so. Scotland wants to protect you. But it may not be able to. That is why,' said Neda, 'I strongly recommend that you get your application in. Right away.'

He nodded, trying to take it all in.

'It's good news,' she said. 'It's great news. I'm just saying act fast, that's all. Don't risk a change of policy at Westminster; they spin with the wind.'

She left the forms and a booklet on his desk and told him she'd meet him at the school. He stared at it thoughtfully, his hand reaching forgetfully to the now empty bakery box.

Chapter Four

In all the great expanse of the universe, in all of space and time, in all worlds created, in all planets, continents, oceans, countries, cities, towns, islands, streets, homes, rooms, in all of those places, there was one spot, one tiny infinitesimal point where Lorna MacLeod felt happy, could always feel happy.

And it was here, this evening. In her bedroom at the back of her tucked-away flat above the tiny Mure museum (usually closed) and the library (only open in the afternoons), in the little home of her own that was cosy with the peat fire in the wintertime, had a sunny kitchen and fire escape to sit on in the summertime. Her blue bedroom, with its windows looking out over the back of the stone cottages, was completely private, completely hers and, at this precise moment in time, shared, under crisp white sheets dried in the fresh clean spring winds of the island, fast asleep, with Saif Hassan. He had had a busy day.

She pulled his hastily discarded shirt around her – she so loved the smell of him – and simply gazed. Part of her wanted to wake him up: they spent so little time together and she treasured every moment.

But part of her was greedy for this, when without words, she could simply drink in the golden sheen of his skin, the softness of the shaggy dark hair, the cast of his absurdly long eyelashes on his cheeks, the mouth, which was usually set pillowy and soft in sleep. He was the most beautiful man, the most beautiful thing she had ever seen. She loved him so much she felt her heart could burst out of her chest. The only sound to be heard other than its beat was his quiet breathing and the distant gulls.

It was almost impossibly difficult for the town's GP to secretly meet up with town's headmistress, who taught the aforementioned GP's children.

In fact, it was a nightmare of secrecy and subterfuge. Flora knew, of course, but was sworn to secrecy. And Jeannie, the practice receptionist, had a pretty good idea of what was going on. But the excitement, the pent-up passion that exploded whenever they were alone in a room together, the desire, the love and muttered words and stolen gasps – they did not always compensate for the lonely nights when the phone could not ring, the occasions and parties at which they would arrive separately, nod politely at each other and either avoid each other completely (that didn't always work well: Lorna's colleague, Mrs Cook, was convinced Lorna disliked him and was worried that she might be a bit racist) or make tortured small talk about Ash's latest school report.

She watched what Flora and Joel had – a love they nurtured, a gradual opening up, a deepening of their time together now with Douglas as well as encompassing Flora's family and Joel's adoptive parents Mark and Marsha, slowly stitching together the tapestry of their lives.

She and Saif could never have that.

Or could they? Lorna never mentioned it, but she hung on to what she knew: that Amena had remarried and had another family.

But even so, they could not charge ahead – how could she possibly ever turn around to those little boys, who had been through hell, who had lost so much, and announce that she, one of the adults they had had to learn to trust in a world that had let them down so badly, that, hey, guess what, kids, their mother didn't want them any more, she had new kids now, and she, Lorna, would be waking up in their father's bed every day! Then teaching them in school! Forget about your mother now!

It was impossible. Unbearable. Cruel.

But ... when? How? She wasn't getting any younger, as she was rudely aware of, babies being more or less everywhere on Mure in their usual nine layers of local wool. She could never say it aloud but her dream of a baby ... with black eyelashes, so long they cast a shadow, with the softest skin ...

She shook her head, cross at herself. It was pointless, picking it over again and again. She glanced at her watch. Plus, he was going to be late to pick the boys up from Scouts. She rolled over, lay down and nestled her back in against his chest. Without even waking, his arms instinctively went round her and held her tight, and he buried his face into the long red hair he so adored. She closed her eyes, wishing she could stay exactly where she was for ever.

His lips in her hair let out a low groan.

'What time ... ?'

'It's all right,' whispered back Lorna. 'They're doing bob-a-job. They'll be late back.'

'I could stay here for ever,' he murmured in her hair, pulling her even closer to him.

'Me too.' Unfortunately, pulling her closer to him had a predictable effect on Saif for the second time that evening, and with the greatest reluctance in the world, he pulled himself away before things got out of hand. Lorna, alone again in the bed, had a terrible pang, the way she always did when he had to get ready, had to leave; as if she was a mistress, or worse.

He showered speedily, then put his tie back on, looking in the mirror, looking back at her.

'I saw Neda today,' he said.

'So did I,' said Lorna, half smiling. She had, of course, been hyper-professional, focusing on the boys, asking no questions about Saif, which Neda of course would not have answered anyway.

'She said ... she said if I apply, I'll get a visa for five years. And after that ... I can apply to become a UK citizen.'

Lorna froze. They never discussed his status, never discussed the future at all.

In five years! It was so long. But Ib would be practically grown up. In five years ... she would only be thirty-eight. People had babies at thirty-eight all the time. They could ... in five years. They could buy a house. He would be able to travel if he had a UK passport. They could do anything. They could live a normal life. They could ...

He looked at her face, unblinking.

'You are pleased?'

She nodded frantically, not trusting herself to speak, and he smiled.

'Always. I ask you to wait,' he said softly. 'Always, Lorenah.'

He came towards her, tucked a stray frond of hair behind her ear.

'Always I ask you to wait longer. Can you?'

Lorna knew she should play tough, demand more than a stolen hour here and there, be strong. Discuss a plan to work out how to tell people; how to deal with the children.

She did none of this. She just nodded.

He came and knelt in front of her in the bed, his hands gesturing out in supplication.

'You are the joy in my life, Lorenah. The boys – they are my heart, my life. You … you are the light.'

She closed her eyes, put her hand out for the last time to feel his strong shoulders, inhale the scent of him, grab him while she could, before they had to go.

Her phone alarm beeped, as did his.

'Okay, okay.' She stood up to say goodbye, but even as he kissed her, even as he murmured endearments in Arabic into her hair, even as she curled up on the pillowcase to hold onto his scent for just a little longer, relive every kiss, every touch, every perfect moment, the loss and emptiness remained; the sadness returned.

Chapter Five

'You're back you're back you're back!'

Joel flew home the following evening. Douglas had gone down without a murmur, even after Joel had gazed into his baby boy's eyes and apologised for leaving him. 'He doesn't seem remotely concerned,' he complained to Flora, 'that I've been gone for weeks. Did you notice the way he—?'

'Talk later,' said Flora with some urgency, who decided she had had quite enough discussing Douglas with Saif, Hamish, Eck, the Fair Isle knitting ladies of the Seaside Kitchen and Agot (mostly about when Douglas would be going to the boarding school).

And whatever it was Joel wanted to discuss about the wedding, that was going to have to wait too unfortunately, as his turning up off the plane, his suit a little rumpled, his tie coming loose, his hair curly and spilling over his forehead, had an entirely predictable effect on her.

She took Joel firmly by the sleeve of his smart suit and

marched him upstairs to their large bedroom, where a fire was playing in the grate and the lighting was soft and all the towels had been put back and a scented candle was burning and, well, frankly Joel noticed absolutely none of this, and Flora didn't care if he did or didn't in the violent tumult until, a shockingly brief time later, they were lying in one another's arms once again.

'You're a witch,' said Joel, breathless, shaking his head. 'You're a mad selkie witch. I don't even know how you do it. Every time feels like the first time, Flora.'

She lay close to him, bright pink, her limbs liquid and heavy, as if every part of her was slowly dissolving.

'Hmmm?'

Then she turned round to face him, her eyes unfocused, the way he loved to see them, and he felt the charge again.

'I think,' he said, 'I am just getting started.'

But it was no use. Flora was fast asleep.

In the morning, jet-lagged, Joel couldn't wake up properly, but lay in a fug as Flora moved around the room.

'Stop watching me,' she ordered, trying to hop into her tights without crashing over.

'I haven't got my glasses on,' Joel reminded her. 'I don't even know that it *is* you.'

They listened to Douglas babbling to himself through the baby monitor. They looked at each other, and Flora quickly fetched and changed him.

'Oh God, it's good to be home,' said Joel, sitting himself up as she handed Douglas over with his bottle. He got heavier every day. 'Tell me everything.'

Flora looked at him and wanted nothing more than to crawl back into the warm bed with her two favourite people on earth.

'I don't want to go to work today,' she said.

'Don't,' said Joel. 'Seriously, screw it. Who needs a job? Let's embezzle Colton's money and take off for Bermuda.'

'Okay,' said Flora. 'What will we do all day?'

'Um, count filthy lucre and drink Mai Tais in the sun? And do that other thing you like.'

Flora grinned and glanced out into the day. The sun was up and everything looked bright, but she knew it was a mirage, that it was still absolutely freezing out there.

'We'd get bored.'

'*Would* we though?'

She leaned back over and kissed his lovely nose.

'Tell me what I've missed,' said Joel.

'While you were mixing with top-level scientists and thinkers and sexy glamorous types at foreign locations?' said Flora.

'You haven't met a lot of virologists, have you,' said Joel drily.

'Ooh!' Flora popped her head up. 'We *do* have glamour.' She sighed. 'Don't fall in love with her.'

'What are you talking about?'

'Olivia Mathieson. Jan's sister. She's flying in! She's going to have her wedding with us!'

'Jan's got a sister? Malcy's got another daughter? I don't see falling in love as a particular risk factor here.'

'She is *so* beautiful and international and successful,' said Flora. 'Don't fall in love with her, I mean it.'

'I was not planning on falling in love with Jan's sister, no. Why, what's she like?'

'Oh,' said Flora. 'I'm ... you know. I don't really know. I haven't met her yet. But everyone else says she's incredibly beautiful and is madly in love with her so don't you do it ...'

'You're beautiful,' said Joel quickly.

'Shut up, sweets!' said Flora. 'I wasn't fishing. I am very glad you like me but if I walked into a modelling agency, like, this morning, they'd assume I was there to take out the bins. Whereas Olivia ...'

Joel shrugged.

'Ah, I've dated models.'

'I know!' said Flora. 'That's why I'm concerned!'

' ... it's just like what happened with you. You have no idea what she is actually like because you're too dazzled with her beauty. So they just think they're awesome all the time. It's very boring. They've had men tell them they're absolutely hilarious all their lives. When they are not hilarious.'

'Well, glad to know I'm hilarious,' said Flora.

Joel nuzzled Douglas's nose.

'And they are very bony.'

'Oh well, I like that more,' said Flora, pulling on an extra jumper.

'And you are very bonny,' said Joel. 'Will that do?'

Flora decided finally to grasp the nettle.

'Okay,' she said. 'Well, I have checked and I guess you don't want to break up with me.'

'What?' said Joel.

'But now you have to tell me what it is we have to talk about.'

'Oh!' said Joel. 'Yes! I told you it was nothing bad.'

'Yeah,' said Flora. 'You said we have to talk. That is often, often bad.'

Joel looked a little nervous.

'Oh my God, *what*?' said Flora.

'Well. You know how we were going to run ours as a trial wedding for the Rock?'

'Oh, we really have to now, because Olivia's having hers with us!'

'What do you mean?'

'She's going to have a huge bash! She wants it to be at midsummer. Which is a lovely date to get married. Well. If we say yes.'

'Oh,' said Joel, frowning. 'Is it going to be all the bells and whistles, that kind of thing?'

'I hope so,' said Flora. 'We could really push the boat out, put the hotel on the map. Good-looking people have good-looking friends, right?' She thought. 'Hey, if they want it at midsummer . . . that's when we were thinking too, right? I know most people plan this for a year but *most* people don't have a hotel!' She grinned. 'I know it's not actually my hotel,' she whispered. 'But I think they might let me pretend, just on my wedding day, don't you?'

Joel felt awful about what he was about to do.

'Listen,' he said. 'I spoke to Mark when I was away.'

'Uh-huh,' said Flora. She adored Mark, who had been Joel's therapist and was now his adoptive father. But it was a bit of a red flag when Joel had to speak to him.

'About . . . I was feeling a little anxious about the wedding.'

Flora knew how hard it was for Joel to be honest about these kinds of things and knew she had to be supportive when he was. Even so, it was dreadfully upsetting to hear it.

'Okay,' she said, aware of his tight grip on Douglas, who was playing with his father's glasses, as if this was his plan right up until the day he inherited his terrible eyesight and needed a pair of his own and he was just getting used to them.

43

'I mean, everyone will be there for you,' said Joel. 'And it's wonderful, and I love that, and I love your family. But ... but nobody will be there for me.'

Flora nodded.

'Mark and Marsha will ... '

'Of course they will, I know that. But apart from that?'

'What about all your friends from London?'

Flora remembered him when he was her boss and she was the lowly paralegal who had a huge, huge crush on him. He was always surrounded by people, going to play squash with other guys or in a big crowd at a bar or, often, with some incredible-looking woman hanging off him.

Joel half smiled.

'I hated those people,' he said. 'No, that's not fair. They were all right. Some of them. But they were just people I worked with. Normally I was trying to work out how to beat them or take their clients or get them into bed or ... well. It felt trans-actional, more or less.'

He pulled her over till she was sitting closer to him, which wasn't really fair. She put her arm around Douglas too.

'I feel so selfish,' said Joel, 'but if you're surrounded by every-one – people who've known and loved you from childhood, all your old friends, everyone you've ever met, I ... It will be hard for me,' he finished. 'Sorry. This is so lame. It sounds so lame when I say it.'

'I get it,' said Flora.

'And I'll just be thinking about my parents, and ... well. I mean. It's your wedding.'

Joel's parents had been teenage drug addicts. It had ended in tragedy when his father had beaten his mother to death, a shame and stigma that had never left the quiet, clever boy with

44

the bad eyesight, who had been shunted around foster homes which had never cared for him, homes where he could not fit in, until, with the help of a kind child psychiatrist, he had escaped to college, where he excelled, pushing himself further and harder than anyone else, working three jobs through law school, and forcing his way up to being a partner in his law firm at thirty-four.

Something inevitably had to give, and it had, near-catastrophically, in New York a couple of years before. Flora had been there then to pick him up and put the pieces back together.

It worried her, sometimes, that he saw her as a healer, as some kind of mystic selkie angel, rather than what she actually was: a cheery, loving, slightly scruffy, utterly normal girl. That she, and by extension the island itself, was some kind of retreat from the 'real' world.

That was why she was so excited about the wedding. The two of them, equals, standing up in front of the whole world, choosing each other. Not just in sickness, she thought sometimes, but in health too. As partners, the two of them against the world. She was conscious of what her brothers thought of him – that he took advantage of her good nature because she loved him so much. She wanted to show the world that he loved her too, properly. In a shit-hot white dress.

'Uh,' said Flora. 'So, what did you have in mind?'

Joel held her close.

'Would you mind? Truly? If we kept it really, really, really small? Just us?'

'Um, how small? Like, a sweetheart wedding?'

'A what?'

'That's what they call weddings without any guests. Sweetheart weddings.'

Flora swallowed hard. She supposed when you put it like that, it sounded rather nice.

'But . . . your brothers will have to be there. I don't mean, like *nobody*. Mark and Marsha of course.'

'So Dad, the boys, Mark and Marsha, that's it?'

Joel shrugged.

'What do you think? I want . . . well. I want you to have what you want though.'

Flora thought of all the pain he'd been through, how difficult it had been for him to get to this point, how much it cost him to talk about his vulnerabilities.

'All I ever wanted was you,' said Flora. 'And this clone,' she said, kissing Douglas on the tummy.

'Are you sure?'

'It's a marriage, not a wedding,' said Flora. 'And I couldn't bear you to be unhappy, not for a second of it.' A sudden lump in her throat took her surprise. 'But would you mind if . . . can I . . . can I have Lorna?'

'Oh sure,' said Joel.

'Plus if Agot is going to be a bridesmaid, I'll need someone to keep her in line.'

Joel nodded.

'Smart thinking.' He kissed her. 'I love you so much. I think midsummer sounds like a wonderful time, don't you?'

Flora nodded and smiled, happy in their little trio.

'There's something else,' said Joel.

Flora frowned.

'No, it doesn't matter; it'll keep.'

'Well, *obviously* it won't.'

'I just . . . Sorry. I did a lot of thinking while I was away.'

'I see that.'

'Okay. Well. It's this. And you have to say if it doesn't suit you because we're going to be married. Be a real partnership. Build this thing.'

'What thing?' said Flora.

'This life,' said Joel. 'This good life.'

'Oh!' said Flora. 'I hadn't thought of it like that.'

It pleased her to think of things in that way, she supposed. That they were getting ready, not just for a wedding, or a fancy day, however small, but for a life together, and that he thought about that too. She had worried, in the past, that she was a dalliance for Joel, a time out from his regular high-pressure life; that she was an escape as much as she was a person in her own right, and as soon as he had his strength restored, he would take off again, back to the ambitious, gym-honed, skirt-chaser he had been when she had met him.

Although those fears were mostly assuaged now – and his adoration for Douglas certainly made her feel better – it had never quite gone away, not entirely. Even though she was sitting here with a ring on her finger – so it was her problem, and not Joel's, she realised. Maybe that was just a feature of getting together with your crush. They always carried that air of unavailability, no matter what you did, and the biggest, fanciest wedding in the world wouldn't change that.

'Well,' said Joel. 'We have this place, unless Fintan wants to move back in.'

They had their beautiful home, which had been left to Fintan. They paid him rent but he didn't want to live among the memories of his late husband.

'Uh-huh,' said Flora.

'And the businesses ...'

'Well, more or less,' said Flora, worrying about the accounts.

'And I'm working part-time for the foundation ... and we're having a tiny wedding ... '

'Are you about to tell me you want to give up everything to become Ultimate Fighting Champion?' said Flora.

'What? No,' said Joel, who didn't get the reference. 'No, I was thinking. With the small wedding and stuff ... I just ... I mean, I made this money in London, but it was all doing horrible stuff, corporate takeovers, tax avoidance, keeping bad guys out of jail,' he continued. 'I just ... I feel the need to atone for it. When I see those waifs and strays Charlie and Jan bring in ... '

Flora still didn't quite catch his meaning.

'I thought maybe we could give the money we might have spent on a big wedding ... There are all those boys out there. Just like me, Flora. I see them every time I help out. We could use that money so well at the Outward Bound.'

Flora looked at him. Of course. How could she say no?

'It is quite annoying,' she said, kissing him, 'that you have turned out to be such a good man, Joel Binder.'

'That's only down to one person,' said Joel.

And he kissed her, too, hard.

'He did *what*?!'

'Do. Not. Start me,' said Flora, gazing miserably at the bottle of cheap white wine they were sharing in the Harbour's Rest, as she had needed to come somewhere where she didn't actually employ everybody there after work to rant.

'He wants to give all your wedding money to *Jan*?!'

'It sounds even worse the more you say it.'

48

'Oh *God*!' said Lorna. 'You have to stop it. What if he wants to give everything away?'

'How can I? He's doing the good and right thing, blah blah blah.'

'For *Joel*. Not for *you*!'

'Oh God,' said Flora. 'I've just thought of something. What if this is just the start of some massive midlife crisis and he starts giving away all our possessions and walking about in bare feet and, like, burning stuff. Oh nooooo!'

'I'm sure it won't go quite that far,' said Lorna, thinking of Joel's expensive Church's shoes.

'Well, I'm glad you're sure,' said Flora.

Lorna grinned.

'He's right though,' said Flora. 'We shouldn't need his money. We both have jobs. There are kids out there who are desperate for help. I've always looked after myself. It's okay for you, you're marrying a doctor ...'

'Stop it,' warned Lorna, who was still extremely superstitious. She had come to share her good news, but had realised Flora had to get this off her chest first.

Flora sighed.

'The problem is,' said Lorna pragmatically, 'you did slightly fall in love with a rich and successful lawyer.'

'But that's terrible though!' wailed Flora. 'So mercenary! And we are absolutely fine!'

'It's not mercenary; it's human,' said Lorna. 'You can fall in love with anyone – Christ on a bike, if anyone knows that, it's me. But it's kind of nice if they've got money. And aren't married to anyone else,' she added quite quietly.

'We can make money,' said Flora. 'I just ... It was just kind of nice to think at the back of my mind that if it ever got too much ... there'd be someone there to take care of me. That's all.'

'He would though,' said Lorna. 'He could go back to work.'

Flora looked doubtful. 'Genuinely, after last time ... I don't think so. I think working for the foundation and doing good stuff suits him fine. Doing corporate sharky stuff, I don't think so. He's happy for the first time in his life.'

'And now you're unhappy for the first time in yours,' said Lorna.

'I'm *not*!' said Flora emphatically. 'I am marrying the man of my dreams; I have an excellent baby.'

'He is an excellent baby,' said Lorna.

'I just ... Being married isn't just about one person, is it? It's about bringing together two lives, two families. It's about your entire community. And that's how it should be. Not skulking away. Sometimes I think ...'

Her voice faltered.

'... I think Joel doesn't care about belonging here. He just wants me to look after him. That I stand for something, rather than being, you know, a person, with, like, mates and things. Who might quite like a party.'

'Tell him that then.'

'But he's so happy! He has good reasons! It's only one stupid day. I just have to stop being up myself and get over it.'

She looked up.

'You could have the wedding here,' said naughty Lorna, flicking her eyes round the rather unbrushed corners of the Harbour's Rest.

'Shut up,' said Flora.

'I hate to tell you this ...' said Lorna.

'This is the second time in two days someone has had

50

something to tell me,' said Flora, 'and I didn't like it that time either.'

Lorna winced.

'Okay, I won't then.'

'Well, you have to *now*!'

Lorna said it quickly, thinking it might be easier that way, but she couldn't bear her friend being gossiped about.

'It's just that everyone on the island thinks all the MacKenzies are totally super-rich because you own everything and you live in the manse and Fintan married an American and everyone thinks you all have Colton's money and the wedding is going to be the biggest thing anyone's ever seen, even bigger than Olivia's, and they're all assuming they're invited. I'm just telling you what I hear at the school gates, that's all.'

Flora very gently rested her head on the table.

'Oh God. Och, no, they'll understand. Everyone will understand. Won't they?'

'Look,' said Lorna, 'you don't have to cancel everything about a wedding, even if it's small. Why don't you just say, okay, this is what it's going to cost, then we'll give the rest to Jan.'

'But men don't know how much stuff costs though!' said Flora. 'They think everything costs £20!'

'That's because whenever Joel says "how much was your new coat?" you say, "£20",' pointed out Lorna.

Joel had indeed gone to Outward Adventures with a smile on his face, to be greeted with a grumpy-looking Jan.

'Thank God,' she said when he explained the situation while

washing up enamel cups in the stream as the boys built shelters. 'I think one ridiculous wedding is quite enough to handle this summer.' And she rolled her eyes and told him about her terrible show-off sister Olivia in such wildly unflattering terms that Joel felt entirely relieved at the end of it that he and Flora had dodged such a bullet by not having a big wedding.

'We thought we'd give the wedding fund to Outward Adventures,' he said, and Jan's face spread in the first real smile it had had all week.

'I think that's the right thing to do,' she said benignly. 'I'm sure Flora thinks the same too. Absolutely the best thing she could have done. She must be delighted.'

Jan did not think this for one tiny second.

Flora and Lorna walked back from the Harbour's Rest along the Endless Beach to give Milou, Lorna's dog, some exercise, even though he was the laziest hound that had ever existed. The sun was just going down at 8.30 p.m. on this chilly spring evening, and the beach was practically empty. They could hear barking from the seals who popped their heads up like little lost people wearing bathing caps, heading to the northern tip, where they congregated round the Rock and occasionally startled people. There was also the occasional baaing from the hillside – lambing was continuing, fast and furious, and there were the lights of quad bikes dotted among the hills; a busy time for farmers. It was fresh and clear and a nice night if you had your coat on, to wander aimlessly with your best friend, and Flora, who had wondered a little about the timing, decided that the best moment was probably now even though there was something undoubtedly a bit awkward about asking someone involved in the most complicated relationship in the universe if they would like to help you celebrate your love affair.

'Lorna,' said Flora. 'I need to . . . I want to ask you something. But if it's too . . . I mean, I'll understand if you don't want to. I don't want to be insensitive.'

Lorna zipped up her jacket a little against the wind and threw a stick for Milou.

'Don't be like this please. I already have enough to put up with from Mrs Cook trying to set me up with people.'

'Sorry,' said Flora. 'I am sorry. Honestly, I thought I'd fallen in love with the most complicated man in the universe.'

'Yeah, yeah, yeah,' said Lorna, but good-naturedly.

'I was going to ask . . . could you be my maid of honour?'

Lorna looked up, surprised and very pleased.

'You mean it? I thought this was going to be tiny.'

Flora nodded.

'I'm going to need you, Lorna. It's going to be so tough without Mum there. You think . . . you think you're going to have your mum at your wedding.'

Lorna nodded.

'Are you going to wear her dress?'

At this, Flora made a noise and scrolled through the old pictures on her phone. She had a file of family pictures, left over from when she'd lived in London.

Sure enough, there was her mum in a full Princess Diana puffed sleeves sateen monstrosity that looked like it might be the before shot in a news story about a terrible fire. Eck was barely visible behind her, buried in acres of material.

'What do you reckon?'

Lorna clapped her hand over her mouth.

'Oh my God.'

'She used to let me wear it when I was wee, don't you remember?'

'Oh my God, *yes*!' said Lorna. She frowned and looked at the photo again. 'We thought it was the most beautiful dress we'd ever seen! We thought it was gorgeous!'

'We *were* eight,' said Flora.

'Goodness,' said Lorna. 'So, when are you going to go for?'

'I don't know,' said Flora. 'If we go for midsummer . . . '

'Wow,' said Lorna. 'That's really soon.'

Flora shrugged.

'Yes, but if you're not inviting anyone, you can do it any time really. Just dinner in the hotel. Gaspard will make something nice.'

Lorna looked at her.

'You're not super-happy about this, are you?'

'No, I am,' said Flora, breathing out. 'I genuinely am. Because Joel is happy and he's right – to fill the room only with people you love, and who love you, there's something very powerful about that.'

'I agree,' said Lorna. 'It'll be lovely. Now all you have to do is explain it to every other person on this island.'

'Nobody will really be expecting an invitation, will they? We already live together and have a baby.'

'Nobody will be expecting an invitation to the wedding of the person who *runs the town café and hotel*?'

'But it's just a wee wedding! We're just doing it for ourselves! They don't even know Joel!'

Lorna snorted.

'OMG. I think you really are going to need a maid of honour. For bouncing duties.'

Flora looked up. She knew better than to ask Lorna what was going on. If she wanted to talk about things, she would. But Flora could never bear to risk hurting her by wading in. She'd seen Neda though, in the Seaside Kitchen.

'What?'

Lorna told her about Saif applying for his residency.

'Oh my God!' said Flora, her face lighting up. She clutched at Lorna's arm. 'That's wonderful news! He's going to stay! Oh my God.'

'I know,' said Lorna, beaming. 'I mean, it's still . . . It's a long way away. Obviously . . . But . . . it feels like . . . it finally feels like we're moving in the right direction.'

She looked at her dear friend, who was looking out at the horizon.

'You know, the boys might like it,' said Flora carefully.

'Don't start talking about *The Sound of Music* again.'

'I'm just saying. *Those* children were delighted.'

Laura sniffed.

'Well, those children didn't have a mother.'

There wasn't much to be said about that.

'Does he mention her to you? Has he heard anything more?'

Lorna shook her head.

'Nobody knows where she is. But she's married, she's pregnant, she won't communicate with him.' She felt a little trembly saying it aloud. 'It's awful. I know it's awful. But . . . he's free.'

Flora looked at her.

'And you discuss it?'

Lorna shook her head.

'It's so hard. How ... how can he tell the boys? Ash still thinks ... Ash still thinks she's coming for him. And we haven't ... we haven't even said "I love you" yet, never mind how complicated everything else is going to be.'

'That's because you've only spent, like, ninety minutes together in two years.'

'I know, I know, shut up.'

'What if it turns out he's really annoying and cuts his toenails in the sink?'

'Well, I don't think he would, and if he does I wouldn't mind.'

'What if he only listens to AC/DC albums and leaves hairs everywhere?'

Lorna smiled.

'I could learn to like AC/DC.'

'He is quite hairy.'

'He isn't actually,' said Lorna primly. 'His chest isn't hairy at all.'

Flora raised her eyebrows.

'Well, there you go,' she said.

She grinned.

'You think he's perfect, don't you?'

Lorna sighed.

'We haven't ... we haven't really talked things over. We can't talk. That's all. But it's quite a big thing, the residency. It's quite ... it's quite final.'

'Joel was the same,' said Flora thoughtfully. 'I still don't know what he's thinking half the time.'

'Maybe that's just all men,' said Lorna.

'Maybe it is.'

Flora half smiled.

'But it's great news,' she said. 'It's wonderful. At least you know now he isn't going to leave! There is a future! You'll have time to work it out. The boys are growing up.'

'The island will go nuts.'

'Who cares? You'll be gossip for two days and then everyone will move on. People want to see you happy. And him. It is genuinely amazing nobody has guessed.'

'I know,' said Lorna. Then, unable to stop herself: 'Is *he* invited to your wedding?'

'Oh lord,' said Flora. 'Oh Lorna, it's so tiny. It's just for Joel.'

'They're good friends.'

'I was thinking my family, you, Mark and Marsha for Joel and, well, that was kind of it ... Actually, I was tempted to invite the entire office from London just so I could go hahaha-haha look I pulled the really hot boss! But Joel doesn't agree for some reason.'

'Okay,' said Lorna.

'But it'll look weird if I just invite him.'

'And the boys. They've never been to a real Scottish wedding! I could have got them to wear little kilts.'

Flora was so torn. She'd literally just agreed to a tiny wedding. But the thought of letting Lorna and Saif share her day was so tempting ...

'Okay. Let me think about it. Anyway, you don't want to be doing any more childminding. I'm only having one bridesmaid. Wanna guess who?'

'Jesus,' said Lorna, going pale. 'You're not. You're not going to make me spend an entire day wrangling Agot.'

'Her mum will be there.'

'I love Eilidh, but you and I both know she'll get stuck into the fizz and be twerking with Innes by about two o'clock in the afternoon.'

This was undeniably true.

'What do you want me to wear then?' said Lorna.

'I am going to get you an exact replica of my mum's dress, except in burgundy,' said Flora.

Lorna stuck out her tongue and they both laughed and tramped on down the beach.

Chapter Six

Jan was sitting in her mother Senga's kitchen, fretting. Christabel was yelling in the highchair, and Senga was about five seconds away from giving the child a lollipop to keep her quiet despite being forbidden to allow the child near sugar under pain of excommunication.

The kitchen was huge and had once been Senga's pride and joy, a vast country-style place in pale wood with curly handles and wooden flourishes on everything. There were flounce curtains at the large picture windows leading out to the conservatory, which was filled with oversized wicker furniture overlooking the golf course where Malcy spent much of his time, his tight checked golfing trousers becoming increasingly stretched over his large bottom.

Now it looked dated and a little faded; the whole house did, huge as it was. There had been money once, but it was nearly all gone now due to Malcy's rather over-confident sense of his own investing abilities. Large brown leather sofas and armchairs were placed around a fake fire in the main sitting room, and there was a plethora of beige with big pictures of Olivia; most of her modelling shots. There was also a single school photo of Jan, wearing pink-rimmed spectacles and a grim expression, and a large, not entirely flattering picture of Christabel, taken in a baby photographic studio on the mainland. She was lying on her tummy on a slightly grubby-looking fur rug, smiling with a clear line of drool running down her chin.

'I can't believe she's coming back now,' Jan was saying, eating biscuits out of a tin, despite her mother's audible wincing every time she helped herself to another one.

'Oh well, we think it's nice,' said her mother. 'Coming home to get married. I thought she'd quite outgrown us!'

'She'll only be coming to show off and pretend she's really kept her roots,' said Jan, 'when she hasn't been here for years and years. She doesn't give a shit, as long as she keeps getting to live her fancy-pants life.'

'Don't you think it will be lovely?' said Senga. 'To have a big wedding at the Rock?'

'What was wrong with ours at the Harbour's Rest?'

Long-practised, Senga changed the subject immediately. Jan's wedding had been lovely, but she'd tried to skimp on the catering and invited many more people than she'd paid for, meaning all Flora's lovely food was gobbled up in five minutes and most of the guests had had to rely on toast and crisps. Jan had somehow managed in her head to blame Flora for this, and had never forgiven her.

'How's Charlie?'

Jan frowned and tried to give some cheese to Christabel, who crossly threw it on the floor and reached for one of Jan's biscuits.

'Darling . . . ' said Senga in that irritating voice.

'I'm fine,' said Jan. 'Don't worry about me. Everyone just go make a big bloody fuss of Olivia. As usual.'

'Have you spoken to her?'

'No,' said Jan. 'Found out about her engagement from Instagram like all her fans. I don't care.'

'Did you drop her a line?'

'Mum, I don't know why you go on about her. She dropped us ages ago. She doesn't give a shit about us. She's going to come back to use us to get some nice pictures for her Instagram and then she'll take off again. I don't know why you're bothered about it.'

Senga looked down.

'I'm sure she'll want to stay and get to know her niece.'

'She sent one stupid Christian Dior outfit that was too small and too stupid to wear,' said Jan, 'and that was it. She's here to show off for a magazine.'

'Well ... at least she's coming home,' said her mother happily, which didn't help Jan's mood in the slightest.

Flora had popped into the Seaside Kitchen first thing, unexpectedly, but she was on the way up to the Rock and wanted to check in on the café. And possibly grab a cheese scone en route. It was a clear, blustery morning, the weather changing every ten seconds as it did so often in spring, and the wind caught the pale-pink-painted door as she came in from out of the cold, her pale eyes shining and happy at the smell of fresh coffee in the air. Iona, who ran it, had adopted a new policy of doing designs for whatever festival or event was occurring that week on a biscuit, and it had worked fantastically well. This week was the shinty finals, so she had little balls and sticks. People looked forward to a Monday morning to see what she had highlighted that week.

Flora had a mental to-do list as long as her arm, part of which included having to get in touch with Jan's sister, Olivia, and talk through what exactly she had in mind for her wedding. Innes, who did the accounts, had pointed out that if they wanted to do a big, expensive, splashy wedding, it could help their financial position considerably.

The bell of the front door clanged. It was nice to hear people coming and going in the café, even as it was running on without her. She loved this place. Flora smiled as she imagined the faces, the nice expression people got when they smelled the baking and felt the warmth of the cosy tearoom.

'For CRYING OUT LOUD, do you listen to NOTHING I say?' a strident voice was yelling. 'I said fourteen and now we only have thirteen and that's another place wasted so I'm bloody wasting my breath, aren't I? Because you never bloody listen?'

Flora froze. Then she tentatively peered through the kitchen door. Yes, she had thought so, but how very odd. Standing in the centre of the café was Jan, even though that screeching voice was one she had never heard before. Normally, Jan used an annoying tone as if she was talking to a not particularly bright five-year-old, who was also you, and you just didn't understand.

Next to her was Teàrlach, or Charlie, Jan's husband. He was a big man, but was standing, face down, staring at the floor.

'Look at me when I'm talking to you, for God's sake,' said Jan, who had not quite recovered from morning coffee with her mother. 'Honestly, I'm wasting my bloody breath yet again.'

She glanced round then – and to her clear horror, saw Flora

there. Obviously, she'd counted on Flora being up at the Rock as she usually was. Her voice changed instantly.

'Okay, darling,' she said in an adoring tone. 'I'll just get you coffee, yes?'

Charlie lifted his head in palpable confusion that didn't really change when he saw Flora standing there. He had no idea of how deeply Jan hated Flora for kissing him once, years ago, when they had broken up – not so much for what had happened, but more that Flora had got over it in about five seconds flat and fallen in love with someone else completely, which Jan found no end of annoying. She had set an ultimatum for Charlie to marry her pretty much straight after that and, being an agreeable sort, he had done so.

Flora saw Jan was standing, with a huge bells and whistles buggy parked right in everybody's way. Jan had been very much about hands-on parenting and never putting the baby down, but Christabel, a sweet child who had her father's affable manner and bright yellow hair, was also built like a dump truck and so that had rather gone by the wayside.

'Hi, Jan,' Flora said, using a voice that always turned bright and sounded fake when she was either scared of someone or didn't like them. Flora was both scared of Jan and didn't like her. 'Hey, Christabel,' she said leaning down, her voice softening. 'Don't you look beautiful?'

Christabel was wearing a baby-sized leather jacket with a huge pink scarf tied round her completely bald head. She had been grimacing and twisting to get out of her buggy but beamed cheerfully back at Flora's open face.

Jan, however, wasn't wearing her normal expression – a faint look of disappointment in everything Flora said or did – but instead looked rather strained. She did make a little effort by saying, 'Where's Douglas?' as she always did, and Flora had to resist the urge to say 'Who?' or 'oh, I left him at home with written instructions to work the deep fat fryer' and explain yet again that while Jan's job allowed her to take a baby along, hers, with quite strict official rules against babies getting their fingers in butter, didn't.

'He's with Hamish,' she said. 'What can I get you?'

'I know Joel's volunteering with us again today,' went on Jan relentlessly. 'It must be so hard for you.'

'It's fine,' said Flora, realising as she said so that she'd fallen into the trap again, and what was coming out of her mouth made her sound not remotely fine.

Jan just sniffed.

'So, Olivia!' said Flora desperately. 'This is so exciting! She's going to come up to plan! I can't believe I've never met her.'

'No, well, you're not really a local,' said Jan, despite the fact that Flora had been born there, raised there, had lived on the mainland for a bit then moved back there and had a baby there.

'I always wanted a sister,' said Flora honestly.

Jan sniffed again and took her coffee. It was, Flora knew, Common Coffee's hand-blend, by far the best coffee in Scotland as agreed by everyone except Joel, who retained a fondness for the horrible burnt jug coffee of his homeland.

'Yes,' said Jan rather stiffly. 'She's amazing. Such an achiever. Of course we're close: why wouldn't we be?'

Flora smiled.

'Goodness. Well, I'll look forward to meeting her ...' She thought about it, trying to remember, and it came out before she even could catch herself. 'Was she at your wedding?'

Jan scowled.

'There was a schedule clash.'

Flora could have kicked herself.

'Oh, okay,' she said quickly. 'Well, I'll really look forward to meeting her!'

Too late again, she remembered that Olivia, via emails sent that morning, was coming up to scope things out and was going to be staying at the Rock, and it was entirely possible Flora would see her before Jan did. Why didn't she want to stay with Jan and Teàrlach? Or her parents?

'Ooooh!' It was Mrs Baillie, one of their regulars, in for a sticky slice of millionaire shortbread before keeping her regular date with the handsome doctor to discuss her digestive issues. One of those people enjoyed these meetings rather more than the other. 'Is Olivia here? I heard she was coming. Oh, that child. You have never seen a more beautiful lass. Like a wee angel, she was. Quite the pride of the island. So famous down in London!'

Flora couldn't even look at Jan. Suddenly everything was a bit clearer: no wonder she could be tricky. That was one good thing about having brothers; nobody was ever going to compare her with Innes.

'This wedding is going to be the biggest thing to happen on Mure in decades!' declared Mrs Baillie. 'Oh no, I'm being daft. Except for that other wedding.' Jan looked up expectedly. 'Fintan and Coltan's. Oh, that was a braw day!'

Chapter Seven

It was a little tricky, waiting for the wedding planner. Flora couldn't help, as she walked the corridors of the Rock, seeing it through her own soon-to-be-married eyes. The little landing stage for the boat – what a perfect place that would have been for them to land, in front of anyone, Joel there looking so incredibly handsome in a smart suit, or a kilt perhaps, her alighting from the boat with a long train to her dress, everyone clapping, the sunshine on the water, Konstantin and Isla coming out with drinks . . .

Well. Small was good, yes, she supposed.

Still. She was going to do one thing. She was going to take a weekend off with Lorna to find a dress. She could still have a dress, at least. They were both very excited about a trip to the mainland.

Old Flora, the sophisticated London type, would have been rather snooty about someone so excited about going shopping in Edinburgh. But these days it was something to look forward to, very much. They were going to book a hotel, and drink cock-tails, and she would catch up with her old college friends, many of whom had settled there – and they would scour the second-hand shops and find something lovely and suitably inexpensive to serve as a wedding dress. There was absolutely no point in going over the top for such a small affair. But she could still find something pretty. There was also someone else to buy for ...

'I have been thinking,' Agot was saying, as she and Flora experimented in the farmhouse kitchen with whether they could make coconut ice to a sellable standard. There was a limit, Flora always felt, to how much desiccated coconut people wanted in the normal scheme of things. Agot did not agree with Flora's assessment. Douglas was having his nap, which suited Agot just fine as she had some important things to discuss with her aunt.

'I have thought about this very much and I have decided: I don't think I need another bridesmaid, thank you,' she said formally. 'You know. For the wedding.'

Flora looked at her. 'But it's Lorna! You love Lorna!'

'She's my TEACHER!' explained Agot, carefully mixing red food dye. 'So, I hate her now.'

'You do not hate her, and don't say things like that,' said Flora, a little cross. 'She is very kind to you.'

'She says "we only do singing in my classroom when it is time for singing in my classroom, Agot Fleur MacKenzie",' said Agot.

'But that's just how it is!' said Flora. 'You have to do what your teacher says. That would be any teacher!'

'And that is why it will be TERRIBLE being a bridesmaid when she is teacher bridesmaid. And she is VERY, VERY OLD.'

'She's not a bridesmaid; she's a maid of honour,' said Flora, sensing on a very deep level that by saying this she was somehow conceding defeat, which was always a mistake. 'Don't lick the spoon.'

'Oh well, THAT is okay,' said Agot, confirming Flora's suspicions. 'So I AM the only bridesmaid.'

'Well, I suppose so ...'

'I have told Mary-Elizbeth and Orla and Maeve to sit in the very front row so they can see my very beautiful dress. I hope they are not too jealous,' said Agot airily.

'Agot ... it's a small wedding. It's not even a wedding like that! There won't be a lot of people invited.'

Agot stopped stirring.

'But everyone is going to want to see me as a bridesmaid.'

'Well, we'll take a lot of pictures.'

'Well, I have told Mary-Elizabeth and Orla and Maeve so maybe just them. And Ash of course.'

She saw Flora's doubtful face.

'Agot, sweetheart, I am not sure we can have all those people at the wedding.'

'But Ash is my BEST FRIEND.'

Flora quickly changed the subject.

'So I was thinking, I am going to go shopping for dresses in Edinburgh, and I wondered what kind of dress you would like?'

But Agot's mouth had turned into a dangerous wobbly line and she was stock-still on the little stool that lifted her to counter height.

'I thought we could maybe look at lots of dresses on the internet ...'

Agot stared mutely over Flora's shoulder.

Well, thought Flora. Lorna already thought Saif was coming. Was it going to look really weird, having only her own family, Mark and Marsha for Joel and ... the town's GP and his kids?

And wouldn't it really shine a spotlight on Lorna and Saif, and basically give the game away? She frowned. This was proving trickier than she thought. And oh God, inviting Saif and not inviting Inge-Britt, for example, and . . .

Agot was still looking at her.

'Okay,' said Flora in a rush, thinking she would worry more about it later. 'Okay. Ash can come, okay?'

'YAY!' shouted Agot. 'My dress is going to be white.'

'I think the bride wears the white dress,' said Flora. 'And that's going to be me, remember?'

Agot frowned.

'But I need a white dress though.'

'I'm sure they do all sorts of pretty dresses for bridesmaids,' said Flora, pouring out the two layers of coconut ice, then helping Agot down and putting the kettle on so they could leave the sweets to set and have a look at the internet.

'Bad. Bad. Bad. Bad. Bad,' said Agot, as Flora scrolled through pages of pretty bridesmaid dresses in ice cream colours.

'You and Lorna have to match,' said Flora.

'I don't think so,' said Agot.

About halfway down the first page, Flora's heart sank. There was an old file picture of Prince William and Kate Middleton getting married – and all her bridesmaids, of whom there looked to be about a dozen, were wearing white dresses.

'Yes, okay, thank you, please,' said Agot, and got down from the chair to go and see if the coconut ice was set even though she knew full well that it wouldn't be; she just liked poking her finger in it.

The dresses were lovely for a royal wedding, but for the stripped-back, small-scale affair they were going to have – well, it would be ridiculous. If she was going to wear something simple and sweet and plain and chic and Agot wanted to wear the full meringue, it would be insane. This was going to get awkward. And of course Innes would want her to have it. Also, Flora knew from bitter experience, trying to get Agot to do something she didn't want to do was not worth the time and energy that would be expended. Few people had forgotten the Easter service when Agot was still in her raccoon period and had turned up in a perfect little dress and cardigan as if butter wouldn't melt in her mouth but then every time she turned around she revealed a massive bushy raccoon tail hanging out of her skirt.

'Well, we'll see,' said Flora.

'We WILL see,' said Agot. 'I am so happy I have my dress! I love it! Thank you, Auntie Flora! I will love being a bridesmaid!'

Innes walked in from the upper field, weary after a day's work, and smiled to see his daughter so happy.

'Daddy! Daddy! Auntie Flora is buying me the loveliest bridesmaid's dress EVER! Come see!'

She pulled Innes round to the internet site and showed him the royal wedding pictures. Innes's eyebrows went up.

'Goodness, sis, didn't realise you were making such a big deal out of it.'

'I'm not!' said Flora.

'Mind you, if you're going full royal wedding, you should definitely put Lorna in that Pippa number.'

'Shut up! It's a very small wedding!'

' . . . Only I bumped into Mrs Kennedy and she was asking about it and I said I didn't really know what was going on but if it's going to be quite a grand affair . . . '

'It *isn't*.'

'I am going to have the most ginormous dress and everyone

will be looking at me,' said Agot. 'Mrs Kennedy will like it and not be cross.'

Agot had recently started Mrs Kennedy's Highland dancing classes and was finding the strict discipline rather chafing. However, the threat – which never worked with school – was to stop going, which would be insupportable, as Mary-Elizabeth would learn to jump higher, and also it would help with her international ice dancing career, being the only local dance class on offer, so she was grimly sticking it out.

'Mrs Kennedy is not coming!' said Flora.

'Oh,' said Innes. 'Because she said you'd be wanting the little ones to do a fling for you.'

Flora bit her lip. The idea of all the little girls of Mure in their kilts and white blouses, their black bodices and their tartan socks, with tightly tied shoes, performing to one of the local pipers . . .

'Oh,' she said.

'I mean, you went to that dancing school for a long time.'

'I am having a *very small wedding*!' said Flora. With, she thought, maybe, possibly perhaps a wee dance. She'd sound Joel out about it.

'I'll suggest her for Olivia's wedding,' she said.

Innes sniffed.

'Oh, I'm sure *Olivia* won't want them.'

'What's that supposed to mean?'

'I mean, she'll probably fly in the Pussycat Dolls or something, won't she?'

'There's a wedding planner!' said Flora. 'She's coming up with her next week. She's sent a lot of rather grumpy emails already.'

'Are you scared of a wedding planner?' said Innes.

'Yes. A bit. No. Yes,' said Flora, sighing.

'Well,' said Innes, who handled the accounts, 'don't give any discounts. I mean it. The Rock can pay its way, but only if you charge properly for it.'

'Of course I will.'

'I've seen you,' said Innes in a warning tone, 'handing out free pies.'

'I do not "hand out free pies",' said Flora very crossly. 'I occasionally help Charlie and Jan out on their charity works.'

'I'm just saying,' said Innes. 'One day it's free pies; the next it's free weddings.'

'Well, I am a professional businesswoman now,' said Flora. 'And I will behave in a professional manner.'

Innes and Agot looked at each other, sharing a smirk that made them look very similar.

Chapter Eight

It was the weirdest thing. Or rather, perhaps it was not because there had been a million weekends just like this, and nothing had ever come together before. They were just due a little luck. The Easter holidays were upon them, it was the last night of Scouts and Saif and Lorna were sitting out on Lorna's back steps drinking tea in the little sliver of evening sunshine. She nestled on his chest talking about her trip to Edinburgh.

Saif smiled, but looked sad too.

'I will miss you.'

'I know,' said Lorna. Then, flippantly, as she always did: 'Just come. Leave the kids with the toaster and we'll hire a submarine so we can sneak out undetected.'

'What are you going for?'

'Choosing Flora's wedding dress! And my bridesmaid dress! We are going to shop and accept free glasses of slightly warm Prosecco!'

Saif looked at the dates on his phone.

'Huh,' he said. 'You know there is a conference then. For GPs. At the Royal College.'

'Is there?' said Lorna, sitting up.

'There is always a conference.' He shrugged.

'I know, I know,' said Lorna. 'Not to worry.'

He smiled. But then later, as he went to the RNLI meetings he attended (as did most of the men of the town), Rigby, one of the sailors, asked whether his boys had signed up or not.

'What for?'

'The water training weekend! Did you not get the form?'

Saif got a lot of paperwork, some of which he read more closely than others.

Rigby passed one over. It was water confidence for children, run by the RNLI – a residential camp over two nights. There would be a lot of mainland children coming, a cook-out, a film night – it looked terrific.

Saif sighed. There was a small swimming pool on the island, and both boys were enrolled, but neither were strong swimmers, and both retained a fear of water. There was no reason to ask why. Sometimes Ash complained so much he let them skip their lesson, even though he knew it was such a vital life skill.

'They don't swim well, the boys,' he said. He grimaced.

Joel, who also attended these meetings, looked over.

'You should send them,' he said. 'It's hard to learn when you're older.'

He spoke from bitter experience. Nobody had cared nearly enough. He had learned to swim as an adult, almost furiously ploughing up and down the lanes of his smart apartment complex pool. But the deep water still scared him. That's what had made him sign up in the first place. It seemed absurd to be living in the middle of the Atlantic Ocean and still be afraid of it, particularly when he was marrying someone half the island thought of as a water nymph.

Fionn, Mure's most seasoned fisherman and now the leader of the island's RNLI unit, looked at them.

'Oh, I'm glad to know I have two non-swimmers manning my lifeboats.'

'I'm not a non-swimmer now,' said Joel. 'I learned as an adult. Front crawl up and down my pool. Exhausting.'

'Your pool?' said Fionn, raising his eyebrows.

'Oh, it wasn't my own pool. It was just in my apartment block in London. I had a trainer come and teach me,' said Joel, not noticing the effect this information had on everyone.

'He's so rich! This wedding is going to be epic,' Rigby whispered to Ewan.

Rigby showed Saif the bottom of the leaflet where it said there were two sections to the camp, for stronger and weaker swimmers.

'You'll have the boys back far better swimmers, I promise you that,' Fionn said. 'After three days of being wet. It's running over the Easter holiday.'

Saif looked up, his heart suddenly jumping. But he couldn't . . .

'Half their classmates are going,' said Fionn.

'Will you take Douglas?' said Joel. 'It might help develop his walking muscles.'

Saif debated with himself. What if he left the island and something happened? And they got into trouble and he wasn't there?

On the other hand, the other times he had left the island was when he'd been summoned to Glasgow to answer questions about Amena. And it had been so awful, so traumatic for him, with a knock-on effect for the children. It might not be the worst thing for them to understand that he could leave without things being about to get worse.

Of course, he thought to himself, those were the days when he had thought they were still married. When he would sit at the water's edge every morning, waiting for the ferry to come in, in case she was on it. Those days were gone now. And there were brighter days ahead.

He imagined himself and Lorna. Just walking the streets. As a normal couple. Booking a hotel room. Being together, out and about, completely as normal, hand in hand. Oh my God.

And also, it was purely selfish. He loved Mure; he loved its safety, its beauty, its healing spirit. But he was a city boy too; born in Damascus, a student in Beirut. He missed the energy of cities; he missed the crowds of people. He missed seeing people he didn't know; people that looked a bit more like him.

And he could shop for the boys, and . . .

He called Neda, who was a reliable moral steer on these things, who knew all about the Lorna situation, and was the only person daring enough to laugh at him and say of course he could go, and by the way he needed one more reference for his leave to remain forms and as he was still sleeping with the local headmistress, she probably didn't count as a good reference, or if she did, she, Neda, didn't really want to hear it. Sometimes, he reflected, when you have a problem weighing down on you so heavily it feels like nothing can help, a joke can. Neda understood.

His absolute favourite thing was breaking the news to Lorna.

Her eyes went completely wide with delight, even though she had been planning on sharing a twin room with Flora and now she'd have to book another. Flora was mildly disgruntled that they were going to sneak off all the time but Lorna assured her that they would definitely have their dress-shopping day together. Saif was actually going to attend the conference so he had plausible deniability, so then Flora could call on some of those super-posh friends of hers from university, who had all bought stupid annoying posh houses in Edinburgh, and hang out with them and be patronising, and Flora said that would be fine except it was more fun when Lorna was there when they were being particularly awful and Lorna said, yes, for Flora maybe . . . so it was settled.

Chapter Nine

By far the nicest way to arrive at the Rock, Mure, is by boat, stepping lightly onto Bertie's sleek little wooden outboard so you putter out of the harbour of the island and feel the sense of being so remote and alone on a great sea, then see the rising gentle slopes of the back of the island, lush and green and full of coos before looking back and getting a wide view on the beautiful frontage of the harbour, all the shops and cafés in different bright colours – the green front of the chemist, the pale pink of the Seaside Kitchen, the black and white of the Harbour's Rest bar and hotel – as well as the small red and green fishing boats, then all the way to the northern tip, behind the great wind farm out at sea, just as you turn the craggy edge of the headland, when Mure no longer seems small, but large and foreboding, looming out of stormy seas, so far from everywhere else it seems astonishing that humanity had made its way there at all, with only the occasional outline of a great slab of a cargo ship on its way across heavy seas in the distance, but often nothing at all between you and the North Pole.

And just as you are perhaps beginning to feel that the boat was, in fact, very small to be out on the ocean, and how often do they do this trip anyway? and if a swell came would it take you all away? and did the winds normally get this strong? and how close were they to the next bit of land? and didn't those crags look rather foreboding now you were up close? and surely if they got smashed against them, wouldn't you just end up as match-sticks? – just as you are thinking these things, the boat changes course and starts putting towards the very tip of the island, and you would, depending on the time of year, get your very first view of the Rock with the sun setting behind it: the beautiful grey stone facade stoutly built by Victorians to proudly face out onto what they had once thought would one day become the North-West Passage, a shortcut on the way to the world's riches; the raked gardens stepping down to the jetty, planted with the hardiest of perennials designed to withstand anything the North Atlantic cared to throw at them; and the jetty itself, gaily lit up with lanterns showing you the way – sometimes also, depending on the wind, lit braziers – plus a member of staff already, in the smart pale blue tartan uniform, ready to give you a hand, and usher you through the heavy front door. Through the vast bay windows, you can see roaring fires and huge, comfortable armchairs; people already sitting, standing, laughing and chatting; drinks being poured and canapés coming round; thick carpets. In the upstairs bedrooms, heavy drapes whisper luxury and romantic getaways. Which is probably the point where you start to relax.

But today, Flora came up the back way in the trusty old Land Rover, happy to see people roaming the back gardens, hoping they weren't getting near the peacocks, who, it turned out, were quite ferocious animals, something Bjårk the kitchen dog had found out to his cost on many occasions as he had gambolled over to see if they would like to play, have sex with him or be eaten by him – he was a very unfussy animal – and had been met by a barrage of outraged shrieks and pecks that made people think someone was being murdered down by the ornamental maze.

Lights were blazing from the windows of the main house as well as from the little cottages Colton had built round the back. Flora as usual was gripped with a mixture of pride and nerves that this entire building was her responsibility. It provided work for people on the island, an income in a place that relied on tourism so heavily. It continued Colton's legacy; his dying wish had simply been for the Rock to succeed, and for Fintan to be safe and loved. It felt like a stake in the future, for the success of the Islands, even for Scotland. Flora knew she was being grandiose, but she believed it, and she wanted to make people proud.

Not in her wildest dreams when she was a legal assistant in London, depressingly in love with the boss who never noticed she existed, and spending on all her money on rent and commuting, could she have dreamed that one day she would be looking out on an establishment she managed, and that the hot boss who never noticed she existed would have bought the ring she wore on the third finger of her left hand.

She sighed with contentment, even as the Land Rover trundled up and a figure appeared at the back of the kitchen door, gesticulating wildly to the point where she thought she was going to run him over. It was her temperamental chef, Gaspard. He had been working there for several months, which appeared to be the longest he'd ever managed to stay in any position anywhere, which Flora supposed was a triumph in some way. On the other hand, the only reason they'd managed to get him to do this was by more or less letting him have his own way on every conceivable matter.

'This is *insupportable*!' he was already hollering, even before she'd opened the door into the stiff breeze. Flora arranged her face into a concerned expression. Things Gaspard had considered *insupportable* in the past included: catering margarine; not being able to serve veal; bread designed to last more than one day; screw-top wine; the existence of Lunchables; and everything everyone in Britain thought courgettes were for.

'Hello,' she said, allowing him to give her his usual tobacco-scented double kiss.

''Allo,' he said, taking a deep drag on a cigarette, his tattoos faded and messy under his bright chef's whites. Flora knew he and Fintan had something going on, but she didn't know exactly what and she didn't like to ask – Fintan, that was; she was sure Gaspard wouldn't give two hoots.

Fintan's love for Colton had been so sure and so strong that she knew he must feel it was a betrayal to be seeing someone else. She wished she knew of a way to make him realise that it was okay, that everyone understood, that Colton would have wanted it (would he? Flora wasn't remotely sure about that. Like most very rich people, he liked to have everything to himself).

'What's up?' said Flora, coming through from the freshness of the garden into the noisy, busy warmth of the kitchen. There was Isla, who used to run the Seaside Kitchen, with her beau, Konstantin; they were laughing and pre-tasting all the different types of cake, but ran up to kiss her hello. It was the big day: the famous Olivia was finally arriving with her wedding planner, and everything had to be perfect.

'Oooh!' said Flora. They were ravishing: what looked like a lemon sponge then a chocolate sponge and one that looked about to be festooned with fresh strawberries. 'That looks amazing.'

'Wedding cake testing,' said Isla with a grin.

'With no gluten! There ees imaginary thing,' said Gaspard crossly. 'Make weather gluten and say in fact "no, I promise there ees no gluten here".'

'No, let's not do that,' said Flora in a hurry.

'I would like sign that says YES, *ICI* THERE EES GLUTEN. Big letters. By the door.'

'I'll think about it,' said Flora quickly. 'Is she here?'

'Not yet,' said Isla excitedly. 'I want to see what she's wearing. I never knew her, but my mum always used to talk about her.'

It was like a celebrity was dropping into town. Flora nodded through the busy, happy kitchen – midweek, they often had lots of quiet older couples staying, which for most kitchens would have been a chance to play it safe with pies and fish and chips, but as far as Gaspard was concerned was actually an incitement to experiment with new dishes, so tonight was *pigeon à la champignon*, the newest, most beautiful tiny pink potatoes and dried seaweed. Flora popped her head into the bar and saw with some surprise a phenomenon: not the expected groups of 'snawheids' – older people who liked to take their holidays out of season when things were quiet – but instead several young people, not together, many checking their phones, some dressed with extreme trendiness including beards and man buns. It had been happening more and more, but today it was striking.

'Who are they?' said Flora.

'Food bloggers,' whispered Isla. 'Because of Iona's 'Gram.'

'Wow,' said Flora. 'What do they do?'

'It's really weird. They come and kind of sit in silence and take lots of pictures and make notes and ask if we can comp the food ... '

Flora gave a panicky look.

' ... whereupon Gaspard tells them to go fuck themselves and they *don't even mind*!'

Flora winced. The problem was she believed in Gaspard and his wonderful food. On the other hand ...

'Are you absolutely sure they don't mind? Could he not?'

'They love it!' said Konstantin, who was playing with a blow – torch and some meringue, and looked very excited about it. 'It's authentic.'

Authentic being an arsehole, thought Flora, looking at Gaspard with some affection even though he had an entire finger dipped in the sauce and was licking it with some enthusiasm. Pretending she hadn't seen, she walked on through to reception, asking Isla to bring some coffee and Seaside Kitchen biscuits into the lounge.

She couldn't help the feelings she was trying to ignore. It would have been nice if she had been tasting her own cake; planning her own wedding. It was lovely to be doing it for another bride, of course it was. But it had only been since Joel had stated his clear, honest and utterly reasonable wish, of course, for a tiny celebration that she had even realised how much she wanted a big wedding of her own. It was selfish though. Joel was already glowing, talking about how happy Jan was with the money they would be handing over; how much good they'd be able to do for the boys.

So. She could make it as gorgeous as she could for Olivia and enjoy it that way, she told herself severely, and count her many, many blessings.

The lounge was quiet at this time of day; most people were still out walking, enjoying the empty vastness of the Endless Beach, or ferreting around the gift shops of Mure harbour. There was a quiet game of Scrabble going on in one corner, and a *Scotsman* being read in another by the window, but the two pale blue tartan armchairs by the fire were empty and she glanced at her watch and looked around nervously. Where were they? This was a big deal for all of them. And then suddenly, the next moment, the wooden entrance way from the reception hall was filled with the slim, tall outline of just about the prettiest girl Flora had ever seen.

Everything about her was lovely. The pale skin. The dark hair with bright green eyes – Jan probably had the same colouring, Flora thought, but her hair was dull and grey, and her eyes were muddier. Olivia's hair was as shiny as a conker, with many different colours in it; her eyes were absurd, a sharp green like limes, with huge thick fringed black lashes. Obviously, some of it was fake, but there was enough to tip you off that, false eyelashes and hair dye or not, they couldn't make someone this beautiful on their own.

But it wasn't just the loveliness of her features. It was something in the tilt of her head, the long delicate line of her jaw, the creaminess of her skin and her delicate shoulders. It was so very odd how you couldn't help but respond to beauty. It must, Flora thought, be hardwired into humans. That when you saw someone who was such an absolute knockout you could barely breathe. She smiled to herself; there was no point worrying about Joel or anyone else falling in love with her: it wasn't a comparison; they were barely the same species.

Olivia was wearing a simple black shift, which somehow managed to look very, very expensive without Flora being able to see how she did it, and silver jewellery, and she stood there looking inquisitive. What would it be like, Flora thought, to walk through life like that? To stop traffic; to have rooms fall silent, just because your cheekbones had turned out a milli-metre or so to the right or left?

Realising she was being rude and gawping, she stepped forward.

'Hi ... Olivia Mathieson? I'm Flora MacKenzie.'

Chapter Ten

The willowy figure stepped forwards and graciously proffered a hand, as if expecting Flora to kiss it. To be fair, Flora very nearly did.

'Welcome.'

'Thank you *so* much,' said Olivia. Flora blinked. She sounded like the queen. There wasn't a trace of a local accent Flora could catch at all.

Olivia looked around.

'Sorry, Jacinth is just looking round the grounds?'

Jacinth was the wedding planner. She had already sent Flora nineteen exhaustive emails just to arrange this visit alone.

'How was your trip up from London?'

Olivia blinked.

'It's such a long way, I forget.'

'It is,' said Flora. 'That's what makes it special. Tea?'

'Hot water and lemon,' said Olivia. She didn't say please or thank you.

Flora nodded at Isla, who was still standing in the doorframe trying to catch a glimpse, and she scurried off cheerfully to fix it.

'So you don't get back to Mure much?' said Flora as they both sat down, Olivia somehow managing to look like she was posing for *Vogue* in 1954, exposing her long elegant neck.

Olivia laughed.

'Christ no, are you kidding? God! I mean, it's not your fault; you have to live here.'

She smiled in a way that suddenly made Flora glimpse Jan.

'You must miss your family.'

'Have you met my family?'

'Uh yes,' said Flora. 'They're very well-respected people here.' How Malcy could possibly have fathered such an exquisite creature as Olivia was hard to fathom. 'So you're coming here to do this for them?'

'*God*. No. This is for my new in-laws. They think it's all marvellous, kilts and hooter choochter and "Donald, where are your trousers?", and I don't want to disappoint them!'

Flora couldn't help but bristle at that. It was all right for foreigners to come in and think Scotland was quaint and hilarious; they didn't know any better. They had never stood by the shore on a bright, crisp morning, as the colours of the sky changed fast above your head, the ancient rocks at your back, the petrels circling higher on the tendrils of mists of the morning, and heard a lone piper in the distance. But Olivia was Scottish. She might not look it, but she was an Island girl too.

Flora tried to bond.

'So, what's he like?'

Olivia preened.

'Anthony? He's divine, naturally. Lets me have whatever I like! He spoils me! The fool!'

'I'm engaged too,' said Flora. Olivia simply raised her perfectly manicured eyebrows and didn't say anything. Flora took her notebook out and noticed the swift glance at the third finger of her left hand, followed by more eyebrow-raising.

She loved her ring. Joel had asked her if she wanted to choose and she had said no, you have good taste, which he did, and it was clearly rather fancier than Olivia had expected from a hotel manager on a small Scottish island. It was three perfect diamonds, the central one larger than the two on either side, entwined in platinum. In fact, Flora was faintly terrified of it and almost never wore it in case she dropped it in a stew or Douglas swallowed it. She had nightmares of having to explain to everybody that she had killed her own baby by letting him eat her very precious and expensive engagement ring.

She had worn it today, though, for this precise reason. Olivia's looked like it could take somebody's eye out, or fell a goat from a catapult. Flora kept finding herself wanting to remark on how pretty she was, but obviously this was pointless, like telling a tall person they were very tall. Not useful.

'So, um, what kinds of things were you thinking you might want for your wedding?'

Olivia shrugged.

'Well, I *suppose* the most expensive, Scottish-y stuff you do. Jacinth will sort it out. Just impress the shit out of everyone, I'm not that fussed. Anthony is *so* generous. Well, his family really . . . ' She frowned. 'I suppose there's a limit to how expensive haggis can be, you know, considering.'

She really hadn't a trace of her Islands accent, not at all. She had simply lost it, thrown it away. It had never occurred to Flora to do that in all her years down south, when people asked her to say things again, either because they hadn't understood her or they just wanted to hear her talk in an accent that was completely normal to her but very strange to other people. It was tiresome and repetitive, and she could have saved a lot of time by just suddenly sounding miraculously as though she came from Kensington, like Olivia did.

'Well,' said Flora, conscious she was now smoothing out her own accent and slightly annoyed with herself for doing so. 'I could serve it with very expensive whisky.'

Olivia's eyes lit up. 'Yes,' she said. 'Now we're talking. How expensive?'

Flora shrugged.

'I'd have to look down in the cellar, but I think it's rather exceptional. Some very old Macallan, I think. Plus some very, very old stuff from the Mure distillery. Rare.'

'Good,' said Olivia. 'Honestly, I don't think my new in-laws take things seriously unless it's completely over the top.'

'Are they nice?'

Olivia wrinkled her perfect nose.

'I am not sure I'm exactly what they had in mind for Anthony. That's why we have to put on a really *monster* show. I mean it. Show them who's in charge. Have them think I'm queen of the island or something.'

She gave a conspiratorial smile.

'According to everyone on Mure, you already are,' said Flora, and Olivia laughed.

'Yes, but I mean people who matter.'

There was a sudden commotion at the door before Flora could respond to this. It had, without Flora noticing, started to rain outside. This was not something you would necessarily remark upon on Mure at any given time of year or day, but the door had swung open and someone was dripping on the floor and looking absolutely furious, wrestling with an inside-out umbrella.

'Excuse me,' she was shouting at sweet Gala who ran the reception desk. 'Excuse me, can you take this please? A little help? Yeah? Thanks?'

Gala scurried over and started trying to take off the woman's wet mackintosh. Olivia and Flora watched on through the doorway.

'Is that ... ?'

'It is,' said Olivia complacently. She rose to her full willowy height.

'Jac! Jacinth! We're in here!'

Jac gave Gala another filthy look.

'Look after that – it's Burberry? That's a brand – it's expensive, yeah?' – she dumped the ruined umbrella on the now-muddy floor and marched through the double doors.

'Olivia! *Darling!* OMG, you look beautiful in this light here. Thinner than ever.'

Jac herself was extremely thin, cadaverously so, thought Flora, who hadn't been to London for a long time, and it didn't look elegant like it did on Olivia. It looked hungry. She was wearing something very strange which appeared to have three armholes, which Flora concluded meant it must be very expensive and directional, and she had sharp, black hair cut very short and sticking up. She looked at Flora, who suddenly felt very square.

'Hi. Jacinth,' she said, thrusting out her hand, which was covered in silver rings. Elaborate tattoos ran up her skinny wrists. Flora suddenly felt incredibly uncool even though she was wearing the most nicest floral dress she had and a soft cashmere jumper. Now she just felt unbelievably frumpy and bumpkinish. 'I'm the wedding planner.'

Just at that exact moment, Olivia said, 'Jacinth is my friend.'

There was a slight pause. Then Jacinth barrelled on.

'Well, I'm certainly not your run-of-the-mill wedding planner.'

Flora hadn't met so much as a run-of-the-mill wedding planner, so she smiled politely.

'Flora MacKenzie. Welcome to Mure.'

'Where even are we?' grumbled Jacinth. 'I woke up in Berlin.'

'We're on top of the world,' said Olivia.

'Well, it's grim,' said Jacinth. 'Christ. Right. What do we have to work with here?'

'Well, all our food is produced locally, and we've prepared a few dishes for you to try,' said Flora.

Jacinth snorted.

'Oh great. You get all your potatoes from a field. Big whoop. What do you have here that's amazing? We need wowed. We need different. Everyone's had enough of those boring Champagne ice sculptures real unicorn Cirque du Soleil weddings. We need something new and different here. Think new!'

Flora glanced at the windows in dismay. Normally, all she would have had to do to impress people would be to gesture to the front windows which looked out on the garden, with its perfect little steps down to the jetty by the sea and the perfect blue waves on the great sea beyond.

It was an extraordinary view, the sun moving behind them throughout the day; beaming in different windows, until it dipped in the evening, resting behind the house over the vast manicured gardens, designed to be suntraps overlooking the cliffs. There was nowhere lovelier than there to sit with the firepits and the pure wool blankets and drink a whisky and honey concoction and smell Gaspard roasting fresh fish inside while watching the sun set. She couldn't think of anything or anywhere nicer; who could?

Except of course today, when it was absolutely hosing it down and visibility was about an inch and a half and the wind was so cutting, tearing off the sea, that it was impossible to tell what was raindrops and what was spray.

'Well, it's a beautiful place to stay,' said Flora.

'Is it though?' said Jacinth. She clearly was unimpressed. 'I mean, is it always like this?'

'No,' said Flora.

'Every fricking day,' said Olivia at the same time.

'Well, we'll need to organise two parties,' said Jacinth. 'An indoor and an outdoor, depending on what we'll get.'

'We could organise a marquee,' said Flora. There was an island marquee which got pulled out for everyone's big parties. She didn't mention that also there was a rumour it was cursed, because every time it was put up it would immediately start biblically chucking it down, rendering the entire structure under about two feet of mud, and the locals more or less thought it was a bit of a rain dance, and had actually discussed erecting it for no reason during an unusually dry spring a couple of years before.

However, both the other women laughed at the very thought of the marquee.

'Oh Christ, how 2002 Tory party conference,' said Jacinth, not kindly. 'No, don't be ridiculous. I was thinking, tepee tents? Or possibly wigwams? Culturally appropriate ones, of course. Or what about a barn?'

'You're not ... You don't want to put up a *barn*?' said Flora. 'There's plenty of barns on the island.'

'But don't they all have ... you know ... *animals* in them?' said Olivia.

'You can't put up a *barn* outside the Rock. Why can't you just take over the whole place and have it inside? You can have in here for drinks, then we'll put all the tables in for the restaurant, then people come back here and we'll move the tables and get the band in for dancing . . . '

Flora's voice trailed off as they looked at her pityingly.

'Flora is getting married too,' said Olivia.

'Oh, that's adorable,' said Jacinth in a very off-hand tone. 'Well, I'm sure that will be just lovely for you. Now, look, I've found a place that can actually build you a medieval library? And you walk through and the roof opens up and it's practically a cathedral space? It'll take a month to build it on site.'

'Hang on, in our garden?' said Flora. Olivia patted her knee encouragingly.

'Don't worry: money isn't an object!'

'But you can't . . . We're running a business over the summer. We can't have workmen in for four weeks!'

'Oh, we'll keep out of everyone's way,' said Jacinth.

'You're building a huge mega-structure in my back garden and you're going to keep it out of the way?'

'I thought we'd have a carousel maybe . . . '

Flora opened her mouth to protest, but shut it again when she thought how much the children of the island would love a carousel. The nearest fair was a long way away on the mainland, and most children never got a shot on one.

'Do we really need one?' said Olivia. 'It's strictly no children.'

'Oh!' Flora couldn't help saying. They both looked at her.

'Oh no,' said Olivia. 'Even with all the nannies, who you also have to feed for some reason. It means the parents just cannot relax. Poor mothers desperate to let their hair down. And the brats cannot behave. Ugh.'

'Your sister had loads of kids at hers,' said Flora, remembering. They had messed up the buffet beyond belief.

'Well, exactly,' said Olivia. 'Yet another reason to steer well clear.'

Jacinth looked outside. 'Is it clearing up? I need to get a look at it.'

It was emphatically not clearing up. Worse, Gaspard and Konstantin were skulking at the restaurant doors. Flora could sense them and assumed, entirely correctly as it happened, that Isla had scurried back to the kitchens and yelped, 'Oh my God, the most beautiful woman in the world is sitting in the bar' and they had come out for a stickybeak. The rumbling noises implied that they were not being remotely subtle about it.

'Oh my God,' said Konstantin, peering through the glass. 'That *is* the most beautiful woman I have ever seen.'

Isla sighed. 'My mum thought after she moved away from the island she might get all big and ugly and spotty and miserable. But I don't think that has happened.'

She glanced at Konstantin.

'Please don't fall in love with her just because she is very beautiful and rich,' she said, 'and then decide you have to have me killed to get me out of the way.'

'I'm just stating that she's beautiful,' said Konstantin. 'It's just a bare fact. I don't fancy her more than you. And I very rarely have anyone killed. Just that one time.'

'She is astonishing,' breathed Gaspard. 'Look at those tattoos.'

'Not that one, you idiot,' said Konstantin.

'Okay, lots to go through,' said Jacinth, as Flora toured the hotel with them and tried to point out local landmarks through the towering gloom. 'I'm thinking we could theme the entrances? Have spring, summer, autumn and winter themes with appropriate flowers and foliage for each so you get a real wow effect as you walk from reception area, to cocktails, to dinner, to dancing. And keep moving it along, so it changes. We can get flowers flown in from everywhere. So in winter ... ' She indicated a big square of nothingness out in the grounds. 'We'll have old mirrors everywhere, old chandeliers, snow on the ground, trees all around, a huge grand piano, cobwebs—'

'You want to buy in cobwebs?' said Flora. 'Because, you know, I probably have quite a few that I can sell you.'

Jacinth ignored her and carried on.

'We could make it look all dusty and then *shazam!*, once everyone is in, we have it snow.'

'Inside the marquee?' said Flora. 'Mind you, June can be harsh.'

'And then pull down the dusty old walls and it turns into a massive coloured discotheque with ice sculptures. A rink.'

'A rink?' said Flora, blinking.

'I am loving this,' breathed Olivia. 'Yes. I would like a rink.'

Flora had tried to be strong all day. Someone else getting a dream wedding. It was fine. Just business. She was very happy and lucky, after all; she didn't have to show off to everyone.

An ice rink, though. An ice rink. All Flora could think of was her little niece Agot, an ice skating obsessive. Twice a month, her mother took her to the ice rink at Inverness, but it really wasn't enough and she could hardly progress at all.

'Um, when you hire an ice rink,' she asked faux-casually, 'I mean, how long would it be here for?'

'Oh, we'd hire it for the weekend,' said Jacinth. 'Have a quick turnaround. The guests are only staying for one night.'

'Is that true?' said Flora.

Olivia nodded. 'We're going to have everyone at Gleneagles –' his was the amazingly famous luxury hotel on the mainland. '– then bring them in just for the day. The idea is we transform the island into this amazing Brigadoon, just for one night. So it's like an island of enchantment. Then at dusk, at nearly midnight, it all fades away again. Don't you think that sounds amazing?'

Flora smiled.

'It does,' she said a little ruefully, partly from jealousy and partly because it would be nice if everyone stuck around and spent lots of money on the island. 'It really does.'

Chapter Eleven

Back in the dining room, Flora found Gaspard. She had told him to make nice, and she could see from his very body language, right from the entrance, that this plea had had the absolute opposite of the desired effect. He was standing with his arms folded, sucking his teeth and looking annoyed. Isla meanwhile was staring at the floor as if she was too shy to look Olivia in the face.

'So, what are we going to sample here?'

'We 'ave duck livers,' said Gaspard, 'in pastry.'

'Pastry, like, oh my God,' said Jacinth. 'Like, flat no.'

'You 'ave not tasted my pastry,' said Gaspard.

'No and I'm not going to,' said Jacinth. Gaspard eyeballed her for a few moments. She eyeballed him right back. Flora didn't like where this was going.

'And this is . . . ' she started, looking meaningfully at her chef.

'Goats' cheese tartlet,' said Isla, when Gaspard refused to speak.

'Dairy. Seriously. Is this a hidden camera show? Am I being punked right now?'

Isla looked up at Olivia as if she was an angel of some kind.

'Are you going to try some?' she asked pathetically.

'Well, obviously I'd *love* to,' said Olivia with a completely fake smile. And then didn't. It was, Flora thought, an alarmingly successful way of not doing something. Everyone was completely wrong-footed.

'Is that beetroot?' said Flora cheerfully. To be fair, this wasn't Gaspard's fault. She had simply asked him to make the most beautiful canapés he could and these were undoubtedly absolutely beautiful. Then they could stay for dinner if they wanted. 'Everyone loves beetroot!'

Gaspard snorted. He thought it was extraordinary that British people would eat food meant for horses but somehow refuse to eat actual horse, but Flora had said local and that's what grew around here.

'What's it with?' said Jacinth scornfully.

'Parsnip cream and fried onions,' said Isla.

Olivia looked pained.

'Alliums,' she mused.

'*Allez oui*,' said Gaspard.

'I'm sure . . . we can sort something out,' said Flora.

'They can,' said Gaspard. 'By going away and never coming back.'

'If I need advice from a terribly temperamental chef, I'll ask any of the nine thousand other ones I know,' said Jacinth. 'It's a booking. Deal with it. What else can you do?'

'With no salt, no sugar, no dairy, no fat, no animals?' said Gaspard. 'For you, nuzzing.'

'See!' said Jacinth. 'Maybe we're wasting our time here. Maybe we should just import all the food.'

'That absolutely won't be necessary,' said Flora, horrified.

'Bah *oui*,' said Gaspard. 'This kitchen is for people who *eat*.'

'Well, don't you have a lot to learn,' spat Jacinth. 'If you're very lucky, we'll let you handle the breakfast.'

Gaspard turned around and slammed out of the dining room, but not before hissing, 'She is *magnifique. Insupportable mais magnifique!*'

'I'm sorry,' said Olivia – but to Jacinth, not Flora. 'It's just . . . I mean, the kind of people who live here . . . You know it's a long way from anywhere. They just don't really know how to deal with a contemporary palate.'

Flora tuned out of this, utterly crestfallen. She looked around the dining room, which she had grown to love; so comfortable, inviting and cosy, with the candles lit every evening, and the crackling fire when it was cold, the soft chairs and beautiful parquet floor. If it wasn't enough for these people . . . well, stuff them. They would have a busy summer. It would be okay. They might not want the food but they'd need the hotel rooms, wouldn't they? Unless they were planning on erecting their own temporary hotel too. She wouldn't necessarily put it past them.

Olivia and Jacinth stood up as if to go. Flora stood up too.

'We can catch that flight,' said Jacinth.

'Are you going to see your mum and dad?' said Flora, genuinely surprised.

'Oh,' said Olivia dismissively. 'They just all have a go at me. For not coming up enough. Even when I do come up.'

'You must want to see your niece though?' said Flora. 'Christabel is gorgeous.'

99

'Oh yes, the baby,' said Olivia. Jacinth looked up from her phone.

'We should maybe get some shots with the baby,' she said. 'You know. For the whole package? Families, coming together, that kind of thing.'

'Package?' said Flora timidly.

'For Instagram. Full coverage,' she said, as if this was patently obvious. 'You won't believe how many people want to give us stuff for free. You're going to be inundated after this.'

Flora held her breath. They needed the money from this booking, they really did.

'So, if there was any way you could . . . ? I mean, obviously bringing in so much money to the island . . . it's going to be a big spectacle.'

Flora looked at the floor.

'But you're sending lots of builders to disrupt everything and rip up our gardens!' she protested.

'Exactly,' said Jacinth. 'Have you any idea how hungry builders get?'

Flora didn't say anything.

The doors to the kitchen flew open again and Gaspard emerged, a grim look on his face, carrying a plate of something that was extremely dainty in contrast with his large hands. He brought the plate forward and slammed it down on the table, then turned on his heel and disappeared again, pausing only to shout, 'EES GLUTEN-FREE!'

The three women leaned over the plate.

There were the tiniest, lightest puffed-up chive pancakes. Flora took one and put it tentatively into her mouth. It was hot and sweet, heavy with lemon and black pepper, with a sharp rendering of Fintan's cream from the dairy, and on top was the local salmon Gaspard had started smoking in one of the outhouses. It had a woody flavour and, with a tiny bit of caviar sprinkled on the top, was like a bite of absolute heaven, as fresh as the sea spray.

Even Olivia frowned and popped one in her mouth.

'You know,' she said, turning to Jacinth, who was nodding her head, 'I mean, hardly anyone is going to eat the food anyway, so does it really matter that much?'

'Yeah, well, maybe, whatever, let him have the breakfasts,' said Jacinth. Flora couldn't help reaching for another one; the canapés were light as air, and absolutely delicious. The other two did not. She sighed. They really did not know what they were missing.

'Oh,' said Olivia, looking at her phone.

'What?' said Jacinth. Olivia showed her the phone, and Flora caught details of Jan's Instagram feed, with lots of pictures of Christabel on it.

'Hmm,' they both murmured, scrolling down and Flora, unusually, suddenly felt furious on Jan's behalf.

'She's very ... pale,' said Jacinth finally.

'Well fed,' said Olivia, but not in an approving way.

'She's very bonny,' said Flora immediately. 'She's gorgeous.'

Jacinth snapped her attention away from the phone.

'So,' she said. 'And of course we all know that venues hike their fees unbelievably for weddings; we all know it's a scam.'

Do we? thought Flora with a sinking heart. They really needed this money.

'And of course, you certainly wouldn't want to do that to a local family.'

Olivia smiled prettily, then held up her phone as if it was ringing and she had to go and answer it, even though obviously it wasn't ringing at all. She left in the direction of the lobby.

'We were thinking ... '

And Jacinth named a figure less than half of what Flora had thought was reasonable for every room and space in the hotel, dinner, breakfast, band and dancing.

Chapter Twelve

Actually, in a way, this made it much easier. If it had been, say, three quarters of what she'd had in mind, Flora would have been more torn. If they'd wanted Gaspard.

But the Rock would get by. It would. She believed in it; she believed in Gaspard. The fact that as long as people wanted to go anywhere, at least some of them would like to sit, looking out on northern waters, hoping to glimpse a whale if they were lucky, happy enough to see the friendly grey seals, drinking a fine Rob Roy in the late evening light. They didn't need to tart themselves out for cheap likes on Instagram which would only – Flora had had some experience of this from Christmas time, when they had briefly been a sensation – encourage other freeloaders to try and get cheap trips too.

She looked around at the care and love Colton had lavished on this place, every piece chosen personally, from the floors to the napkins to the ridiculously heavy and impractical silverware, from the paintings to the blackout liners on the curtains for jet-lag and the white nights in the summer when it never got dark, and how he had entrusted the place he loved most in the world to her and Fintan.

'Sorry,' she said finally, her voice quiet – she was quaking inside. 'No.'

Jacinth looked at her.

'But this is the wedding of the year! Olivia and Anthony Forbes! It's massive! International!'

'That's great,' said Flora. 'And you know, the Harbour's Rest would definitely try and accommodate you.'

'Oh my God, is that place still open?' said Olivia, coming back in. 'It was falling down when I was here. I had my first drink in that place. Cider and black. Oh my God. This place never moves on.'

'Well, I think we do,' said Flora, standing her ground.

'Christ,' said Jacinth, shooting daggers at Flora. 'We could maybe stretch to—'

'I pay my staff a fair wage,' said Flora. 'I use the best local ingredients I can find. I am not making a killing out of this, I assure you. But I can't do it for that.'

The annoying thing, she explained to Joel later, lying with her head on his tummy, was that they had already flown up! Just for a quick visit! That was already expensive!

'That's rich people,' said Joel. 'They'll spend money in ways that seem crazy to us, and yet for all the big things they'll haggle like crazy. I suppose they didn't get rich by throwing their money around. Well done, you, though.'

'I know,' said Flora. 'I'm proud of myself. *"No!"* I said. Well, maybe bit quieter than that.'

'You have to stand up to the Jacinths of this world,' said Joel. 'Otherwise they'll eat you alive.'

'I think she might do that anyway,' said Flora. 'Well, she would if she ate anything.'

'Did they really not sample anything? Gaspard must have been furious.'

'They did try the pancakes. Nothing else. Actually, I think he was oddly respectful,' said Flora. 'It was very strange.'

'Gaspard being strange,' said Joel wryly. 'Amazing.'

He tickled her.

'See? Aren't you glad you don't have to bother with all this ridiculous fuss?'

'Uh-huh,' said Flora. Then she perked up. 'But *then* ...!'

The pair had been readying themselves to leave and Flora was seeing them, rather apologetically, to the door.

As happened so often, the weather had passed over and the world outside had changed on a dime. A vast rainbow had appeared to the east, on the back end of the grey sheeting clouds which were heading rapidly towards Norway, and in their place was a freshly washed blue sky with a clothes-drying wind and the sun behind it.

The grass of the garden that descended to the pontoon was so green it glowed; the immaculate little hardy beds of succulents and the rigid lines of daffodils waving in the wind looked glorious. The beautiful wooden boat bobbed at the jetty, as if it were simply waiting for a perfect, classic bride to step from it and make her way up the landing stage to crowds of friends and family waiting there, clapping and whooping, the sun high overhead, the drinks and the waiters emerging in this heavenly calm and peaceful environment, where the air was so fresh you could taste it, where the only sound above in the atmosphere was the birds, curlews creaking across the surface of the water and distant spring songbirds behind, busily arranging their nests.

Flora stood back and let them emerge together to see if they felt it. If they couldn't look out at the outgoing fishing fleet, those hardy men sailing into cold waters; couldn't contemplate the vastness of the ocean that stopped nowhere between them and the North Pole; couldn't feel in their hearts the breath-stopping beauty of the place ... well. There was nothing she could do.

Olivia stood stock-still. Then she turned round.

'I forgot,' she said. 'You know? I forgot it gets like this. All I remember is the bloody rain.'

'It doesn't ... I mean, it rains a *lot* ... ' said Flora.

Olivia took a step forwards, the sulky look on her beautiful face softening.

'Oh, I did forget ... '

The peacocks chose that exact moment to chase each other, grumbling and squawking madly, across the lawn.

She turned round.

'But what if we don't get weather like this?'

'You know what they say,' said Flora. 'Don't like the weather in Scotland, wait five minutes.'

Olivia nodded.

'And you know what else they say: there are two seasons in Scotland – winter ... and June.'

By the time they got round to the Land Rover parked up at the back of the house, it wasn't entirely settled, but Flora felt a little more optimistic.

'It will impress the in-laws,' Olivia admitted grudgingly.

Flora smiled.

'I promise we will do everything in our power to make sure this is perfect for you,' she said. Then thought about it and added: 'As perfect as it can be.'

'Midsummer night,' said Olivia. 'That's what we want, isn't it? A perfect full light night. The grounds an enchanted fairyland?'

'I thought you wanted cutting edge and up to date?' said Jacinth. 'I'm not going to be buying stupid little painted driftwood boards that say "Live Laugh Love" on them, and making everyone drink out of fucking jam jars.'

'I like jam jars,' said Flora.

'I bet you do,' said Jacinth, just as another old Land Rover drove up in a great rush and Jan got out, in a guddle, red-faced, Christabel bawling her head off in the car seat beside her.

'OLIVIA!'

Imperceptibly, Flora could feel Olivia stiffen next to her, but she remained as poised as ever.

'You didn't say you were coming! Ewan had to tell me.'

'I'm glad the bush telegraph works as well as ever,' said Olivia. 'Hi, Jan; it's good to see you.'

Flora had never had a sister, and often wondered what it would be like to have a girl in your life to chat and play and trade make-up tips and clothes with.

On this evidence, though, she hadn't missed very much.

'Were you just coming down to see Mum and Dad?'

'It's such a flying visit,' said Olivia, pouting her perfect mouth. 'We have to catch the plane back.'

As the plane wasn't leaving for two hours, this wasn't remotely true, but Flora just kept her eyes fixed firmly on the middle distance. This was absolutely none of her affair.

It was odd, though, how often she had felt the sharp edge of Jan's tongue. You'd think she'd be pleased that it was now Jan's turn to feel small and edged out. But of course, Flora didn't; one never does. She felt nothing but compassion and squirming awkwardness.

'Do you ... don't you want to meet your niece?' said Jan, trying to get Christabel out of the very awkward car seat apparatus while the child screamed unmercifully, as all very small children must do when they know you are trying to impress someone.

'Of course!' said Olivia. 'You know I am going to be back and forth so much as we get the wedding organised ...'

With an air of triumph, Jan finally managed to free Christabel, who let out a huge wail. She had obviously been eating some fruit purée, and there were stains all the way down her grey Babygro, which had seen better days, and Flora rather thought she needed a change.

'Say hello to your Auntie Olivia!' said Jan, waving Christabel about. Jacinth made a face of extreme distaste and stepped backwards in case she had to dirty herself by touching a baby in any way.

Olivia, on the other hand, took a deep breath, then knelt down until she was eye level with the baby.

'Well, hello there,' she said in her sweet, soft, English-sounding voice, and as if a switch had been clicked, Christabel stopped crying right away, and instead her face took on a look of awe as she reached out to touch the pretty lady.

It was like a miracle, thought Flora, that this tiny child, not even a year old, already responded so very strongly to beauty. Christabel grabbed a lock of Olivia's shiny hair and twisted it round her chubby little hands.

'Well, it's nice to meet you,' said Olivia to the hypnotised baby.

'I was hoping,' said Jan, 'she'd be walking by June. So she can be your flower girl.'

The silence that fell afterwards was deathly.

'Uh-huh,' said Olivia, flashing that smile that meant absolutely nothing at all. Jacinth's face didn't change at all.

She turned away to speak to Flora.

'Where are you getting your dress?'

'Oh, I was going to have a look in Edinburgh,' said Flora, who was looking forward to it immensely. 'They have lots of vintage shops there too, so I'm going overnight and we're making a girls' trip of it.'

'You know vintage clothes are very small,' interjected Jan sullenly. She was back holding Christabel, who was squirming towards Olivia.

Olivia's eyes widened, for once in pleasure rather than disdain.

'Do they have a lot of vintage shops there?'

'Yes . . .' said Flora.

'And you're going with your . . . mum?'

'I haven't got my mum,' said Flora a little stiffly. 'I'm going with my friends.'

'Oh my God, that sounds great!' said Olivia.

'Well, I don't . . . My mum isn't alive,' said Flora. 'And I don't have any sisters. So it's the next best thing to going with my family, I suppose.'

Olivia, despite having a mother in rude health and a sister who was standing right beside her, nodded vigorously. Flora felt a scratch of sadness; she knew one of the reasons for needing to have such a small day was that neither she nor Joel would have their mothers there; a thing that bound them close, that made her hug Douglas till he struggled. His adoptive mother Marsha was amazing, of course – Flora adored her too, her wise twinkling eyes, her little birdlike ways – but it wasn't quite the same thing. Joel's need to barely mention his parents . . . It was best.

'Oh, but that sounds *amazing*,' said Olivia, her eyes shining. 'Girls' trip! What do you think, Jacinth?'

'I've already spoken to the atelier,' said Jacinth glancing up from her phone. 'The fittings are all booked.'

Olivia grimaced.

'Honestly, sixteen hours having pins poked into me in Paris. I honestly could do without it.'

'When are you going?'

For a second, Flora nearly lied. She and Lorna had been looking forward to it for so long. Mind you, Lorna was getting to take her boyfriend with her.

'Weekend after Easter,' said Flora grudgingly. She couldn't possibly get away over the holiday itself as they were going to be mobbed, but she could risk a little time then.

'Great, that'll work,' said Olivia.

'Um, I'm probably really busy that weekend . . . ' said Jan, and with a start, Flora realised she hadn't expected Jan to want to go with Olivia – understandably – but also that Olivia hadn't expected her to either. Goodness.

'Oh, that's such a shame,' Olivia cooed, gathering herself. 'Never mind.'

Just at the exact moment as Jan said, ' . . . but I can probably shift some things around . . . '

Chapter Thirteen

'I'm just saying,' said Jan, 'you should take the boys kayaking.'

Joel stared out at the water mulishly.

'I'd really rather not,' he said stiffly. 'I'll do bush craft.'

Jan was making plans for being away on that weekend.

'Well, being scared of water is just stupid,' she said.

'I'm not *scared* of it,' said Joel. 'I just have ... no fond-ness for it.'

He looked out on the darkness of the waves – it was a brooding day – carefully. They made him want to shiver. It was astounding to him that Saif had escaped his country on a boat, genuinely amazing. That's why he went to the RNLI meetings – to try and get over his phobia. Thankfully, so far it had just been a lot of drills and planning. That he could handle.

'Flora is looking forward to the weekend.'

Jan sniffed.

'God, really? I'm just there for my sister,' she insisted. 'I don't know why people want these showy, expensive weddings, I really don't. Just showing off at the end of the day, isn't it?'

'Flora isn't like that,' said Joel proudly.

Jan rolled her eyes.

'Women always say that,' she said. 'It's going to be a mad bunch of girls.'

Then she scowled. 'Oh, and don't forget to update the emergency aid list. Dr Hassan's away that weekend too. There's a locum in.'

'How on earth does nobody notice that Lorna and Saif are away on the same weekend?' said Joel.

Ever since Flora had sworn him to deepest secrecy and told him about Lorna and Saif the previous year, to his genuine shock, he had subsequently found it impossible that two of the only single thirty-somethings on the island (farmers excepted), who held complementary roles in the life of the community, and who could be – in the normal way of things – expected to spend a lot of time in one another's company, ruthlessly avoided speaking or looking at each other in any public forum whatsoever.

'It just makes it really, really obvious,' Joel said. 'It's insane people don't realise.'

'People don't pay attention to anything that isn't shoved in their faces,' said Flora, politely not mentioning that Joel hadn't noticed when she was nearly five months pregnant.

'I mean, it's just so *completely* obvious,' said Joel.

'Mrs Cook thinks they hate each other. She thinks Lorna

is a massive racist and Lorna just has to bite her tongue all the time.'

'Oh no!' said Joel. 'Poor Lorna.'

'Well, quite,' said Flora. 'But given now he's going to stay . . .'

'I know,' said Joel. 'Mind you, wait till they find out that they're getting a massive racist for a stepmother though.'

Flora hit him with a pillow. He lay back, watching as she cheerfully started packing, full of relief for his unshowy bride.

'So is Olivia going to pay for it all?' said Senga in the kitchen.

'Well, the mysterious *Anthony*'s family is,' said Jan. 'But she pretends it's her. You should have seen her, Mum, swanning around the place like she owned it. She's worse than Flora.'

'Who *does* own it.'

'No, she doesn't! She's just staff!' Jan sniffed.

'Well, I'm happy to have Christabel if you want to go dress shopping,' said Senga, doubtfully. 'Be nice for you two to have a little bonding time.'

'We had an entire childhood of bonding time, Mum!' said Jan. 'Didn't work, remember? She treated you like a skivvy, she treated me like dirt, then she took off without a backwards glance. And you let her.'

'Well, yes, excuse me for my two daughters' incredibly successful lives,' said Senga crossly, giving Christabel a biscuit on purpose. 'Try and enjoy yourself, love.'

Flora was picking Douglas up from the farmhouse, ready to hand over to Joel as she left for Edinburgh.

'Hey, is there going to be room at the hotel for Tripp? He's asking.'

Fintan was lying on the sofa, making faces at Douglas, who was rolling on the rug playing with Bramble's fur. Bramble didn't care a bit. Flora slightly did as it meant that between the old stone floor and the old fuzzy-wuzzy dog she was going to have to retrieve him absolutely filthy, and with some very strong objections vis-à-vis getting washed.

'What?' she said. She glanced at the accounts Innes had left out for that very reason – to get Flora to pay attention to them, you had to insert them in the direct eye line of the baby she was already looking at.

Innes had got them in as clear a layout as he could manage so she could see exactly what was coming in and going out. There was a lot going both ways. A lot. Staffing, power, goods, everything. But they were busy. They were in the black. Just about. As long as nothing went terribly wrong. Colton had left them the properties, but after that they were on their own, sink or swim. It wasn't quite either, thought Flora. It was treading water, with a faint air of panic.

Think of the cheque from Olivia, she kept telling herself. Play nice this weekend. Get her to hire Gaspard, spend all the money she can.

'For the wedding? He just wants to know where's best to stay.'

Tripp was Colton's estranged brother, a proper redneck to boot.

'Tripp?! Tripp isn't invited to the wedding! Why would I invite your brother-in-law, who is an absolute homophobic bastard, if you remember, to my tiny, intimate sweetheart wedding?'

Fintan looked surprised.

'But he's Colton's family!'

'He wasn't even at *your* wedding!' said Flora.

'No, but he's changed.'

Flora snorted. She liked most Americans – most people, in fact – but the charms of the good ol' boy Tripp had rather passed her by.

'He has,' insisted Fintan. 'Do you know what he's doing now? Trying to get people off conspiracy theories! Trying to explain to people not to believe in all the crazy stuff they read on the internet! Do you even know how hard that is? Especially where he lives! He does that all day! It's very lonely and everyone hates him.'

'Oh,' said Flora, sitting up. 'I hadn't realised.'

'Look,' said Fintan, and he sent her Tripp's Facebook page where he was indeed trying to debunk conspiracy theories, and all his friends were calling him a coward and a cuck, whatever that was.

'Wow,' said Flora. 'He's doing that for you?'

'More or less. So doesn't he deserve a little jaunt away to spend time here where he has so many friends and he is, after all, family?'

'Yeah, *your* family!'

'*Our* family,' intoned Fintan piously.

Flora sighed.

'Joel said only people we loved in the room.'

'Joel doesn't love me!'

'Well, one: he likes you very much, and two: I do,' said Flora. Fintan bit his lip.

'Yeah, whatever,' he mumbled, but she could see he was pleased.

Flora sighed. If Saif was already in the mix, this might help cover it up.

'Oh God ... maybe bring him as your plus-one?'

'Oh *God*, vom – don't be disgusting – OMG, what's the matter with you?'

Flora rolled her eyes.

'Are you bringing Gaspard?'

'Well, I can't, can I? You're locking him in the kitchen.'

She glanced at him. 'Is this ... are you two still a thing?'

Fintan shrugged.

'Who knows? I don't want to ... I don't want to call it any-thing, okay? I don't ...'

Gaspard and Fintan had started having an affair at Christmas time. Everyone had rather expected it to burn itself out, but so far it hadn't. Though nobody had quite put a name on it.

Fintan sighed. 'I don't want to lead Gaspard on. I don't ... I mean, I'm not really up for a relationship. I'm ... I was married. I had a husband. That's how I think of myself. Anything else, I'm not going to put a label on it.'

'Fair enough,' said Flora. 'Does Gaspard know about this?'

'I was hoping it was just going to be ... I don't know ... a fling. Something to help me get over Colton. But this is such a small island ...'

'Are you falling in love with him?'

Fintan shook his head. 'Are you even listening to me?'

'Oh,' said Flora. 'Well, here's the thing. He's the best chef we've ever had, so could you possibly pretend for, like, as long as possible, and maybe for ever?'

Fintan sniffed and looked back down at his laptop.

'So, I'll tell Tripp just to maybe pop into the reception?'

'You invited him yonks ago, didn't you?' said Flora.

'You're the one who said it was at midsummer! That's just a really easy date to remember! I figured it was set in stone.'

Flora frowned. That was the date Olivia wanted. Mind you, did it really matter if she and Joel were only to have a tiny ceremony? The thought that they could probably fit theirs in while Olivia was still getting ready made her sadder than she could admit.

'They're non-refundable tickets,' said Fintan, frowning. 'Come on, sis. He absolutely promises to behave himself.'

'Thank you,' Inge-Britt said as she handed Lorna and Flora their pre-mainland trip gin and tonics. They were having a very quick end-of-the-day drink before going home to pack in huge excitement. And they were in the Harbour's Rest so Flora didn't have to jump up every five seconds and help confused people who wanted to know where Mure's Starbucks was or why they couldn't access Netflix, or work out what all the shouting in the kitchen was and try not to wince too much when Bjårk the dog started meandering round the main reception area. Although she had found that on the whole the punters absolutely loved him and the idea that he was the official Rock dog. Konstantin, his owner, kept a variety of jaunty neckerchiefs for him which somehow made him even more popular. Flora would have liked to put up a sign telling people not to feed the dog from their breakfast plates, because he was irritatingly ingratiating when they served sausages in the morning, but was nervous about tipping off Environmental Health, so had decided to turn a blind eye. Hence the bar at the Harbour's Rest, which was a little dirty, a little sticky but always bustling and busy and full of people and noise and absolutely nobody suggesting that Flora come have a look and see what was bunging up the drains again.

'I'm so pleased you're not having the wedding here!' said Inge-Britt. 'It means I can come and enjoy the whole day! Plus presumably we'll all be booked out with guests, but that's okay. They can have a late breakfast.'

Flora blinked.

'Oh, I . . . I mean, it's going to be a tiny wedding. Just family and so on.'

'And your friends from the mainland will be coming,' said Inge-Britt.

'I mean, it's going to be . . . I mean, not everyone.'

'Well, that'll be even nicer!' said Inge-Britt. 'Just us girls at the wedding then!'

Lorna shot Flora a 'told you so' kind of look, but Flora smiled broadly and mentally filed it away to worry about later. She was enjoying Lorna's buzzing excitement too much to let anything spoil her mood.

Sitting a few stools down from them though, clutching his hand round a solitary beer and staring into space, was someone very unexpected – Charlie. You never really saw him out drinking – he worked too hard, and he was never separate from Jan, not really. The girls smiled at him over the bar.

'*Ciamar a tha thu a, Teàrlach?*' said Flora. 'How are you, Charlie?' Gaelic was his first language.

He shrugged.

'Come join us!' said Lorna, whose happiness was bubbling over today and who was worried she might accidentally say something about Saif that Inge-Britt would hear.

To their immense surprise, he did so, his large body scraping the old stool over the rather sticky floor.

118

'What's up?'

'Oh, I dunno,' he said, looking sadly at his beer. 'Not really wanted at home, I don't think.'

'Well, it must be pretty tiring,' said Lorna sympathetically. 'You and Jan work so hard. And you're together all the time.'

He shrugged.

'I never minded it,' he said. 'I think she's just about had enough though.'

Flora frowned.

'What do you mean?'

'Oh well. We were kind of fine. I mean, it's been weird since the baby came – it always is, right?'

'I mean, good weird . . . ' said Flora. 'But yeah, weird.'

'But this Olivia thing. God. She can't stop going on about it. How easy Olivia has it. How big Olivia's wedding is going to be. I mean. I *liked* our wedding.'

'You had all those wee lads playing football,' said Flora. 'It was cute.'

'Exactly,' said Charlie. 'Now she's going on about money and posh tents and I don't know what people do for weddings.'

'A *lot*,' said Flora, who was coping with about ninety jillion emails from Jacinth every day, with mysterious subject lines such as 'formation dance specialists tuition times', '99 important lighting cues (daytime)', 'flower allergy checklist' and 'camera rigging'.

'I didn't think she cared about stuff like that.'

'She doesn't,' said Flora. 'It's just a sibling rivalry thing, isn't it?'

'Aye, maybe. And of course the bairn is still up five or six times a night, which helps naebody.'

'I *knew* it!' said Flora, then immediately went silent again as

119

she'd been inappropriate, but Jan had basically sworn blind that Christabel had started sleeping through the night at ten weeks.

'Then she's exhausted, and apparently I'm not pulling my weight even though I keep suggesting we get more help. Then she complains about her mum and the whole thing comes round again ... ' He stopped talking then, and took a pull of his beer. 'Sorry, I'm talking too much.'

'Only for you,' said Flora, a small smile tugging at the side of her mouth. She wondered who else he had to talk to. It was difficult on a small island, she knew, when everyone wanted to know your business.

'It's not uncommon after a baby,' said Lorna gently. 'Even for parents of kids at school, it's hard.'

'I know,' said Charlie. 'I know. I'm a patient man, or at least, I try.'

He was a patient man. It was why he was so wonderful at his job, running the Outward Adventure courses for corporate types (which was where they made their money) and deprived children (which was where they spent it), treating all alike with the same steady calmness he normally attempted to bring to his marriage.

'And I do my share. But I feel like she's so blinded by how much she hates Olivia, and sometimes I feel ... sometimes I feel she almost hates me.'

He looked at Flora.

'Do you hate Joel?' he said almost hopefully. Douglas and Christabel were more or less exactly the same age.

'Erm ... ' Flora cast around for something. 'Sometimes he can't find his glasses and he's so blind that I have to get them for him no matter what he's doing or he has to crawl around on his hands and knees. It's not his most attractive look.'

'That's not his fault though.'

'Oh goodness, no,' said Flora. 'Bless. When I get all old and wrinkly, I'm going to hide his glasses anyway. So he can only ever see me through a lovely gauze.'

'*That's* your futureproofing plan?' said Lorna. 'Blindness?'

'Yup,' said Flora. 'Come on, it's the only way. He's obviously going to stay gorgeous for ever; you can see it in his hair. He's going to get a tiny distinguished bit of grey on the sides and a really sexy little furrow in his brow and that'll be like it . . .'

She sighed happily then remembered the task in hand.

'Marriage is difficult though,' she added quickly. 'Everyone says that.'

Charlie looked more disconsolate than ever.

'It's even worse with all this Olivia nonsense.'

'That's just sister stuff,' said Lorna.

'She thinks,' said Charlie heavily, 'Olivia is getting all the love and romance. And I'm just an old boring farmer and she settled too soon.'

There was an immediate silence. This was such a shocking thought.

'Don't be daft,' said Lorna, filling the silence in a rush. 'What makes you think that?'

'The way she keeps saying it,' said Charlie, his eyes getting slightly wet. 'I mean, I know I'm not very glamorous and I'm from farming and running the Outward Adventures, that's just what I do . . . I mean. I don't know how to change that. I can't get interested in Hong Kong or designer shoes; I just don't know how. I can't . . . I don't even know what she wants. Except it isn't me.'

He was genuinely teary now.

Flora felt absolutely terrible. She had never been in love

with Charlie, but she had always liked him very much. He was decent and kind to his very bones; attractive and funny and open. If Jan didn't think that was enough and that there was a lot better out there, she was very much mistaken.

On the other hand, she knew that it was difficult after a baby to carry on working as if nothing had happened. To pretend everything was fine after life had taken you and shaken every single thing about you – every single thing you had ever thought about yourself – and given yourself a new centre to your world. You had to play it down but it was still pretty dramatic. Feeling sorry for Jan wasn't something she would ever have considered. But she did.

'Oh *Teàrlach*,' she said. 'I'm so sorry. You know, it is weird, the year you have a baby. Lots of people feel this way.'

'It'll blow over,' said Lorna. 'It will.'

She patted him on the hand.

'Maybe she should go see S— the GP,' she said. 'I mean, they can do things with low mood and . . . '

'She doesn't believe in anything like that,' said Charlie. 'Thinks it's weakness.'

'What's wrong with weakness?' wondered Flora. 'I nearly fall apart about twice a year. So does Joel. So does everyone.'

Lorna agreed.

'I cry, like, nine times a week,' she said.

'Do you?' said Charlie.

'Yeah,' she said. 'Loads.'

Then she put her hand to her mouth as if she'd said too much.

'I mean, loads of people do.'

'Totally,' said Flora quickly. 'This will pass.'

'Now she's spending this stupid weekend away with Olivia,' said Charlie gloomily. 'She is so jealous of her it's not even funny. I think if I were more glamorous or wore different clothes or had an amazing job . . . Maybe I should turn into Joel!'

Everyone quickly looked away at that little comment.

'Just for a bit,' said Charlie hastily. 'I wouldn't get into any of those suits anyway.'

You couldn't imagine Charlie in a suit; it would be like dressing up a horse.

'I don't know, maybe . . . just keep your head down?' said Flora. 'Maybe just till after the wedding? Maybe if she has fun and then Olivia goes away, she'll be back onboard again?'

'Or worse than ever,' said Charlie.

'The fact that this is making you so sad,' said Lorna, 'is a great sign for your relationship.'

'That's true!' said Flora, pleased. 'If you didn't care, you wouldn't even be sad!'

The door of the bar flew open and Jan strode in, Christabel strapped to her back, yelling her head off cheerily.

'*Here* you are,' she said. She shot a filthy look at Inge-Britt.

'No babies in the bar,' Inge-Britt returned in passing.

'And spreading gossip with . . . '

The expression on her face was as if Flora and Lorna just crawled in from somewhere. She was horrified.

'I just came for a quick drink,' said Charlie meekly.

'Of course, he never takes me out,' she said, as if she was joking.

'I could take you out!'

'No babies in the bar,' said Inge-Britt again.

'Don't give yourself the trouble,' said Jan. 'I'm fine. I'll just go and do all the paperwork, shall I? You stay and enjoy yourself.'

And she had turned around and was marching out the door already.

Charlie gave them both a meaningful look, then slowly stood up to follow her.

They let him go, then as soon as he'd left both put their hands over their eyes.

'Oh God,' said Flora. 'It's not funny. It really isn't funny. Poor, poor Charlie.'

'Poor Jan,' said kind Lorna.

'I know. I know. But seriously. She has a lovely husband, a lovely baby, a good job – honestly. If she's not well, she should get help from Saif. If she's fine and just being a pain in the arse, maybe she should stop being a pain in the arse.'

'Surely she'll be better on the trip,' said Lorna. 'She will be. It's going to be a fun trip.'

Flora made a groaning sound.

'My brilliant fun weekend away is dribbling through my fingers second by second.'

Even Ib looked excited at going with his mates on the RNLI course. But Ash was ecstatic.

'I am going to be Aquaman when I grow up, I think,' he said. Ib rolled his eyes.

'No, you aren't, mate. That is the stupidest thing I have ever heard.'

'Well, if I was Aquaman, you wouldn't say that,' said Ash equably. 'One day, I will be. But I think I will be merciful. With my TRIDENT!'

He picked up the kitchen brush and started gesticulating wildly in Ib's direction.

'Stop that!' shouted Ib. '*Abba!* Stop him!'

'You cannot stop the wrath of Aquaman,' retorted Ash.

'Put it down,' said Saif.

'Okay,' said Ash. He put it back by the fridge. 'But after the swimming course . . .'

'Yeah, whatever,' said Ib.

'Now, I'm going to be on the mainland . . .' started Saif.

Ash crept a little closer.

'Is it one of your special visits?' he asked nervously.

'No,' said Saif truthfully, lifting the boy, who was still very small for eight, up onto his lap.

'So you're not going to talk about . . . Mama?'

The boy so rarely said the word these days it even sounded strange. Particularly since – and there seemed to be absolutely no way he could stop it – Saif would speak to the boys in Arabic, but they now would only answer him in English.

Saif became aware of Ib standing stock-still, pretending not to listen. He always told them stories of Damascus, of the old days, of the songs Amena used to sing and the stories she used to tell.

'It's okay,' said Ash. 'I don't think of her very much now. Only at night sometimes. Miss Lorna says it's all right to be sad.'

'Well . . . yes that's quite right,' he said. Then: 'What else does she say?'

'If I hurt myself or fall over in the playground –' Ash's leg still wasn't perfect, having been badly set in the past. '– she always makes sure I am fine and tells me everything will be all right and gets me a plaster. Which I think is like what a mummy would do. Except she is not allowed to cuddle me because she is my teacher. I know because I tried.'

Saif froze at that, his mind darting.

125

'What about you, Ib?'

Ib shrugged.

'She's not my teacher.'

'No. I mean, talking about your mother.'

Ib paused for a while, thinking about someone else at school. He shrugged.

'I like Lindsey all right,' he said finally – and Saif knew immediately what he meant.

Lindsey Pettersen's mother had died the previous year from pancreatic cancer, Saif's least favourite diagnosis. It was such a filthy disease. She had hung on as well as she could, but it had looked bad from the second she had arrived at the surgery with the whites of her eyes tinted yellow and the weight dropping off her, so there was nothing useful he could do, except check in constantly, and keep her in as little pain as possible.

'How is he?' said Saif.

'It's like other people are all right,' said Ib, kicking his leg and staring at the floor, 'but they don't really get it. They don't really know what it's like. And they keep forgetting. They'll be nice for about five minutes, then they want to go back to doing their thing so they'll just forget all about it all the time, but you've still got it. Lindsey, he knows though.'

'I suppose he does,' said Saif. It was difficult sometimes, when life had done bad things to you, to remember that there were bad things happening all over to all sorts of people. Lindsey's father, also Lindsey, was in the RNLI too and a good man. Saif knew he should spend more time with him. It was just that sometimes he found spending all day in the surgery listening to people's worries and concerns took quite a lot out of him, and it was hard to continue to extend the courtesy. He tried to remind himself to do so.

'But is Miss Lorna nice to you?'

'Suppose,' said Ib. 'She's just one of these people who's nice to everyone though, isn't she?'

'No!' said Ash. 'She is especially nice to me because she likes me. But sometimes she has to shout a teeny-tiny bit at Agot because, YOU KNOW.'

Saif did know.

'What about Mrs Cook?' he asked Ib, who shrugged.

'Mrs Cook is not so nice,' whispered Ash, who shared with many of the younger class a defined terror of the older class of children, although Mrs Cook was a perfectly good teacher who, when you were teaching every age group from Primary 4 to Primary 7, simply required a sharp edge to her tongue every so often.

'Mrs Cook is very nice!' said Saif, confused.

'She eats children who are naughty,' said Ash. 'Agot told me.'

Saif strongly believed that Ash's best friend was a witch.

'Well, Agot is talking nonsense yet again,' he said. 'Did she eat Ib?'

'Ib would taste disgusting,' said Ash, and the boys immediately started squabbling again. Their conversation about their mother seemed to be forgotten. How curious children were, thought Saif, that their minds would immediately bounce from one subject to another, while the adults got mired for so long. Resilience, he thought. An astonishing gift. One he wished life had not needed to bring them.

'Okay,' he said, putting up his hands. 'So you don't want to go to swimming camp then?'

'No, no, we do! We do!' said Ash. 'Watch me with my trident! WHOOSH!'

Chapter Fourteen

Flora and Lorna headed down first on the Friday flight to pick up the train. It would of course have been completely fine if they had taken the daily flight on the same day as Saif – durr, it wasn't as if you didn't expect to know every single person on a Mure flight who wasn't a tourist. Nobody would have thought a single thing about it. But Lorna's paranoia ran deep. Flora was just relieved that she didn't have to put up with them canoodling in public. She was very fond of the tall, grave doctor, but she felt no need to be in a general canoodling situation.

'*Oh my God!*' said Lorna, as they belted themselves into their tiny little seats. The plane that hopped between the Islands and the mainland was more like a little school bus, often filled with excited holiday-makers and ornithologists, as well as people heading for shopping and the bright lights of Glasgow, Edinburgh or, at a pinch, Inverness. 'I don't have any marking! Nobody has just thrown up in my immediate vicinity! Nobody has asked me a question about dinosaurs in at least two hours! Oh my God!'

Flora smiled.

'Do you know what kind of bread we're having at dinner tonight?' she said.

Lorna shook her head.

'No.'

'*Neither do I!*' said Flora. 'Yay! I don't even care!'

She sat back with a sigh of happiness.

The plane journey wasn't long enough for a drinks service, but Flora got them both ensconced on the Aberdeen to Edinburgh train – not only that, but with advance purchase first class tickets as a special treat, which made them both laugh and then sob when Flora said, 'Enjoy this, as this is the last time I'll be able to afford it before Joel gives every penny to the starving orphans', and they cheerfully opened gin and tonics in tins and watched the beautiful spring-laden flowering Highlands pass by them in a blur of gorse, thick bluebell woods and lambs jumping and bouncing everywhere as they sped south. It was glorious.

'Okay,' said Lorna. 'Run me through it.'

'Tonight: hotel bar and the most exotic restaurant we can find,' said Flora, who didn't often miss the city, but she did very much miss the massive variety of food on offer. 'There's a brand-new Korean barbecue place I really want to try.'

'Ooh!' said Lorna, who had plainer tastes but was happy to indulge her food-mad friend.

'I made us a super-early reservation because if we're staying in a posh luxury hotel I want us back there super-early in bed watching terrible television and drinking the mini-bar.'

'You don't want to hit the town?' said Lorna mischievously.

Flora gave her a look. 'One: no, and two: it's Edinburgh. Their definition of "hitting the town" is "kill five foxes and then brag about it in Waitrose".'

'Flora!'

'I'm kidding! Anyway, we have a busy day tomorrow. What time is Saif free?'

'After lunch. I have a plan though. We're going to be dress shopping, right?'

'Oh yes,' said Flora. 'Morning is us finding something amazing in the vintage shops. Then we have to meet up with Olivia and Jacinth at the proper scary wedding shop. And then slag them off later if they're mean to us.'

'Okay,' said Lorna. 'Well, there's a café in Edinburgh. Run by Syrians. Look.'

She showed the web page to Flora. It looked lovely – pink and full of sticky-looking sweets.

'It serves loads of Syrian food. I'm going to stick him there for a couple of hours. Then, um . . . well, we'll see you later.'

'Are you going to join us for dinner? Please don't leave me at the mercy of the two terrifying people.'

'Um . . .' said Lorna. 'Sorry. I feel bad about this being our girls' weekend and everything.'

'It's all right,' said Flora. 'I've got in touch with some old mates; I want to see them too. Except they're going to spend a load of time teasing us about living in the middle of nowhere. It's quite deadly. I could do with the back-up.'

'I really am sorry,' said Lorna again, although her pink cheeks betrayed that she was not in fact that sorry at all.

'Let me never stand in the way of a dirty weekend,' said Flora. 'Honestly, I am most looking forward to not getting up tomorrow morning. I am going to sleep and sleep and sleep and sleep and then have a big, long bath *all to myself* and then sleep and sleep some more.'

She looked at the messages piling up on her phone from the Rock, and frowned.

'Do you know what I need? A mainland SIM. One that only works for here, so I only get messages from you asking me if I want another Margarita, which I do.'

Lorna smiled, but noticed her friend's fingers still flicking through her phone.

'Stop that,' she said. Unconsciously, Flora was looking at old photos of Douglas.

'Come on,' said Flora, holding up another picture of her curly-haired, brown-eyed son. 'Isn't he just so adorable?'

'He is,' said Lorna. 'Put your phone away.'

'I will. I have. I am. I am not an old frumpy mum who works in hospitality. I am a lovely bride.'

She looked sadly at the empty bag of Mackie's crisps which lay between them.

'I probably shouldn't have eaten those, should I?'

'Girls' weekend away!'

'I bet Olivia isn't eating them.'

'Too busy sleeping in a glass case surrounded by dwarves,' said Lorna. 'I wouldn't worry about it.'

The hotel, on a little triangle just back from the old town, turned out to be everything the girls had wished for: big comfortable beds, clawfoot baths full of endless steaming hot water, a cosy bar. Flora was running her eye over everything to see if they did anything better than the Rock and, if so, what could they learn, but that settled down after the first excellent Dark and Stormy.

It was so wonderful to be able to chat without worrying that they were being overheard or without being interrupted every two seconds by the concerns of very small people; to be able to get to the end of a conversation without constantly leaving the dangling threads that busy women so often have to do.

They talked about marriage and the future, safely for once, without Flora having to worry about Lorna not having found anyone. It would be complicated, of course it would. But there was a way through.

They talked about Joel, and Flora, free of her brothers, could confess how very difficult it had been when Joel was at his lowest ebb, and Lorna, her tongue loosened by the cocktails, could finally confess how dreadfully they thought he had treated her when he didn't think he was ready for a baby and how worried they had all been, and what a relief it had come good, and while Flora was obviously in full agreement with this on one level, she couldn't help feeling very slightly pissed off as you do when you think someone is amazingly awesome and someone else disagrees even in a very tiny way, and Lorna very quickly said that it was only because he was so handsome and looked like a male model and now she knew him better she loved him too and so did everybody else and Flora had been right all along, which was absolutely the correct way to go, and Flora said she'd been worried about Lorna too but it turned out Saif was absolutely perfect, and they were both very happy with the conversation in the end.

They pored over wedding magazines and shapes and dresses, and enlisted the woman working behind the bar, forgetting that she wasn't Inge-Britt but in fact a lovely nineteen-year-old from Poland who did her best nonetheless. She imparted wisely that in Poland all the dresses were as big as possible and she personally thought if you were only going to get married once you should go large and Lorna said see, that's what she'd been saying all along, and Flora, who had not had a night out in a while said, no, this was the whole point this was a tiny, simple wedding OMG she had no money how many more times did she have to say this to make it clear? The barmaid said, small wedding, that is so sad, and Flora frowned and Lorna quickly said, well, even more opportunity to dazzle everyone with a dress, no?

And in fact they did not end up in bed nice and early after all but they did have an absolutely brilliant time, although Flora did wake up at five a.m. feeling rather peaky. She managed to drink lots of water and get back to sleep again, not before reading a rather dry message from Joel saying thank you for the twenty-odd messages she had sent him last night saying how much she loved him; it was much appreciated in a getting-married situation.

An extremely hearty Scottish breakfast set them both up for the day ahead, although Flora was slightly concerned about trying on lots of things in her undies. She had packed some Spanx to put on in the changing rooms and consoled herself that the thing about Edinburgh was you always ended up walking about fifteen miles whether you wanted to or not, so that should work quite well.

It was a bright, cold sunny morning, and they stumbled up past the great National Museum of Scotland close to their hotel, and the funny little Bedlam Theatre, heading in the opposite direction, down to the Southside where the students were, and therefore also the vintage clothing shops.

'I am going to find something very, very cheap,' said Flora. Lorna decided to keep quiet about their bar bill from the night before. 'And very chic and divine so that everyone will be amazed about my good taste. And something lovely for you that will go with your gorgeous hair but also not make Agot have a total shit fit.'

'I cannot wait,' said Lorna with heavy sarcasm. 'Can I have unicorns top to toe?'

Flora grinned, but slightly nervously.

'Agot and I don't have to look the same, do we?' said Lorna.

'Noooo . . . ' said Flora. 'But . . . it's such a little wedding. I'd quite like something to be kind of uniform, do you know what I mean? Rather than Agot looking like a weird child bride and us looking like we have nothing whatsoever to do with it.'

Lorna nodded.

'Absolutely,' she said. 'And this is your wedding. You should have whatever you like, and I will wear whatever you choose. Except for pink maybe,' she added quickly, pushing back a strand of her rich red hair.

'No pink,' said Flora instantly.

The vintage shops of the Southside were many and varied and a lot of them were quite lovely. Unfortunately, what passed for vintage, particularly when you were looking at wedding-y styles, was the 1980s – great big puffball meringues, forty years old now amazingly, yellowing and tired, with sateen bodices, ruffles and highly flammable materials.

'Goodness, did everyone want to look like Princess Diana?' said Flora. '*Why?*'

Lorna picked up more yellowing brocade. This was from a fishtail horror that had no top, thus rendering the bride entirely naked from the armpits up.

'No,' she said. 'Some people wanted to look like tarty mermaids.'

'Oh,' said Flora briefly. 'I mean, I suppose I kind of *am*—' And then she saw the monstrosity.

'Never mind,' she said quickly.

'Do you have anything slightly older?' she asked the intimidatingly cool shop assistant, who had rolled-up sleeves and rolled-up hair and bright red lipstick, like a super-cool land girl.

The woman vanished and re-emerged with a shimmering, tasselled gown from the twenties, with long strands and a silk underbody.

'Ooh!' said Flora.

'Ooh,' said Lorna.

Flora nipped in, rolled the Spanx on with some difficulty and slipped the cool rippling silk over her shoulders. Thank goodness, it fitted. It smelled a little musty ... but it felt so cool and pretty.

She twirled round, ready to catch sight of herself in the cramped dressing room mirror – and what she saw completely dismayed her.

Chapter Fifteen

'You look *fine*,' said Lorna. 'You're not going to love yourself in the first dress you see, don't be ridiculous!'

'But I look . . . I'm such a hideous old matron!'

'You're not!' said Lorna soothingly. She would have to wrestle Flora back out of the dress before she either stained it with her tears or tore it off. 'It just doesn't suit you, that's all. Those flapper dresses are made for people with no hips or tits, and you have both.'

'That's true,' said the shop assistant, who was hovering warily. 'They don't really look good on anyone with a waist.'

'I look . . . I look like a box,' sobbed Flora. 'A great big shoebox!'

Lorna rolled her eyes.

'Don't be mad. You've just still got massive boobs from breastfeeding, which Joel completely loves anyway.'

'How do you know that?' said Flora screwing up her face.

'You told me last night. Look, it's just the first thing

you've tried on. Of course not everything is going to suit you. Honestly, Flora, you're gorgeous. You're just being a bit mad.'

'It's because I'm working all the time or stomping around in my stupid wellies and there's no clothes shops on Mure. I barely look in the mirror. And so now I come shopping for the first time in two years and I look like a big, frumpy, matronly *shoebox*!'

'We're taking this off now,' said Lorna in her Primary 1 voice. 'Sorry,' she said to the shop assistant, who waved her hands in a friendly manner.

'Fifties,' she said to Flora as she was led off, sniffing, back to the changing room. 'Fifties, that's what you want. Little waist, lovely shoulders, good knockers.'

'But I wanted to be *elegant*,' wailed Flora.

Nobody said anything. The bell tinged.

'HERE YOU ARE!' trilled Olivia happily. 'I knew we'd come across you sooner or later.'

'Good God, what on earth are you wearing?' said Jacinth.

The change in the shop assistant was instant as Olivia breezed in, wearing sleek white trousers and a white cashmere top. Who even wore white trousers in Scotland in the spring-time? Flora found herself thinking. That was unheard of.

Jacinth was in black leather, scowling. Seriously, she was as far away from Flora's idea of a wedding planner as Flora could imagine: her short, dark, spiky hair, wearing her thick glasses – there were so many choices of thin glasses frames on the market these days, Flora thought, so she must be doing it on purpose as a kind of reproach to vanity. And bringing up the rear was Jan, wearing the same waterproof trousers and climbing boots she wore to climb the hills on Mure.

'Oh my God, seriously, is that what you're wearing?' she said, even more rudely than Jacinth if that were possible, staring at Flora, who was already bright red in the unflattering dress and didn't exactly need the extra attention.

'No,' said Flora, 'I was just trying it on.'

'Everything is worth a shot,' said Olivia.

'Oh no, you definitely should wear it,' said Jan with a snigger. 'Let me just take a photo.'

'*No!*' said Flora, storming off.

'Now,' said Olivia to the shop assistant, 'I'm looking for a wedding dress too. We're girl shopping! Do you have anything that might suit?'

'I have just the thing,' said the woman, who suddenly looked a lot more friendly. She disappeared into a room neither Lorna nor Flora – who emerged from the changing room mutinously annoyed, hot and refusing to try anything else on – had seen before; it obviously wasn't on show to the general public. The girls swapped a quick glance when they saw Jan there, both of them silently agreeing to pretend the scene with Charlie hadn't happened.

'So, how's Christabel?' asked Lorna politely.

'Oh, could you send over some beginners' reading books?' said Jan.

Lorna gave her a look.

'But she isn't one yet . . . ?'

'Yes, I know but she's definitely showing signs. She knows all her animal noises and can do baby sign.'

Lorna didn't look at Flora. Douglas could just about roll over. Every time he tried to clap his hands he kept missing.

'I think she needs to keep her brain stimulated. She's very gifted; it's just not fair to ignore that.'

138

'Oh Christ, babies are dull,' said Jacinth, for once, Flora thought, being rather useful.

Olivia had been discussing things with the shop assistant, who had brought something over wrapped up in a plastic sheath. She vanished into the changing room for what seemed like milliseconds, then reappeared, and a hush fell over the group.

She was wearing a long jumpsuit in a white material which managed to seem fitted and skim her at the same time. It had a deep V-neckline which would have made Flora look like a barmaid in a 1980s soap opera, then high-waisted trousers which made Olivia's legs go on for miles, and curled round her immaculate bum. She looked like Bianca Jagger in 1970. Everyone let out a small sigh, even if Flora had to do it with her arms folded.

'Let's see you?' said Jacinth, motioning for Olivia to turn.

'Well, it's not a wedding dress,' said Jan, 'for starters. And you can see your gusset. I mean, if that's what you were going for.'

For just a second, Flora saw it. Beneath Olivia's perfect face – and she did look so lovely in an ancient jumpsuit that would have made anyone else like they were going out to an ABBA tribute night but made her look like a goddess – her face fell. All the haughtiness dropped out of it. It was astonishing. Someone as stunning and otherworldly as Olivia could still be brought low by a mean comment from her big sister.

'Ignore her,' said Jacinth quickly. 'It's ideal.'

'What?' said Flora. 'You've chosen a wedding dress? That's it? We're done?'

'It's not even a dress,' said Jan sourly.

Jacinth sniffed.

'No. It can be one of the dresses. Possibly taking us from day to night? Or evening leaving depending on the weather?'

'Stop talking about the weather,' said Olivia. 'I can't bear it.'
Flora blinked.

'You're going to have more than one dress?'

'Oh, I should think so,' said Olivia carelessly, looking at her perfect rear in the mirror. How was she so smooth? thought Flora sadly. With no lumpy bits.

'Flora won't need two dresses, will you?' said Jan innocently, although her face was beaming with self-satisfaction. Flora was suddenly so cross she couldn't help it. She lashed out.

'Actually, I'm really sorry but I don't think I can shop with everyone this afternoon,' she said. 'Honestly, I'm not really in the mood for people being ruthlessly honest.'

'You'll get it from me,' said Jacinth. 'I'm tough but fair.'

'I don't care!' said Flora, pink in the face. 'You're not doing my wedding. This is my and Lorna's day and I don't think we need this. You look absolutely beautiful, Olivia. Come on, Lorna. Bye, everyone.'

Lorna, completely blindsided by this turn of events, got up with a start.

'No, no!' said Olivia suddenly. 'No! Don't leave me! Can I come with you?'

'Can't handle people telling you the truth?' said Jan, folding her arms.

'It's a wedding!' said Flora in exasperation. 'Nobody wants the truth! We want joy and hope and love and excitement and the triumph of optimism!'

'Exactly!' said Olivia, suddenly moving over to Flora and taking her hand.

'You didn't even bloody *come* to my wedding,' shouted Jan suddenly. 'You couldn't even be arsed. And *you* –' She meant

Flora. '– charged me a fortune and pretended you were too good for it, in between trying to steal my fiancé.'

'That's not *exactly* how I remember it,' said Flora, astounded. She had worked her head off for Jan's wedding, catering beautifully, only to have all her work destroyed by a large group of extra guests who'd piled in.

Jacinth glanced at her watch. Olivia always tried to insist they were mates, but in fact she was on an hourly rate so this all worked in her favour.

Soft-hearted Lorna tried to ameliorate matters.

'Always emotional, weddings,' she said soothingly. 'Come on, Jan, let's just have fun. Here we are in the city; freedom and a lovely fun time.'

'Yes, don't upset Olivia,' said Jan crossly. 'Everyone has to run around panicking about what Olivia wants and do what Olivia would do.'

Everyone looked at the floor.

'I should have come,' said Olivia eventually. 'I'm sorry, Jan. I didn't realise it was such a big deal for you. I remember when you emailed to tell me, you said it was going to be a small affair because weddings were stupid and just an excuse to get people to spend loads of money on nonsense and a total waste of the earth's resources.'

'They are!' said Jan.

'So I thought you didn't want me to fly all that way, and you didn't send me an invitation.'

'That *was* the invitation!' said Jan, pink in the face.

Lorna couldn't help it. She clicked into primary teacher mode.

'Well,' she said in her jauntiest voice, 'isn't it amazing what a misunderstanding can cause! And, Olivia, well done for saying sorry! And Jan?' Jan sniffed. 'Because I think it would be lovely if we could all go to the next place together and then enjoy a nice lunch, don't you? It's such a lovely day, it would be a shame to waste it. Come on then, everyone. Olivia, you get changed, and let's go; thanks so much.'

This was to the shop assistant. Flora was slightly stunned as, firstly, Jan muttered an apology, and secondly, Olivia vanished to get changed.

'You're like a terrifying Primary 1 witch,' she said in awe.

'You too, Flora MacKenzie! Out you go, right now, and we'll all meet you on the pavement!'

Chapter Sixteen

Everyone was strangely mollified as they reached the wedding shop where Jacinth had booked them in. It was an exceptional contrast to the vintage shop, and they entered the scented-candle air almost in silence.

'I feel like I should take my shoes off,' said Flora. They had been quiet in the cab down, except for Jacinth who had taken a phone call which involved her shouting loudly at suppliers in a way Flora correctly thought was an attempt to intimidate her.

Olivia was looking pensive. Jan was staring out the window looking mulish. Lorna and Flora traded glances. Flora was genuinely stunned by the depth of ill feeling between the sisters.

Heaven Wedding Store was in an old grey Georgian house in the New Town of the city. It had huge high ceilings, gilded mouldings, soft voile curtains and thick pale carpets which Flora thought must be a devil to keep clean.

Even so, after the cramped vintage shop with its unflattering mirrors, it felt unfathomably luxurious and much more, Flora thought, what wedding dress shopping should feel like. She had now officially taken against the whole of vintage clothing as a concept.

Here, they were invited to sit down on pale brown suede couches, given magazines and glasses of Prosecco as predicted, and two charming assistants started pulling dresses out from the rack they felt might suit.

'A double wedding,' cooed one of the assistants. 'Are you sisters?'

'No!' said both Olivia and Flora rather too quickly.

It didn't really matter what you sent Olivia out in, thought Flora, settling back with her Prosecco. She looked ravishing in everything, the raven dark hair against the creams or bright whites. However silly the ruffles or blinged up the frock, she seemed to rise above it. It was hard, exactly, to see what she should choose. Each dress sat on her, turned her into a Barbie, or a shepherdess, or a Grecian urn. They were all flattering.

None of them said 'wow!' though: she always looked like a model modelling them rather than a born bride. She tried on one after another, looked lovely, got photographed, but nothing was quite right. Meanwhile, Flora was worrying more and more about when it was going to be her turn.

'Maybe more bling?' said Lorna.

'No. Absolutely not. Do you know what you need, babe?' said Jacinth finally. Olivia looked up.

'Think Meghan Markle.'

'What, drummed out of the country by a vile, hostile media?' said Flora. The bubbles were slightly reactivating the alcohol still in her system from the night before.

'Remember her dress?'

'Not really,' said Olivia, screwing up her nose. 'I remember Kate's.'

'*Exactly!*' said Jacinth in triumph. 'She had the plainest dress in the world. They basically sent her out in a napkin. And why? Because she's so goddammed beautiful she didn't need a pretty dress to make her look even more beautiful. That dress was a massive "screw you" to the very idea of fancy dresses. They should have realised then they couldn't cage her.'

'So you're saying I should walk down the aisle . . . in a towel?' said Olivia doubtfully.

'You totally could, babe.'

She turned to the assistant.

'Bring me the plainest thing you have. Bring me something a nun would wear. And not a naughty nun.'

The assistant blinked. Not very many people asked for the dullest dress they had in stock.

'Hang on,' she said, then disappeared and reappeared carrying what looked like a duvet cover in a plastic wrap.

'It's from the modesty range,' she explained. 'It's a one-off: they made samples but it didn't go to a full range. You'll fit the sample though.'

Olivia took it and vanished for a few moments.

'Maybe,' said Flora, 'it'll look like a gigantic sack. Could you look like you're wearing a huge sack, Olivia?' she said, loud enough for Olivia to hear. 'We're all going to lie and tell you it's terrific.'

Even Jan almost smiled at this. Lorna on the other hand turned round.

'No more fizz for you.'

'I know,' said Flora morosely, putting her glass down. 'I'll get beer goggles and start thinking I look good in things.'

Lorna gave her a hug. 'Don't be stupid. We're going to find something you look amazing in.'

'Well, we already know they do sacks,' said Flora.

The assistant pulled back the curtain of the changing room. There was a podium in the middle of the floor where you could stand and see mirrors all around and let the skirt puddle down onto the floor, and Olivia progressed slowly towards it.

But really, she didn't have to.

Jacinth, it turned out, had been absolutely right. The dress was incredibly plain, cut from heavy silk in a pure white. There was a boatneck, which seemed to carve out Olivia's swan's neck and her narrow shoulders, framing her lovely head. The top had, they were informed, some Lycra woven in, which gave it a tiny stretch, like a dancer's leotard; the long sleeves emphasised the grace of her lovely arms; the skirt was full, but not too full. There was no beading, no diamanté, no ruches or ruffles at all.

She looked like a black and white photo from the past; a perfect, untouchable, slightly haunted beauty.

'Whoa!' said Flora eventually, when she could speak again.

Jan surprisingly burst into tears.

'You ... look ... so ... beautiful,' she sobbed.

Immediately, everyone turned towards Jan.

'But you looked lovely too,' said Lorna.

'I didn't look like *that*.'

'Nobody does,' said Lorna soothingly.

'And it's going to be the same thing all over again. People saying, wow, didn't Olivia turn out lovely and what a shame about Jan.'

Lorna had to bite her lip a little hard to be able to say the next bit.

'Jan,' she said through slightly gritted teeth, 'you had a lovely wedding. You have a lovely husband who loves you very much. You do a very good job in a very necessary field and help loads of people. And you have a beautiful baby girl. And there are a lot – a *lot* – of people who would like the tiniest fraction of what you have.'

Her voice nearly wobbled then.

'So if you want to look like Olivia, fine. Lose ten kilos and get contact lenses and plastic surgery, who cares? But if you're going to sit here bleating about your terrible luck all day, let me know, as I can't listen to it.'

'I just say things as I see them,' said Jan, wiping her eyes.

'Maybe you don't always have to do that?' suggested Flora.

Olivia was standing still as a doll. Flora stood up.

'It's perfect,' she said finally. 'You look exactly right.'

'Do you think?' said Olivia, her eyes blinking, seeming much softer suddenly. 'I do . . . I do want to look perfect.'

'For him?' said Lorna with yearning in her voice.

'Oh, just in general really,' said Olivia.

'It is perfect,' said Jacinth.

'Like it was made for you,' breathed Lorna.

'That's why I stay sample size,' said Olivia. 'So everything is.'

'Is it really hard?' said Flora, who normally couldn't in her life countenance exchanging a piece of toast in the morning for even the most beautiful dress in the world.

'Very, very hard,' confirmed Olivia, although she was still looking at herself with a timidly pleased look.

There was a silence. Then, with a bad-tempered sigh, Jan stood up.

'Sorry,' she said. 'It's a lovely dress, Olivia,' she added. 'Everyone will think so.'

'Thanks,' said Olivia almost shyly. And Flora took some

photographs, and Jacinth told her she wasn't allowed to put them on any social media as it was restricted due to the terms they had with a magazine.

'It's okay,' said Flora. 'I'm going to send them back to Joel and tell them it's me.'

'Hush,' said Lorna.

They broke for lunch, the idea being to do Flora after lunch, which Flora grumbled about, meaning she couldn't have much to eat. They went to the very posh restaurant in Harvey Nichols, the designer clothes shop, where at least Flora was happy to see they did very tasty tiny salads for people who were deliberately depriving themselves; she had one of those. Jacinth and Olivia had them too. Jan had fish and chips, which smelled amazing, and Lorna slipped away.

'Where's she gone?' said Olivia.

'Oh, she's meeting another friend who lives here,' said Flora vaguely. 'Just for lunch. She'll be back.'

Jan's ears pricked up.

'No! Has she got a boyfriend? Or a girlfriend? That would explain a lot.'

Flora looked up, suddenly very nervous.

'Would it?'

'Come on! She's the biggest spinster on the island! She didn't even notice when Wullie Mulligan got divorced!'

'That's because Wullie Mulligan is a toerag and his own coos know it,' said Flora.

'... And she's not *that* ugly. Honestly. It's always been a mystery. But if she's seeing someone in Edinburgh ... Yup. That explains it all. Is he married? Ooh. Is *she* married?'

Flora considered the question in her head. Would this be helpful or not? Probably yes.

'I couldn't possibly comment on any Edinburgh friends of Lorna's. Who totally live here,' she said. 'But I do know she always loves coming to the city ...'

This was all she would say, and it definitely satisfied a bit of the need for gossip. Flora could tell from Jan's eyes that this would be going straight back to Charlie, and half the island, and that was absolutely fine by her. And it brought Jan back into the conversation, which was something.

'So,' said Flora, desperate to take a new tack, 'tell us about Anthony.'

Olivia wrinkled her perfect little nose.

'Oh, he's a poppet,' she said. 'Honestly! Spoils me rotten!'

'What does he do?'

'Oh well, he's still looking for a purpose,' said Olivia rather vaguely. 'So he's dabbled in this and that ... the leisure industry, imports ... he hasn't quite found his métier.'

Flora was puzzled.

'But he has a lot of money though?'

'Oh, it's family money really,' said Olivia, frowning. 'Why do you think we have to put on such a good show for his family? All good family people!'

Jan sniffed loudly, but everyone was used to that.

'Are you bringing him up beforehand?' said Flora. 'Do we get to meet him?'

Olivia's face turned dull.

'Oh lord no, he's far too busy for that. Don't worry. Anthony will do exactly what I tell him!'

Chapter Seventeen

Even at Waverley station, the teeming hub in the middle of Edinburgh city centre, Lorna was cautious, looking around amid all the hundreds of people coming and going, all of them ignoring her in their own big-city-busy way. She didn't know anyone here. Nobody else was coming to Edinburgh from the island this weekend. Jan was packed away in Harvey Nick's with Flora keeping an eye on her. There was no way she was going to run into anyone she knew. None at all.

With the flood of people coming off the Inverness train, she hovered just at the ticket barriers, looking at everyone coming through, filled with joyous, nervous excitement, feeling like a teenager on a first date rather than seeing a man who came to pick up his kids at her school every day of their lives.

Finally, his head tall among the crowd, she saw him, dressed smartly for his conference in a dark grey suit he didn't normally wear at home, a crisp white shirt and a tie, carrying a leather overnight bag. Her face cracked into a beaming smile, which he returned and, as soon as he was through, he gathered her in his arms right there in public under the huge departures board, in front of anyone and everyone and nobody would have thought a thing of it.

'It's so good to see you!' she said, surfacing from kissing him, and even though they had not been apart, he knew exactly what she meant.

Curled up in one another, she walked him up the bridge to where she'd planned lunch for him, not far from his conference at the university. On a busy street, they found it: a sideways sliding door that led into the tiniest café. Saif looked alarmed and then delighted as he noticed the menu and the friendly face of the proprietor over the countertop. It was the Syrian restaurant.

'No way!' said Saif looking around.

'You are going to eat, then I have to rush,' said Lorna. 'Because dresses and stuff. But you can stay and drink coffee ... '

Saif was already running his eyes up and down the long wooden bar, covered in mirrored sequins, where there was a display of every imaginable pastry, filled with pistachios and spun sugar. The scent of fresh flatbread and carraway seeds filled the air.

'Oh! Lorenah!' he said.

Lorna smiled.

'Surprise!' she said.

He beamed at her suddenly.

Saif approached the counter tentatively. There was a table of men speaking loudly in Arabic, and the radio too spoke in a language very far away from a busy Edinburgh street. The nice owner smiled at Saif's surprise: this was nothing he hadn't encountered a million times before. They addressed each other, and Lorna could follow just about enough (she had worked

151

incredibly hard to learn a little bit for the boys when they had started at the school) to know that Saif was being royally slagged off for being from Damascus and not Aleppo. Then Saif ordered rapidly and laughed when the man told him something even Lorna understood meant that he had ordered too much food. He shrugged and they sat down at a little pink table and ate and talked about everything and laughed, and she had never seen him so carefree and couldn't bear to tear herself away, even if she must, as the proprietor was coming over with tiny cups of coffee for them, anxious to make conversation.

'I'll need to take some pastries back,' said Saif.

'You do that,' said Lorna, laughing at him. 'I should have brought a spare suitcase.'

And she left him, strong coffee brewing in the tiny kitchen of the café, loud voices all around him, feeling happy and safe and secure and much less upset at Jan and everyone else in the world getting married except for her, and headed back down the road, looking forward to the rest of the day and evening ahead very much, and determined to find something lovely for Flora, who, okay, might not be technically as beautiful as Olivia, but was, to her loyal friend's eyes, very lovely indeed.

Saif chatted with the proprietor, who had kind eyes and did not press too much. Saif wondered how many sad stories he had heard coming through this door. It was the oddest sensation though: the scent of the food and coffee in the air, the pistachio nuts and heavy syrup, the Arabic-language newspapers, the radio, the prayer weavings on the walls and the voices of the tables chatting behind him. If it hadn't been for the cold spring wind breezing in every time someone arrived, he could have been . . . he could have been back home.

He tuned in to the men talking.

'They wouldn't,' one was saying. 'Not here. Not in Scotland.'

'That's what they thought in Denmark,' said another. 'And they sent them home. All of them.'

'That's not Scotland.' The first man sounded very definite. 'Scotland is kind. It protects its refugees. I think people want us here.'

'Well, I want to go back.'

This was from a much younger man, no more than a boy really. The two elders laughed at him.

'To what?'

'To opportunities! To build the country up again! There will be money to be made! Things to be made better!'

'What use will you be?' said one. 'What are you going to do, leave your lovely home here and your job and your education and go carry bricks? You won't like Syrian pounds as much as British, I can tell you that.'

'It's our country,' said the young man stubbornly. 'We owe it to go back. Rebuild.'

The older man snorted.

'As if you could do anything,' he said. 'Too used to the good life here now. You are soft now, brother. It's not like you're someone they really need or anything.'

Saif froze. He didn't move or betray he was listening.

'We should all go,' said the younger man, still full of bravado.

'Yeah, you say that,' said the first. 'As if I'd drag my kids away from their brilliant school and all their friends. They can go to university here! Get a good job! They can do and be whatever

153

they want! If you think I could take all of that away from them, think again. It is ... This is all anyone could ever dream of for their children.'

'Also, your wife would kill you before the militias did,' said his friend.

'Also, my wife would chop me into a million tiny pieces,' said the man, and they all laughed, and Saif felt oddly pensive all the way to Gordon Aikman Lecture Theatre.

Chapter Eighteen

Back at Heaven Wedding Store, Flora felt oddly nervous, particularly when Lorna turned up, glowing.

'Where have you been then? Is he or she all right?' said Jan, but Lorna simply grinned and blinked in a disarming way and completely ignored her.

'Where did you have lunch?'

'I grabbed a sandwich,' said Lorna vaguely, faintly concerned Jan was going to ask for a receipt.

'Okay!' said the shop assistant. 'So lovely to see you back. I have ... ' She was obviously used to difficult atmospheres within bridal parties and was looking very sweet and positive. 'I've looked out a few things I thought might really suit you,' she said to Flora, who had been increasingly trepidatious.

'Oh good,' said Flora. 'Lorna, come with me to fasten me in.'

'Wilco,' said Lorna.

'And stop grinning like that,' she said once they were safely inside the huge luxurious changing room. 'You look so happy

I'm worried they'll get really super-suspicious and give me a Chinese burn till I end up betraying you both. Although I would try *really* hard not to, obviously.'

'Um, well, good,' said Lorna, trying to stop smiling but being unable to help herself.

'Anyway. Help me into the big knickers.'

Lorna helped her roll up the tight elastic pants.

'Are you sure about this?' she said. 'Do you really want to be in absolute agony all day?'

'*All* day,' said Flora. 'I insist on it. If I have even a moment's comfort that will mean I'm failing as a bride.'

'I'm glad you're not wearing a napkin,' confessed Lorna as she brought down a lovely bodice dress, with tiny seed pearls sewn in to make it glint. 'I like a bit of fancy stuff.'

'I hope so,' said Flora as Lorna and the assistant, who had popped in to check on things, carefully brought it down over her head. It had a V-neck in chiffon, flattering half-sleeves, a low waist and a full skirt, and it felt cool and heavy, as if she was wearing water. It was a very pretty dress indeed.

Flora advanced out into the middle of the floor, tentatively approaching the full mirror.

'Ooh!' said Olivia.

Jan looked up from her phone and sniffed. Flora raised her gaze tentatively, nervous to see herself transformed.

'Oh!' she said.

It wasn't the shape – the small waist suited her, the chiffon around her pale skin was intensely pretty and as she actually had a bust, unlike Olivia, that worked fine too. It was the colour. Flora had almost colourless hair, very much the result of her Scandinavian ancestry, and her skin was as pale as milk, so white as to be translucent, the result of her vitamin D-starved

Scottish ancestry. Her eyes were a pale green-blue-grey which seemed to change with the water and the sky.

On Mure, with the blue-grey-green sky and sea, and the endless white beaches and pale grey stones and shingle, she fitted in, was at one with the landscape. In London, Joel had never noticed her. In Scotland, she seemed to be something elemental.

But in a white dress, on a pale carpet in a grey city, she looked like she was going to disappear completely. The contrast of Olivia's raven hair and white dress was stark and beautiful, but there was no such contrast for Flora. It was quite difficult to tell quite where she ended and the dress started.

'You look *nice*,' said Lorna encouragingly. 'And it's a great shape.'

Everyone murmured and talked about what a great shape it was.

'Let's try something else,' said the sales assistant, and they tried a flared fifties-style dress, with a thick waistband. Again, the silhouette was pretty on Flora; anything which emphasised her creamy shoulders, her generous bosom and her tiny waist was flattering. She wasn't nearly as chunky as she thought she was; she'd just spent too long standing next to Olivia, and looking at brides in magazines.

But the colours just didn't work. They tried bright white, ivory, cream and parchment. Every single one of them made her look consumptive, except for the bright white, which made her look liverish.

'I can't believe we never thought this might be a problem,' said Lorna, marvelling.

'It's just your colouring is so unusual,' said the shop assistant.

'I know, I know,' said Flora, incredibly disappointed. She'd thought with this huge cornucopia of dresses, of fancy, beautiful silks and brocades, of embroidery, tulle, pearls, netting, chiffon and satin that although not a frilly person in general, for once – for just once – she would find something lovely, which would make her feel so special, just for a day. So she could take the apron off.

'Maybe a contrasting trim . . . ' the woman started.

'Stop!' said Jacinth, who had been more or less ignoring everything and been glued to her phone, which Flora would have taken a lot more personally if she had liked Jacinth in any way and if Jacinth hadn't treated absolutely everyone and everything like this, probably including her smear test.

Jacinth raised an eyebrow as if already incredibly bored by what she was going to announce.

'What have you got in bridesmaid colours?'

The woman shrugged.

'Well, I have lilac . . . rose gold . . . peppermint . . . '

'No, no, no,' said Jacinth, shaking her head. 'Have you got anything strong? Proper strong? Black?'

'There isn't a lot of demand for black bridesmaid dresses,' said the woman.

'Hmmm,' said Jacinth. 'What about red?'

'They tend to . . . I mean, we do a couple at Christmas, but . . . '

'Go fetch them,' said Jacinth; then, grudgingly: '*Please.*'

The woman was gone a long time.

'I'm not . . . I don't think I want a red wedding dress,' said Flora. 'Doesn't it indicate that everybody in the room is about to be brutally killed?'

'In China, it's lucky,' said Jacinth. 'And will make you rich.'

Flora's eyes flicked to Lorna, who shrugged.

After what seemed like an age, the assistant came back with several dresses wrapped up in polythene.

'Let me have a look first,' said Flora, with a warning glance around the room. 'I'm not coming out if I look like a strawberry pudding.'

Lorna didn't join in the desultory chit-chat as they waited for Flora: she was miles away, thinking of Saif sitting in his lecture, taking notes. She thought of his long fingers, listening in English, writing in Arabic.

Eventually, the curtain pulled back just a little, and Flora emerged, a little pink in the face from the zip.

The dress was lace on top, quite tight, over a bodice which made her waist look tiny. The skirt was barely material at all, just a poppy-red tulle like a ballerina's, layers and layers of it shooting out around her to just below her knees. The lace lay across her shoulders like petals of a flower, her skin gleaming like fresh snow beneath it.

'No *way*,' said Jan crossly. Flora's eyes went anxiously to Lorna, who jumped up nodding madly, absolutely delighted.

Jacinth stood up, came over and examined her critically. 'Needs lipstick,' she said. From which Flora took to mean, quite correctly, 'It's completely great.'

It was. It was the loveliest, most glorious dress, and even Flora at her most hungover and in post-baby body and critical about everything could not deny that it was absolutely lovely. That it was her wedding dress.

She burst into big fat tears.

'*I want my mum*,' she sobbed onto Lorna's shoulders, who nodded and held her, and made sure she didn't streak mascara onto the frock.

Flora didn't want to take the dress off. She was completely entranced by it. Lorna had photographed her from every angle and promised faithfully to keep the pictures in a top secret file in her phone and not tell anyone Flora was wearing a coloured dress.

'But what are *you* going to wear?' said Flora to Lorna eventually, as if the thought had just occurred to her. Lorna had been very much thinking the same thing. 'It can't be red.'

'And no pink,' said Lorna quickly, conscious of her hair.

Everyone was quiet for a moment.

'Agot wants white but I don't think . . . '

'Hang on,' said the sales assistant, frowning, and she disappeared into the back room again, re-emerging with two dresses, one larger, one smaller.

'Come on then.' She beckoned to Lorna, who followed her into the changing room.

This dress was a green so pale it was practically white. It was made of chiffon, with a V-neck over the shoulders and a ribbon waist. The soft chiffon skirt again fell just below Lorna's knees. This palest, most delicate of green washes gently highlighted her glorious red hair, and complemented her skin without washing her out.

'It's really a wedding dress,' said the assistant. 'But I think . . . '

Lorna stepped out next to Flora. She looked like a leaf curving round a rose. They were perfect together. They stared in the mirror, grinning heartily, holding hands.

'Well, *get us*,' said Flora.

'It looks like Lorna getting married,' observed Jan.

160

'*Does* it?' said Flora, not even able to let Jan get to her. And Lorna felt a familiar twinge that she too would have liked to be getting married . . . coupled with a slight, tiny root of hope. That it wouldn't be now. But it wouldn't necessarily be never. And she thought about that night and how they would get to spend it all together, and a huge grin spread over her face.

'I absolutely love it,' she said.

'Do you really?' said Flora. 'Because obviously sending you down the aisle in something that made you look like a massive purple pincushion would be hilarious and I was quite looking forward to it.'

'And there's a child-sized one,' said the assistant.

'Good, good,' said Flora. The girls looked at themselves in the mirror and leaned their heads together, the pale and the red.

'Our mums . . .' started Lorna.

'No,' said Flora. 'Don't go again. I mean it. I can't do it.'

She turned to Olivia and Jan though, quite sternly.

'Your mum should be here though.'

For once, Jan wasn't ready with a sarcastic answer, and both of the girls glanced at each other, almost shamefacedly.

Flora had been so carried away with the soft carpets and the Prosecco and the sweet, expensive-smelling candles and the gauze that she had almost forgotten when it came time to put down the deposit. She whistled when she saw the amount.

'That looks expensive,' said Jan pointedly.

'Yeah, yeah, all right,' said Flora through slightly gritted teeth. Lorna crept up.

'I can pay for my own dress,' she said softly.

'Don't be daft,' said Flora. 'That's not how it works!'

'But it's so lovely! I can wear it again ...'

'No, it'll be fine,' said Flora heavily.

It was so odd, she found herself thinking, that she and Joel had had to struggle through so many barriers to be together, so many things which had been incredibly difficult to talk about – his childhood, his fear of commitment, her worries that she wouldn't suit him, her life on the island – all of that, they had made it through and were out the other end. Until now, she felt she knew him better than she had ever known anyone; that she could look as deep into his soul and he could reach into hers; that she felt known to the depths of her being, and strongly believed that they carried each other's hearts in their hands ... and she still hated talking to him about money.

Chapter Nineteen

Much later, Saif glanced at Lorna with a challenging look in his eye.

'What?' she said.

He glanced out of the turret window of their hotel room. Down below, there were screeds of people, crowds pouring in and out of the bars and over the cobbled streets, laughing, shouting, enjoying their weekend.

'You know what we could do?'

'I don't want to do anything,' protested Lorna, who was languid and sleepy with love in their little private universe of the tiny high-set bedroom.

'Let's go out,' he said. 'We never go out.'

'That's because where we live there is no "out",' said Lorna, smiling and yawning like a cat.

He looked at her.

'You're serious?' she said. 'We have room service. It's freezing out there.'

But then she saw his face.

'Walk down the street?' she said softly, a spark of excitement building in her. 'Arm in arm? Just like that?'

'It's late,' he said. 'We're not going to see anyone. And I want ... I want to be out with you. Show me the city. Go just to a bar. Have a drink. Like people who are normal.'

Lorna jumped up.

'You're going to have to walk with your arm around me,' she said. 'In full public. Otherwise, I'm going to freeze to death.'

'I can do that,' he said, smiling and pulling on a beautiful purple cashmere jumper Lorna had bought him that he never ever wore because it felt too much of a giveaway, although it went with his shaggy dark hair rather wonderfully.

Giggling like children, they hit the wet late-night streets of Edinburgh, skirting the noisy crowds of young people, loud students and smartly dressed folk coming out of the many theatres and concert halls. They wandered down from the bridges, where the glowing lights shone all around the city: from the castle, floodlit at the top, to the riot of lights around the Balmoral and the noisy fairy-lit outdoors bars of Waverley, past the beautiful bookshops of Victoria Street with their gorgeous displays, to the depths of the Cowgate, where gangs of drunk and loud people marched up and down, circumventing cars before disappearing into the bottom of the vast grey tenements that towered up the strange vertical city. They pointed things out to each other, talking about history – Saif talked too about Damascus, how it grew and spread so fast, but how ancient roots lurked around every corner – and they found themselves in the Grassmarket, the large open space at the foot of the castle, where noisy restaurants chattered and they squeezed each other tight as bars beckoned to them to come in, because to the world, here, they were just any other young couple on a Saturday night out – they could be anyone; they could have just met, as simple and as uncomplicated as that, and they both felt it.

They stopped in one bar and had a glass of Champagne, but it was noisy and hard to talk and they suddenly had so much to say to each other, when they could be loud and noisy and nothing was off limits. So they came back outside again and found an ancient set of steps – Lorna knew where they led but Saif did not, so when she hauled him up them, both of them laughing at the toll Edinburgh took on your legs, he was silent as they emerged at the very tip of the city itself and onto the forecourt of the castle, empty and imposing at this time of night.

'Wow!' said Lorna, breathless in the spring chill, her cheeks pink. 'Look at it up here! It's amazing!'

'Like the city is ours,' said Saif, looking out over the top of her head, holding her close. 'Look at it. Amazing!'

Lorna pointed over the Southside, back the way they'd come.

'That's the university,' she said. Then, almost without thinking: 'The boys could go there; it's a great university.'

They both stared out into the night then, Lorna wanting to bite her tongue. His head was resting on hers, so she couldn't tell what the expression on his face was, not at all. Had she gone too far?

Her many little fantasies about the future – coming to visit the boys, sending them treats from Mure, telling them all the village gossip, bringing them home for Christmas – oh, she was letting her imagination run away with herself, as usual. It was a terrible habit, born of far too many nights alone. But Ib – despite his disdain for written English – did have a marked talent for maths and science.

She turned round to face Saif, concerned. His face was miles away, as if it was staring out, completely lost in thought. He was genuinely blindsided by the comment. It had simply never occurred to him until today. That one could think that far ahead. That there was something so far ahead. That, whatever happened, the boys would grow up. Would forget their own heritage.

'Sorry,' Lorna said. 'I just . . . '

He shook his head.

'No,' he said. 'Only . . . it has been so very long. Since I was able . . . even to dream of a future. Even to think beyond one day, and then one more day.'

He stayed, rooted to the spot, staring out at the glittering horizon. He was thinking it, Lorna knew. He was thinking beyond the now, beyond the everyday. The government papers had changed everything. If the boys went here . . . if their lives were here . . . if he broke the links in the chain, started completely afresh . . .

But it meant putting away a part of himself and a part of his life, for ever. It meant loss.

She squeezed his hand, and he pulled her in and put his arms around her waist, hugging her tight, still staring out over her head at the glittering city, full of life and hope and promise.

They ambled back down, his arm still around her, more quiet now, looking at the lit-up ancient buildings of the Royal Mile which led down from the castle, with groups of people still darting to and fro even at this late hour. They were hugging together closely, and though Saif was more withdrawn than he had been, Lorna hoped sincerely that he was thinking about things; about the future, now the future could be real and could be grasped.

He squeezed her tighter suddenly, as if reading her mind, and she felt her fears assuaged as she laid her head on his shoulder and felt his familiar solid warmth next to her, happy and secure in his arms as they walked down the cobbled roads and through the ancient streets.

Jan had not had a good evening. First of all, everyone had given her nothing but grief all day, just for being honest and telling it like it was. Secondly, everyone just wanted to talk about stupid boring weddings all the time and not about Christabel and all the amazing things she, Jan, was doing on the island and all her charity works. It was all about Olivia. It had *always* been all about Olivia since as far back as Jan could remember.

And now bloody Flora getting in on it too, being all fancy! Meanwhile, Jan had phoned home and bloody useless Charlie had had very little to say apart from the fact that Christabel had thrown mashed carrot on the floor and that was the end of the conversation and she didn't know how to do anything, it felt, except express her disappointment, to tell him off. Every time she vowed not to be mean to him, not to be annoyed, she would see him or hear him, and he would immediately set her off and she would feel cross all over again. His stupid puppy-dog eyes, the way he was always apologising for stuff – for goodness' sake, why couldn't he just be a man about it? He was just so irritating all the time.

All the while, Flora and Lorna were going doolally about all the romance and getting married and mushy stuff – which was some cheek of Lorna, seeing as she didn't even have anyone, or was having an affair or whatever – and Olivia was marrying Anthony with his stupid boats and houses and cars which some-how made down-to-earth, trustworthy Charlie look even worse by comparison. Charlie, who had been wearing the same pair of boots since she'd known him.

Then Flora and Lorna had dashed off, giggling, with some stupid secret agenda. Jan didn't really have female friends; they were stupid and annoying.

But she was stuck with Olivia and Jacinth, who had insisted on the poshest restaurant they could find in the whole city, which turned out to be this mad place covered in cobwebs – deliberately – and lit by candles, and they thought this was screamingly funny and had ordered Champagne and lots of food which they had then ignored as Jan had stoically munched her way through it (it was absolutely superb: shellfish bisque, gin-smoked salmon, langoustine and crab, then red deer). Every single thing was local and delicious and if Jan had been a more generous person she would have told Flora to visit, and to take Gaspard who, although a fabulous chef, only really deep down believed in French cuisine, and would simply incorporate any great local produce to match his own prejudices. It might have been a good way of broadening his sensibilities.

Meanwhile, Olivia and Jacinth screamed and laughed and talked about parties and people Jan had never heard of and had no interest in, and rather than people being annoyed, other tables glanced at Olivia, who was wearing a yellow dress that on anyone else would have looked sharp and overdone, but on her looked fun and young and lovely, and you could tell – you could just tell – that Olivia being there was making the other people in the restaurant feel good, that just by her indisputable glamour, they felt they were in the best place they could be.

The serving staff brought them extra amuse-bouches, and the chef came out to see if they were having a good night. It just looked as though they were sprinkled with fairy dust. Then – worse – a band came in, who had just played a gig somewhere in the city, and even Jan vaguely recognised them, and rather inevitably Jacinth knew somebody in it because she was so obviously the kind of person that would run into someone she knew in any city in the world, and they'd be in a bloody band. So tables got pushed together and the Champagne kept flowing and the noise levels got even higher and nobody but nobody was talking to Jan, who was sitting, make-up-free, short tidy hair styled to the side for the evening, in her black top and a skirt on, a skirt being the biggest concession she could make to trying to dress up.

'I think I'm just going to head,' she said to Olivia, who widened her lovely eyes and said was she sure, they were just having fun and Jan nodded and pulled out her key – Olivia had paid for the hotel rooms, except somehow Olivia had a suite and Jan had a tiny room at the back overlooking the bins, and Olivia said, okay, have a great time! which as Jan was going back to sit in her tiny bedroom overlooking the bins didn't seem terribly promising. She rather passive-aggressively took out her wallet to offer to pay her share and her share only of the incredibly expensive dinner, but Olivia and Jacinth just stared at her in horror, and she was sure Jacinth was mouthing 'oh my Gawwdd' as Olivia waved her money away.

Jan turned and marched off, shoulders down, through the exit and out into the Lawnmarket on the Royal Mile, which was full of weekend revellers and happy couples. In fact, there was one now, all snuggled up into one another in some moony dreamworld of their own, as if they were the only couple who had ever been like this, in a way Jan couldn't remember her and Charlie being, ever. She scowled at them just as they passed beneath a street light, and then she realised who it was, and gasped aloud:

'LORNA!'

Chapter Twenty

All three froze.

Lorna's first instinct was to jump away, but she and Saif were so closely entangled: he had his hand in the back pocket of her jeans; she had hers tightly around his waist. They couldn't and didn't manage to spring apart, but more had to unfurl themselves.

'Uh . . .' said Lorna, cursing and cursing her luck. She had said, hadn't she, that they should stay in? Stay hidden. And it had to be bloody Jan. Of all the people in the world. Of all the bloody thousand or so people on their bloody island and eight billion people in the world, half a million of them in this bloody city alone.

Jan, meanwhile, had let her mouth drop open and was gaping like a fish, looking from one to the other.

'You . . . you! You . . . !'

Saif put his hands up in what was meant to be a reassuring way.

'Jan, I . . . '

She stared at him.

'You send your boys to us! You send the boys to the Outward Adventures! Is that when you want to . . . sneak off with your fancy woman?!'

In truth, although Lorna was genuinely taken aback by Jan's shock and anger, it was not that hard to understand this reaction from a woman who genuinely had been feeling that the whole world was madly in love except for her, to be confronted by yet more evidence. And though to Lorna it was indeed incredibly aggressive, to Saif it was more. It was frightening. This could affect everything: his application, his good standing in the community . . . his citizenship.

'So that's what we're doing, looking after your children . . . ? Aren't you married?!'

Saif swallowed, turned red.

'It is very complicated.'

'Not from here,' said Jan, full of fury and right up on her high horse. There she was, putting up with dull, bloody irritating Charlie while her sister was marrying a billionaire, Flora was flouncing about the place flaunting how in love she was and now even pathetic single lonely old Lorna was carrying on – with the most attractive man on the island! Nothing was remotely fair.

'Jan,' said Lorna. 'Jan. Please.'

'Oh my God,' said Jan. 'You teach his kids! Oh my God!'

'Jan! *Please*.'

'How long has this even been going on? Oh my God.'

'Jan, it's just . . . we're just two people . . . '

'Flora told us you were seeing someone in Edinburgh!'

'Jan . . . ' Lorna was getting more and more upset. All her dreams about how this might not be such a big deal, that people

172

would get used to it pretty fast, that everyone would come around . . . all of these ideas seemed to be slipping out of reach.

'And what, are you going to be Ib and Ash's new mum? Oh no, I forgot, they already have a mum. Looks like I'm not the only person who forgot. If I was going to look out for the boys, I'd probably have started with that.'

Lorna burst into tears.

Jan felt a powerful mixture of emotions: jealousy, sadness, but most of all as if she'd been left out again. Nobody told her anything. Nobody included her. It made her prickly and cruel.

'Yeah, Ash cried too on the Outward Adventures,' she found herself saying. 'Missing his mum. I didn't mention it.'

Saif squeezed Lorna, then walked forwards towards Jan. She was furious at how large his brown eyes were, trained straight on her, so handsome and so sad.

'I understand,' he said in his low, quiet voice, the accent a real mix of Middle Eastern and a Highland lilt that was oddly seductive, 'that this is difficult for you to see. I wish you had not seen it. I apologise with all my heart for the shock. I was very grateful when you took the boys – not because of this, but because of how much they loved being with you and doing your courses. You taught them so much, Jan. They learned so much from you and Charlie. And they did let out their emotions with you, and it was so good for us, Jan. It helped us so much as a family. But, Jan, I cannot go home and Amena . . . ' He sighed. They had managed not to reveal this to the rest of the village, nor tell the boys. They barely talked about it to each other. But if no one knew, what was the point? 'Jan, if I tell you something now, can you keep it a secret? It is the heaviest part of my life. Can I trust you with it?'

Jan shrugged.

173

'That depends. I don't know if I can believe anything you say.'

'We never lied!' Lorna hissed furiously from behind Saif, but they both ignored her.

'Jan, Amena has moved on. I realise this does not make it better. But we know this. This is the situation. The boys do not know this. They believe – they must believe – that they have a mother who still loves them.'

Jan's mouth flapped open even more.

'Please,' said Saif. Lorna sank further into the background, realising he was much better placed to deal with it than she was. 'Now you know my life. My whole life. You are holding it in your hands. Please, Jan. My boys mean the world to me. My life is never simple. But please, I must beg you to keep this secret not for me – and you see, I am weak of course, I see how that must look –' Lorna might have done a small Miss Piggy snort at that, but she understood Saif's strategy. '– but please . . . for them.'

'But—'

'I have a chance, Jan, to stay in this country. With the children. But a scandal . . . ' He shook his head. Then, scared for his boys, he pushed it even further. 'That would ruin me. It is even possible the Home Office would send me back if they thought . . . if they thought I was of bad moral character.'

Saif didn't even know if what he was saying was true or not; he was so desperate, so terrified in that moment, that everything would spill out, that everything would be ruined, that he found himself doing something he had never done to the people smugglers, to the people who had found him, to the British authorities. He begged.

'My life is in your hands, Jan. I do not think . . . You are not the person who would do this to me.'

174

Jan still looked at him; the gaze on his handsome, slightly strained face was so sincere.

'Do you love her?' she found herself asking bitterly.

'I love my boys,' said Saif steadily. 'I want them to have a future. They are all that matter to me.'

Jan felt rather triumphant, and she glanced at Lorna, who stood feeling humiliated even as she tried to tell herself he didn't mean it.

'Would they really send you home?' said Jan.

'It's entirely possible,' said Saif. 'My application is going in.'

She nodded curtly.

'I would not do that to you.'

'I would owe you my life.'

She blinked.

'Fine,' she said. 'I didn't see you.'

'Not even ... please. Not even to Charlie? Please, Jan, I am begging you. I have for you the gratitude of a million lifetimes,' he said, bowing his head. 'I owe everything to you.'

Saif stood there, head bowed. Jan felt a sudden urge to give him a cuddle – she hadn't touched Charlie in months, hadn't had any close contact with anyone except a slightly snotty baby. She stared at him, then nodded quickly and scurried away.

Lorna watched her go, as she stood in the shadows of the ancient buildings, looking at Saif, his outline on the cobblestones.

Chapter Twenty-one

Somehow, the evening had grown even colder. Nights in Edinburgh in the spring were never warm and Lorna shivered without Saif's arms around her. Jan had gone down one of the tiny closes and stairwells that lined the Royal Mile, simply vanished from sight. The revellers too seemed to have vanished; the cobbled street, in the shadow of the great castle, was empty and echoing. Lorna walked on alone, stung and hurt beyond belief.

'Lorenah!'

The voice that she loved beyond all others, saying her name. He ran to catch her up and she shook him off.

'You know I had to . . . I had to say that to her.'

Lorna nodded numbly, marching onwards.

'Of course you did.'

'I could not say . . . I could not say the truth.'

'But it was the truth,' said Lorna with clarity. 'You would do anything to keep your boys safe. Of course you would. If she'd told you to dump me, you would have. In a heartbeat.'

'Why would she do that?'

Lorna shrugged.

'Because she's mean.'

Saif looked confused.

'I had to say the first thing . . . that would save us.'

Lorna nodded stiffly, not stopping walking.

'Us, Lorenah.'

He stopped her then, took her hand.

'Us. You and me. Us.'

'I don't understand.'

'If I can keep you out of this . . . I think that will be easier for Jan to keep it a secret maybe?'

Lorna shrugged.

'Like she'd do anything for you but not for me?' she said, feeling it sting.

'No,' he said. 'Not for me. For the boys. That she will not betray my sons.'

Lorna nodded reluctantly.

He took both her hands, pulled her closer.

'Do you think,' said Lorna, her voice trembling, 'we should break up then? In case? So we're not a couple, so you can deny it if the boys do hear?'

His eyes closed briefly in pain.

'I think it would be –' His hand waggled slightly. '– after the destruction of Basra.' His face screwed up and Lorna frowned. 'That does not work in English in any way. I mean, too late.'

'Oh,' she said, realising. 'You mean, closing the barn door after the horse has bolted.'

He looked confused.

'That does not work in my language.'

'No,' said Lorna. She paused. 'But it doesn't explain ... it doesn't explain what you're going to do.'

Her voice went quiet, and she stared at the damp, shining pavement, the street light bright, high above her head.

His face looked confused suddenly, as if he had only just realised something.

'But, Lorenah,' he said softly, lifting up her head in his hand. 'You do know that I love you?'

Lorna stared at him for a long time.

'I did not know,' she said finally. He frowned.

'I did not show you that I love you?'

Lorna shrugged.

'You didn't say it.'

'I did not ... I did not think I needed to say it.'

'Because everything gets so complicated?'

He shrugged.

'Everything is already very complicated. My love for you was a very simple thing in my life. Until now,' he said.

Lorna swallowed.

'I ... I love you too.'

He nodded.

'I ... Good,' he said.

Lorna half smiled.

'You just already assumed I did?' she said. He looked away, a smile playing on his lips.

'I did not ...'

'You did! Wow, so arrogant!'

'I am many things,' said Saif softly. 'But that, no. I know how many flaws I have.'

Lorna kissed him.

'Loving you is easy,' he said. 'It is everything else that is difficult.'

'And for me, it's the complete opposite,' said Lorna. 'You are the most difficult thing in my life.'

'And I am sorry for that.'

They wended their way back down towards their hotel, keeping an eye out for whoever else would be around, too scared to consider or discuss the consequences if Jan went nuclear and told everyone. Tentatively, they took each other's hands once more when they reached the lobby, Lorna gathering this new knowledge to her to keep her warm.

He glanced around once more at the door, as if checking Jan wasn't behind them; that nobody was on his tail.

'To bed, my love,' said Lorna quietly in his ear. 'Come to bed.'

Chapter Twenty-two

'Shit!' said Flora.

'Don't,' said Lorna, as they huddled in the corner of the train carriage. They had met at Waverley station, Flora late and overslept, Lorna quiet and still coming to terms with the night before. She and Saif had ended up wrapped in one another's arms, but without being able to talk about what would happen next. Because there was nothing they could do except trust Jan. And hope for the best.

'But . . . Shit!'

'Please,' said Lorna. 'Oh God, I have to tell you. I was having a really, really, really good weekend.'

Flora looked at the expensive gold-ribboned boxes of the bridesmaids' dresses on the luggage rack. Her own dress would need to get altered later. She was already doing her best not to think about the cost. Well. Anyway. There were more pressing problems.

'Why did it have to be Jan?' said Flora. 'She hates us!'

'I know,' said Lorna.

'I wish I'd been nicer to her,' said Flora. 'Shit.'

'You were nice to her!' protested Lorna loyally. 'Up to the point where it became absolutely impossible because she was being such a monster.'

'She's not going to see it like that though, is she? She's going to think, "I was being perfectly reasonable and realistic about marriage and those idiots bullied me."'

Lorna sighed.

'Well, maybe it won't be about us,' she said. 'Come on, she can't be that evil. Charlie wouldn't have married her otherwise.'

'You mean miserable poor old sod Charlie holding up the bar at the Harbour's Rest because he's so depressed he married a witch?'

'And surely,' said Lorna, 'she'll see that it would hurt the boys. Her whole life is looking after boys, kids from difficult backgrounds. It's everything she does. She wouldn't mess the boys up like that.'

'She might see it as telling the truth.'

'Well, if the truth is so destructive ... oh God. We talked about breaking up.'

Flora's face fell.

'Oh, darling. What, and just denying everything?'

Lorna's face was a mask of misery as she nodded.

'That's pointless,' said Flora. 'If it gets out, it'll get out; it won't matter if you're still seeing him or not. The fact is that you were, so it's too late.'

'And Basra has fallen,' said Lorna incomprehensibly. 'I know. But then now we'll just be sneaking around even more. And it'll be worse because we'll know that people think that it's terribly wrong.'

'Well, I don't,' said Flora. 'Do you mean people with a moral compass? Or busybodies who like to tell everyone else off and point fingers and throw stones?'

'I don't know,' said Lorna. 'All I know is I was so happy. And it felt like everything was ... going. Moving somewhere. And now, it feels like I'm back at square one. Worse.'

Flora took a sip from her cup.

'Would it really be the worst thing ... ?' she said. 'I'm just playing devil's advocate. But what if she just told everyone and everyone was like, oh well, okay?'

'Even the boys?' said Lorna. 'No. I don't think so.'

'No, but ... I mean, like ripping off a plaster. You're not going to live the rest of your life like this, are you?'

'No. But it's definitely not the time. Ash is just a baby. At least let him get his right to stay first.'

Flora put out her hand and patted Lorna.

'There is one thing ... ' said Lorna, and she told Flora about not only his saying 'I love you', but the clear and obvious message that it had never, ever been required.

'Oh well, that's good,' said Flora. 'Although it remains absolutely astonishing what men don't quite think is required.'

'I know,' said Lorna. 'But even so.'

She thought for a minute.

'It's a bit monkey's paw though,' she said. 'As if I wished for something and got it in the worst way possible. I'd still rather he hadn't said it, and that Jan hadn't seen us.'

Flora leaned forwards.

'I am sorry this happened,' she said, 'and if I hear of her breathing a word of it to anyone I am going to kill her. I am going to actually cut her hand off with that stupid penknife she keeps in her belt.'

'I don't think that will be too easy.'

'I don't care. Slow is better,' said Flora bullishly. 'Sod her fat baby.'

'*Flora!*' Lorna played with her coffee cup. 'I think Jan needs attention,' she said. 'I think she's lonely somehow. I think maybe if we showered her in positive attention, she wouldn't feel the need to tell people about us.'

Flora stared at her in horror.

'You're telling me I have to be *super-nice* to Jan?'

Lorna shrugged.

'It's all I can think of. You saw what she's like when Olivia is there.'

'Oh God. Please can't I just kill her with a rusty pen-knife? *Please?*'

Saif got off the train and then sat on the ferry in a state of surprised calm, waiting for the guilt, the usual all-encompassing pain, to hit him like a hammer blow. It didn't ... Well. His life was so complicated.

He tried, though, to ignore what had happened to Jan, and instead just to remember the sensation of happiness, of the sheer uncomplicated pleasure of being with Lorna when they could shut out the world, when they could build their own private universe, just the two of them, cast everything behind them, everything away. It was heaven. Which meant, of course, it wasn't real life. He kept his eyes on the sea; the rain was thudding down steadily. It had been a very changeable April indeed.

He thought of Lorna's skin, the laughter, the sticky Syrian

cakes they had eaten in bed ... but that made him think again of the men in the café, talking about his home country. He tried to remember again their whispered promises in the darkness before dawn, the almond scent of her hair ... He worried again about how the boys were getting on. Ib had a phone but he wasn't terribly good at answering it, and had only responded in grunts when Saif had called him the previous evening.

They would be fine. Of course they would be fine. And he ... he felt guilty even telling himself what he told his patients day in, day out: look after yourself. You can't look after other people if you always put yourself last. But putting himself first felt wrong. Just wrong when he had no idea what was happening elsewhere, when the world was still so awful a place, when Amena—

He swung off the road towards the ferry port and cranked up Radio nan Gàidheal to distract his swirling thoughts.

At the campsite, the boys were waiting, Ib was looking sulky, which was not the most unusual state of affairs. Ash ran to Saif and threw his arms around him as always.

'Was it fun?' said Saif, unable not to smile.

'YES! I can swim now and there were slides and I could punch a shark not a real shark a blow-up shark but I think maybe a real shark and Ib got in big trouble and I dived in without sitting down on my head! I dived on my head! I can dive! And sharks!'

'Ib what?' said Saif, trying to disentangle himself.

'Yes, hi,' said old Iain, who had run the weekend. 'Well, I

didnae want to call you at your conference, ken. It wasn't that much of a bother, I didnae want everyone to get worked up, but ... I mean ... '

'What happened?'

'He hit a lad, like.'

'Ib?' said Saif, turning with genuine sadness. Ib stood motionless, his mouth a determined line.

'Why didn't you call me?' he asked Iain. 'This is unacceptable.'

'He was provoked, like,' said Iain. 'We figured it was for the best. The lad didnae tell his parents either. I think he had the more to be ashamed about.'

Saif looked at Ib, still confused.

'He said the "p" word,' said Ib quietly, and it took Saif a moment to deconstruct what had gone on; that the other child – a mainland child of course, not an island boy – had been racially abusive.

'Ah,' he said.

'I didnae ... I mean, I understand your Ib,' said Iain. 'Of course he won't be able to fight his way out of it at the high school.'

'He won't,' said Saif, sad and cross and angry and proud all at once. 'Ibrahim! You know this is unacceptable. You can't ... '

'Why not?' said Ib.

'The other lad apologised, aye,' said Iain, who clearly thought Ib had done completely the right thing.

'There are better ways to fight your battles,' said Saif.

'How would you know?' said Ib in full rudeness. 'I hit him and he stopped.'

'Not a bad right hook either,' said Iain. Saif did his best to smile under the circumstances, even though inside he

185

was churning. The welcome they had received on the island had been so warm, so all-encompassing, especially for the children, that he genuinely hadn't considered he would need to brief Ib.

The boys got in the car, slightly soggy, Ash very anxious to show Saif his swimming in the bath the second they reached the house.

But Ib would have to go to the mainland later this year to get his education. He'd have to share with these lads. Saif had thought of racism being distant, something happening in England maybe, or America; places far away. Not on Mure.

But the outside world could encroach, even on Mure, as he knew only too well.

'I don't care if you punish me,' said Ib from the back seat.

'I'm not going to punish you,' said Saif, who had never chastised either boy in his life and wasn't about to start now.

'He said sorry!' said Ash, the peacemaker as always. 'The other boy said sorry! Because he was a bad, bad racist! He was the baddie and Ib was the goodie.'

'Okay, that's enough,' said Saif, an edge to his voice. He parked up outside the manse and turned around.

'I have seen where aggression leads,' he said. 'So have you. That is why I do not want you to fight.'

'But when things are wrong, you have to fight,' said Ib. 'If I didn't do it quickly, he'd do it for ever. Then all his mates would start doing it too. Then they'd do it to Ash.'

Saif blinked.

'You're going to send me to the mainland by myself,' said Ib. 'I'm going to have to learn to stick up for myself.'

'Uh-huh,' said Saif.

They got out of the car. Saif put his arm around Ib, who

186

shook it off and stalked into the house. Ash, on the other hand, was very up for a cuddle.

'Agot says you should most probably have got us a present,' he said. 'Did you most probably have got us a present?'

'I have,' said Saif, pulling a pink box of pistachio and honey cakes from the back of his car. Had it really only been the previous day he had bought them? So full of hope for them all?

'But I told you I don't think I will be wearing the same as HER,' said Agot, quite reasonably as far as she was concerned.

'You don't say "her",' said Flora, slightly annoyed. It was raining on Mure, but the farmhouse on this Sunday afternoon was cosy and warm, the fire blazing, nobody at work, a chicken roasting happily in the oven. She'd head on up to Joel and Douglas, but first she'd wanted to store the dresses in her old room where nobody would find them, and show them to Agot. Lorna had come with her in an attempt to get Agot to see her out of a school environment, and also because she wasn't desperate to get back to her empty flat all by herself.

'I think it's going to be fun!' said Lorna.

'You said that about the story of nine,' said Agot defiantly.

'Okay,' said Flora. 'Let's see what you think.'

The dress was in a beautiful stiff white and gold box, wrapped in gold rope and layers of tissue paper. What the wrapping alone cost, Flora couldn't bear to think about.

Agot very carefully untied the rope with suitable respect and pulled the lid of the box up carefully. Innes came over to have a look. Flora filmed it. With due reverence, Agot pulled back the tissue paper. Then she pulled a face. Flora could cry.

'Um, what is it?' she said.

'I think,' said Agot, 'they have given you the wrong dress? Because my dress is white and this dress is GREEN?'

'It isn't green!' protested Flora. 'It's the most beautiful white with a tiny, tiny, tiny hint of green.'

'So, is green.'

Lorna rolled her eyes, but out of the way because that is not the kind of thing teachers do.

Flora came over.

'Just try it on,' she said. 'There is a reason for the green.'

'What?' said Agot immediately. Flora thought on her feet.

'Because of you of course, silly,' she said.

Agot eyed her suspiciously.

'I'm not green though.'

'No, it's because you look like a mermaid.'

'I thought I looked like an angel,' said Agot.

'And also a mermaid. A beautiful mermaid rising out of the sea,' said Flora. 'With hair all the way down and a beautiful shimmering sea-green gown.' She held up the dress. It was exactly the right size. 'Because you are a mystical sprite from the depths of the waters who will enchant anyone she sees.'

Agot was clearly considering this.

'Like the Little Mermaid?'

'Yes,' said Flora quickly.

'I mostly like raccoons better than mermaids.'

'I realise that,' said Flora. 'I'm just saying what people will think when you wear that dress. Here comes Agot, the mysterious mermaid from beyond the sea in a white dress with just the tiniest hint of sea-green.'

'I AM mysterious,' said Agot, nodding.

She pulled off her Fair Isle jumper and cord pinafore but left on her best stripey tights. Bramble perked up, thinking she might be going out for a walk, then strolled to the farmyard door, heard the rain pattering on the flagstones and heaved himself back over to lie in front of the fire again.

The dress shimmered over Agot with a rustle. Flora took the white-blonde hair – Agot normally made a big deal about people not touching her hair, but Flora was allowed – and let it flow down her back, and tied the wide green ribbon at her waist. The children's version was slightly different to Lorna's, with puffed sleeves that Agot instantly took to.

Everyone stood back and folded their arms.

'Let me see! Let me see!' said Agot and, ignoring Flora's suggestion that she went to her old bedroom and looked at herself in the big mirror, scrambled up on the chair and onto the old dining table where she could see herself in the old spotted glass above the mantelpiece. Flora and Lorna held their breath.

'Oh!' said Agot, twirling around. She hopped and danced up and down.

'Well. It is not so bad for being green.'

'You look lovely,' said Flora.

'Like a proper mermaid!'

'Like a proper mermaid.'

'Say thank you to your auntie,' said Innes.

'And get down off the dining table,' added Flora quickly.

Agot got down.

'Do I have to say thank you to you?' she said. 'I think you should say, "Thank you, Agot, you are an exactly perfect mermaid bridesmaid to have at my wedding even if you have to wear green, *tha thu cho breagha.*"'

189

Flora hugged her.

'You are,' she said.

'... I don't even think you need the other one any more,' went on Agot inexorably, shooting Lorna a filthy look behind Flora's back.

Chapter Twenty-three

Douglas was delighted to see his mum again and Flora, after such a long weekend, fell on him like she was starving for his affection, his beam, his little fingers pulling hard at her hair.

'He missed you,' said Joel, looking tired.

'Did he though?' said Flora. 'What did you guys do?'

'Oh, I helped Charlie, with Jan being away.'

'Oh God,' said Flora, diving onto one of the sofas with Douglas held over her head, as he chuckled mightily. 'If I never hear the name Jan again it'll be too soon.'

'She's all right,' said Joel. 'She's a decent sort.'

'Hmmmmmmm,' said Flora.

'So, how was it?' he asked, once they'd settled with tea.

'It was, um ... mixed. Great and occasionally terrible,' she said. 'Although I barely saw Lorna at all.'

Joel shook his head. 'And now they have to go back to completely ignoring each other's existence?'

'Maybe that adds to it,' said Flora. 'I always like it when you go away and come back.'

He smiled at her.

'Likewise,' he said. 'But I don't think I could keep that up.'

'No,' said Flora. 'But I did get a chance to see loads of people I haven't seen for ages.'

'Okay.'

Flora didn't mention the fact that they had had a hilarious catch-up and everyone had absolutely assumed they were coming to the wedding and she hadn't quite got around to disabusing them.

'Maybe ... ' she said, 'maybe we could have a little ... little after-party? After our wedding?'

Joel frowned. 'God, really?'

'I mean, later ... ' said Flora quickly.

'Anyway,' said Joel, 'I have a surprise for you!'

Flora blinked at him.

'I thought we weren't going to do any more surprises. After New York. And ... uh ... Douglas.'

'I don't like you surprising me,' said Joel. 'But I have noticed that normal people seem to quite like it.'

'Uh, okay?'

Flora smiled patiently; she was extremely tired. Joel handed over an envelope and she opened it carefully. It took a little while for the print to swim into focus.

'Oh!' she said, looking up. 'Goodness!'

It was the banns, the official wedding registration form. Flora's face lit up.

'Oh my God, this is actually happening!' she exclaimed.

'Well, didn't you get a dress?' grumbled Joel good-naturedly. 'I thought since we'd organised absolutely everything I should get up to speed with the paperwork.'

She glanced at the date.

'Twenty-first of June.'

'Midsummer!' said Joel. 'That's what we agreed, right?'

'It is lovely,' said Flora, her last dreams of managing to pull off a party vanishing rapidly. 'That's Olivia's day.'

Joel shrugged, not noticing her face.

'But they'll all be organised and outside, won't they? And that scary woman is running it, right? In fact, that's perfect: inside the Rock will be empty. Or Gaspard could come and cook for us at home! That would be even better!'

At home! That was even ... that meant nobody would even see her, or her dress, or Lorna and Agot.

Flora bit her lip. Don't you want, she felt like saying, to show you love me in front of everyone, instead of hiding me away like your Emotional Support Bride?

Joel smiled. 'I'll let Mark and Marsha know.'

Chapter Twenty-four

Flora was pondering her predicament the next morning when a short, mousy woman wandered into the Rock, looking rather fretful, and Flora recognised her as Jan and Olivia's mother.

'Senga,' said Flora, with a smile. 'Hello!'

'Hello.'

'I thought I'd see you on the dress-picking trip!'

Senga sniffed and was very like Jan all of a sudden.

'Oh, my Olivia wanted to surprise me, I'm sure. That's why she didn't invite me. So I could get a lovely surprise on the day.'

Flora nodded.

It was almost impossible to reconcile the high-cheekboned perfection of Olivia in Senga's features – although there was a lot of Jan there – but if you peered closely enough you could see large, deep-set dark eyes and thick hair that might once have been lustrous. Then Malcy of course had a large straight jaw which in Jan looked heavy and in Olivia looked absolutely amazing, like a model from a Duran Duran album. How strange genetics were.

'Well, hopefully it'll be a wonderful day,' said Flora.

Senga sighed.

'Aye. And now . . . '

The door burst open and Jan walked in. Flora did her best 'hello, Jan' smile, which as usual came out horribly fake and awkward.

'Olivia wants . . . What does Olivia want now?' she said, rolling her eyes. Christabel was on her back in an uncomfortable-looking shawl contraption, bawling her eyes out.

'Hello, sweetie,' said Flora, feeling on much safer ground with the baby. 'Aren't you looking lovely?'

She felt in her pocket; one of the remote controls in the rooms had broken and she had snaffled it to take it home to Douglas, who was profoundly and seriously interested in pressing buttons. It was markedly better for everyone when those buttons didn't actually do anything.

'Would you like to play with this?'

'We only have wooden and educational toys,' said Jan quickly, unravelling Christabel rather awkwardly. 'Right,' she said, sitting down heavily. 'What's she done now?'

There was no question about who Jan meant. Senga let out a sigh.

'I'll leave you girls to chat,' said Flora, heading back behind the reception desk to speak nicely to someone who wanted a bigger room for a view when they had actually booked the cheapest room available and there were lots of pictures of every available room on the website when you booked.

Meanwhile, Jacinth was sitting with her arms folded.

'Why? Why do you want to have your hen night up there? I was thinking Santorini, babes. Speed boats and topless waiters bringing Bellinis . . . No, hang on – Negronis. No – something brand-new we make up for next summer because all the drinks are totally over.'

Olivia picked at her nails.

'Because,' she said, 'I'm sick of how everyone is being up there. All snotty and treating me like a foreigner. I'm sick of Jan being an absolute pain in the arse. I'm sick of my mother looking nervously at me all the time and everyone treating me like I'm some kind of exotic alien. I'm going to shower them with money, get Flora and Lorna on *my* side and show that I totally am still an island girl. I need to impress my new in-laws, and they've probably been to Santorini.'

'Well, it's, uh, their money,' said Jacinth.

'There's all sorts of boring yachts and money and other people in Santorini,' said Olivia dismissively.

'No, we need you Flora,' said Jan. 'It involves you anyway. Olivia is only bloody dumping the hen night on us, can you *believe* her?'

'I don't know what people are going to think,' said Senga, fretting. 'They're coming all this way; I just don't think it's going to be any good.'

'I haven't heard anything about this,' said Flora.

'Really?' said Jan. 'I thought you and she were *best friends*.'

'Darling,' said Senga with an edge to her voice, 'should Christabel be eating that table?'

'It's very clean,' said Flora, looking at the baby gnawing the edge. 'And wood.'

'Well, you pick her up then,' said Jan to her mother with bad grace.

'I was just saying—'

'You weren't saying,' said Jan. 'You were just criticising.'

She grabbed Christabel, who pouted and looked about to howl once more.

'Want to say anything about my hair now?'

'No, but you know Olivia's looks so—'

'Yes, yes, Olivia's the best I know. Shall we get on?'

'Get on with what?' said Flora.

'Well, we can't have the hen night at the Rock because that's reserved for the wedding, so Jacinth doesn't know where to do it.'

'London?' said Flora, suddenly exasperated. 'St Tropez? Hong Kong? I don't know why this is my problem. Why do they want to come here twice?'

'Jacinth said to ask you.'

'You want the Seaside Kitchen? Why not the Harbour's Rest?'

'Because it's mucky,' said Jan.

'Yes, but . . . ' Flora thought about it. 'Plus I don't have a licence for the Seaside Kitchen,' she said. 'If I wanted to do it. Which . . . I'm . . . I'm really busy.'

Jan sighed.

'Fine. I'll tell her it's all ruined then. Because some people couldn't be arsed to work for a living.'

'Look,' said Flora, 'why don't you speak to Inge-Britt, offer to send in cleaners. I'm sure she wouldn't be offended.'

'But Inge-Britt won't send out all the old fishermen drinkers lining up the bar.'

'That could be local colour,' said Flora. 'Could be nice.'

'It'll prove to Olivia I can't do anything,' said Jan. 'Is that what you want?'

Flora looked at Jan curiously. She wouldn't – now she knew Lorna and Saif's secret – she wouldn't use it for leverage, would she? Surely not. Surely she wouldn't . . . Mind you, Flora wouldn't put it past her.

'I'll suggest the Harbour's Rest to Jacinth,' said Flora hurriedly just in case. 'Although I genuinely cannot imagine why they want to do it there.'

Her phone pinged and she checked it; her mouth opened in surprise.

'What's that?' said Jan irritably.

'Actually, it's Jacinth,' said Flora, deflating. 'She wants to know how you're getting on.'

Jacinth was annoyed. She wanted the Seaside Kitchen. But Flora was adamant; she couldn't get an alcohol licence in time, even if she wanted one.

'Put the pressure on,' Jacinth was saying to Olivia, who was also fretting. Her new mother-in-law, Mrs Forbes, had already turned down two offers of tea at the Savoy and drinks at Claridge's, claiming to be too busy. Olivia needed to impress her. She was, more than anyone else, aware of the disapproval of Anthony's family; aware of her own sell-by date as a beauty at thirty-four. This had to work. It had to. Because if it didn't . . . Olivia didn't want to be out there again. Against the younger models, more and more every year, so beautiful, from every country in the world, fishing in the same pond of rich men. She didn't want to go back to sharing a grotty flat, living on tiny commissions from travel magazines and the very occasional sponsored post, eating ramen and nothing else. She had hooked Anthony. She had to land him. Nobody on Mure would understand; they were happy marrying the first farmhand that came along. They had no idea how she struggled.

'I need to show them,' said Olivia, 'that I really am a decent, honourable girl and not some . . . '

'Gold-digging wench?' suggested Jacinth, but Olivia ignored her, staring at her phone.

'I have an idea,' she said. 'Get the islanders onside. Flora MacKenzie is completely skint, right?'

'Does it matter?' said Jacinth lazily. 'They only barter with buttons and stuff, don't they?'

Olivia put on her very meekest voice, the one that made men melt.

'So I was going to ask . . . I was wondering . . . if . . . if you would like . . . to share my hen night. Seeing as you're getting married too.'

Flora blinked at the phone, astonished.

'Sorry – what? You mean, what, I invite all my female friends and then we'll have one together?'

'As long as . . . you know, they maybe don't mind being photographed for Instagram?'

'Oh, so you just want my good-looking friends?'

'Nooo!' said Olivia. Then: 'There's apps for that!'

Flora laughed. Olivia didn't know why; she hadn't been joking.

'But,' said Flora, 'I wasn't really going to have one. I don't really have the cash right now and we're not having a big—'

'Oh no, it's on us. Completely,' interjected Olivia quickly.

Flora paused.

'Are you *sure*?'

'Don't even consider it,' said Olivia. 'I mean it. Call it our wedding gift to you. I absolutely can't wait for your wedding.'

The news that Olivia also expected an invitation to Flora's wedding rather got lost in Flora gradually taking in what this actually meant. This might be it! The solution to her problem! If she invited all her friends to the hen night – well, surely they wouldn't want to come to the wedding too! This would get everything done in a one-er, she could have a party and, amazingly, they would still have Joel's precious donation money! It was a great solution.

'I just thought,' said Olivia, 'that it would be so lovely to have a lot of people.'

Flora's heart leapt. The chance to have everyone … Oh goodness.

'It's going to be a bit basic though,' she said. 'You know that, right? If it's not at the Rock, it's going to be a little bit … rough and ready …'

'That's perfect,' said Olivia. 'I think it just screams authenticity.'

'Well, it screams something,' said Flora. 'Normally, "buy more bleach".'

Inge-Britt was absolutely delighted for the business even though Flora wanted to tell her to clean her pipes but didn't quite dare.

'Hey, but if she wants to bring all her friends,' said Inge-Britt, 'all my Reykjavik friends are super-hot on Instagram *and* they know how to party.'

'Go for it!' said Flora, who had been so thrilled to be able to send out invitations to her friends far and wide, and was feeling happily generous. Her friends didn't mind a bit of rough and ready. And if that was really what Olivia wanted ... she couldn't imagine it, but there we go. But on the other hand, how much money could they really spend at the Harbour's Rest after all? Olivia could probably buy up everything in the place and not even notice she'd lost the pocket change. Jan had point-blank refused to do the organising once she learned Flora was involved so Olivia had hired Jacinth again (while implying that Jacinth was doing it as a massive favour for her friend).

Everyone said yes. Everyone.

'Where are they going to stay?' Lorna wondered, who was doing her marking at the bar at the Rock because Flora was doing a very boring stocktake and needed the company.

'Well, the wedding party can't all stay here because they're staying here for the wedding and apparently Jacinth doesn't want to spoil the "surprise". So the mother is here but otherwise they're half at the Harbour's Rest and half at the Airbnbs.'

'But ...' said Lorna.

'I know!' said Flora. 'Don't tell me.'

'Half of the "Airbnbs" are just cow sheds!'

'I know!'

Airbnb had been a novelty on the island. As soon as people had realised you could lease out more or less anything, a surprising number of outbuildings had been 'repurposed', i.e., throwing on a coat of paint and a sleeping bag.

'Then every single one of my friends is coming from the mainland, which is good because they won't expect to be invited to the wedding.'

'Once again, I am not sure how that's not going to make them even more convinced they're coming to the wedding,' said Lorna.

'I'm going to make an announcement,' said Flora.

'Well, you'd better make it early. If it's anything like most hen nights, people will be off their faces on Vodka Bru by about 6.30.'

'Oh yeah,' said Flora. 'Anyway, I have six people staying at mine, there's four to a room here . . .'

'I know I should take some of your mates,' said Lorna, 'but there's the *tiniest* possibility I might get lucky at some point . . .'

Flora smiled ruefully.

'I'm guessing they're not on the Outward Adventures.'

Lorna rolled her eyes. 'No, but but you never know – he might get Mrs Laird for an emergency.'

'She's not coming?' said Flora in disappointment. Mrs Laird had been such a massive help when they'd set up the Seaside Kitchen.

'She says the last time she went to a hen night they were all off their heads on Vodka Bru by nine p.m. and she spent the entire evening cleaning up sick, thank you very much.'

'Nine p.m., huh? Very restrained. Anyway, this is Olivia's. I can't imagine it'll be like that.'

'Nobody thinks it will be "like that" when they enter the Harbour's Rest,' predicted Lorna wisely. 'Then it all goes tits up and there's carnage everywhere and you don't even know how it happened.'

Flora smiled.

'Well, if they all pass out in a field that would definitely help my bed situation.'

'I wonder what she's doing for food?'

'Bacon rolls and crisps if I know Inge-Britt,' said Flora. It was meant to sound snooty but came out sounding rather fantastic.

'Hooray!' said Lorna.

Chapter Twenty-five

They were, Flora thought, two weeks later as she walked home from the Rock to the farmhouse the day before the fabled hen night, very lucky with it. She meant the weather. She rather thought Olivia was probably pretty lucky with everything. Douglas was in his buggy, babbling at the ducks which crossed his path and the peacocks which screamed at him. He pointed at the latter cheerfully even though Flora was reasonably sure they would peck out his eyes given half a chance, and so gave them a wide berth.

Even with the pesky peacocks, it was as lovely as May can be. There was a cold breeze of course, but the sun shone down over the top of it, and everywhere the world was springing into life. There were so many rabbits, and the hills were alive with the sound of the lambs playing – Douglas could watch and point for hours at the little ones playing and hopping in the fields, leaping over brooks and sticking their heads through the fence to get at the juiciest grass. The birdsong started earlier and earlier, Joel had observed to her that morning, as that was generally when Douglas woke too, and the haar that greeted them out of the windows would dissolve in the sun as the days grew longer.

The short, potent bluebell season was in full bloom; that extraordinary purple eruption in the most unlikely of places with the heavy yet delicate aroma that raised the hearts of anyone who fell across the thick vales carpeted with them. It was a wonderful time of year, and a wonderful time for a party, as the thick scent of early flowering gorse filled her nostrils. The sky above her was scudded with little clouds, the sun coming and going, the sea in great patches of glistening light or grey shadow.

To the north, the great sea field of windmills was spinning merrily, and to the south shone the wingtips of the great metal sculpture that stood below the school and above the harbour, dominating the scenery; it was a huge tourist attraction in its own right (too much, people would occasionally mutter, trying to pick their way around people posing next to it for Instagram – there was an angle where it looked like the wings belonged to you and people lined up to take their shot at it). Flora never complained, partly because she loved it, but also because usually the next thing you would do once you'd taken your photograph at the statue was come and have a lovely cup of coffee and a slice of millionaire's shortbread at the Seaside Kitchen.

Today, people were out and about, hanging washing to dry in the sunny breeze, and children were scuttling home from school. Even the youngest children could walk home on their own on Mure as there were so few cars, and Flora made out the bright white hair of Agot standing at the top of the steps down from the school, her carefully sourced Torvill and Dean backpack almost larger than she was.

'Hello, sweetie!' Flora waved. Agot's face was stony. It became clear she was waiting for her aunt.

'Hello, Auntie Flora. *Ciamar a tha thu?*'

'AAAH!' said Douglas, pointing and chuckling. The meaner Agot behaved towards him, the more Douglas adored her. Flora couldn't help slightly worry about how this would develop as he grew up.

'Be quiet, That Baby,' said Agot. 'I have to have a proper talk with your mummy.'

Then she walked round to the back of the buggy and tried to take Flora's hand, even though getting the buggy down the incredibly steep, winding path that curled around the school steps was a job at the best of times, never mind one-handed.

'So,' said Agot, 'I need to talk to you about this party.'

Flora looked at her.

'What party?' she said, assuming she meant someone at school. Agot tutted as if Flora was being unfathomably dense.

'Your chicken party,' she said. 'What am I wearing please?'

'Oh Agot,' said Flora, realising what she meant. 'Darling, that's a grown-up party.'

It was true there were very few things on Mure one would truly refer to as just a 'grown-up party'. Most socialising was communal: the garden at the Harbour's Rest overflowed with children on sunny days and at weddings; at ceilidhs of course children were expected to attend and learn their steps. In a small community, everyone did tend to get together as a group.

But this was different. Everyone was flying in the next morning and Flora was going to make up beds for some of them at the farmhouse. She'd be driving back and forth to the airport too to collect everyone. She was excited and a little nervous at the same time.

Agot frowned.

'But you're inviting the chickens.'

'I'm not,' said Flora. 'It's called a hen party but I'm the hen. Well, Olivia is the hen. I'm kind of runner-up hen.'

'You are dressing up as a hen? I will just come as an ice skater.'

'I'm not dressing up as anything.'

'Mary-Elizabeth said her mum said you were going to wear a crown and a veil.'

'Oh yeah,' said Flora. 'Well, maybe a bit of that.'

'I shall wear my skating costume,' said Agot, adding quickly: 'And also a veil.'

'Agot, it really isn't a children's party.'

'Mary-Elizabeth said her mum said she hoped there wasn't going to be too much Irn Bru. But I love Irn Bru.'

'Yes, but it isn't a children's party.'

'Mary-Elizabeth said *she's* going.'

'Well, she most certainly is not,' said Flora.

'She said she is,' said Agot, folding her arms.

'I don't want to get into this,' said Flora, realising with aggravation that she was quite clearly getting into it. She waved cheerfully to the people she knew passing by as if to show everything was perfectly normal and she certainly wasn't being harassed by a six-year-old.

'It's a grown-ups' party and there are lots of people arriving but they are all grown-ups, okay?'

Agot looked mutinous.

'This will be very, very bad if Mary-Elizabeth is at the party,' said Agot.

'She isn't coming!' said Flora.

It carried on back at the farmhouse, even as Innes was trying to encourage Douglas to cling onto his fingers and clamber up to standing although Douglas seemed intensely disinterested, as Flora made tea for Eck back at the farmhouse, and Agot marched in and out in a variety of different dressing-up dresses, admiring herself in the old spotted oval mirror above the fireplace which she made Innes angle so she could see. When Innes enquired what she was doing, she simply remarked, 'Oh, just being on the SAFE SIDE,' with a ferocious and meaningful look over at Flora each time she did so.

Flora's phone rang and she saw to some surprise it was Olivia. Recently, all the calls about the wedding had been from Jacinth, and they'd increased in volume depending on how many mysterious deliveries were expected or how many workmen were about to land and do things. Flora had to keep her cool and pretend that she absolutely knew how rich people did things as in fact she had done this many times and obviously it was all going to be fine.

'Hi!' said Olivia, gushing as if they were best friends. Flora on the whole was a very friendly person but she found this a little bit suspicious. Olivias didn't normally make friends with Floras in her experience. Birds of a feather and all that. It was why some people were still unflatteringly amazed that she had ended up with Joel. But on the other hand, she was incredibly grateful for Olivia hosting the party.

'Hey!' said Flora. 'If you're phoning to check whether or not we'll clash tomorrow, I'd have to ask you how much Per Una you've bought online recently.'

Olivia laughed in her tinkling way as if the thought hadn't crossed her mind, which it patently hadn't.

'Darling,' she said, 'you know my in-laws are arriving tomorrow?'

'I do,' said Flora. 'And your friends, right?'

'Um ... yes,' said Olivia quickly. 'Well, anyway. I wondered if you could ... ?'

'I'll be at reception of course, to welcome everyone.'

'Would you mind terribly joining me at the airport?'

'Um ... sure that shouldn't be a problem.'

'And ... staying with us for a bit at the hotel ... ?'

Olivia sounded tentative and nervous.

'Um,' said Flora. 'And when exactly are Jan and Senga showing up?'

There was a pause.

'I'm not sure,' said Olivia. 'I'm sorry.' Olivia was trying to get reinforcements. But there was truth in it too. 'You've rumbled me.'

'You're looking for reinforcements?'

'I just felt ... it's the first time the families have met, that's all. I just wanted ... I just wanted everything to be nice.'

'Is Anthony not coming?'

'No, he's in Baku. It's my hen night anyway.'

'I know, I just thought ... '

Something occurred to Flora.

'Olivia, have Jan and Senga met him *at all*?'

There was an even longer pause.

'The thing is,' said Olivia finally, 'Jan wasn't talking to me for so long, and Mum was being so down on everything all the time and ... his family is so important to him.'

Her voice had got quieter and quieter.

'Oh right,' said Flora,

'And now ... my new mother-in-law is coming ... '

Her voice sounded genuinely pained.

'Would you mind terribly? Coming along and being Switzerland? I think Jan behaves herself more when there's an outside observer.'

Flora thought how much she would hate to imagine what they were like when she wasn't there, but she agreed nonetheless.

'All part of the service,' she said. 'All my mates are coming in on that flight anyway.'

It was not, in the end, that difficult to tell the difference between Flora's friends and Olivia's in-laws, although Flora's friends made enough noise for them all. And the Forbes family looked rather stiff, as if they were unsure about travelling in such a bumpy little plane, as indeed they were.

They disembarked first, an older but incredibly well-preserved woman in a beautiful suit, her hair honey-blonde, with a gorgeous, very petite woman who was presumably the mysterious Anthony's sister. They looked around them. Flora couldn't help beaming; it was such a treat when people arrived on Mure for the first time and didn't hit a sheeting rain day or a heavy haar day, when you couldn't really see your hand in front of your face.

To get a day like today, when the breeze blew fresh but the sun was doing its best, with the crazed tumult of spring in a wet climate making everything spill over, the windblown flowers in the verges tumbling into the roads, the new unfurling gorse

(Gaspard had sent everyone out to pick some to make gorse syrup the summer before and everyone had returned with horribly scratched hands and sunburned arms complaining mightily and that had never been tried again although it was a shame, because it was absolutely delicious in a gin and tonic) was perfect.

She expected people to get off and do what they normally did – take in a great breath of bracing air – but both the Forbes looked rather discombobulated. Flora went to step forwards but found herself immediately engulfed by Kai and her other London friends as well as her Edinburgh chums, and she had to spend some time hugging everyone and showing off Douglas, whom she'd brought along, and who dealt thankfully very calmly with being picked up and pinched and prodded.

At the back were half a dozen tall girls who looked like supermodels, or a girlband as they did look as if they'd been put together by committee, all very tall and very slim with expensive luggage. They were all staring at their phones, wondering when the signal was going to come in.

Olivia was saying hello rather formally to her in-laws. Behind her stood Jan and Senga, Jan looking stolid and sullen, Senga looking nervous and whispering at Jan.

'I need to sort everyone out,' said Flora to her mates. 'I'm working here!'

'No way!' said Kai. 'We're on *holiday*!'

Everyone held up tiny bottles of Prosecco and cheered. It was clear the Edinburgh contingent and the London contingent had bonded rather well on the plane.

'Good, good,' said Flora. 'Right, you guys head off.' Innes had followed her with another vehicle, and she instructed them to follow him.

'Did you bring the tractor?' shouted Kai.

'Aye, aye,' said Innes, smiling and taking Douglas with him.

'TRACTOR! TRACTOR! TRACTOR!'

Laughing, Flora turned her attention back to Olivia's guests.

'Hello!' she said. 'Sorry about that. Welcome! Welcome to Mure; we're so delighted you're here.'

The women smiled politely.

'So, this is what Anthony has chosen,' said the sister not particularly nicely.

Olivia swallowed rather nervously. 'And this is my mother, Senga.'

'Finally,' said Senga with a kind of odd half-laugh. 'I thought she wasn't going to introduce us. Not good enough for the fancy in-laws!'

Mrs Forbes smiled rather carefully at this and proffered a beautifully soft hand to shake.

'Ooh fancy!' said Senga. 'Get that, Jan.'

Jan mumbled like a teenager and glanced halfway at Anthony's sister, whose name was Lucy.

'Hi,' she said.

'This is my sister, Jan,' said Olivia.

Jan didn't smile, just kept up the surly expression. An awkward silence descended.

'Well, how lovely,' said Mrs Forbes finally. 'We've been to Scotland before, of course. Many of my environmental charities sit here. But never *quite* this high up, I don't believe! Goodness, Olivia, it's not the kind of place I was expecting at all. Of course, my Anthony fits in with all sorts of people.'

To be fair, they were in a tin shed that functioned as an airport so it didn't feel entirely right to judge the island on that. But even so.

'Okay, well,' said Flora, bustling into the conversation. 'I have the Land Rover here, and Gala is going to bring up your friends . . . '

The tall group of unsmiling girls, all of whom were still engrossed in their phones, barely moved, then wandered up and one by one air-kissed Olivia.

'Hey, Livvy,' said one casually. 'It's been yonks.'

'Yeah, tell us everything,' said another in a bored tone, without looking up.

The atmosphere in the car wasn't fraught exactly; there was just a sort of low-level anxiety coming off everyone. Mrs Forbes, in the front, seemed perfectly composed, however, and Flora found herself babbling as she pointed out the beach, the harbour and the big statue of course, glistening protectively over the rackety rooftops of the streets below.

' . . . So,' she concluded, 'it's probably a bit different from the Cotswolds. But we do our best to be environmentally friendly.'

'I'm happy to hear that,' sniffed Mrs Forbes.

Jan tutted from the back as if this was the stupidest thing she'd ever heard.

'Well, rather,' said Mrs Forbes in a way that implied there was absolutely no comparison. 'Still, it's not like Anthony is going to have to *live* here. He has . . . You know he is used to . . . rather . . . different surroundings.'

'Did you really spend your entire childhood here?' said Lucy, looking around. 'Is there, like, another town on the other side of the island? Like, a resort or something?'

Olivia laughed.

'Nope. There's some farmsteads as you go on up but . . . no. This is pretty much it.'

'But . . . I mean, it's really . . . there's nothing here.'

'We have a post office!' said Flora, stung. 'And a school! Compared to Benbecula, we're Las Vegas!'

'Very good,' said Mrs Forbes, as if Flora was a little slow, and she looked at the lambs gallivanting by the sides of the road. 'And of course, to keep in touch with your authentic heritage in this way, maintain the original ways . . . I think it's so important. To keep your roots. To keep close to your family. That *is* important. Even if . . . '

She waved her hand at the countryside.

'Well, you know.'

There was a taut silence in the car.

'Well, I wouldn't say Olivia—' Jan started. Flora jumped on it.

'So tonight,' she said in a hurry. She couldn't think of what to say suddenly.

'Um . . . the local bar is doing the party for us . . . There will probably be some authentic local dancing, and drinking . . . uh . . . the authentic local spirit.'

'Whisky?' said Mrs Forbes, looking worried. 'It really doesn't agree with me. Such strong stuff.'

'Oh no,' said Flora, pivoting. 'It's called Vodka Bru.'

She found herself pronouncing it 'wodkabrúé', like the Russian sailors did, without even trying.

'I thought I'd heard of all the cocktails,' said Lucy. 'Is this new?'

'Not exactly,' said Flora. 'But you do find it at a lot of hen nights. Bit of a local speciality.'

'Ooh!' said Lucy.

'Goodness,' said Mrs Forbes.

Mrs Forbes's face brightened slightly at the comforting crunching of gravel under the threadbare tyres of the old Land Rover as they arrived at the Rock. Instead of taking them into the main house, Flora immediately led them each to one of the little cottages in the grounds, perfect little buildings with underfloor heating, amazing water pressure (one of the great underappreciated island qualities is where you live anywhere on sea level with an awful lot of rain, amazing water pressure is pretty much a given) for the super-powerful rainforest showers, luxurious high thread count linen and widescreen TVs. Joel had lived here for a year when he'd first moved up to Mure, and Flora could never enter one of the cottages without a little frisson and happy memories. Oddly, things had seemed simpler then, though it hadn't felt like that at the time, not at all. Mrs Forbes looked at it and said that it would do, although Anthony was – and Flora had mentally said to herself, yes, yes – used to the finer things, and wondered what on earth kind of ninny Olivia was taking on.

Chapter Twenty-six

It had been a busy day for Lorna. The blustery weather was good for the children, who could tear about outside; the worst days were the very few when the weather was considered too awful for the children to venture outside. Mure children were hardy from necessity, but on the days when the winds from the high oceans swept in at gale force speeds, with stinging hail or sideways sheeting rain, they had to be kept in watching a film at breaks and lunchtimes, which invariably led to bad tempers, pent-up energy and general dismay.

But a bright spring day, with gusting winds and scudding clouds, brought out the best in the little tykes, who dashed around the playground with their anoraks upside down over their heads, trying to take off. It was also Friday, which brought a happy, busy air to the proceedings as Lorna tried to hand out her marking.

Ash looked up at her with wide eyes as she went over his

story, gently trying to show him how to hold his pen correctly and form proper letters. The problem was – and it was her weakness, she knew, which she was trying to overcome – that his past had been so difficult, and his demeanour so sweet and heartbreakingly desperate to please, that when he looked up at her and said, 'Was my story good, Miss Lorna?' it was very, very difficult to be harsh to him and tell him that it was almost completely illegible.

'It was a wonderful story and you have a great imagination,' she said to him, and he beamed wholeheartedly. 'But we're going to have a bit of practice of your curly cat Cs, aren't we?' she added, and he nodded as she sent him off as usual with a sheaf of handwriting practice and not a huge amount of hope. Over-encouraging children wasn't usually seen as a problem, though in this case she suspected a little more tough love might be good for Ash. But Saif was in no position to give it. Neither was Mrs Laird, who adored him and spoilt him silly; Eilidh, Agot's mum, likewise. Which left her, Lorna, his teacher. But he trusted her so completely. The idea of making that gorgeous face of his crumple up in confusion or misery if she even raised her voice a fraction . . . Plus, who knew what would even happen in the future? Possibly the not-too-distant future, she thought, with the horrible eruption of anxiety she got in the pit of her stomach and the back of her throat when she thought of the terrible Sword of Damocles Jan held over them.

'Double practice!' she called after them. There was an alter-cation going on in the reading corner in what should have been 'Golden Time Quiet Choosing'. She was unsurprised to notice Agot and Mary-Elizabeth going at it, both of them holding tightly to a corner of a Maisie Cat book.

'Come on, you two,' she said, heading over. 'There's plenty of Maisie in the library.'

'I need something to read AT THE CHICKEN PARTY,' said Mary-Elizabeth. Little Agot's pale face was creased in fury.

'You are not going to THE CHICKEN PARTY!'

'I's AM!'

Lorna deftly retrieved the book before something irrevocable happened, and ordered both girls down on their chairs, hands on the desk, not a single word, thank you, I said not one single word, Agot MacKenzie.

Agot came up to her to put her side to it, but Lorna immediately told her to stay in her chair until she was dismissed.

'But!' said Agot.

'I don't want to hear it now, sweets.'

'You must be going to the party too,' said Agot, watching Lorna's expression closely. 'You ARE!' she shouted in an accusing tone at Lorna's face.

'But I AM A BRIDESMAID! I WANT TO GO TO BRIDESMAID PARTY!' She folded her arms.

'Agot, it's for grown-ups.'

'Mary-Elizabeth is going.'

'She isn't,' said Lorna. 'She really isn't. Now, it's time you both went home.'

Agot stamped her foot.

'I hate you. I think it's good you don't have any children. You would be MEAN to them and NEVER LET THEM GO TO ANY PARTIES.'

And she stormed off.

218

Lorna looked out of the window at the clouds and closed her eyes. Maybe Agot was right. I mean, the two of them were only meant to be bridesmaids together and she couldn't seem to get on with her at all. Maybe she really wouldn't be able to ... to love a child. Properly and specifically, rather than in the abstract way she slightly loved all of her pupils, even Burton Jorgison, who ate bits out of his nose all the live-long day.

I mean, if she couldn't even rub along with her best friend's niece, stealth hellion or no stealth hellion, how could she possibly consider ... well ... possibly ... maybe ... becoming a kind of stand-in or substitute or whatever for Ibrahim and Ash?

It was silly to think about it. But she couldn't stop thinking about it.

'MARY-ELIZABETH MACINTYRE, YOU ARE A BIG FAT STINKY POO!' came drifting through the open window. Lorna sighed and went to see if Mrs Cook had any coffee brewing.

Flora was adamant that she wasn't going to drink too much on her hen night. First, it was unseemly. Second, a day with a hangover and a baby and a job was nine thousand miserable hours long and she didn't want that to happen. Third, she was going to have to keep half an eye on Olivia and Jacinth and make sure they were all right in case they had a terrible time and withdrew their business altogether. Finally, she had to check that Jan didn't get drunk and spill the beans. Oh, and she had to keep all her friends together and make sure nobody wandered off the side of a cliff into the sea or anything, all under the disapproving eye of Mrs Forbes. That would probably put a dampener on things.

'This is going to be the least fun hen night ever,' she complained to Lorna as they were getting ready in her posh bedroom in the manse, Joel and Douglas banished downstairs to the large kitchen. 'I can't even wear a little veil in case Agot notices and has us all killed.'

Lorna was pensive; she told Flora about the school outburst.

'Don't be daft,' said Flora in a brisk way that made Lorna feel better almost immediately. 'Parenting Agot is like being a crocodile keeper at the zoo. It's not really like parenting. She is not at all typical.'

Lorna sighed.

'Come on,' said Flora. 'You must see that. You're a teacher.'

'I know,' said Lorna. 'Although if there's one thing I've learned, there's no such a thing as a normal kid.'

'One thing at a time,' said Flora.

And then Innes phoned.

'This party tonight . . . '

'I am not having a conversation about this,' said Flora.

'But Mary-Elizabeth—'

'*Nothing! Zip! Nada!* If you keep on at this, I'm going to remove her as bridesmaid.'

Innes sounded haunted.

'You wouldn't do that.'

'Try me,' said Flora.

'Phew!' He paused. 'All your mates are here. I can't believe you're getting all dolled up for a night at the Harbour's Rest.'

'Well, it was either this or I had to host it,' said Flora.

'I mean, are you all just going to hang round the bar?'

'I suppose so.'

'How are they going to stop Wullie just turning up?'

'Aha!' said Flora cheerfully. 'This is the brilliant, brilliant thing! I have absolutely no idea! Not the foggiest! I sent Jacinth and Inge-Britt off together because it is *not* my establishment and I don't even have to know!'

'All right then.'

'Didn't you want any input?' said Lorna as Flora hung up. 'It is kind of your party too.'

'Nope,' said Flora. 'I want to see my dearest female friends, and I want to talk about boys and shagging and drink Vodka Bru (within sensibly agreed limits) and dance in a liberated fashion without any old drunken farmers leaning against the bar going "Och aye, ah sees that Flora MacKenzie isnae as young as she was, ken." *That* is what I want for tonight and that is all I want.'

She beamed and looked at her swirly pink skirt in the mirror. She had ordered the dress from the mainland in three sizes, shopping being tricky on Mure, and was consoling herself with the middle one.

'It swirls,' she said. 'And it has pockets.' She frowned. 'Oh man, how am I going to lose weight for my wedding?'

'Why do you need to lose weight for your wedding?' said Lorna. 'You look lovely. That's the weight you're meant to be. You've always been like that. You have great tits and a tiny waist; I don't even know why you're moaning about it.'

Flora sighed.

'You're just meant to be skinny though, aren't you? All the magazines talk about bridal diets. You're meant to be like, the *thinnest ever* on your wedding day.'

'That's because magazines are trying to make you miserable so you have a really unhappy wedding,' said Lorna. 'So you'll buy more magazines to try and make you happier. Also ...'

'What?'

'... Remember for the rest of your life, people will look at your wedding photos and you want to be able to say, well, of course I can still get into my wedding dress, because you will always be able to get into your wedding dress, whereas if you went on some mad maple syrup crash diet it would make you really snappy and bad-tempered, and you'd never be able to wear that dress again and people would make Meaningful Comparison Looks.'

'You have a point,' said Flora thoughtfully. 'Does that mean I'll be able to eat crisps tonight?'

'Jings, I should hope so. That's probably going to be all there is.'

Flora glanced in the mirror and put on some pale grey eyeliner.

'Oh *God*,' she said. 'It's only just really occurred to me that we are putting all the very fashionable and rich people who have just arrived for their very first night on Mure through a night out at the Harbour's Rest.'

Lorna started laughing.

'Oh, come on, it's not that bad.'

'It's dirty and needs painted and it's sticky and smells of chips – OMG!'

Flora covered her face in her hands. 'I thought this would be funny, but what if people think it's my hotel?'

'They won't. You've told them, haven't you?'

'Okay then, maybe they won't, but what if they think *we* think it's amazing? That it's the high point of our social lives?'

'It is the high point of our social lives though!' pointed out Lorna. It was true. The Harbour's Rest, for its many faults, was where the locals gathered, celebrated their birthdays, weddings, parties and funerals. Many rites of passage had taken place there down the generations. It was part of the landscape.

'I think when people say they want authentic they don't mean authentic,' mused Flora. 'They want a decked-out barn covered in fashionably clean hay bales with fairy lights strung everywhere.'

Lorna thought for a second.

'We should probably have just done that then.'

'Ugh, shut up,' said Flora. 'Oh man, you're right. What are we going to talk about, the shinty trophy cabinet?'

'The graffiti in the ladies?'

They both giggled.

'I don't think Anthony's mum has ever even smelled disinfectant,' said Flora. 'I think her entire world smells of Jo Malone candles.'

'She's gorgeous,' said Lorna. 'I wonder if we could look like her at her age.'

'I can't look like her at my age,' grumbled Flora. 'I am going to attempt not to let it faze me. I think it takes a lot of money to look like that.'

'Maybe when you're rich they give you special soap?' mused Lorna. 'Maybe they say, hahaha, those fools who just have showers and stuff; now enter the magic floral cleansing zone we all have.'

'That would explain a lot,' said Flora. 'Well, I shall be interested to see whether the magic floral cleansing zone can get rid of that old stale cooked breakfast smell that gets in your pores after a night there.'

'Let's see, shall we?' said Lorna. They stood in the long mirror looking at each other, Flora in a sweet pink dress with a poufy net skirt, Lorna in a rather saucy emerald satin. Flora squeezed her tight.

'Better than mortal man deserves,' she said, their old catch-phrase, and they grinned at one another.

Joel dropped them off at the farmhouse, where they entered to a chorus of whoops and catcalls. The London tribe was here; everyone had happily got stuck into Eck's elderflower wine, which he was always trying to offload on visitors, and was as surprised as everyone else how well they'd taken to it. Hamish was also having a fantastic time.

Agot's mum, Eilidh, was wearing a bright yellow rara skirt and was full of beans, and there was a huge pile of pink balloons and a tiara for Flora. Agot was nowhere to be seen, but from her bedroom came the loud sound of 'Bolero' being played on repeat, never a good sign.

'Okay, okay.' Everyone started to get up and grab coats (the ones who'd been to Mure before had brought their proper winter ones).

'Hang on,' said Flora, briefing the others before disappearing to Agot's little room. Eilidh did occasionally say how much she would like to move to one of the new (when she said new, she meant built in the nineties) bungalows on the north end of Mure, which had proper glazing and central heating that worked all the time and let you have an actual full bath, but Innes was used to working the farm and collapsing in the cosy farmhouse, plus it was good for Eck to have him there and there was plenty of space for Agot to run about outside with the chickens while desperately hoping for icy winters, and he didn't really see the point of moving.

Agot was sitting on her *Frozen* bedspread, ignoring Flora in a very dramatic way. She was humming loudly and making her Sylvanians perform elaborate ice dance rituals.

'Hello,' said Flora.

'I am very busy,' said Agot.

'I can see that,' said Flora.

'What do you want?'

'I wondered . . .' said Flora. 'We were going to have a special pre-party. In the kitchen. With everyone. There will be a dancing song and it needs someone to go in the middle in a very good dress.'

'Your dress is pink,' said Agot.

'I know,' said Flora, unpinning the tiny veil the others had pressed on her. 'I hoped that person could wear this as well.'

The little face was unbowed.

'Is Miss Lorna there?'

'She is. If you can't dance for us, I think she'll have to dance in the middle.'

Agot's face changed all of a sudden, and she leapt up.

'No! I will do it!'

She thought for a second.

'I will have to put on my bridesmaid dress,' she said. 'Even though it is GREEN.'

'You can totally do that,' said Flora, wondering how many times she'd have to have it washed before the big day.

'And my ice skates.'

'It isn't really an ice skate dance,' said Flora. 'But you can wear this L plate.'

'What does that mean?'

'It means L for learning. Like if you're learning how to be a bride, you haven't done it before.'

Agot frowned.

'But you and Joel have That Baby.'

'Yes, okay. Well, do you want to wear it or not?'

Agot wriggled into the bridesmaid dress – even though Flora had suggested to Eilidh she lock it away, this obviously hadn't happened (and Agot of course could be extremely persuasive). The dress was already fringed with mud stains, and grass stains along the bottom.

'Agot!' said Flora. 'It's all dirty.'

Agot eyed it disinterestedly. 'It's not a very good dress for ice skating in, Auntie Flora. And it is not white.'

'Could you possibly keep it clean till the big day?' said Flora.

'But I can wear it now?'

'Yes. But this will be the last time,' said Flora, mentally putting aside an afternoon for coming over to scrub it.

Agot eyed herself in the mirror.

'Well, *I* look very beautiful.'

'You do,' said Flora. 'Okay, are you ready?'

She took the little girl's hand and led her outside the bedroom.

'Cue!' she shouted. Kai pressed the button and 'Dancing Queen' came out of the old stereo at top volume and Fintan turned on the hastily acquired disco lights app on his iPad, and everyone leapt up and formed a ring and Agot, wearing her slippiest socks, performed her very best ice skating moves in the middle of everyone, who clapped and danced around her, and then they gave her an ice lolly, a big kiss and the slip, and headed out down the road from the farm, laughing and feeling quite geed up for the night ahead.

They joined with the group from Edinburgh, who had bed and breakfasts and Airbnbs all along the harbour, and made a merry band as they walked out together in bright colours and finery against the soft pale grey of the May evening.

Many older residents of Mure came to their doors and windows to see the young party pass, chattering and as bright and beautiful as birds in pinks and reds, full of youth and optimism. They gave joy to many of those who worried about the future of the island, with the loss of so many of its young people to the bright lights of Inverness, Edinburgh, Toronto and Auckland. To see the hen party on the streets gave many people hope. To others, it was more bittersweet to watch joyful youth pass by on a fine spring evening, ignoring the disappointments love can bring, and disdainful of the pressing down of life's cares.

The chattering, laughing, colourful flock moved on, heedless to all of this. For this one night, they were enjoying being by the sea, the world wide open, the future full of flowers and kisses and joy: Flora was looking pale and lovely in pink in the centre of the throng; Lorna, her red hair shining, her normally anxious look wiped clean from her face, making her look like a teenager again; the Londoners, swept away by the quaintness of the buildings which lined the harbour, pink and green and dark red, talking about how much they would cost in Notting Hill; the Scots, many of them never having visited the Islands of their own country before, enjoying the wild strangeness, the fierce gorse scent on the air; the local girls pleased to be togged up in their mainland clothes for once, to have a big occasion.

'Now just remember, this is *not my place*,' Flora said for the millionth time as everyone rolled their eyes and yelled 'Yeah, yeah!'

'... Mine's the really posh one on the hill, okay? This is *local colour*.'

'You mean rough as arses,' shouted Eilidh, prompting laughter.

But as they approached the old three-storeyed creaking black and white hotel at the very end of the harbour, just before the Endless Beach, Flora pulled up short, the rest of them too, and just stared, open-mouthed in amazement.

Chapter Twenty-seven

The first thing that caught Flora's eye was Jacinth, who was standing outside in her normal black jeans and shirt, arms crossed, barking orders into a headset. As soon as she saw them, she slipped into the shadows.

But Flora's attention was soon dragged away as they got closer. She had barely been in town all week, either at home with Douglas and Joel, or working long hours at the Rock, trying to make it run smoothly as the summer system cranked up and the hotel was more or less full at all times. She'd also wanted to make it as lovely as possible for Anthony's family, with as many personal touches as she could manage, and she hoped she'd succeeded. But it had been tiring, and she hadn't popped into the Seaside Kitchen or been down to the seafront at all. And of course, everyone else had been sworn to secrecy, which meant it came as much of a surprise to her as it did to her friends and relations.

The whole of the front of the Harbour's Rest had been

completely transformed. It was completely unrecognisable. There was something not quite right about the windows ...

Flora squinted upwards. All the slightly wonky angles of the Harbour's Rest, which had been built in the early 1800s and not had quite the maintenance it might have done – the uneven windows, the slanting floors – all of that seemed somehow worse. The black window ledges sloped alarmingly and the windows had changed shape and were tiny or huge. She screwed up her face. And the doorway had ...? What was it? It was completely covered in what appeared to be a hedge and covered in rose bushes painted red and white. The entrance was completely gone.

As everyone was watching in disbelief, there was suddenly a noise, and a pink light shone over the building illuminating – where the horrible old side return filled with broken glass and the odd cigarette butt normally was – a string quartet of women, all in huge red ballgowns, playing an odd discordant version of what Flora came to realise was a Rihanna tune. Meanwhile, pink and red spotlights came on and danced around the building, highlighting the new wonkiness of the windows even more.

'*What?*' said Flora, her hand covering her mouth. 'What on *earth* is going on?'

'Oh, my tails and whiskers!' came a voice. 'I'm late! I'm late!'

Something dawned on Flora, and she turned round slowly. Sure enough, there, running up the harbour, was ... a white rabbit, wearing a long chequered coat and pulling a watch from its waistcoat pocket.

'No way,' she said in astonished joy.

'I'm late!'

And it ran past them, towards where the door of the Harbour's

Rest used to be, now a great wall of roses – and somehow, it opened and let him in.

Everyone stared after him for a moment in amazement. Then, as Jacinth waved them forwards, laughing and delighted, they followed through under the heavily scented arch of the bower – which opened and then closed behind them, presumably to start over again for the next arrivals – and were immediately confronted with a corridor, in near pitch-black, only a starry ceiling effect to guide them, with cloth walls where the reception would normally be, which appeared to get smaller and smaller as they advanced through it, until they reached a tiny door at the end, no higher than their knees; it was a pure optical illusion.

The door was locked. Flora and her friends looked around nervously until somebody glanced upwards and saw the roof, which was festooned with tiny keys. Kai grabbed one, barking with excitement, and Flora unlocked the tiny door. Inside was a diorama of a beautiful, sunshine garden – and a bottle of Champagne, with 'Drink Me' written on it. Flora grabbed it, to much cheering and giggling, held it up and pulled out the cork, only to unleash a huge explosion of confetti, which made everyone scream – at which point, the black curtain to their right dropped down and the room beyond was revealed. The bar was completely transformed, with pink lights playing everywhere, and fantastically attractive men walking around topless except for large playing card tabards, holding trays of drinks and canapés for the throng. The cocktails were in perfect little china cups and saucers, as if it were a tea party.

'Oh. My. God,' said Flora, shaking her head. Someone came forwards and popped a crown on her head. It was Alice. Or, as Flora saw when she looked closer, Inge-Britt, dressed in a

231

highly fetching blue dress with a white apron, a hairband in her long, messy, blonde hair.

'You're the Red Queen,' she said, smiling. 'And there is the White Queen.'

Olivia was already standing there, waving benignly. In fact, as Flora's friends surged in behind her, it felt like everyone was there, and it was absolutely amazing.

Flora grabbed a glass – it was a jam-tart Martini – went over to Olivia and gave her a huge hug.

'Okay,' she said. 'Oh my God. I mean ... we said this was going to be just the down-at-heel traditional hen night and ... I mean ... oh my God, we were feeling *sorry* for you!'

Olivia smiled and shrugged. 'Oh, Jacinth did it all really. When she saw how shabby the Harbour's Rest was looking, she just decided to go with it.'

'The windows ...'

'Yeah, I think they're done with plasterboard and ... it's all set dressing anyway. It's just a bit of fun. Do you like it?'

'I ... I *love* it,' said Flora, shaking her head. 'I've never seen anything like it. It's amazing. Did you send Anthony the photos?'

Olivia shrugged. 'Oh, he wouldn't be *remotely* interested! Men!'

Everywhere, the attention to detail was just breathtaking. The canapés were tricks, so a jam-tart would actually be made of ham and cheese, or what looked like a mushroom would be white chocolate. In the corner, a 'caterpillar' sat on a huge mushroom, blowing bubbles and twisting them into extraordinary shapes. Alas, Flora's first thought was, 'Oh my God, Agot would have *loved* this.' Everywhere, girls were squealing and chatting and admiring each other's outfits.

'Wow!' said Lorna, coming up to Flora. 'I mean, this is ... '

'I know!' said Flora. 'Oh my God, being rich-adjacent is *brilliant.*'

Over in the corner, she suddenly caught sight of Jan and Senga, who were sitting by themselves at a table. Jan was wearing a checked shirt and jeans and a furious expression; Senga was casting her eyes around miserably. At the next table was Mrs Forbes, sniffing and looking as if she was finding the entire thing rather vulgar. Senga and Jan were not making the slightest effort at conversation.

'Uh-oh,' said Flora, pointing them out to Lorna.

They glanced at each other. 'I'll be over on the other side of the room,' said Lorna quickly.

'Should we say hello?' said Flora. 'Try and keep Jan sweet? Is that our play?'

'No!' said Lorna. 'The last thing I want to do is remind Jan that I exist in any way at all. Might encourage her to start something. I am absolutely terrified, Flora.'

As if overhearing them over the noise, Jan suddenly lifted her head. Fortunately, however, before she spotted them, as if on cue, the doors to what was normally the fairly ratty car park at the back of the Harbour's Rest were opened.

'This is ridiculous,' said Flora.

Because outside in the grim old car park behind the old, shabby hotel was – a garden. A garden the likes of which Mure had never seen. There are very few trees on Mure; the stern Atlantic winds see to that. But here ... here was a garden full of trees.

The local girls all gasped. It was beautiful. There were fruit trees and rose bushes, everything dotted with tiny fairy lights. Olivia stood with her group of very skinny, slightly smug-looking friends, all of whom stood very tall and were performatively refusing the canapés while trying to get the others to eat them.

'Oh my,' said Flora in astonishment, walking towards it as the White Rabbit sent them all out into the garden and divided them into two teams because waiting there was a full croquet set.

'I am not playing . . . croquet!' said Flora, helpless with laughter as one of the playing card waiters handed her a stick.

'You're leading a team,' said the White Rabbit in quite a commanding tone of voice. 'You're the queen!'

'Oh! Well, okay!'

Although Olivia's team was noticeably smaller than Flora's of course, it did unfortunately include several people who had played croquet before, and they didn't attempt to wield their mallets like golf clubs as the Scots did.

It also had Jan and Senga. Senga wasn't much use, complaining heartily about the handholds and how the artificial grass was too difficult to roll croquet balls on and what was the point of all of this anyway. But Jan was fiercely competitive, head down, grimly knocking the balls through while Olivia cast slightly worried glances towards her mother and, on the opposing team, Flora, Lorna and all their friends fell about laughing about how terrible they were. It was a rout.

Flora and Lorna laughed so hard as the final scores were announced – twenty-six to four – that they had to hold each other up, beckoning one of the playing cards over to refill their glasses from the cocktail teapot he was holding. Then everything got slightly worse when they heard Kai exclaim 'Chuffing hell!' and turned round. In their absence, the floor of the bar in the Harbour's Rest had somehow, by magic, been turned into a chessboard pattern, disco lights were plying the area and, to Flora's horror and delight and amazement, an army of Magic Mike-style dancers, all wearing bowties and waistcoats and – no – yes – tiny rabbit's tails, had taken to the floor in a synchronised routine.

You could hear the screaming up at the MacKenzies' farm.

'Jings!' she found herself saying, but the dancer, whose name was Sanchez and was the epitome of a decent sort, smiled and took pity on her, long experience at these matters teaching him the difference between the girls who wanted to go all out for once, and those who genuinely didn't want to be up there at all but didn't want to disappoint their friends. For the first lot, he had some extremely hot and heavy moves to show them a fun night. For the Lornas of this world, as Tom Jones came over loud on the stereo, he gently twirled her around and bent her back and forth, to Lorna's profound relief, and she soon found that actually, as everyone whooped and cheered, it was wonderful, brilliant to dance with a properly trained dancer (even if he was half naked), who expertly pushed and pulled her everywhere she had to go. She found herself laughing and spinning around absolutely unexpectedly, getting into the music to everyone's delight. Flora took so many photographs she barely saw it all; Lorna's face tossed back in laughter, having the time of her life.

Lorna did not normally behave like this, not at all, but it was so funny and, not really being a drinker, the cocktails had shaken her loose somehow. At any rate, the lead dancer of the troupe (which didn't consist of, Flora had been slightly relieved and her London friends had been very disappointed to learn, *full* strippers, at least not tonight) had hollered that he needed all the bridesmaids up on the floor. Three thin disinterested friends of Olivia's had reluctantly slunk up and started gyrating in a bored kind of a way, and Lorna had thought she probably didn't want to go up on stage and dance, but there was no help for it – Flora and Isla were on either side of her, shoving her towards the stage, everyone else baying and calling her on from the sidelines until, reluctant and bright red, she was standing in front of a huge dancer with muscles glistening with baby oil.

It was quiet up at the Manse, though it was Friday night so the boys got to stay up a little later and there was the unusually quiet sound of them actually cooperating – they were building something together on Minecraft – rather than fighting. It was nice, Saif was thinking, if a little unnerving. He was heating up one of Mrs Laird's chicken pies and a large amount of peas, not being remotely in the mood for the broccoli discourse tonight, and he thought it would probably be a quiet night on call, unless the hen night got out of hand. Lorna had been so excited about it. He wished he could see her all dressed up, maybe in something shiny that he could unwrap, like a gift or a sweet.

Anyway. His plan for the evening, as the boys had commandeered the television, would be a little reading, and possibly a play on the old piano. There was one in the Manse which used to sit in the church, and he'd started Ash on lessons (Agot had informed him she needed someone to play while she practised her ice dance steps) but he'd found himself getting into it a little, just tinkling the notes, messing around. He found it calmed his mind. And afterwards, they could all watch *Floor Is Lava*, which the boys adored and he found utterly incomprehensible, then would begin the tradition of wrangling Ash into bed.

'*Awlad*,' he shouted into the sitting room as the oven pinged, knowing it would take at least five repetitions of that before it infiltrated their Minecraft-y heads. Finally, they got up, Ash babbling about what they were building and how there was an upside-down horse and Ib's house had a swimming pool and could they have a swimming pool and could they go to the swimming pool on the mainland and could they swim in the sea this summer? Then Ib frowned and said, we're not having broccoli are we because broccoli on a weekend night just wasn't right man, and Saif said, no, don't worry it's peas and Ash said peas were being reclassified as not a real vegetable they had learned it in Miss Lorna's class and Saif had looked worried and said, that couldn't possibly be true, could it?

He managed to get them to wash their hands and sit down properly and pick up a knife and fork, one of them even getting it in the correct hand, and then got Ib to put down his phone. This was so much progress that Saif was feeling rather proud of himself when his own phone rang.

It wasn't the surgery number, thankfully, and he wondered briefly if it was Lorna. She never ever rang him though; it was just coincidence that he was thinking of her. Though he was always thinking of her.

It was Neda's number flashing up. He frowned and glanced at his watch. It was after eight o'clock. Not work hours. Not a routine call.

He stared at it.

Something in him did not want to pick it up. Ash's voice was still wittering on to Ib about how he was going to build an even bigger swimming pool in HIS house it was going to make Ib's look rubbish and Ib was going, shut up squirt it'll be stupid and he'd put a shark in his pool and that would make it better and Ash

237

was saying, no it WOULDN'T, and separating the peas from the carrots that were spilling out of the pie, so he could eat everything in his preferred order, and music was spilling out of the radio and everything was normal, so normal, the boys bickering, steam rising from the pie, the music playing, the lambs on the hills outside, the cool spring wind blowing the long meadow grass, the nights getting longer so quickly it felt like a miracle every night and the log burner crackling away. Normal. His normal life.

It stopped ringing, then started again.

'Daddy!' said Ash. 'I think that is the telephone, you know!'

Ib, on the other hand, flicked his eyes to his father, nervousness in them.

'Eat,' Saif said. *'Ta'akul!'*

He snatched the phone and took it into the sitting room. Then, on second thoughts, he went outside. It was chilly in the wind off the sea, where the big tankers were going past in the far, far distance and the seafield of windmills was going round nineteen to the dozen.

'Yes?'

He was uncharacteristically short. Maybe it was something about his right to remain application; maybe she was late doing paperwork. Maybe it was something very small and insignificant and she would apologise and they would get it cleared up in no time, no time at all.

'Saif.'

The dancers beckoned all the women to the floor as the undying opening chords of 'Dancing Queen' made everyone pour towards the dancefloor. Jan and Senga excepted, they all got up with a great scraping back of chairs and clattering of high heels, Inge-Britt scrambling, as the tallest woman, to get hold of the tallest dancer before anyone else nabbed him.

Olivia, who had been fully adopted by Flora's London friends, was wearing an expression that looked as if she couldn't quite believe that she might actually be having ... fun? Even her model-y friends were shimmering away quite cheerfully; there was definitely something in those jam-tart cocktails. The lights glowed, the noise and laughter rose and Flora genuinely couldn't believe that this was their party, that this was Mure, surrounded by the people she loved, her best friends, at a fantastic party, in a sea of smiling faces and some half-naked men, all so that in a month she was going to marry the man of her dreams. She glanced over at Lorna, who was still dancing with the chap she had started off with, and got a huge grin in return; Flora reached out and squeezed her hand.

'I'm sorry to disturb you at night.'

'That's okay,' said Saif, still gruff.

'I just didn't feel it could wait until Monday.'

Even up here at the Manse, at the very upper end of town, Saif could hear something. It was loud music playing in the far distance. He squinted over the ridge of meadow grass at the edge of his drive, desperately trying to somehow get away from the phone call. There were flashing pink and red lights out of what appeared to be the Harbour's Rest.

'Uh-huh?'

'We've found her,' said Neda.

Dunes crumbled, sand collapsed, the rocks became dust in his hands.

'You have said this before,' said Saif in his quiet, measured way.

'Yes, but ... we have confirmation.'

His heart felt like it would not go, like he needed to pound himself hard in the chest just to get it to keep on beating. The music from the Harbour's Rest had been joined now by high-pitched laughter and shouting, girls' laughter, joyous and free.

Neda named a refugee camp on the Jordan border. Saif nodded. He knew of it.

'She is ... she is well?' he said. Again, the cutting to his heart, the blade: *she never contacted us. She would not speak to me.*

'She is ... as well as can be expected in that place,' said Neda slowly.

'She would not answer my messages! What about her children? She had no phone? She had no chance?'

The bitterness in Saif's tone was harsher than he had realised; he moved further away from the house so the children could not hear.

'She is adamant,' said Neda, choosing her words carefully, 'that she did not want to endanger your status, ever. Nor that of the boys.'

'She would not have done that. She could have joined me. Joined us,' he said, his voice low.

He knew, of course. He knew. He had known since he'd seen that photograph. But this was the final confirmation. She'd moved on.

The party grew livelier and livelier, even though it was still early. Mrs Forbes had looked horrified at the strippers, but elsewhere people were going absolutely crazy. It felt like the winter had been so long, that it had been a while since there'd been a proper chance to let their hair down, and the local girls wanted to show the fancy foreign people that they knew how to party as well as anyone, and the people who had come from away obviously were there now so they might as well go for it, and the copious cocktails obviously didn't hurt either, as well as the huge effort that had gone into making it all such fun.

The DJ was great, with a seamless feel for exactly what everyone felt like hearing, whether that was 'Shake It Off' or 'Happy' or 'Hey Ya' or Janet Jackson, and before long all the different groups of friends had bonded in the loos, which had been specially cleaned for the occasion, with both sets given over to anyone's toilets, and chairs placed inside so the girls could sit and gossip. To everyone's amazement, except Olivia and her friends, there were boxes in there with perfume, lipstick, tampons, hairspray – anything anyone could want or wanted to try out – so there was plenty of bonding going on until the dancefloor would reverberate with something utterly irresistible and they would charge off again.

'So. He is there. The husband?'

'He hasn't been seen,' said Neda. 'He may have died in the fighting. We don't know. Amena does not know.'

'She looked so happy in the photograph,' he said quietly.

Then he asked the question he had to ask.

'The child lives?'

241

'No!' Lorna was saying. 'NO, NO, NO, NO!' But she was doubled over with laughter.

'Yes,' said Flora, trying to keep a mock-serious expression on her face. 'It's the law.'

'It is absolutely *not* the law,' said Lorna.

'HANDS ON MY WAIST!'

'Conga! Conga!' shouted Isla and Iona, dashing over behind Lorna and grabbing her by the waist too.

'Oh no!' said Lorna, but it was too late – Flora was off, her tiny scrap of veil still lifting up from her pale hair, lipstick everywhere, making everyone in the room join the conga, which then proceeded to circle the croquet garden/car park before making its way out along the harbour. Mrs Forbes declined with a tight smile.

The fishing boats, heading out on their tough night shifts in the freezing fishing grounds of the North Atlantic, all honked their horns cheerfully and the girls waved in response – island girls waving to the men leaving on boats, a way of life on Mure that had not changed in a thousand years or more.

Saif screwed up his eyes. There was a long parade of women somehow dancing their way up and down the harbourside. It was not something he had ever seen before and looked completely bizarre. There was a lot of whooping.

'She does,' came Neda's voice.

242

'It's a girl,' said Saif, swallowing hard. They had hoped, once ago, back in another lifetime. Back in another world, after the two boys were born, someone had said to them, and now a daughter to complete your world, and they had been so happy then, so happy with their two perfect sons, they had brushed it off, because they had plenty of time, because the world was before them and everything was possible and they had everything to look forward to and how could they be happier than this?

He half watched the girls, laughing and dancing along, revelling in their freedom and joy. Amena had a daughter. Ib and Ash had a half-sister. It was so strange.

'I see,' said Saif stiffly.

'She won't contact you,' said Neda. 'She thinks it could put you in jeopardy, put the boys in danger. She's terrified of them losing their citizenship.'

He nodded shortly. He had plenty of evidence in the UK as to how people responded to women who married fighters.

'And frankly,' continued Neda, 'it is possible ... that there would be consequences for her if she did.'

His heart froze.

'But we do have a message for you.'

Chapter Twenty-eight

The boys were still happy playing Minecraft until Ib realised it was long after their bedtimes, even on a weekend, and pushed Ash with his feet and told him to go to bed, and Ash said NO WAY YOU DON'T TELL ME WHEN TO GO TO BED, and they were rolling on the floor but still their father did not come, and that was when they got up to go to him and see what was wrong, because normally that would have attracted his attention.

Their father was sitting in the darkening kitchen. He held his phone in his hand but he wasn't looking at it; he was staring into space.

Immediately, Ib's hackles were up. He remembered. He told people he didn't really because that made them feel better, he could tell. Ash had it easier: he really couldn't remember; it was as if he was a blank slate. But Ib did. He remembered the adults staring at their phones, then off into space. Sitting in rooms when it went dark, because there was no electricity.

Ash marched up. 'WHAT IS IT, *ABBA*?'

Saif looked up. And Ib caught something in the haunted look in his father's eyes that he had not seen since the very earliest days they'd arrived on the island, and he was terrified.

Saif made a snap decision. He had to.

'Nothing,' he said, forcing himself up. He glanced at his watch.

'Look, look, it's bedtime,' he said. Fortunately, Ash was distracted by the lights down in the village.

'Agot said they were having a big party without her,' he said thoughtfully. 'Is that the big party?'

'I think so,' said Saif, observing, as it grew dark, that the Mure Angel, the huge statue below the school, was itself lit up in red and pink. Ash shook his head.

'She is going to be very, very cross about this.'

Saif put his arms around him.

'Don't worry about it.'

Ash shook his head. 'I don't. Miss Lorna said if people are upset, often they are not upset with YOU but the SICHWATION.'

Saif looked at him. God. Lorna. The only person he would desperately like to talk this over with was the only person he couldn't mention it to.

'She is very wise,' he said, reflecting that indeed she was, and suddenly feeling a desperate craving to be with her, somewhere, anywhere, safe in her arms.

He put Ash to bed, kissing the boy, finding comfort in reading to him, noting that he was growing out of his pyjamas again. He was bad at buying clothes for the boys; you had to send away for them and he wasn't used to it at all. He didn't know that most of the families traded hand-me-downs, had

245

done for generations, but nobody dared pass them on to him in case they were mistaken for charity cases just because they were refugees. As a result, the boys wore a motley collection of things that had caught Saif's eye, Saif not realising that the first thing that catches your eye when you are shopping is rarely the thing you should buy. He himself dressed as his father had, but the way his father – an arch anglophile all his life – had dressed and the reason Saif had the right medical qualifications in the first place, was because they believed all doctors should dress, like something out of *Dr Finlay's Casebook*.

At any rate, Ib rarely wanted to wear anything other than his beloved Hibernian shirt, which didn't bother Saif too much, and both the boys favoured shorts in all weathers, like their hardy island mates.

'You are all right, *Abba*?' said sensitive Ash once more, drowsily, as Saif switched on the nightlight that sent patterns of whales and dolphins spinning around the walls.

Saif stroked the little boy's forehead. What could he say? I know where your mother is? This safe comfortable world you live in, I could crack it, like an egg; I could break the only peace and security you have ever known, the only safety you could ever remember. The best future you could ever have.

'*Naeam*,' he said. 'All is well.' And the little boy closed his eyes and slipped into a peaceful sleep as if he was stepping off a ledge. Not a furrow crossed his brow. Saif kissed him once again, then stood up, feeling a hundred years old.

Ib was still there, lingering in the doorway.

'Will you tell me?' he said severely.

By the time the conga finally finished, Flora was having such a good time. People flopped back down, and the DJ wisely pulled right back on the music and gave everyone a chance to catch their breath, drink some water – or in fact Champagne, which was now in circulation in preparation for the toasts. Everyone was sweaty and giggling, and it was no longer possible to tell who had originally been Olivia's friends and who was from the island or the mainland. Everyone had bonded over the dancers, the toilets and the cocktails.

Well, almost everyone.

Olivia had been enjoying the cocktails too, and – possibly as a result of a wedding diet even more strenuous than usual – they had had quite the effect. She also was used to always being looked at, rather than surrounded by a clutch of carefree lassies absolutely hellbent on having a great time. It was hardly surprising, really, that she'd got carried away. She was yabbering away nineteen to the dozen in the loos to anyone and everyone, and when Flora went to the bathroom too, she flung her arms around her and said, 'This is the *best*! I love you so much,' and Flora smiled nicely and said, 'I'm so glad you're happy, but you did it all,' and Olivia said, 'No, you brought the fun people ... not like bloody Jan out there. Did you see her? Face like a fucking misery machine. God, I wish you were my sister, not her.'

Flora screwed up her face and indicated the opening cubicle door. Olivia set her lovely face in a pout as Jan emerged, pink and hot-looking. She had already been pink and hot before she even got into the cubicle, but this wasn't helping. The entire washroom immediately went quiet, waiting to see what would happen. Several people were secretly rather delighted that this already fabulous party was about to become even more legendary by also including a huge fight.

'Jan,' said Olivia sulkily, then turned on her heel and stumbled out of the bathroom.

To no avail: Jan was right on her heels, into the middle of the room.

'It's fine,' said Jan. 'I didn't want you as a sister either.'

'Well, you always made that perfectly clear.'

'What do you mean by that?'

'"Go away, Olivia!" "No, you can't play!" "Get out of my room!" "Get off my stuff!" First thing I remember.'

'Yeah, you only did that when you were sick of making cow eyes to all the adults within a ten-mile radius.'

'I was *four*! And you hated me from the minute I showed up.'

'"Ooh, everyone look at Olivia, she's so pretty, everyone clap Olivia." It is so *sickening* and *so boring*.'

'That's not *my fault*!' said Olivia.

'And starting the Big Fat Jan Club? Whose fault was that?'

'The "Big Fat Jan Club"?' said someone incredulously.

'Because you never let up being mean! Not for one single second.'

Mrs Forbes was watching all of this, mouth hanging open, as the girls screeched at each other like alley cats.

'Uh, girls,' said Flora. 'Come on. Don't fight. It's a lovely night, it's a lovely party, let's just head to the garden maybe . . .'

'It's a stupid party full of show-offs and you throwing your money about,' said Jan. 'Or Anthony's money about. Do they know that? Whose money is paying for all this?'

Olivia bit her lip and a huge flush rose in her cheeks. She shot an incriminating glance towards Mrs Forbes, whose mouth was now a narrow straight line.

'Come on,' said Flora more firmly. 'Don't make me get Inge-Britt!'

248

'You didn't have to come,' shot Olivia, completely ignoring Flora.

'Yes, I bloody did, didn't I?' said Jan. 'Keep up the "Everyone Loves Olivia" little world you live in. Impress the new in-laws. Pretend we're all a big happy family when you couldn't even be arsed to come to my wedding. Or meet my daughter.'

'Maybe because you made it *perfectly* clear I wouldn't be welcome and you hate every minute of my presence and have done since I dared to be born,' said Olivia.

'GO!' said Flora, and with some friends' help took an arm each and more or less hauled them off the dancefloor.

The DJ moved to the mike to try and improve things.

'So ... eh ... let's hear it for the brides!' he hollered, and the entire room cheered. Olivia, bright pink, and Flora looked at each other in horror.

'Speech! Speech! Speech!' was the chant that started up.

'Yeah!' shouted Kai, pushing Flora towards the floor.

'Uh ... ' said Flora, looking beseechingly at Olivia, whose hair was mussed and wild, and whose eyes seemed to be looking in different directions.

'Speech! Speech! Speech!'

Lorna was giving her a ferocious look and Flora couldn't at first remember why that was, then it suddenly came to her: keep Jan sweet. Calm everything down. She took the microphone and thanked everyone for coming, everyone for being ace, told everyone she loved them, told Jacinth she'd done an absolutely amazing job at the Harbour's Rest, who could possibly have believed it, she certainly hadn't, which had the unfortunate effect of implying that a) it usually looked terrible and that b) she, Flora, hadn't thought Jacinth would do an

249

amazing job at all, therefore managing to completely insult an entire raft of people at the same moment. Lorna was still staring at her, so she then took a breath.

'Thank you so much for coming to this from near and far, everyone. I know we all owe it all to Olivia . . . '

Everyone cheered, and Olivia rallied and beamed that killer megawatt smile at the party, as if the fight had never happened. Mrs Forbes was still unsmiling.

' . . . and I'm so glad I can have you here, given Joel and I are only having a . . . private family wedding . . . '

The room fell completely silent.

'What?' said Kai. 'Because I've hired a kilt already and it was very expensive.'

'Um . . . ' said Flora, feeling absolutely awful at the lovely happy faces of her friends being disappointed because they wouldn't get to share her big day.

There was quiet in the room, when suddenly Olivia loudly snatched the mike off her.

'Yeah,' she said. 'But I love Flora – she's like a *sister* to me.'

This was spat more than said.

'And she's getting married on the same day as me – and I've decided we're going to have a *joint wedding*!'

She put her arm around Flora's shoulders.

'*Joint wedding!* And it's going to be awesome!'

She looked around the room.

'I know you don't all know me. But I feel as though you have taken me in and welcomed me home like I'd never been away.'

Flora, completely stunned, glanced at Jan, whose face was mutinous.

'And to those of you I have just met, it has been an absolute delight. As if I'm not already lucky enough to be marrying the best man in the world . . . '

Whoops, thought Flora, her mind spinning in circles. I forgot to mention Joel at all.

' . . . in the most beautiful setting in the world . . . '

There was a hearty cheer from the assembled. Dang, thought Flora. I should have mentioned the island as well.

'Thank you so much, my sister bride, for doing this with me . . . and I wish everyone as much love in their lives as there is in this room tonight,' finished Olivia, and it was so obviously heartfelt and sincere, if slightly slurred, that people yelled louder and louder. 'And let's make this the *best joint wedding ever*!'

Next time Flora glanced over to where Jan was, she had disappeared. So had Mrs Forbes. But she had barely time to think that when a huge cake was wheeled out – huge, bigger than a table – and *BOOM!* out of it, waving her hands in the air, and to mass whoops and applause, burst a tiny little Alice in Wonderland.

Or, as Flora belatedly realised, Mary-Elizabeth MacIntyre.

The shouts and roars just about reached up to the distant Manse, amplified by the gently rolling hills as Saif sat in the kitchen with his eldest son.

'Mama is there?' said Ib. Saif was determined not to break the boy's heart, not to hurt him. His life had been tough enough already. He was only young, and he had had quite enough of the harsh realities of life.

Ib stared stubbornly at the cup of warm milk Saif had placed in front of him. He was at that stage of very early adolescence when bits of him seemed to be growing all at the wrong time. His ears were too big for his head; his straight black hair falling messily around them; his body was very thin; his feet absolutely huge. He had a pointed nose that would one day be Roman and handsome like his father's, but for now looked beakish; his eyes were huge and wary. Looking at him, on the very cusp of leaving his boyhood behind him, Saif felt his heart overflow and crack; one day there would be only traces left of the boy Ibrahim had been. The man he would become felt in the very balance of Saif's hands.

'It's possible,' said Saif quietly.

'And we could see her?'

'I don't know.'

Ibrahim frowned.

'But she wants to see us?'

'Mmm . . . ' said Saif.

'I never thought she was dead,' said Ib scornfully. Saif blinked. He couldn't believe his child even had to entertain the thought.

'No,' said Saif. 'Neither did I.'

'Ash did,' said Ib. 'He's such a baby.'

'Did you talk about it a lot?'

Ib shook his head. 'He just says it sometimes because it's easier than having to explain,' he said. 'And everyone's nice to him. He's *such* a baby. He only does it for attention.'

'At school?'

Ib snorted. 'No! Miss Lorna wouldn't let him away with that.' He sounded approving. 'But at swim camp and stuff.'

'Oh,' said Saif.

There was a long silence between them. Ib looked up, his dark eyes huge. There was, Saif noticed again, the lightest line of hair on his upper lip. It took Ib all of his courage to ask the question.

'So. Are we going to have to go . . . back there?'

Chapter Twenty-nine

Feeling emboldened by the general love in the room, Flora headed outside – dancing was continuing but in the garden, suddenly hundreds and hundreds of twinkling lights had appeared strung overhead and somehow, as if from nowhere, little burner stoves and high brazier lights had been lit all around to blast out warmth, and soft tartan blankets in pink and red were draped over sofas and comfortable chairs.

At the end of the garden, two ballerinas dressed in white masks and chequerboard skin-tight costumes were performing a pas de deux. People had got so used to the amazing things at this party, they were barely watching. Flora found herself slightly tipsy with excitement. Joel could hardly argue if they were going to give away all their money – every single penny of it now could go to Jan and Charlie and their boys' charities! So there would be a few people there for them, and then they could join the main festivities after dinner – have a quiet ceremony, just the small group of them – then join the huge party! With everyone there! It was such a perfect solution! She couldn't wait to tell him.

Of course, it was not all love in the room.

Jan had gone to march out, unfortunately knocking over one of the beautiful ornate garden tables as she went, shattering teacups and spilling cocktails all over the plastic grass. She brushed past Flora in the garden, who said her name, only to be ignored. Lorna wandered up beside her.

'Should I go after her?' said Flora.

'You are literally the last person who should go after her,' said Lorna. 'Well, maybe the second last.'

Olivia was talking urgently to Lucy, her soon-to-be sister-in-law. Lucy's body language seemed to indicate she wasn't terribly engaged in the conversation. Meanwhile, Mrs Forbes was loudly saying to anyone who would listen, 'This isn't the kind of thing my Anthony likes. Not at all. This is wildly inappropriate.'

Flora glanced at Senga, who had the lip purse on again. 'Are you going to go after her?' she asked.

Senga shook her head. 'I've had it up to here with the pair of them,' she said. 'I could never make one of them happy without making the other one unhappy. I'm fed up.'

They both looked at Lorna.

'No way,' said Lorna.

'Someone has to go after her,' said Flora. 'And she'd throw the rest of us in the harbour.'

'It can't be me,' pleaded Lorna. 'You know why.'

'But you're so sensible and gentle,' said Senga. 'You can see why you're such a good teacher.'

'That's true,' said Flora. 'She deals with huffs all the time.'

'But, Flora, you know . . . '

'All the better reason,' said Flora gloomily. 'If you can bring her round, she's less likely to . . . '

'Do you think she would?'

'In the mood she's in, she might be capable of anything,' said Flora, and Lorna, exasperated, ran out into the night.

Saif had answered Ibrahim's questions as honestly as he could. Yes, they could stay on Mure; they wouldn't have to leave. No, there was no longer much fighting in Damascus. No, their house would not still be there. No, he did not know if they could speak to his mother.

Ib was so hungry for information, and he had to be reassuring. No, he didn't know if they could 'visit for a bit', but he had to say it was very, very unlikely. And yes, Amena would have come and found them if she could have, but she wasn't allowed. And he did not think she could be contacted.

Every word, every line was another drop of pain straight into the boy. It reminded Saif of having to treat very young patients, when the treatment itself caused pain. Except then it generally made children better. He didn't know how this could.

'Your mother,' he said finally, 'is very, very happy that you are here. That you are safe, in a nice house, with nice friends, and a safe place to stay, and plenty of food to eat and electricity that stays on all night, and there is schooling. This is what she wants for you. This is everything we both want for you. Then, when you are more grown and you can travel on a good passport and can always be safe and have your own car, then, then … things will be simpler and we can be together again. It will just take a little time.'

Ib stared straight ahead.

'In many places,' Saif said, 'mummies and daddies must go away from their families; they are torn apart by war, or work, or other terrible things. You are not alone, Ib. And your mother will never forget you. But the biggest thing a mother will do is sacrifice herself for you so that you will have a good life, even if it means that she cannot. She would do anything for your happiness.'

'Even be in prison,' said Ibrahim in a very small voice.

'Gladly,' said Saif softly. He pulled the boy to him. 'It is not a prison. And these are grown-up things,' he said. 'I wish you did not have to know them. I wish you did not have to be a grown-up.'

Neither of them felt like going to bed, although Saif was worn out from a long week. Instead, he did something he rarely did, which the boys often wished he would do: he sat down at the television, Ib next to him, and put on a daft Marvel film at random, and they watched the film together companionably until the boy's breathing finally started to slow and his taut long body relaxed in sleep, and he laid his head on Saif's shoulder, and Saif, normally discouraged these days from touching him, gently stroked his hair.

'*Abba?*' came a sleepy voice beside him as the film played on. 'In Damascus, does everybody look like me?'

Lorna ran out – it was still mostly light at half past ten on a May evening in Mure, the white nights just about upon them now – but couldn't see any sign of Jan anywhere. She wasn't stomping up the Endless Beach; she wasn't down in the town on the harbour, where a cheery Friday-night queue had formed, made up mostly of men, outside the chippy. Perhaps she'd gone home, nursing her wrath to keep it warm. What would she do? thought Lorna. She could threaten Olivia, threaten Flora, threaten herself. Lorna found herself remembering the story of the Prodigal Son, for whom the fattened calf had been brought out. She hadn't thought it was a very fair story when she had been younger. She guessed she wasn't alone.

There was a chill in the air, and she turned to go back and confess that her mollifying teacher skills had been unsuccessful on this occasion. As she did, she looked up at the pink- and red-lit statue. It always made her feel better somehow.

Saif walked out into the garden after putting a blanket on Ib, who was still fast asleep on the sofa. The boy was now too big for him to carry upstairs to bed, he had noted, or at least not without heaving him into a fireman's carry. How fast they grew. How fast they changed. The time, dashing away so quickly, pouring through his fingers.

He looked down the hill, where the noise of happy girls beginning to go home caught his ears. It must be later than he'd realised. The angel was still lit up. He liked looking at it. It felt . . . it always felt comforting somehow.

There was a figure there, standing quite still. As he watched, it turned in his direction, almost as if it was looking straight for him. And then the figure waved at him heartily and, not knowing what to do, and aware everyone on the island knew him, he waved back. Then he turned and went back indoors.

Chapter Thirty

An hour later, the party was finally breaking up. Joel was up with Douglas, who was restless, and he decided to see if Flora wanted a lift home rather than try and clamber up the hill in those ridiculous heels, or rely on the village's one rather unpredictable cabby. There was a hard core in the Harbour's Rest bar settling in with shots, Flora noticed. Lorna hadn't returned, and Mrs Forbes and Lucy had also gone. Olivia ... Olivia was having a very passionate drunken heart-to-heart with Jacinth, who was trying to look interested while also looking at her phone.

When Joel texted 'Want a lift?' she happily moved towards the door. Outside, there were bits of red hearts all over the ground; confetti, sparkles, spilled cocktails, cigarette butts; the end of a party. Flora smiled. What a great party though. Lorna came back, looking grave; no sign of Jan. Flora shrugged. These things got sorted, didn't they? Everything would be okay in the morning.

She went up to Olivia, who really was babbling drunk – although still looked irritatingly gorgeous, naturally – who flung her arms around her.

'You're my sister now!' she heaved dramatically. 'We're going to have the most wonderful wedding.'

Joel turned up at the door, looking around in consternation at the mess of the bar.

'Goodness,' he said. 'Looks like you had quite the knees-up.'

'No boys! No boys!' shouted Flora's friends rather hypocritically, seeing as they were all madly chatting up the dancers who had stayed behind too because they were staying upstairs and really had nowhere else to go. And Kai was there too. Inge-Britt had gone back behind the bar, still wearing her Alice band, her apron a little askew.

'I know, I know,' said Joel, with his hands up. 'I'll just collect my wife-to-be, if that's okay.'

There was mass awwing as everyone leapt up to hug Flora.

'We can't wait for the wedding,' they said. 'Oh my God, it's going to be even *more* amazing than this!'

Olivia launched herself at Joel.

'You're Joel! The famous Joel! I didn't think you'd be quite so ... Have we met?' she said, looking up at him.

'I don't think so,' said Joel, although it wouldn't have surprised him; she looked like a lot of people he used to know. He knew the type well.

'I can't believe we're going to have a double wedding! You're better-looking than Anthony! I'd better keep him on his toes or I'll marry the wrong person! Hahahaha!' She put her hand on his shoulder. 'I think I might be a little drunk.'

Joel looked around for someone to relieve him of Olivia but didn't see anyone.

'Okay,' he said, bamboozled by her statement. 'Uh, Flora?'

'I'm coming, I'm coming,' said Flora. 'Cor, there's a lot of shoes around here. Okay. Bye, everyone!'

'See you at the wedding!' yelled everyone cheerfully, embracing her as Joel walked with her, rather stony-faced, back out to the car, where Douglas was clucking cheerfully at the moon.

In the car, bouncing up the path, Flora couldn't see the problem.

'So I know you wanted the money to go to Jan,' she said, 'but now, Olivia is going to pay for *everything*. It'll be like five pence to her! So we can have a tiny ceremony just for us, just like you want – then everyone at the big party! Organised by Olivia! It'll be brilliant – look how well tonight went!'

'Actually, half your party was catatonic and half appeared to be missing,' said Joel rather shortly.

Flora looked at him.

'*And* Jan is going to get *all of our money*,' she said, slightly wobbling off the point. 'Don't you think I'm a total genius?!'

Joel looked at her.

'Flora, I only asked you for one thing.'

'A tiny wedding! We're doing that! Do the vows just us! *Then* we just add on to a huge wedding, like a huge, brilliant, amazing wedding with everyone there, and we get the best of both! It's perfect!'

The jam-tart Martinis had rather numbed her to what had absolutely seemed like the best idea, but even in her befogged

262

state she realised she wasn't getting quite the reaction she was hoping for.

'It solves everything!'

Joel pulled up in front of the house.

'I wasn't aware,' he said stiffly, 'that there was anything to solve.'

Chapter Thirty-one

There were some very sore heads among the female part of Mure's population the following morning. Everywhere you went, you could smell the restorative scent of sausages – veggie and local – being cooked up for useful hangover breakfasts. There was indeed a shoe still hanging outside the Harbour's Rest, indicating that someone had got caught in the wrong fairy story. Otherwise, it was like magic, as if elves had stolen in during the night and dismantled what turned out in the morning simply to be plywood and tarpaulin after all. The dingy car park was returned. The fairy trees had gone.

Flora had woken early, feeling grotty and, not quite ready to face Joel, she'd made coffee and taken Douglas outside. It was bright and blustery, grass bending in the wind, and she felt she needed that moment to keep the cobwebs away. She had drunk a pint of water and taken two paracetamols before bed, so it could be worse, but even so, she was a little fuzzy.

She had felt so happy though. It had seemed like such a good solution. Olivia had her infinite money, and it was her desire to invite everyone on the island and treat them to a rollicking brilliant party, while she and Joel could still donate the money and have a private ceremony of their own when everyone else was witnessing Olivia's. She was under no illusions that Olivia cared about her particularly; Olivia cared about Olivia looking good in front of her new in-laws. But surely they could turn it to their advantage?

She had looked at Joel's face, stony even in sleep, though he always looked so vulnerable without his glasses on. She'd closed the door as quietly as she could and stuck a cheery Douglas in the sling. He weighed an absolute ton, but she liked the warmth of him next to her, his little paws playing with her hair, and she felt strangely drawn to the Endless Beach that morning, wanted to feel cool sand between her toes.

Nobody was about except for Bramble, on his regular morning trip to pick up the paper, and she scritched his ears as he trotted past with an impatient stop that seemed to say yes, I want my ears scritching, but only for a second as I am on important newspaper-fetching business as you can surely see.

There was a heavy sea fog, but pinpoints of blue in the sky which normally indicated that the sun would triumph eventually, and people would spend the day discarding layers of clothing one by one. The Endless Beach was hers alone this early; even the dog walkers were not yet abroad. Flora thought and thought about the night before. She winced at Olivia and Jan's fight – she had tried everything she could there, but some wounds, she supposed, were too deep to cover up with Martinis and fancy dresses. She made a mental note not to fall

265

out with her brothers, ever. It couldn't possibly be worth it. She texted Fintan.

'Just to say, I like you a lot,' she typed.

'Oh Christ,' came back two seconds later. He still didn't sleep very well. 'What have you done now? What do you want me to do? Oh crap.'

She unfastened Douglas and held him up on the beach.

'Come on, you nine-month walker,' she whispered as Douglas promptly grinned, plonked himself down on the sand and started eating it.

She sighed. She had thought this was a good solution. But Joel was ... he was ... well. It was his right to have his ideal wedding too, of course, she thought to herself. Even though most husbands of her acquaintance had simply let the wife have whatever she wanted for her dream day ... although of course, she thought again, she didn't want most husbands. She wanted one. This one. Complicated as he was. Maybe she would talk to Mark.

But she'd already agreed to it, that was the problem. She'd said yes when maybe she hadn't meant it. That ... that was not an ideal way to start a marriage either. She sighed to herself.

She went completely silent, tilting her head, keeping half an eye on the horizon and half an eye on Douglas to make sure he didn't swallow any more sand. There it was. A low level crooning. It wasn't seals; seals barked, clear as you like. In fact, she could hear them, agitated. As if something was unsettling things; something in the water.

She screwed up her eyes. Was that a splash, just out, halfway towards the horizon? Where the tankers balanced, on grey cloudy mornings like this one, where the sea and the sky were indistinguishable from one another, and the boats appeared to be floating in mid-air?

266

There it was again. One . . . two . . . and a deep, heaving sigh.

'Oh my goodness,' said Flora to herself, her worries forgotten. She lifted Douglas.

'It's the pod,' she whispered. 'It's the pod, my little whale boy. They've come to visit. Say hello.'

Douglas looked at his mother and smiled at her because she seemed so excited.

'Welcome,' she said, then she frowned. It wasn't good if the pod came and settled. Whale watchers would swoop in from all over the place. It didn't matter how many times you told people you couldn't sail out to the pod or disturb them, somehow people found a way. People were welcome to come and watch, but somehow, sometimes, things got spoiled when there were too many. Maybe that's how Joel felt, she thought. The whales needed peace and quiet; mating season was over and the cows needed tranquillity in their pregnancies. They might not get it.

If it was up to her, she wouldn't tell a soul. Unfortunately, even now the pod would be pinging on the radar from Bergen to Newfoundland. People would come, no matter what she did. And the animals would be hemmed in and claustrophobic . . .

She turned round. Maybe she could get back to the house before Joel woke up . . .

He was working in the office, never normally a good sign. She took him in a cup of tea.

'How are you feeling this morning?' he said in a slightly loaded tone.

'Fine, thank you,' lied Flora. He gave her some side-eye.

'Really?'

'Yes!'

'Okay, good. Don't breathe too many fumes on Douglas.'

Well, at least he was talking to her.

'So, I was thinking about the wedding.'

Joel lifted his hands up.

'Don't worry about it. I see you've got it all planned.'

'It was just an idea. Of Olivia's. That I thought you'd like.'

'Why?'

'Because we're still having our wedding ceremony ourselves ... then there's just a kind of ... party we could go to.'

'With everyone you know there.'

'She's the one making a big splash,' said Flora. 'And it means every penny can go to Jan.'

'You already said that,' said Joel. 'It's fine. You do whatever you want. I can see you're hellbent on dragging the entire island into this thing no matter what I do so I might as well just deal with it.'

'Don't be like that," said Flora.

'Be like what? You never ... you never considered doing it my way for a second, did you?'

'I did!'

'Really? So how come *Saif* is coming? I mean, I like the man, but Flora, he's my doctor!'

'That was for Lorna.'

'Tripp's coming! And nobody likes him!'

'Did you know all this?'

'No. I did some digging this morning. Because up until last night, I thought ... I thought we were all sorted. All organised.

You and me. In a room full of people who love us. Properly love us. Not the usual rubberneckers and bar flies. Not people that don't give two shits about me. I've had that my whole life, Flora. My whole life. People staring at me who don't care, or who are curious or prurient about my parents, or weighing me up, seeing if I'm good enough for them to get work out of me or something else out of me or . . . something transactional. You were the first girl I ever met who wasn't just after the money and the attention.'

He swallowed.

'I can't . . . I hate to think I was wrong. I never wanted an Olivia.'

Flora looked at him steadily.

'You weren't wrong,' she said. 'But part of me is my family, my community, my island. You didn't just fall for me. You came to take part in this life. And hermitting yourself away from people, that's no use. That's not how people see you. You are valued here. People do care about you. I just wish you valued yourself enough to see it.'

They stared at one another, astounded, amazed they had got to here, neither of them able to see the other's point of view.

'Fine,' said Flora, turning. 'I'll tell Olivia.'

'Don't bother,' said Joel. 'It doesn't matter what you do. I'm sure people will find out where we are and just turn up anyway. I might as well go through with it.'

Flora suddenly turned round in fury.

'"I might as well go through with it",' she repeated in disbelief. 'Why . . . ? How could I ever marry someone who said "I might as well go through with it?"'

And she stormed out of the room, Douglas in her arms.

Chapter Thirty-two

It was one of Joel's volunteer days so he found himself down the docks waiting for a new intake with Jan, who looked as solemn as he felt.

'Hey,' he said. 'Did you have fun last night?'

Jan snorted.

'Christ no. Bunch of screaming ninnies.'

Joel almost smiled.

'I can't believe you agreed to all this double wedding nonsense,' she said. 'Bunch of bloody rubbish.'

Joel winced.

'It doesn't appear I have much of a choice.'

'God no,' said Jan. 'Olivia always has to have her own way. In everything. Flora too, I suppose. And all the local freeloaders.'

Joel shrugged.

'It's good news for the Outward Adventures though,' he said. 'Even more cash if we don't have to pay for dinner, I suppose.'

Jan's face lit up. 'Well, that *is* good news.' She thought about it. 'We could replace all the tents! And all those cruddy old ground mats!'

'New boots all round,' said Joel.

Jan nodded. 'I wonder if . . . Sometimes I want to send them home with the boots when they turn up in those old stinky trainers with holes in them, and you know those are the only pair of shoes they have.'

Joel nodded vehemently. 'We should be able to do something about that. Strike a deal with a shoe company or something'

Jan shrugged. 'Mind you . . . if it isn't Nike or Vans, the kids don't want them.'

Joel sighed. 'Got it.'

Jan looked at him rather slyly.

'So is . . . Saif coming to your new wedding then? With anyone in particular?'

But Joel's attention was grabbed by something out at sea.

'Is that the ferry? What is that?'

Jan picked up her binoculars.

'Oh lord,' she said.

'What?'

'It's a pod of whales. They've obviously made their way across.'

Joel thought.

'Oh. That would be why Flora would have been out there this morning.'

'This stupid . . .' Jan remembered herself. 'Does she really think she can talk to the whales?'

Joel shrugged.

'She certainly hears them.'

'Well, it's good for her, I suppose. This place full of whale watchers too as well as this ridiculous bloody wedding. Whole bloody island turning into a circus, everyone getting their pictures in front of that bloody statue. We're not a fricking theme park.'

She sighed. Joel could not disagree. He shivered. Even now, in summer, the water looked cold and unwelcoming.

They watched the ferry arrive, knowing what would be inside: another mouthy, scared, prickly cohort of young boys either in care or at special schools, these five days a holiday that would bond them, make them complain vociferously, tire them out and give them friends for life. It was hard work, but it was always worthwhile.

Olivia woke up with a very sore head indeed, and she checked her phone to see if Anthony had rung. He had not. She padded down quietly for breakfast at the Rock – a super avocado toast, as it happened, who'd have thought it? – and drank about a litre of coffee before looking around to see where Mrs Forbes and Lucy were.

'They took the early flight out,' reported Jacinth, entering the room with her clipboard, looking the same as ever.

Olivia stared in shock.

'But today I was going to take them to the statue ... to the Seaside Kitchen ...'

'Yeah. I don't think they were too happy about last night.'
Olivia winced.

'What, because Jan and I had a bit of a family fallout? Come on, everyone knows families do that.'

Jacinth shrugged.

'Maybe also because ... you committed them to paying for another wedding?'

'Oh, come on!' said Olivia, pouting. 'It's the same people. It's nobody extra, for goodness' sake.'

'Yes, but I think they feel you should probably have run it through with them nonetheless.'

Olivia sighed.

'Oh, for goodness' sake. *Whose* wedding is this?'

She picked up the phone and called.

'Hello, darling,' she said, her voice purring. 'Oh, I just loved seeing your mum again; she's such a poppet! And Lucy. I'm sure we're going to be best friends, I could absolutely tell. It was just fantastic. We had an amazing time. Okay, my love. Love you! See you very soon!'

Jacinth gave her a look.

'What? Just getting my side in first,' said Olivia. 'Anyway, as soon as I see him, he'll come round.'

'To getting married standing next to some guy he's never met?' said Jacinth.

Olivia frowned.

'They're the ones who keep saying family is super-important,' she said. 'They should be impressed by how many people want to come and what a happy community their precious Anthony is marrying into.'

'Impressed isn't what I'd have called it,' said Jacinth, scraping the avocado off Olivia's toast and helping herself to it. 'I'd better get my invoice in PDQ.'

Olivia looked up, startled.

'You don't think they'd ... ?'

Jacinth shrugged.

'Rich people can be weird, man.'

273

Olivia sighed.

'And I've got all the builders arriving soon,' said Jacinth, looking worriedly at her watch. 'So much going on up at the Rock. Listen, darling, I just . . . I have to move, okay?'

Olivia blinked up at Jacinth blearily.

'Yeah, speak soon,' said Jacinth, who was almost backing out of the room in her hurry to get away.

All by herself at the table, Olivia tried to look as if she wasn't remotely worried. But she was. Little Isla came out to see if she wanted anything else, but Olivia chased her away.

Chapter Thirty-three

June dawned, with little change – Joel and Flora were still tip-toeing around each other, both of them scared to say any more. The vicar wanted to get them together to have a small discussion about marriage and it seemed a very bad omen that they couldn't even do that much. The plan was to have the wedding in church, for Eck really, but the vicar was quite adamant they were needed there for Christian chats as well.

Meanwhile, vast supplies of mysterious things were turning up at the Rock almost daily, mysterious things which required a lot of puffing and panting and complaining from Konstantin and Hamish, who'd been drafted in to help; they were dispatched to a shed awaiting the mainland construction firm. Flora couldn't feel excited, though, as she saw exciting boxes that said things like 'dry ice' or 'snow machine'; she guessed it was going to be amazing. But her friends, all in the throes of planning their trips back, were beside themselves.

However, the one person she cared about was out,

volunteering all hours with Jan, who Flora did not think for one second would be a good influence on this situation at all, and whenever Flora timidly mentioned discussing the wedding and what would be a good alternative date maybe if he didn't want to do it with Olivia and Anthony, he'd simply shrug and say that Mark and Marsha were all booked so they might as well go ahead now, don't worry, if it was all sorted; Jan was happy about the money, so that was good enough for him.

That did not sound good enough at all.

The worst of it was everyone assuming that Flora was over the moon, soon to be a bride at her own hotel, the happiest of situations. The old ladies at the Seaside Kitchen, many of whom now appeared to be coming, could not stop wittering about it at all. Flora smiled as widely as she could with the feeling of something that ought to be so wonderful and so happy charging away from her faster and faster, out of reach.

And June was here. Oh, June. Everywhere in Scotland, statistically speaking, June is your best bet in terms of when to visit. A lot of people from further south than Mure, which is pretty much every single person who ever has been born, think that August is a summer month, but any Murian and indeed any Scot will tell you quite emphatically that it is not, and that August and autumn sound almost exactly the same for a very good reason. July and August are wet and cloudy months.

May and June, however, are bright and piercing and glorious and a well-kept secret. In June particularly, when it never gets dark, and you can find yourself, wide awake, wandering the Endless Beach at 11.30 at night, completely confused and hailing the other residents who are doing the same thing, because they also got confused about when precisely they were meant to be in bed. Schools break up in June, which is a good thing as, near the end of term, everyone is exhausted and overworked, and it seems cruel to keep the children, who have been inside all winter and half the spring, indoors on the beautiful meadowslip days when the island is a riot of a thousand shades of green, and the heavy scent of the heather hits your nostrils as the sun warms your neck and the wind is gentle in your hair.

Add to this the school's sports day with, as had to be repeatedly reinforced, no ice dance component sadly, as well as the school talent show, which was a constant battle between children taking it very seriously and adults of the island trying not to laugh at people who weren't notably talented getting up and having a go. Lorna MacLeod was absolutely exhausted. You could faintly sympathise with her after the first sixteen minutes of Ruaridh Brodick's drum solo, and then the magic act, the less said about which the better although it did not reflect well on anyone in the end.

She had barely seen Saif, and when she had, worse, he had been distant – something she was used to, but it worried her nonetheless: now that he had told her he loved her, was he going to pull back? Men did, she knew. It happened all the time. They got in over their heads and panicked. Even exceptional ones, even the very best of them. She hadn't even seen him during the Cubs' jamboree, which filled her with fear.

And things were getting real, feeling more intense, she knew that too. That instead of spending their lives dreaming of an impossible future, there was a real future out there. A difficult future, but not an impossible one. But one that would require difficult choices, difficult conversations. She was worried that she was driving him away, and there wasn't a damn thing she could do about it.

It wasn't that though, she told herself sensibly. They were

both terrified of Jan. It made sense to cool things down. Every time she passed Jan in the street, she smiled broadly and complimented her on something she was wearing, which with Jan could be quite challenging. Jan had always smirked at her, making it very clear she was enjoying the power she had over her. No doubt she was the same with Saif.

So all Lorna could do was hold him in her heart while he felt further and further away, and it terrified the life out of her. She knew that she had to find her feminist courage, step up to the plate, ask for what she wanted. But he knew what she wanted. It was . . . a little more complicated than that.

She hadn't even confided in Flora because Flora was just so patently happy that she was happy, so glad that things seemed to be working out that Lorna was genuinely too terrified to suggest that they might not, as if she would be a spectre at Flora's wedding.

And also – she didn't want to say this out loud – she was happier with Flora thinking everything was great with them. As if that might make it so. It would just take Saif a little while to get used to it, she told herself. Just to get used to the idea. But once he had sent his paperwork away, then it would be real, and the boys could start thinking about passports, and citizenship tests and all of that stuff. She just needed to be patient.

Saif told himself to stop googling. He had to stop. It was bad for him, it was doing him no good, it was upsetting and he was terrified that the boys would get hold of the history on his browser, though he had a firm lock on the laptop and the boys didn't have internet access on their iPad, a stance Ibrahim complained about endlessly. But Saif was too terrified. It was so beautiful and safe here that you could kid yourself, fool yourself into looking the other way. Most people did. He did not blame them.

But he could not. It had been easier to shut things out when he did not know. He had read the message from Amena, forwarded by Neda, had looked at it for a long time and thought he understood what she was really saying, loud and clear: 'Do not bring my sons here.' It made perfect sense. She was obviously in a situation where it simply was not safe to talk – because of the other refugees, or her family, he could not say.

But now he knew how she lived. He knew a mother ought to know her sons. And he did not know what to do about it.

Lorna didn't exactly specifically tell the children they were making things for Father's Day, although that was what it was. It was for a significant male person in their life – a grandparent or an uncle, or, in the Jameses' case, a hippyish family who had moved up to Mure from Surrey to experience the Good Life, whereby the father had decided after about five minutes that he completely hated the Good Life and wanted back his central heating and Deliveroo and railway stations and traffic jams and Amazon Prime, and had scuttled home with his tail between his legs to a semi-detached house, by which time unfortunately the four children – Esmerelda, Oona, Crispin and Caraway – had become completely feral and roamed the island at will, terrorising sheep and cats alike, wearing trousers held up with pieces of string, cheerfully joining in the harvesting and the shinty, refusing to wear shoes from May to September and frankly becoming completely incapable of ever being civilised again. Lorna thought they might be a little *too* embedded into the island lifestyle – they spoke with accents thick even by Mure standards, peppering their language with Gaelic that drove their very posh mother to despair – but she had been too thrilled at how they had lifted up the roll for their tiny school to complain too much.

There was another reason for making the cards too: with Ib and Ash in the school, they had barely marked Mothering Sunday over the last few years. On the last Friday before Mother's Day, they had taken half an hour to wrap paper daffodils which, Lorna had murmured, could be given to anyone. Ash had come up at the end of the day and given his to her. She had waited until she got home to have a small cry. She had not told Saif about it and had never quite known why when usually she wanted to tell him everything. But no. Being given flowers by his son for Mother's Day ... that one could probably wait. Though, of course, Ash had announced it in quite a matter-of-fact way at dinner that night, then looked worried when he saw his father's startled face and asked Abba if he had wanted the flowers – it was okay, he could make him another bunch; he just needed green crepe paper and yellow tissue paper and some Copydex and some wire and some newspaper – and his father had said no, no, that was quite all right, but had filed it away in that endless ticking corner of his brain.

The vast majority of children were lucky enough to have a father at home, or one who they saw regularly, and were perfectly happy making wooden boxes which involved glue, shells and rather a lot of dropped sand, and left quite a distinctive fishy smell around the classroom, Lorna couldn't help but

280

notice. Nonetheless, it was a happy project, and she enjoyed supervising it.

'It's for people who look after us,' Agot was saying. 'I should really make one for Daddy AND Hamish and Fintan and Eck and Joel. They will have to share.'

'Well, I am making two,' Ash announced suddenly.

Agot, next to him, frowned. 'No, you are not. Nobody is allowed two.'

'I am,' said Ash. 'I get two.'

'MISS LORNA!'

Agot had no compunction about summoning her despised nemesis when there was tattling to be done.

'Ash says he is making TWO SEASHELL BOXES when everyone is making ONE SEASHELL BOX. *Chan eil sin cothromach?*'

'Ash,' said Lorna pleasantly, 'we're just all going to make one seashell box.'

'But,' said Ash in a small voice, 'my dad is a mum and a dad. He counts as two.'

Lorna bit her lip.

'I know,' she said. 'And he is very good at it.'

'But it WOULD NOT BE FAIR,' said Agot, 'IF YOU TAKE ALL THE SHELLS.'

Ash's little face started to crumple. Agot sighed, sounding ridiculously grown-up.

'ALL RIGHT,' she said, regarding her own pile and removing the smallest and brownest of all the shells.

'You can have THIS ONE of my shells. LOOK, Miss Lorna, I am SHARING.'

'Thank you,' said Lorna, and the other children, one by one, eager to join in, proffered their own shells to Ash, whose large

281

brown eyes suddenly became more cheerful, as the pile in front of him grew higher.

Ash was still very thoughtful though when he arrived home that night.

'Do you think,' he said, 'and this is not me giving away the surprise I am not giving away any surprise it is just a FOR EXAMPLE.'

'Okay,' said Saif, who was stirring lentil soup on the stove.

'FOR EXAMPLE, are you very, very excited about Father's Day?'

Saif blinked. He had been completely unaware it was happening.

'I . . . ' He looked at Ash's face. 'Um, I suppose so,' he said.

'And would you be very, very excited about . . . a BOX? For example.'

'I . . . Yes, a box is always useful.'

'And would you be very, very excited about SOME SHELLS?'

'I do like shells yes.'

Ash let out a big sigh.

'Because you know it is Father's Day and that is all for you and you will be SO HAPPY and excited when you get, FOR EXAMPLE, a box.'

'No, he won't,' said Ib, coming in from football, his beloved Hibs shirt covered in mud. 'It'll be absolute rubbish. I made one when I was in that stupid class, my first year here.'

'Did you?' said Saif mildly. 'I don't remember that.'

Ib frowned.

'I didn't bring it home. It was stupid.'

In fact, he had smashed it up in front of the other boys, leaving them feeling awkward and scared. It had taken Ib a lot longer to settle down and learn the language than Ash. Even now, and only through football, had he really come into his own.

'But,' went on Ash inexorably, 'I have two bo— two things. But I can give one to you. But I can't ...'

'I'm hungry,' said Ib quickly, trying to head a meltdown off at the pass. 'What's for dinner?'

'Lentil soup,' said Saif as both the boys made a face. 'And warm bread from Flora's.'

Ib perked up at that, but Ash wasn't letting it go.

'There's a Father's Day,' he said. 'But why isn't there a Mother's Day?'

Ib and Saif exchanged looks.

'Uh,' said Saif. 'I think ...'

'There is, stupid,' chipped in Ib.

Ash's face was confused and upset.

'But then why ...?'

'It's when you make that stupid daffodil.'

Ash's eyes went wide.

'But Miss Lorna said that was for anyone who helped us in our lives!'

'Yeah, well, for most people, that's their mum.'

Ash frowned.

'But,' he said. Then he went quiet.

'Is there really a Mother's Day?' he said. Ib and Saif exchanged a glance again.

'Only here,' said Saif quickly, sensing danger. 'Not in Syria.'

'But if it was Mother's Day, wouldn't your mother ...?'

'Let's eat,' said Ib. 'I'm really hungry.'

But Saif knew he couldn't sweep it under the carpet.

'I don't think Mama would have known it was Mother's Day,' he said gently to his youngest son. 'But she would have been thinking about you all day, like she thinks about you every day.'

It wasn't dark. It looked like three o'clock in the afternoon, even though it was after eleven p.m. Saif didn't know how anyone got used to it: you could live here all your life, surely, and still find it absolutely astonishing that it stayed light all night in the summer months, just as the days were pitch-dark in the winter. Coming from a land where sunset didn't vary by more than two hours throughout the year and that change was barely noticeable, this insane swing was completely discombobulating.

Flora sold absolutely shedloads of coffee to people who couldn't remember what time they'd gone to sleep, or been awake from three a.m. with the bird noise. The blackout blinds in the Rock were all in full use. People got a little strange this time of year too, when the white nights hit them.

So Saif was in bed, trying to make himself sleep but acutely conscious of the sunlight pooling around the curtains, when he heard the deep and silent sob of someone crying but trying not to be overheard. He crept in. Ash was in a little ball, sobbing his heart out.

'*Habibti*,' he said. He glanced at Ib in the next bed, who was awake, watching them grimly, his face full of pain.

'I want my mama,' Ash was saying, half asleep, over and over again. 'I want her. I want my mama! Mama!'

Saif held him tight, rocked him, not quite awake, not quite

asleep, just saying his mother's name, over and over again, quite frantic. He looked over at Ibrahim.

'You see why we can't tell him,' he said, expecting solidarity from the boy who understood, who knew just how much they all had to lose, who was so terrified of leaving.

Ibrahim's face turned to stone.

'I want to see her,' he said, his voice almost impossible to hear beneath Ash's wails. 'I want to see her. Why do I have to be the grown-up? Why do I have to be without a mum, *Abba*? Why is it always just Ash we have to worry about?' The older boy's eyes were now wet too. 'You said she's alive. You know where she is. I want my mum. Why can't I see my mum? I want my mum.'

Chapter Thirty-four

Dr Mark Philippoussis loved his adopted son Joel and his daughter-in-law-to-be very much, but he remained constantly surprised by their inability to remember the time difference between the tiny island they lived on and the Upper East Side. Marsha was excited to see the white nights when they headed there in a couple of weeks' time; at the moment, Mark would have settled for another couple of hours' sleep. He wasn't getting any younger.

'Flora,' he said, putting on his glasses.

'Mark,' said Flora. Then: 'What time is it there?'

'Doesn't matter,' he said, as Marsha rolled out of bed next to him and went to put the coffee on. Sun poured through their windows; it was going to be another scorching, humid Manhattan day. 'What's the weather like on top of the world?' he said.

'Breezy,' said Flora. 'Kind of scudding. Fresh.'

'God,' said Mark. 'That sounds awesome. Well, we'll be there soon. I can't wait. There's no fresh air in New York at all; it's all been breathed in and recycled about nine million times.'

There was a pause. Uh-oh, thought Mark.

'Joel . . . ' said Flora. And then she explained.

Mark's phone beeped. Joel was on the other line.

'Give me a sec,' he said to Flora.

'Joel?'

'Hey, Mark. How's the weather?'

'How's Flora?'

'I hate it when you do that.'

Mark stood for a minute staring out at the skyline, which was already shimmering in the heat of the dawn. Marsha handed him a cup of coffee and looked at him meaningfully.

'Knock their blocks together,' she whispered. 'You're not his therapist any more.'

'I'm not the head-knocking type either,' grumbled Mark. He thought for a second, then spoke into the phone.

'Joel?' he said. 'Okay, I'm in a rush so I'm going to be quick. How you get married doesn't matter. The only thing that matters is if you are lucky enough to have found someone in this life who loves you and who you love too, and who isn't evil. Only an idiot would get caught up worrying who else is in the room when it happens, okay? It doesn't matter.'

He clicked off and was left with only Flora.

'Flora?' he said. 'Okay. I'm in a rush so I'm going to be quick. How you get married doesn't matter. The only thing that matters is if you are lucky enough to have found someone in this life who loves you and who you love too, and who isn't evil. Only an idiot would get caught up worrying who else is in the room when it happens, okay? It doesn't matter.'

Marsha snuggled up to him. Even as he'd got older, his beard

287

filling with grey, the waistcoats he wore to work expanding, the bags under his large dark eyes getting slightly heavier, the forehead a little higher, she'd never found him less attractive. For his part too, he still loved the little bird qualities of her; her bright eyes, enquiring look, small bones.

'You're brilliant,' she said.

'I don't think either of them thought that,' said Mark.

'Don't be silly; you were quite right. And I need to up my baggage allowance for all the toys I'm taking Douglas.'

Chapter Thirty-five

I will, Flora told herself, as she headed up for the final meeting for Olivia's wedding, I will. Mark is always right. I will swallow my pride, tell Olivia it's off, tell everyone we're just having a small thing – oh God, they'll all think that Joel hates them. They'll think we think we're too good for everyone. Or that we're really, really tight. And oh God, Joel's already committed the money so we can barely have dinner. And I did so want everyone to see my lovely red dress. No. No. I won't. I just want him. There is absolutely nothing Jacinth can say now that can make me change my mind.

Jacinth was standing waiting for her at reception in the Rock, Gala indicating she had an appointment.

'Hey,' said Flora. 'How's it going?'

'Busy, busy,' said Jacinth. 'Hey, are there really whales in the bay?'

'Yeah,' said Flora. 'You can't go out or near or anything like that though.'

'Really?' said Jacinth, wrinkling her nose. 'You'd think it would be a good money spinner. Great for Instagram.'

'Yes, well, not so great for whales . . . How's Olivia?'

'Hungry,' said Jacinth. 'Shall we walk it through? Given it's your wedding too, apparently?'

'Hmm,' said Flora, non-committedly.

'Are you and Thingy all right?' said Jacinth suddenly.

'What? What do you mean?'

'When you have personally overseen 186 weddings,' snorted Jacinth, 'you can't help picking up on a frisson or two. Ridiculous institution.'

'My fiancé isn't too keen on having a lot of people,' said Flora.

'I just organised one for 1,700 guests,' said Jacinth. 'Now *that* was a bash.'

'Wow,' said Flora. 'What was it like?'

'There were elephants,' said Jacinth. 'This will be quite intimate by comparison. Although it would be so lovely to incorporate the whales . . . '

'Forget about the whales,' said Flora firmly.

She led Jacinth out the back of the Rock, where the kitchen garden was.

'Okay, good,' said Jacinth. 'We are starting from . . . '

'DO NOT—' came a voice.

'Oh no,' said Flora. 'Gaspard. If you are going to keep banging on about your . . . '

'DO NOT touch *mes choux*!'

'I've told you a million times! The construction starts *after* the kitchen garden! They won't tread on your cabbages.'

'People with 'igh-'eeled shoes! They think, cabbages cabbages, I do not care.'

Gaspard grimaced and lit up a cigarette. Jacinth looked at him; he tossed her the packet and she took one.

'Oh, so I see *smoking* around your cabbages is completely fine,' said Flora crossly. 'I mean, I like high-heeled shoes; I am not a monster. But there is *no respect.*'

'How's breakfast coming along?' said Jacinth, as Gaspard growled.

'Eediots. You waste my skills.'

'It's going to be amazing,' said Flora quickly. 'Everything local, everything fresh ... '

'They make me egg chef,' said Gaspard. '*Me!* That is my plan. I make omelettes. For my skills.'

As a matter of fact, Flora was already well aware of Gaspard's plans for the wedding, i.e., siphoning off the unbelievably good vintage Champagne that had already been delivered, and replacing it with the Prosecco that people drank happily in the hotel but which he thought was abominable, before getting cheerily squished with Fintan and Konstantin.

She had accused him several times of being about to commit an actual crime, and a crime moreover that would now also deprive her own guests, but he denied it with so much flouncing and fury that she couldn't press the matter, considering that her own guests would be perfectly happy with Prosecco anyway, as would she. But she had caught him, more than once, passing a keen eye over the delivery schedule and clearing out the cellars in anticipation. A heist, however, was low down on her list of current priorities.

'So we all enter here, from the boat,' said Jacinth, making copious notes. 'Okay. So first off, we have a huge receiving chamber, here, with Champagne in the ice castle.'

'An ice castle,' repeated Flora, shaking her head.

291

'It's the theme,' said Jacinth. 'It's not real ice. Although obviously there will be ice sculptures everywhere.'

'Obviously.'

'Then the mini cathedral will be here ... You will walk down the aisle, one after another, Olivia first, naturally, past all the rows of red velvet mini thrones.'

'Mini thrones.'

'Meeny thrones,' echoed Gaspard, but not in admiration.

'Gaspard, are you up on the lunch service?' said Flora as strictly as she dared, which wasn't very.

'I do not know. I am mere omelette chef now,' said Gaspard.

'So, now we're in Snow White's ice palace ... the red queen and the white queen ... It's about thirty feet high; it's quite something. Heaters if cold, plenty of ice if not.'

'Ooh,' said Flora, trying her hardest not to be impressed.

'So we do the service, all very lovely, do you take ...?'

'Joel,' said Flora.

'Yeah, whoever,' said Jacinth, ticking something off on her clipboard. 'Marry marry marry wedded wedded wedded then ... *pouf!*'

'Pouf?' said Flora, who was absolutely, definitely on the point of explaining that she and Joel wouldn't be getting married there.

'Pouf!' said Gaspard with some satisfaction.

'The walls collapse – *boom!* – and ...'

She spread her arms wide, even though they were only looking at the pasture that led down from the Rock towards the gravelly road. It was thick with cow parsley, the grass high and filled with poppies.

'We're in the spring room! Flowers everywhere, vines twisting, birds tweeting.'

292

'Real birds?'

'Real songbirds, absolutely. Tinkling fountains, string quartet, young spring maidens serving drinks. A little stream.'

'We're having a stream?!'

'Absolutely. You can dream it, etc. Then, depending on the weather, we can either let people roam outside, or if not, the tables will be hung under the vines for dinner.'

'Ees not deenner,' said Gaspard. 'Ees nothing.'

'... salmon, light summer salads, ices, watermelons, olives. Then – *boom!* – we move on again to the *hot Ibiza nightclub*. Summer summer summer all night long.'

Flora bit her lip, imagining it and how much everyone was going to absolutely love it.

'Everyone they will be so 'ungry,' said Gaspard sadly.

'And we have summer food – hot dogs, burgers, ice cream, lollies, fish and chips.'

'I will remember not to fill up on salad,' said Flora, shaking her head with longing. 'Oh my God. It's going to be amazing, isn't it?'

'Then, to the side we have the autumn room: brown leather Chesterfield sofas, fires, blankets as it becomes evening, and we have speeches, and toffee apples and hot cider and marshmallows. And the ice cathedral becomes an ice rink with boots and so on. So all night everyone wanders between the seasons, wherever they want, to dance, to sit, to skate, to take lots of pictures of themselves by the flower walls in springtime. It will be marvellous, darling. Right, let me just make sure we've got all the measurements.'

She took out her phone to call her site manager, who'd been up checking the plasterboard.

'Wow,' said Flora, shaking her head. 'Olivia talked about it, but I didn't quite realise ... I mean, it's a massive production.'

'Ees ridiculous,' said Gaspard. 'A kees and a good deenner – what more is *necessaire?*'

But poor Flora's eyes were full of stars, full of the amazing visions that were going to be built at her hotel, the amazing party that was going to be there, with her a vision too in the centre of it as one of the brides, and surely, when she explained it to Joel, surely he'd realise this was special, a day in a million, something they would never do again, a wonderful celebration, a way for her to feel glamorous and lovely again after the baby. Surely when she explained how wonderful it was going to be . . .

Chapter Thirty-six

'I don't believe you.' Neda sounded exasperated but that was as far as her professional nature would allow her to disclose herself: inside she was absolutely furious.

'The deadline is Friday! Where is it?!'

'I've ... I've been thinking.'

'You don't have time for thinking! If the home office doesn't get your form, that's you – you can't stay! And it has to come to me first to sign you off and write a reference about the boys!'

Saif swallowed. He hadn't slept for a week; he had walked miles and miles and miles up and down the Endless Beach, trying to figure things out, trying to work out what was the best thing to do. For some reason, he couldn't forget the men talking at the Syrian café in Edinburgh, teasing each other about how useless they would be rebuilding a country.

He would not be useless.

He wouldn't be dealing with people's minor ailments here as anything serious or genuinely concerning was passed on to the big hospital on the mainland. There, he would be right in the thick of it, helping anyone who needed it. Images of children who had lost limbs in bombings haunted his mind, as he lay in his comfortable bed. Children just like his. Children he should be helping.

'Saif,' said Neda, in a warning tone. 'Saif, your children. How can you do this to your children?' she said. 'You'll lose everything.'

Saif was silent.

'My mother,' said Neda, 'worked three jobs cleaning offices her whole life. Never got used to it. Never got used to the cold. Never got used to the abuse. Ever. But she did it so I could go to school. Get an education. Get a job. So I could have chances she never had. So I could have everything. She sacrificed that.'

'They don't want everything,' said Saif in a quiet voice. 'They just want their mother.'

'They may not be able to see her,' said Neda. 'You know that? If she's married, you could get in the line of fire of some very, very unpleasant people too.'

Saif closed his eyes.

'I think,' he said, 'I could certainly help there. And I have money saved now ...' He half tried to make a joke. 'Rent in Damascus is not expensive. And there is an international school for the boys ...'

Neda's heart sank. He was organised. He was prepared. The same determination, she suspected, which had brought him to the very tip of the world, against all the odds, would take him back again.

'Have you talked this over with anyone?'

'No,' said Saif. 'But since Ibrahim found out ... that I knew where his mother was ... it is all he desires, Neda.'

Neda sighed.

'I *get* it. But you still shouldn't do it. And if Amena was here, she'd agree with me. You saw her message. You know what she wants.'

'But she is not here. That is the problem,' said Saif, his voice still quiet, his eyes, glancing once more at the white unfilled form which sat on his desk.

'Do you *want* to leave?'

'No,' said Saif fervently, with all his heart and soul. 'No. Of course I do not want to leave.'

'Then for heaven's sake, *why?*'

Saif's voice, when he finally spoke, remained very quiet and low.

'I think, perhaps, it is my duty.'

Chapter Thirty-seven

Things moved on even faster. The Rock was overflowing with deliveries, plans and orders as well as the normal summer holiday visitors, overrun now with people coming, hoping to catch a glimpse of the whale pods. There was an official boat from ORCA, and most people were respectful, watching through telescopes from the headlands, but there were skirmishes with people bringing boats from further away. The coastguard wasn't happy about it at all. The whales were out of bounds until they were further from the shore and weren't at risk of beaching themselves; those were the rules. Not everyone wanted to keep them though.

Flora lay awake at night, the checklist of things she had to do circulating round and round her head, making her feel sick with anxiety and nerves, and she could hear them, deep in her bones, communicating to one another. She still hadn't spoken to Joel, who was working all hours with Jan and Charlie. Her sensible side said, forget about it. It doesn't matter. Her island side couldn't bear not to share her day with everyone. And another part still couldn't help longing for the loveliest wedding Mure had ever seen.

Joel for his part had a litany every day from Jan of how much money was being spent, how much fuss, how much waste for one silly over-the-top day when that money could do so much good elsewhere. He genuinely couldn't understand where Flora was coming from at all. He would do it her way, of course he would. But he could not deny he was disappointed.

Saif finished his rounds, checking up on some patients, particularly the older ones. It was tough in the white night months for people who already found it difficult to sleep.

The boys weren't shouting or banging around or blowing things up as they usually were. Since that terrible night, they had grown silent, occasionally whispering together, a sound that stopped as soon as Saif entered the room.

He walked slowly to the house, nervous. If only he could talk things over with Lorna. If only. She would have a solution, surely. She would know the best thing to do. Perhaps she would see a loophole. Perhaps there was some solution that would allow them to come and go.

He was being a coward. He couldn't bear it. He couldn't face it. He couldn't admit to himself that . . . he couldn't even think it.

And the boys. He was going to take them away from everything they knew, from everything safe. It had seemed right, when he had finally decided in the early dawn of two a.m., when he had finally thought he had made up his mind.

But what if . . . ? What if they did not want to go after all? Here was safety and their friends and football and tablet, and the long days that never ended, and the wind across the meadows. They loved it. They were happy here, but Saif could not let himself think of the ways he had been happy here.

And to disrupt their lives again. It was a terrible thing. Especially for Ash, as Scottish a child as any other.

He approached the big old chilly Manse, which had sheltered them so well, anxiously. Was he making the right choice? Was he doing the right thing? He had sent, as ever, a message to Amena's old email account. It had bounced back, as they always did. Her Facebook account had been deactivated a long time ago.

The boys looked up as Mrs Laird put on her coat, clucked at them both as she always did and headed off down the drive, not before reminding Saif to heat the stew through. He thanked her, as she always did, and she headed down the road worrying about him, as she always did.

'*Taeal alaa huna*,' said Saif, beckoning them to him. Ash scampered up onto his knee immediately; Ib, who would normally hang back, reluctantly came over and sat on the arm of his chair.

He was so nervous, terrified, of what he was about to say. But what was the alternative? For his family to spend for ever apart; for his children to grow into men who thought their mother had not loved him?

She had. She did. He had to believe that.

'We have a chance,' he started quietly, 'to go back to Syria.'

'To see Mama?' said Ash immediately, his face wide-eyed and astonished.

300

'Yes. Probably.'

'YAYYYY!'

Ash leaped up and started running round the room in a victory dance.

'But if we go,' went on Saif, 'we cannot come back.'

Ash stopped abruptly. Ib stared straight ahead.

'But we live here,' said Ash, his little face confused.

'We would live in Damascus.'

'But there are bombs and soldiers,' said Ash, creeping back into his father's arms.

'Not any more,' said Saif. 'Not like that. They aren't fighting any more.'

'Would we go home?' said Ib, who remembered it.

'I don't think it is there any more. But we can find a place to stay. There is a school that teaches in English I think you would like.'

He pulled up the little school on his laptop. The children looked as happy and cheerful as children anywhere.

'And we can visit Mama?' said Ib.

Saif swallowed hard.

'I think so,' he said.

There was a silence.

'But we can't come back here?'

'I very much hope one day you can,' said Saif. 'This is Scotland. It's a good place. Maybe one day you can study here, yes? At the big university in Edinburgh?'

'Can Agot come to visit me?'

'I ... I don't know,' said Saif.

And then, to his amazement, both of the boys got excited and started looking on the internet at parts of Damascus they might visit, and where they might live and what their school would

301

be like. Children, he thought, looking at them. Their amazing resilience. Their amazing ability to cope. Far better than me, he thought. Far better.

'When?' said Ash.

'Very soon,' said Saif. Without his leave to stay, they'd be required to go pretty much immediately if they ever wanted to visit again. On the other hand, it was like pulling off a plaster. Best done quickly. As to how to explain about their half-sister, everything else . . . One thing at a time, he thought to himself.

He went in to see the boys that night as he prepared himself for another sleepless one. But they were both fast asleep, soft and gentle breathing, as if everything was going to be okay. He wished he shared their optimism.

He had told them in no uncertain terms that they were absolutely not allowed to mention it at school until he had had the chance to talk to their teacher, and had texted Lorna asking to meet. He was almost as terrified of this as he was of telling the boys. No: more. Because there was no happy upside to this meeting. None at all.

He reiterated the instruction to them again as he straightened their collars and flattened down Ash's unruly hair: there was absolutely no telling anyone, not Agot, not anyone, until he had done it. Otherwise, they might not be able to go. This was a ridiculous lie born of desperation which completely puzzled Ash but terrified him into silence nonetheless. Fortunately, Agot didn't notice as she was very busy explaining to him what a triple Salchow was, and how much he was going to enjoy the wedding. Ash was absolutely beside himself – a wedding, which he'd never been to, and *then* his amazing secret thing, going to see his mum! He was the happiest boy on the island.

Chapter Thirty-eight

Jacinth had arrived to oversee the builders, who were already beginning the fantasy land of the wedding castle, and to have a couple of good stand-up fights with Gaspard about what exactly he was going to serve for the two a.m. breakfast, both of which left them breathless and pink-faced; frankly neither of them could have enjoyed it more.

She was exceptionally happy about the weather forecast, which looked up and down for a week, then followed by a settled spell showing up from somewhere. She loudly proclaimed everywhere that she had a special military weather-based function that worked better than everyone else's, which raised a few eyebrows among some of the fishermen, who could read the weather rather better than they could read a newspaper. They didn't agree with the forecast, not at all.

Olivia was there too, signing the paperwork and checking in with the registrar all by herself. Anthony was golfing on the Algarve. Her loving messages were stepping up. She still hadn't heard from his utterly bloody mother. And Flora, of all people, who ought to be incredibly grateful for everything she was doing for her, wasn't even returning her texts! It was absolutely ridiculous; people were doing nothing but taking advantage. She sat up in bed, pouting. Jacinth was looking out of the window.

'You need exercise,' she said. 'You're going to look scrawny, not toned, in that dress.'

Olivia sighed.

'Do you think?'

She examined her face in the mirror once more.

'Nobody up here even does a vampire facial,' she complained. 'I'm going to look ancient.'

'You're going to look fine,' said Jacinth pointedly, '*if* you get some exercise.'

'There's not even a decent gym or yoga studio!' said Olivia. 'I just don't know how you survive up here.'

'Come paddleboarding,' said Jacinth. 'Good core workout and I can take some good early shots for the wedding photographer.'

'Always on the job,' said Olivia ruefully.

Jacinth smiled. 'Ah, come on, it'll be fun too.'

'Ooh!' said Olivia then frowned. 'But – wetsuits?'

'You can look good in a shortie from the right angle,' said Jacinth.

'Okay then.'

The sun was high in the sky, looking as if it intended to stay all day, as they made their way down, having hired the boards from the little kayak shack round the north side of the island. It was, Olivia had to concede, rather beautiful on a day like today. She supposed. In the pictures it was going to look like somewhere wildly more expensive. They wouldn't even need that many filters.

Jacinth started to take photos of the sun glinting off the water, Olivia posing elegantly on the board. 'Hashtag: livingmy-bestlife,' shouted Olivia. 'Hashtag: notacareintheworld.'

This was not remotely true of course, but Jacinth was all in. Suddenly they both paused. There was a noise, an odd sort of hooting, coming from the pond-flat waters. They looked at one another.

'I wonder if that's those whales everyone keeps going on about.'

'Oh my God!' said Olivia. 'Let's go see them! We have to! Come on! Think of the photos! And then Anthony's mum will see what a humanitarian I am, saving the whales and all that and it will be— This is a great idea.' She sighed. 'I feel, the more I want her to like me, the less she does.'

'You're not allowed near the whales,' said Jacinth.

'Oh for God's sake,' said Olivia. 'You sound exactly like bloody Jan.'

She looked out over the beautiful blue sea.

Lorna hadn't been sleeping well and so had popped into the Seaside Kitchen, hoping to find Flora first thing, which she did.

'Hey, what's up?' said Flora, quiet.

'Saif texted!' said Lorna. 'At last! I thought he was ghosting me! He wants to meet after school when Ash is at Scouts! I thought … Honestly I thought after Edinburgh, he'd gone off me.'

'Oh good,' said Flora, but without her customary enthusiasm.

'What's up?' said Lorna, and Flora explained.

'Well, do it Joel's way, and just tell everyone they can't come,' said Lorna. 'Come on, they'll understand. Don't get so twisted up about it.'

'They won't!' said Flora heavily. 'They'll think Joel is some kind of spoiled outsider who hates them all and deeply resents them and that he doesn't want to be part of our home and our culture and doesn't want to belong and it'll make everything worse than ever!'

Lorna frowned.

'Well, just do it your way then.'

Flora shook her head. 'I'd be dragging him to the altar.'

She sighed.

'Argh! I was thinking … of postponing? I mean, people postpone all the time, right? Just say we're waiting for Douglas to walk me down the aisle?'

'Any sign?' said Lorna. Flora shook her head. 'But that's not the point. He's unhappy about it, I'm unhappy about it, it would be stupid to do it. And it's bad for Olivia too: her mother-in-law went nuts about the extra expense. If we withdraw … just for now …'

'I hear Tripp's flying in today,' said Lorna. 'And when are Mark and Marsha arriving?'

'Oh God, yes,' said Flora. 'I never thought a wedding would be so complicated.'

'So speaks somebody with absolutely no experience of weddings,' said Lorna. 'But you two will be all right, won't you?'

Flora sighed.

'I mean, if we can't even decide on something like this, that doesn't even matter . . . what's it going to do for us in the long run? What if something actually difficult happens?'

Lorna nodded.

'You should really talk it through.'

'Ha!' said Flora. 'Is this from the person who has been absolutely refusing to talk things through with the man she loves for *four years*?!'

'We're different,' said Lorna, going pink nonetheless. 'But you should. Talk about it properly.'

'I know,' said Flora. 'I know, I know. Good luck today.'

'Thanks,' said Lorna, giving her a hug. 'You too.'

The sea was like glass, and it was further to the plashing of the whales than Olivia could imagine.

Jacinth was behind her, keeping up but looking concerned.

'You sure about this?' she yelled, but Olivia kept ploughing forward, a determined look on her face.

What happened next was an accident, that was all.

Agot had arranged a fake wedding in the playground – excitement around the festivities, and the children's whispered exaggerations about what exactly was being built up at the Rock – certain variations on Disneyland had been mentioned – had caused island excitement to rise to fever pitch, and Agot was attempting to run a mock wedding with of course herself as bride, poor Ash as the groom, inveigled into the event even though his own gentle nature still didn't particularly want to do it, and a few favoured acolytes very much not including Mary-Elizabeth MacIntyre as bridesmaids.

During the event, several people were given the chance to provide 'the band' (a lot of rock banging and pencil drumming) and there was marching and a game of Grand Old Duke of York which enabled the 'couples' to tear through without too much mushy stuff. They made a merry sight, covered in green rushes in the playground as Lorna and Mrs Cook supervised together, drinking their cups of tea and laughing.

'It's going to be frightening when Agot is world dictator,' observed Mrs Cook.

'I know,' said Lorna. 'Let's just enjoy it while we can, and hope she spares us.'

The bell rang to mass groans, the children still enjoying their 'wedding party', Agot's daisy chain headdress becoming increasingly askew, but they dragged themselves back into the class reluctantly, even though Lorna planned to take them back out again for story time. Although, she thought, glancing up, there were clouds gathering in the distant north that could race towards them fast as anything; perhaps not best to make promises.

'*A h-uile duine a staigh*,' she said, rounding up the stragglers. Agot carefully took off her daisy chains.

'Tra-la-la,' Ash was singing to himself quietly, as he dragged his feet on the cobbles. 'I am going to a play wedding at the school and then I am going to a REAL WEDDING and then I am SEEING MUMMY! La la la la la!'

He didn't know Lorna was there. He was just a little boy in the sunshine, having a lovely day and celebrating his good fortune.

For Lorna, it was as if someone had poured ice cubes down her back.

Mure was now far behind them. Very far, in fact. But the whales didn't seem much closer. Although, oddly, the great oil tankers on the horizon did. It was very strange indeed.

Olivia sat down on her board. It was drifting towards the whales, so that was good, right? Get her there without having to do much. She was, she realised, exhausted. Pilates and yoga were all very well, but paddleboarding was actually much more knackering than she'd thought. Jacinth was sitting too now, with a slightly worried expression on her face, staring at the rapidly piling clouds in the corner of the sky.

'Got any water?' shouted Olivia back to Jacinth, who shook her head. Then Jacinth took out her phone. There wasn't a signal out here.

Lorna followed Ash into the classroom.

'That was a nice song, Ash,' she said as steadily as she could. His immediate, haunted look as his head whipped round confirmed her worst fears. He was singing something he shouldn't, and he knew it.

'Oh!' he said.

'Don't worry,' she said, swallowing hard. 'Your secret is safe with me.'

And he beamed. His face lit up. His secret was okay; it was safe. He was the happiest child Lorna had ever seen. He was going to speak to his mum.

Maybe it was a phone call, thought Lorna. It must be that. Maybe a Facebook call, right?

But why would that be a secret? Because of the home office? Maybe it was part of the citizenship paperwork, that ... maybe Amena had to sign it off in some way? He wouldn't sing 'seeing Mummy', the thought nagged at her. He wouldn't. Not like that.

Flora arrived bearing cakes, lots of them, to the campsite where the lads were learning forest-craft and attempting, with some rather fruity language, to weave themselves a bush canopy.

Joel looked up at her trudging up the hill, Douglas on her back, two huge bags in either hand, puffing rather in the unexpected warmth, and felt his heart melt. Sitting here in the sun, surrounded by noisy chatter, seeing his boy, feeling useful ... suddenly his objections felt silly, shallow. He stood up, arms wide to greet her.

She arrived, shyly smiling, instructing the quietest-looking boy to share out the cakes, a responsibility that young Luke Hoyer took very seriously indeed, getting to his duties, his dark curly hair falling over his forehead.

'My darling,' said Joel, opening his arms.

'I've been thinking,' said Flora. 'You know, we could just postpone a little bit, do you think? Would that be a better idea?'

Joel's mouth fell open.

'Call it off?' he said. 'Good God, Flora, these are lawyer tactics.'

Chapter Thirty-nine

'We need to go back,' said Jacinth. 'I don't think this is going to work.'

Olivia pouted. 'Oh for God's sake. I can do nothing right these days.'

'I just don't think ... I don't think we're going to make it to the whales. But I can photoshop them in, darling!'

'Fine. Whatever.'

She stood up, turned around and set the board towards shore and started paddling. Nothing happened.

She frowned.

'Why isn't this board moving?'

Jacinth looked down herself. She didn't allow any panic to creep into her voice.

'Uh. I think. I think ... '

Now Olivia was paddling to stand still, it was becoming increasingly obvious, now they weren't moving at the same rate, that Jacinth was floating off behind her, further and further out to sea.

'I think ... there's a current. God. Olivia.'

'Paddle!' said Olivia, her voice rising. 'Paddle towards the shore then!'

Jacinth stood and started paddling but was hardly moving; she simply going hell for leather just to stand still.

'Oh crap,' she said.

How Lorna got through the rest of that day she would never know. There was a quite vast amount of bad behaviour which carried on unseen, and the Curriculum for Excellence would have to be even less excellent than it normally was, because she was churning up inside, running on autopilot.

'Are you all right?' asked Mrs Cook at lunchtime. 'Are you sickening for something? You should go see Dr Hassan. He's actually an all right doctor, you know. Once you get used to him.'

Lorna stared at her, unseeing, and muttered something non-committal. He was due at her flat after school. She'd talk to him then. It would be a simple misunderstanding, she knew. It would be cleared up easily. And everything would be fine. It would be. It had to be.

'You don't want it with everyone around,' said Flora. 'I get it. But I can't ... I can't explain. For me to say now, oh you all can't come, we don't care about our family, the island, the community, it's just for us ... it would be so selfish, Joel. I know it isn't

314

meant that way. But it would look like that. It would be such an awful way to start our married life. Whereas if we just postpone it for a while ... We've already got Douglas. I just think it's a better solution, don't you?'

'Your solution to us is – calling off our wedding?'

He shook his head and stared at the ground. It had taken him so long to get to this point. It had been a long and difficult road. And now she was throwing it back in his face.

'But Mark and Marsha are coming.'

'And so is everybody else,' said Flora. 'It's okay. We'll figure something out. We'll all go to Olivia's wedding; it's going to be quite the fancy thing.'

'And that's what you wanted all along. A fancy, wasteful, expensive thing.'

Flora shook her head vehemently.

'I wanted you,' she said. 'I wanted you and my family and our home and our community. I didn't realise it was too much to ask.'

'You didn't ask!' said Joel bitterly. 'You said it was all fine! Then I find out you'd just gone right behind my back and organised your own wedding anyway!'

Flora stepped up towards him.

'Joel,' she said softly. 'I love you. You know I do. Heart and soul. Weddings don't matter. You matter, and Douglas matters, that's all. So rather than have some stupid ceremony neither of us is happy with, let's leave it. Just for now. It changes nothing.'

He looked at her.

'But you said before that having a sweetheart wedding would be fine, and you didn't mean it.'

'Because I thought it would be,' said Flora. 'Then I realised, when everyone was there, that it wasn't. That the reason for

getting married is to tell the world who you are. That's why ... '
Her voice wobbled. 'That's why Colton and Fintan's wedding was
so important. They needed to stand up and be counted for their
community, for their world. Colton was so brave to do that ... '

Joel sighed.

'And I'm not.'

'This is going so wrong,' said Flora. 'Let's ... let's leave
it for now.'

He watched her walk away, completely stricken. She didn't
know what it was not to belong to her world.

It was all he knew.

The speed of it was the first real indication of fear. What had
started as a tiny cloud in a pale blue sky had raced in with terrifying speed, and now huge thick grey clouds, piles of them,
were covering the sky, some so dark as to be almost black.
Already on the horizon you could make out the odd slanting
light of a rainstorm at sea.

'Shit shit shit *shit*,' shouted Olivia, the two of them sitting on
their boards, drifting further and further away from the island.
'Oh my God! Shit! Why can't we get back?'

'There must be some tidal current,' said Jacinth, who
was furiously stabbing at her phone. 'Oh my God, come *on*.
Honestly.'

'Why didn't the paddleboard guy warn us about this?'
said Olivia.

'Oh, he did,' said Jacinth. 'There was a safety briefing, but
you were on your phone.'

'And you heard it?'

'No, I was on my phone. I'm just guessing.'

It was getting colder and gustier by the second.

'They'll see us,' said Olivia stoutly. 'People will be watching for the whales, won't they? If we steer towards them, someone will see us through a telescope.'

This would have been a better idea had visibility from the island not gone to zero, and the whale watchers had all crowded to the Seaside Kitchen for toasted sandwiches thick with local cheese on the best crusted white bread, served with small pots of sharp tomato salsa and vast mugs of tea, and were having a very lovely time indeed.

'This couldn't . . . '

The girls were having to shout at each other now over the rising wind. Despite their wetsuits, which were only short, they were still adrift in the North Atlantic. It was getting very, very cold.

Flora stumbled along the headland, straight into the stormy weather sweeping in from the north. She unloaded her bag and took out the cagoule no Mure inhabitant ever left home without; after all, you never could tell. She pulled Douglas round to her front in a clumsy movement so he could look where he was going. He cooed appreciatively, putting his hands out as if he could feel the low cloud, the roaring wind.

Then she stopped, decided. She was being absolutely ridiculous. They were sweethearts. They would have a sweetheart wedding. Nothing else mattered a whit. She was being stubborn and ridiculous and she was going to sort it out right now. Enough prevaricating. Just do it. Do the right thing. She turned around . . .

. . . the noise came on suddenly. She stopped, hushed Douglas and stepped up on a hillock to hear better.

The island people had said it about Flora all her life: she was part selkie, attuned to the island's creatures as her mother had been and her mother before her, stretching back as long as recorded time. Flora had always shaken it off as superstitious nonsense, particularly when she lived in London, but she could hear it now, clear as day. A lowing sound from far off in the water; a deep tremor; a vibration that stated to Flora, clear as day: something is wrong. Something is wrong.

It had to be the whale pod. But what? Not the storm, surely? That wouldn't worry them. Frowning, she stumbled back to her car, determined to go up to the Rock, where there was a state-of-the-art telescope Colton used to love, before he got too sick.

As she reached the car, though, her mobile signal picked up reception again. It was Gala – Shugs, from the board rental, had been in; had she seen Olivia and Jacinth?

Immediately, Flora knew. She knew exactly what the whales were saying; she knew exactly what had happened. How could they have been so stupid? Olivia, forever trying to look the best and the coolest – of course she'd gone to see the whales, despite being specifically told not to. Everyone knew not to go out there. Everyone except stupid spoiled girls who weren't remotely island girls, not any more.

She called up Fionn at the RNLI, who immediately sent out the call. Meanwhile, the weather was getting worse and worse. Rain was throwing itself at the island now, the bright skies and gentle sunlight of an hour before completely forgotten, and she shivered. She'd go to the Rock, make sure the heating was turned on in their rooms. It would be okay . . . wouldn't it?

Oh God. Joel would have to go out with the lifeboat, it struck her suddenly. Oh God. He'd only been trying to train with them to get over his phobia. He wasn't . . . Suddenly, she was terrified for him. He shouldn't be on the water.

The whales groaned their warning once again, their sombre song hanging in the blustering air.

Chapter Forty

Saif had finished surgery and was taking the boys to Scouts, not really listening to their chatter, terrified of what was to come. Lora would understand. That it wouldn't be for ever. That it would be temporary. She might even have a good solution, a practical route he and Neda hadn't thought of so far. There would be an answer. Yes. Where he could come back.

Maybe there was a way of rotating, coming and going every two months, for locum work maybe, the boys could do terms here and there. She would see him and say, of course, let's do it this way, it will be absolutely fine, I have a perfect solution, I love you, this is all going to work out perfectly.

The boys splashed through the puddles ahead, laughing, as he dropped them off.

'Is there Scouts in Damascus?' asked Ash, then glanced around to see if anyone had heard.

'You cannot talk like this,' said Saif. Then: 'If there is not, I think we can start one.'

'Yay!' said Ash, charging into the hut next to the church.

Saif watched the boys go, just as his emergency beeper went off.

Joel was quiet as he helped the boys check their tents were all watertight before they got in them to take part in a quiz while sheltering from the storm, full of excitement and tall tales about how they had all somehow been struck by lightning before, but made miraculous recoveries. The emergency channel on his phone rang. He frowned.

'What's that?' he said.

Jan tutted.

'Oh for goodness' sake, are you on the lifeboat or what?'

'Oh my God,' said Joel, suddenly nervous. 'Well, yes, I am but I never thought . . . you know. That anything would actually happen.'

Jan rolled her eyes. 'Sunny morning, unpredictable storm? It'll be some idiot in a dinghy – go, go, go! I can manage here.'

'Are you sure?'

Jan nodded and shooed him off out into the storm. It wasn't until he'd gone that she thought to check her own phone; it was on silent – but with message after message after message piled up.

Lorna sat in her beautiful flat, as the rain pelted the windows. A sweet candle burned, and there was tea on the stove and little biscuits set on a plate. Her heart pounding. He was late. Of course, it might be a patient; that could always happen.

But he always texted or called whenever he was delayed. He never left her to sit and stew like this. Never. She thought back to Ash. It couldn't. But what could it be?

'Right, crew!' shouted Fionn, no longer the slightly sullen boatman in charge of the RNLI cohort, but a man of action. He looked out on the eight indistinguishable men and women in their yellow all-weather outfits. 'Flora reckons they're up by the whales; Jan also says they mentioned they were going to go take a look at them and she also wants us to know that, um, she told them not to.'

The boat was manoeuvred down the slipway. Saif and Joel glanced at each other. Although they were with experienced lifeboat people, this was their first ever actual rescue. Both of them were incredibly nervous, Joel more so, and they grinned to each other underneath their hoods. Innes was up front; Hamish was on land, untying the ropes.

'Just follow your training, lads,' said Innes. 'You'll be all right.'

At sea, it was a maelstrom. The lifeboat had practised in calm seas often; it toured children's groups and gave lectures on sea safety. But actual people in trouble – this was new.

Flora couldn't see a thing through the telescope. The weather was furious now and visibility was practically at zero. She came down to the Rock to be confronted, in the foyer, with eighteen small and very wet little boys. And, sitting by the fire, sobbing her heart out, was Jan, with Charlie and Christabel by her side.

'She's my stupid sister,' Jan was sobbing. 'She never listens! But I don't want her to die!'

Flora took charge immediately.

'Isla!' she begged. 'Please would you mind taking these boys into the dining room and feeding them as much cake as you can uncover?'

'Yay!' said the boys, gladly following. This week was turning out to be much more exciting than any of them had hoped.

Charlie looked up at Flora, who tried a half-smile.

'You really reckon they're with the whales, aye?'

'Um . . . ' Flora felt silly to say it out loud. 'I think it's possible.'

'Well, there we go; they'll find them easy,' said Charlie, trying to perk Jan up, who kept on sobbing.

'Wee dram?' mouthed Flora to Charlie, who nodded, and she fetched the whisky. Normally, Jan would have turned her nose up, but she accepted it gratefully, and even let Charlie put his arms around her.

The boat plunged up and down without respite and Saif grabbed the seat hard. He had known how hard he would find this. That was one of the reasons he did it, because he had no good memories of boats. None. Everything flashed back to that terrible journey he'd taken once, away from everything and everyone he had ever known. What he had done for his family once.

What he would do again, gladly. He closed his eyes briefly. When he opened them, Hamish, who was always on RNLI duty in case they had to row like fiends, was patting him gently on the arm. He nodded his thanks.

Fionn was worried. They had good radar, but paddleboards were absolutely tiny. It was like looking for a needle in a haystack. And visibility was absolutely shocking.

Jacinth, practically, had grabbed the two paddleboards together and laid their paddles side by side. But they were entirely at sea now; the island was a dot in the distance and huge tankers seemed massive, looming up ahead.

'Will they see us?' said Olivia, sobbing. Jacinth thought it was extremely unlikely but kept this to herself. They were freezing now.

'Why didn't I tell anyone where we were going?' moaned Olivia.

'Well, you mentioned it to Jan and she told you that you were evil to want to disturb the whales,' said Jacinth.

'I was!' wailed Olivia. 'I was! Selfish and unthinking and now ... now ... '

Suddenly, out of the cloud and gloom came a huge, long, groaning, lowing noise. Both girls screamed, and Olivia, unsettled, toppled right into the water.

They had been up and down every cove where the boards might have washed up or got stuck, but nothing. Now the only thing to be done was to turn the boats out to sea and consider scrambling a helicopter from the mainland. Helicopters couldn't really help much in these conditions though; the fog was so thick you could hardly see a thing, and the spray and wind so strong you couldn't hear yourself think.

Then they all heard it: a low, groaning noise. Fionn glanced at Joel.

'You think Flora's right?' he grunted.

Joel shrugged.

'She does have a weird ... big fishy mammal thing,' he said, shrugging, and several other Mure men, who remembered her mother, nodded in agreement.

'Well,' said Fionn, turning the RIB around at speed. 'Can't hurt to start somewhere.'

And he accelerated north-north-east, in the direction of the whale sound, the boat ripping along the tops of the grey rolling waves.

Olivia was screaming and panicking, thrashing at the boards and threatening to upturn Jacinth. The creatures, somewhere in the fog behind them, made another groaning noise, and Olivia's face sank beneath the waves.

'Oh for Christ's sake,' said Jacinth, wondering whether or not she could reasonably put in for danger money. She leaned over both of the boards, positioning herself very flatly across them.

'Get my hand,' she said. 'Take my hand, Olivia. Just take my hand.'

Joel was peering out of the port side as Fionn, flying practically blind, aimed closer and closer to where the animals appeared to be. There was another one.

'You'd swear they were telling us,' said Joel, his rational lawyer's brain completely turned around. He'd always known the island was full of stories and fairy tales of selkies and mysterious visitors from the sea, of man and the sea communicating. But he'd seen it as just romantic tales, old superstitions.

The great lowing came again. There was nothing romantic or storybook about it. It was a warning.

'Hush,' said Fionn. 'We're getting closer.'

'COME ON, OLIVIA!' Jacinth was shouting. Olivia was at least hanging onto a paddle, her face a mask of panic as she slipped up and down in the waves.

'Come on! Hold on!'

From the very far distance, just as she felt her strength beginning to give out, Jacinth thought she heard something above the roaring of the water and the moaning of the unseen whales, as she tasted the salt in her mouth and watched Olivia's shapely head bob up and down once again beneath the waves.

Chapter Forty-one

'YES!' It was Joel, wiping the condensation from his thick glasses, who saw them, which was odd, given how little he could see ordinarily.

'There's only one,' said somebody else, and everyone's face was grave.

'No,' said Fionn, pulling up the boat. 'There's one in the water.'

He pulled out the loudhailer and turned the lights on to full beam. The figure lying across the boards turned round and waved frantically, much to their relief.

'STAY WHERE YOU ARE! THIS IS THE RNLI! PLEASE DON'T MOVE,' shouted Fionn.

'There's someone in the water,' said Joel. 'Where's the lifebelt?'

He grabbed it and sent it out, where it landed painfully short.

'They can't get over,' said Fionn. 'The current. It can't catch up with them. Plus, they'll be done. Too exhausted to move.'

He took the boat round to the other side, where it bucked unmercifully in the wind, crashing up and down. From here, though, great waves were just thrown back into the boat. The conditions were horrific. 'We can't get closer,' said Fionn. 'If we keep stalling like this, we'll flood the engine. I can't see the other lass, if she's still there.'

There was silence in the boat. Then Joel stepped forward.

'Take it round again,' said Joel. Fionn looked at him.

'Aye, all right,' he said.

Joel had never learned to swim as a child. Neglected children are rarely taught. It had taken him a long time to learn, to force himself as he had forced himself through so much of life. But he had, and he prevailed. He could overcome anything. He could.

Joel attached himself to the rope and the lifebelt, and jumped into the water.

The freezing shock of it hit him like a slap in the face.

'God,' he said, his first instinct being to struggle and panic. He felt the water get into his mouth, felt his mind going white with the panic.

Then he thought, for one second, of the people waiting, of the person who had told him where to look.

And now he could hear the boys were cheering him on as the current bore him forwards and he started ploughing with the regular, perfected crawl stroke that used to take him up and down the swimming pool of his incredibly expensive private members' gym in London a million years ago.

The fact that his vision was poor didn't even matter; there was so much spray and fog and water in his face. He moved by instinct, the boys shouting him the way, until he found himself at the boards, bumping against each other. He could do this.

'Thank Christ,' said Jacinth. 'Get her!'

Olivia was still only just keeping her head above water, dipping and retching, her eyes distant. She looked very close to slipping under completely. Joel threw the lifebelt over her, grabbed her in the lifesaving position and tugged the boat to come get them.

As he hurled her onto the boat, he turned back, kept one hand on the side of the boat and managed to grab the paddle-board hook to pull Jacinth towards him.

'Sometimes this is a *very stupid job*,' she spat. And then: 'Is Olivia all right?'

Flora looked up from where she had been frozen in front of the telescope. The whales had stopped.

'Coffee. Flasks. Blankets. Now!' she ordered Isla.

'You can't . . . Have they found them?' said Isla, frowning.

'I hope so,' said Flora, her mouth a line. *How* had they found them? That was a different question.

The boat came limping back slowly to the harbour to find the entire island was out to greet them. Everyone was concerned, then, when they heard the girls were okay, ecstatic. A couple of photos had already found their way online.

Saif had checked them both out and recommended a very hot bath for Olivia as soon as she got back – he didn't feel it was necessary to call an ambulance – and they used the RNLI gurney to bear her straight off to the Rock. Jacinth, once warmed up and with Flora's hot coffee down her, was actually not doing so badly.

But Jan, tumbling down after Flora, went ballistic, screaming and rushing over to where Olivia was lying, chilled and as white and pale as a beautiful statue. She looked like Sleeping Beauty lying there. Jan looked at her for a long time. Trembling, she put out her hand and very gently stroked her sister's hair. She didn't say anything. But she took her place at the head of the party taking her to the Rock.

Flora hardly had a second to take in this scene, however, when Joel bounced off the RIB. He looked ten foot high. The other men clapped him all the way off.

'Our hero, ladies and gentlemen!' he shouted to the crowd. 'The man who jumped in!'

A huge round of applause burst out as Joel, filled with life and spirit and happiness, jumped out of the boat and ran to Flora and Douglas, sweeping them both up in his arms. They were surrounded by a vast group of well-wishers, patting him on the shoulders and thanking him. He blinked once, twice, amazed at the reception, full of people he knew well, all absolutely delighted. It was astonishing.

'That's okay!' he said, suddenly beaming from ear to ear. 'No worries! Can't wait to see you at the wedding! Saif, my man!'

He thumped the good doctor hard on the back.

'What a team we were out there, eh? What a team! Can't wait to have you at my big day.'

'Uh, Joel . . . ?' said Flora carefully.

'These people,' said Joel, putting his arms out. 'Best gang in the world. I want everyone there and I want *you* to have the best day of your life.'

Flora frowned.

'No,' she said. 'I'm sorry. I was wrong. I just want us. That's all. I was so wrong. Just us, Joel.'

He got his mouth very close to her ear so she couldn't misunderstand him.

'There was a moment there,' he whispered, 'when I thought I might never come home again. And I suddenly knew exactly where home was. And I promised, if I did, we would celebrate like this island has never seen.'

Olivia was sitting up in bed, feeling very sorry for herself. Jan was guarding the bedroom from everyone, making sure her beloved sister was all right.

'I can't believe you went out in that,' she would say from time to time.

'I know, I know,' Olivia said. 'I was such an idiot.'

'It doesn't matter,' said Jan. Then, shyly: 'Sorry I was jealous.'

Olivia shook her head and took another sip of Flora's irresistible hot chocolate.

'Why?' she said. 'Why? You have everything. You're happy here, you have a lovely husband, a nice job, Mum nearby. You have no idea what it's like out there.'

Jan shrugged.

'So you keep saying.'

'No, I mean it. When you don't have any skills ... to make money ... I couldn't model; there are a million younger kids than me who'd do it for nothing. All those jobs; they pay absolutely nothing. They're for people with private incomes to meet other rich people. I was holding on, just trying to get on – oh my God. Turning thirty, Jan. You can't imagine what it was like. So awful. So, so bad.' She sighed. 'You're so lucky. Imagine just being able to wear ... '

She indicated Jan's handmade canvas top of which Jan was rather fond.

'I can't imagine. Your life is so much easier than mine.'

'But Anthony ... '

Olivia shook her head. 'His family,' she said. 'They just put so much pressure on him. Money ... it's not what you think. It's a control. They use it like a leash. I think his mother told him to get engaged, and then he did and now she's horrified that it's to me.'

She burst into tears.

'It's all such a mess!'

'There, there,' said Jan. 'If that stupid snotty Mrs Forbes thinks they're too good for you, they have another think coming.'

'But I was wrong,' said Flora, sitting in the bar of the Harbour's Rest, as the town turned up to pay its respects to its brave and valiant lifeboatmen. 'I was selfish. I wanted a big fancy wedding and everyone to see me ... '

'And so you should,' said Joel. 'It's your big day. I want it to be fabulous for you.'

The returning sunlight – as usual in Mure, no weather lasted for long – hit the dirty windows, and Flora looked around, laughing at the Harbour's Rest restored to its grubby old self.

'God,' she said. 'It's going to be insane, you know? There's teams of workmen up there. There's an ice rink going in on Tuesday! A living flower wall being flown in!'

Joel shrugged, still getting his back slapped and drinks bought for him that he did not want and was happily sharing out among the cheerful fishermen at the bar. Inge-Britt was having a great time.

'More the merrier.'

She leaned over and kissed him on the nose.

'Now I am marrying a *great hero of our times.*'

He giggled.

'Don't be daft.'

'I'm not being daft; they'll be talking about this for decades.'

'And how the selkie guided him home.'

He was looking at her with an intense look she knew very well and went to get up to escape the festivities and drag him straight back to the Rock, when Jacinth, fully recovered, marched up to her, holding up a phone.

'Can you take this?' she said, mouth a straight line. 'It's Mrs Forbes.'

'Hello?' said Flora.

'Have you seen the internet?' said Mrs Forbes.

'What, all of it?' Flora was inclined to say but merely replied, 'No, we've been ... quite busy.'

'That girl! Disrupting those whales' natural habitat! Nearly getting herself killed! It's gone viral, you know. Idiot risking the work of the lifeboat service!' Her voice was like steel. 'I sit on many important committees, Ms MacKenzie, to do with environmental protection. I'm afraid I can't condone this. I just can't. And as we are the people ultimately paying for the wedding – and I believe you are caught up in this too, although that was Missy's bizarre idea, nothing to do with me, so I don't know why I should have to apologise to you, but regardless – the wedding is off, do you hear me? And with any luck we'll have nothing to do with your little island ever again.'

Chapter Forty-two

'Yikes,' said Flora, after the phone had been passed back.

'Well, that's that.'

Joel gathered her to him.

'Oh goodness. Are you disappointed?'

'Not a bit,' said Flora, realising as she said it that it was true.

'But we'll have to tell Olivia. Oh God. She'll be ... I mean, this will be the end of it. I don't even know what she'll do. She's always seemed a bit lost. I think this wedding ... '

'Surely her fiancé won't back out?'

'The way she talks about him,' said Flora. 'And the way his mother talks about him ... I think if it became a choice between her and all his money ... I wouldn't want to be Olivia.'

'Oh God. Poor Olivia. That's what they say, isn't it?'

'What?' said Flora.

'You marry for money, you earn it.'

Saif left the crowd at the hotel and went to Lorna's house. There was nobody there, only an unopened bottle of wine and the scent of her perfume on the air, waking in him the most terrible longing.

He knew exactly where she'd be. He found her right at the edge of the Endless Beach, with her little dog Milou bringing his mistress sticks to attempt to cheer her up. It wasn't working.

As soon as he saw her face, he knew she knew. He approached her slowly. The weather had calmed, but there was nobody out; everyone was back in the village.

'Lorenah.'

She stood up very slowly, the tearstains clear on her face.

'Is it true?'

'I'm sorry . . . I got called away to the lifeboat.'

She shook her head.

'Not that. I don't care about that. I mean Ash. What Ash was singing.'

Saif swallowed.

'I told him not to . . . '

'He didn't,' said Lorna fiercely. 'He didn't mean to. He was terrified. That was too big a secret for a child, Saif. He's only little. You should have talked it over with me.'

'I was . . . I was going to talk to you. Tonight. I was coming to tell you, I promise . . . '

'So it *is* true.'

She stared at him, eyes burning.

336

'They have found the boys' mother, Lorenah.'

Lorna nodded, trying to take it all in.

'Right,' she said. 'Right. So. You're leaving? Just like that?'

He looked back at her.

'I do not think there's anything else I can do.'

'Of course there is!' she said. 'You keep your kids here where it's safe! You're completely mad! Completely!' She was shouting now. 'It makes no sense! NONE! You're crazy! You're mad to do it! You would be absolutely insane. You can't do it. You just can't! And Amena would agree with me. You know she would.'

'I do know that,' said Saif, his head bowed.

'Can't you just speak to her? Until it's safe? Skype her with the boys?'

'I cannot speak to her,' said Saif. 'It's not safe.'

'It isn't!' said Lorna. 'That's why you can't take the boys there!'

She swallowed.

'I . . . ' She took a deep breath. 'Darling. Go. Find her. Bring her back. But leave the boys with me. Here. Where they're safe. I'll move into the Manse, whatever works. You go and . . . sort things out . . . and we'll be here when you get back. People will understand.'

Saif's face contorted.

'I would . . . ' he sighed. *'Habibti*, if I leave the UK I can never, ever come in again. And although I think you would be wonderful, I can never— I left them once . . . ' He shook his head. 'Never again.'

They walked on, Lorna staring at the ground.

'She doesn't even want to speak to you,' said Lorna.

'She passed on a message.'

Lorna kicked the sand.

'What was the message?' she said bitterly. 'Is it that absolutely everyone who cares about those children is going to tell you not to go? You idiot. Neda must be fuming.'

'She is,' said Saif quietly.

Lorna looked up at him.

'What was the message?' she asked again.

He could barely get it out, his voice cracking. 'The message was, please find someone to help you raise the boys. And please make sure they are kind.'

They trudged back, apart.

'Change your mind,' said Lorna. 'It's right for everyone. You know it is.'

She looked at him, her eyes wide and full of tears.

'Unless . . . unless you want to go.'

He stared at her, utterly stricken, unable to talk. All he could do was shake his head, not trusting himself to speak.

This gave Lorna hope. Of course. It was madness to go back. Amena herself had told him as clear as she possibly could to stay for the sake of the boys. It made sense. It was the only thing that made sense.

As they drew within sight of the town, Saif prepared to peel off to the old rectory at the top of the town.

Lorna, no longer furious, went up to him, laid her head on his familiar chest. He kissed the top of it, his eyes closed.

'Stay,' she said, with confidence. 'I know you will. You

know it's best. It doesn't even have to be for ever. Just for now. Change your mind. Tell the boys next year. It will be all right, I promise.'

She carried on, not looking back as he watched her go along the Endless Beach; she was too terrified to turn around in case he had already disappeared.

Chapter Forty-three

Flora and Joel trudged back up to the Rock, Flora not looking forward to breaking the news to Olivia.

'Maybe I should let her have a good night's sleep,' she said. 'She definitely needs it. Saif is going to check in on her anyway, so I had better stay out of the way.'

'She'll know already,' predicted Joel gloomily. 'So she could probably do with some comfort. Jan is probably throwing a victory parade.'

'God,' said Flora. 'You're right. I'll just check in on her. You take Douglas home and get him changed and fed; I have some quite big plans for ocean-going bridegrooms when I get back.'

Joel smiled.

'I will do that, my selkie mistress.' And he kissed her. Then he looked at the hotel and frowned.

'Oh crap!' he said. 'All our boys are still here!'

'Oh lord,' said Flora, hurrying in. 'Oh my God. What on earth will they be up to?'

She hurried up the steps; they were not exactly expecting skateboarding in the foyer, but you could hardly blame them for being wary. There was not a sign of any of them.

'Oh God,' said Flora. 'They've made a break for it.'

Joel shook his head.

'They're good lads,' he said stoically. Gala looked up, smiling, and nodded them towards the kitchen.

In the kitchen, in absolute ignorance of every health and safety rule in the book (although their hands were all washed), the clutch of young lads were all happily chopping and stirring under the watchful eye of Gaspard, who was shouting orders at them from time to time, Charlie and Jan taking part too.

'You use knives PROPERLY,' he was hollering at them. Flora and Joel raised their eyebrows at each other.

'I'll stay here,' said Joel. 'Catch you later.'

She squeezed his hand tightly.

'God yes,' she said. 'I have very much missed you, Joel Binder.'

'Likewise, Mrs Binder,' he said, and she felt a thrill run through her that had absolutely nothing to do with flower walls.

Flora knocked on the door of Olivia's room gently. There was a sound inside and Flora took this as an assent.

Olivia looked beautiful in the glowing light – the day now looked completely innocent as if nothing bad could ever have crossed its mind – standing and looking out of the window. Flora went over and stood next to her and saw what she was looking at. The workmen were striking the buildings beyond Gaspard's cabbage patch – the huge white ice castle marquee; the wall set to receive thousands and thousands of blooms; the tent that was to have been transformed into the autumnal library – all of it just flat-pack after all, a stage set for a performance, nothing more, being loaded up onto lorries and driven away.

'Oh Olivia,' said Flora, gently touching her arm.

'It was your wedding too,' said Olivia.

'Yeah, that doesn't matter,' said Flora, because it didn't. She looked at Olivia. 'You haven't heard from him?'

Olivia shook her head. 'Mrs Forbes has released a fricking press release.'

'You're well out of it then,' said Flora, hugging her gently. 'Also, you know, you never sounded so hung up on him. There's a million blokes that would fall over backwards for you, not one you hardly care for. You barely mention his name.'

Olivia sniffed, then turned to Flora, her face a mask of sadness.

'Oh *God*!' she said. 'No! That's the thing! I've been playing it cool for so long! You know what men are like! And God, to be really into someone . . . I mean, OMG so naff . . . Everyone would just laugh at me. God . . . '

Flora looked askance.

'What on earth do you mean?'

'I adore Anthony!' said Olivia, bursting into tears. 'Okay, so he's spoiled and relies on his family money. But he's so sweet and funny and gentle and I . . . compared to all the other horrible, horrible sharks out there, Flora. They're awful. They're just awful. It's a snake-pit. And Anthony . . . he was always kind. Proper kind.'

'You're making it sound like being incredibly beautiful isn't actually that much fun,' said Flora, putting her arms around her. 'There, there.'

'And now his horrible mother will tell him to break up with

me ... and he will, just to keep the peace, I know he will. He probably already has.'

The tears were dripping now. 'And that's it for me. I'm thirty-four!'

She said this in the way someone else might say 'I'm ninety' but Flora didn't mention it.

'... Or twenty-nine if you're asking him.'

'Don't be silly,' said Flora. 'You just need to talk to him. And keep the ring,' she added quickly. 'You can probably buy an apartment with it.'

'He's not picking up,' said Olivia, in floods. 'He's breaking up with me and won't even tell me. And have you seen the internet?'

'No,' lied Flora.

'They're calling me the whale killer!'

'Well, you killed no whales, so I wouldn't worry too much about that.'

'I've ruined everything.'

'There, there,' said Flora again. 'You have had a terrible day. I think I am going to tuck you in and sit with you.'

Just at that moment, however, the door knocked. It was Saif, checking up on his patient. He looked dreadful, worn and with huge bags under his eyes.

'Hello, brave sailor,' said Flora kissing him. 'Christ, you look worse than Olivia.'

In the white night, as the sun didn't set at all, Olivia lay in bed, trying to both glance at and not look at her phone which had a lot of people contacting her for bad reasons, and nobody for good.

Saif lay awake, turning it over in his mind again and again: Lorna so resolute, so sure. Amena too. The men made war, he thought, not for the first time. The women suffered, and fought for the peace.

Lorna sobbed until she couldn't sob any more; started a thousand messages to him; picked up the phone; put it down; told herself sternly he would come round, he wasn't crazy, of course he wasn't, this was better for the boys, better for everyone. If only she could get Ash's happy little face out of her mind. It wouldn't be what he thought, she told herself sternly.

But what was he thinking? Only that he wanted to see his mum, that was all.

Jacinth, having finally shouted enough to extract a promise from Mrs Forbes that work to date would be paid for in full, marched up to the Rock kitchen in triumph and proposed something absolutely eye-wateringly filthy to Gaspard and Fintan, who immediately decided to make a night of it.

Flora and Joel lay entwined in each other's arms.

'I can't believe you're going to get your own way after all,' she said, smiling at him.

'Ah,' said Joel. 'About that. I might have accidentally re-invited Tripp. And the entire Highland dancing school.'

'You're telling me you're going to arrange an entire wedding in a week and a half?' said Flora.

'Watch me,' said Joel.

Chapter Forty-four

Flora went to see what everyone was up to bright and early in the morning, passing the people taking away the last of the fuss. Well, she thought, you don't miss what you never had, after all. All her sympathies were with Olivia.

The early-morning ferry was departing, filled with the elaborate fixtures and fittings from the wedding, and Flora made a mental note that somehow – somehow – they were going to have to talk to Agot about the ice rink. Well. One thing at a time.

Arriving at reception were a few people from the ferry, here to enjoy the white nights and the supposedly settled weather they were in for, and to watch the whales – of course they were. Publicity strikes again, thought Flora, although it was good for business. She would instruct Gala to tell people under no circumstances were they to approach the pod. The RNLI was going to set up a cordon anyway.

'Excuse me,' said a sandy-haired person. He was very short,

with a wide face covered in freckles, ears that stuck out at right angles to his head and a cheerful expression. He looked about fifteen; the only giveaway was the fact that he was wearing a watch the size of a dinner plate. 'I'm looking for Olivia Mathieson?'

Flora looked at him for a very long while, a smile starting on her lips.

'Your name wouldn't be . . . Anthony, is it?'

'Yah! That's me, yah! Anthony Forbes! Charmed!'

And he beamed, showing off large friendly teeth which seemed too big for his head.

Flora thought of the David Gandy mysterious millionaire figure they had conjured for Olivia. This chap looked like he'd just left secondary school.

'Wow!' she said. 'Hang on . . . are you here to be nice to her or to break her heart?'

'This is what I would call jolly strict for a set of check-in questions,' said Anthony, still beaming.

'Well, we like to look after our guests,' said Flora.

'Well. Uh. The former, yah? Seeing as she's the loveliest creature I ever did meet in my *life*!'

Flora beamed.

'Well then. I think . . . I think she'll be very happy to see you,' she said, pointing him in the direction of the bungalow. Then, she leaned out the door, so she could hear Olivia's happy cry of surprise.

'Well, well, well,' she said, shaking her head in amazement. And people thought island life was quiet.

347

Chapter Forty-five

The next ten days were a blur of quiet organisation – Gaspard, Konstantin and Isla suddenly had an entire wedding to cater for after all, on a budget of about five buttons. Anthony turned out to be completely charming, if very nervous every time the idea of his mother came up – she had not softened her original stance in the slightest, and they had found themselves entirely cut off. The idea that they'd actually both have to get jobs was a bit of a shocker, although Anthony's best man was still coming, and assured him there were plenty of jobs in the City as long as he could talk posh which Joel confirmed was absolutely true.

Olivia didn't care a bit. She clung to Anthony, even as she rather towered over him, a picture of happiness, wearing hardly any make-up in the endless sunny days so her little nose started to freckle, and she didn't even notice that, walking barefoot with Anthony on the beach, careless of her own pedicure.

'I say,' Anthony had been heard to say one night in the

Harbour's Rest, 'such a jolly place here. Perhaps we should stay?' Olivia had slightly choked on her warm white wine; there were limits, even if she was going to have to get a real job.

And of course Flora and Joel had done the natural thing: invited them to share their own celebrations, which had been heartily accepted. 'At least I know you're not one of those fillies after me for my money,' said Anthony. 'As I no longer have any.'

Olivia had smiled and kissed him. 'Till one of his aunts dies,' she whispered to Flora on the side.

Flora herself was busy and happy and was still secretly trying to encourage Douglas to walk down the aisle with no success whatsoever, but she took time out to see Lorna. She was shocked at the news. Surely he wouldn't go? He couldn't, not with the life they had here. He wouldn't.

But the near-midsummer deadline came and went with no word.

'Maybe he's put it in and you just don't know?' said Flora. 'Maybe he did change his mind and he's just waiting till it's all done.'

'He'd have told me,' said Lorna, her face so unhappy. 'Of course he'd have told me.'

'He'll be thinking it over,' said Flora reassuringly. 'You know what he's like. So careful. He'll be dotting the Ts and all of that.'

Lorna sniffed.

'He is, isn't he? He'll show up with the letter when the application has gone in. Won't he?'

'Totally,' said Flora. 'Or maybe he's applying for a visitor visa so he can go there and come back.'

'Can you do that?' said Lorna doubtfully.

'Of course! Maybe he'll go for the summer and take the boys, then come back for the new term. Come back to you.'

'Yes!' said Lorna. 'Yes. Maybe that's it. Maybe he's just finalising everything. And he'll run in clutching a piece of paper.'

'I'm sure it is,' said Flora.

'Do you know what I wish?' said Lorna, her face white and drawn. 'I wish Jan had told every last bugger on the island. I wish she'd forced the issue. I wish we'd come clean. Moved in together. Shocked the whole bloody lot of them.'

Flora looked at her, indeed shocked. But yes. The worst thing they could have imagined two months ago was not the worst thing at all. Not by a long shot.

But Ash showed no signs of being less happy as the joyous end-of-year rites of school commenced. Lorna heard nothing except a cheerful stream of how excited he was to be going to the wedding – with, it seemed, every other child in the class, despite Agot telling them it was going to be rubbish without an ice rink or a proper white dress.

Agot had, to Flora's total astonishment, been an easier person to talk round than she'd been expecting. She and Olivia had decided to tackle it together, becoming closer friends day by day, and they'd sat Agot down together with Innes.

'Um, there isn't going to be an ice rink now,' Flora had said, bracing herself for the onslaught. Instead, Agot had thought-fully kicked her heels up and down.

'Well,' she said. 'Sometimes things do NOT go to plan.'

Flora and Innes looked at each other in astonishment.

'Um, you realise ... that this means there won't actually be an ice rink at the wedding?' said Flora, in case Agot hadn't quite got it first time round.

'There are sadder things happening,' said Agot.

'Oh my God,' said Flora. 'Oh, Agot, you're growing up.'

And she nearly burst into tears, tears not being too far away from the surface for Flora at the moment.

'Agot and I have a plan,' said Olivia, as they winked at each other, or rather Olivia winked, and Agot gave a big double blink.

'A secret plan,' nodded Agot, 'for people who had green bridesmaid dresses and didn't—'

'Ssh!' said Olivia, and Agot managed to close her mouth.

'What do you mean, sad things happening?' Innes asked.

'Oh, my best friend is leaving FOR EVER,' said Agot, taking on a tragic expression and hopping down. 'It is terrible. It is very, very hard to find a best friend, you know.'

'He told you this?' said Flora, stricken. She had believed Saif would come to his senses. 'For definite?'

'He said it's a secret,' said Agot. 'Oh, I forgot that bit. But it's not for AAAGES.'

'Oh. Phew. Really? Well, that's good,' said Flora.

'AAAGES,' said Agot. 'After the wedding! We are so excited about the wedding!'

'Agot, the wedding is this weekend.'

'AAAAGES!'

Chapter Forty-six

Flora had told herself not to be disappointed about the weather. It was ridiculous, even at the height of summer, to expect a good day when you lived at the top of the world. Sunny weather was for built-up southern places, with hotel blocks lining concrete roads and pools and exhausted dusty roads. Here was fresh air, green space, the best water in the world, friendly people, and long, long days: it was the most wonderful place on earth. You couldn't expect amazingly hot weather too; that was just being silly and spoiled.

She didn't look at the forecast or talk to the fishermen. And when she woke, on her wedding day, it was to a thick haar, and that was fine, she told herself. It was better than fine. It took her a moment to realise that of course she was back, once more, in her old childhood single bed at the farmhouse, Agot sleeping with her mum and dad for the night. Flora's old Highland dancing trophies and Mod certificates still lined the walls. Joel was at home with Douglas, then that night the baby would go home with Eck and they would stay in the honeymoon suite at the Rock, the beautiful vast suite on the very top floor. She was excited to think of it; excited about everything. There was already the sizzle of bacon frying in the kitchen, but she didn't think she could eat a thing. She tiptoed down the passageway anyway to be greeted by all her brothers, clapping and bringing their teacups.

'Here she is,' said Fintan. 'Another blushing bride in the family.' But his voice wasn't bitter, and he was smiling.

Agot was already sitting up and dressed. 'Aren't you ready yet, Auntie Flora?' she said.

'It's five hours away, Agot,' said Flora. 'Can I maybe have a coffee first?'

The time, though, felt like it was slipping through their fingers. Flora was leaving her long pale hair natural and down, with a plait around it to hold up the heavy red-rose coronet – no veil, Agot was horrified to see. And, tempted though she was to go for heavy make-up, she wasn't entirely convinced anybody needed to see her in baby blue eyeshadow and pearlised pink lipstick, so she was sticking to a bold black eyeliner and red lips that matched the dress perfectly. She wouldn't look like Olivia of course – but she would look exactly like herself.

Lorna turned up at eleven, and Flora's happy footling and long baths plans suddenly came crashing down. Her friend had lost weight and looked pale and as if she could barely stand; her red hair was lying limply down her back.

Flora hugged her.

'I think . . . ' said Lorna. 'Flora, I think he's definitely going. I think he tried to tell me; he did tell me, and I wouldn't listen. I wouldn't listen, Flora.'

'You don't know that,' she said quietly. 'Oh Lorna. I'm sorry. I'm so, so sorry.'

Lorna let out a tortured sound and sat down on Flora's bed.

'Oh God,' she said. 'Oh God. I can't. Oh God.'

She looked up.

'I don't think I can do today, Flora. Not if he's going to be there.'

'I'll disinvite him,' said Flora instantly.

'No, you can't . . . Ash has been talking of nothing else,' said Lorna. 'I'm not disappointing that child.'

She swallowed hard.

'Well, someone else can bring Ash,' said Flora stoically. 'Eilidh will do it. I don't want anyone to be sad today.'

Lorna lay down on the bed.

'Oh God. I'm so sorry, Flora. I'm so sorry. On your special day.'

'It doesn't matter,' said Flora.

Lorna sniffed.

'Agot will probably be happier without me anyway.'

Suddenly, the door was pushed open and the little sprite appeared.

'*Ciamar a tha hu*, Miss Lorna,' she said. 'Oh.'

She came over curiously, inspecting Lorna's tear-filled face.

'You're sad,' she said.

Lorna nodded without saying anything.

'Are you sad because you are not really a proper bridesmaid?'

Agot frowned, trying to puzzle things out. She tried again.

'Are you sad because you're not the bride?' she said. Flora winced.

'Well,' said Agot. 'I think you should not be too sad. I think I won't mind really if you are another bridesmaid.'

354

Lorna looked at Flora imploringly.

'You might feel better,' said Flora, 'rather than just staying at home dwelling? Maybe?'

And that is how, when Flora emerged from her bedroom, ravishing in her scarlet wedding dress, her sea green bridesmaids came behind, the little one supported the big one with all her might.

Eck was the first to crack in the old kitchen.

'Well,' he said. Then he tried again. 'Well.'

His old eyes grew rheumy.

'This would have been something your mither would have liked.'

The boys immediately got a bit wobbly too.

'Stop it, Dad!' said Flora. 'You can't ... you just can't. I've got waterproof mascara on but that only lasts for so long. Come on. Don't ...'

And she was in his arms.

'I miss her so much,' she said. 'It's not fair when you can't have your own mother at your wedding.'

'It isn't,' said Eck, patting her back. 'It isn't, I know.'

Her father steadied her in the boat, led by the trusty Bertie, who was wearing an all-black kilt in honour of the fact that this was absolutely the final nail in his hopes of Flora. But he did his duty nonetheless, carefully motoring the boat round the headland, their little team of five, towards the Rock.

Flora looked out on the horizon. Was that ... a tiny patch of blue? No, she would not think of it. It was a Mure grey day, perfectly normal. Nothing to worry about. They could retint the photos. Anyway, she was marrying the man she loved. Nothing else mattered. Nothing at all.

As they rounded the headland, what a sight greeted them.

Not a flower wall. Not a huge ice cathedral or a vast bower or a row of black-tied waiters armed with glasses of expensive Champagne and fussy vegetable canapés.

It was just all their friends and family, arrayed in their best, waving frantically. They didn't even have chairs. One of the island's ceilidh bands was playing 'Mairi's Wedding' with full vigour. The vicar was smiling at them on the deck. Joel, and Mark beside him, were standing there, both in matching, ancient tartan kilts and tweed waistcoats and jackets, Mark already looking rather hot, Joel holding Douglas, who was not standing, but was nonetheless wearing his own tiny kilt and a little white shirt that looked like it would not stay white for ten minutes flat, and the sun, just for a second, poked a shaft out from behind a cloud, and Flora stood, quite still, and let her heart flood over.

There were no fancy personalised vows written by a professional scribe. There was no expensive flown-in choir. There was a massed communal bawling of 'How Great Thou Art' followed by the children performing 'Oh the Love of My Lord Is the Essence', as trained by Lorna, which left very few dry eyes around the place.

As Flora stepped off the boat, she felt surrounded by a sea of happy faces, every single one of which, apart from her excited clusters of mainland friends, had known her since she was Douglas's age. She looked at Joel, who grinned at her.

'What can I say? My wife was right,' he said, as she reached him, embracing Mark, then Joel all at once. He held her at arm's length.

'Supermodel,' he said.

'Shut it!' said Flora.

They took their vows under the shadow of the Rock at the dock, as the sun gradually burst through behind them, and the noise of the waves rather too loud for people to hear them speaking, so it was basically private, Flora pointed out later. Lorna stood, staring out to sea, refusing to look at the crowd. Agot waved enough for both of them.

As the vicar handfasted them, tied their wrists with ribbons of blue and white for Scotland, and red, white and blue for America, they kissed, Douglas grabbing at his mother's flowers, which she did not mind in the slightest. Agot vanished, but nobody noticed too much, except Innes, who knew what she was up to.

Then Joel and Flora turned on the dock to face the throng – and, to the band starting up again, out walked Olivia, followed by a triumphant Agot who, even in straitened circumstances, was wearing the whitest, widest, flounciest dress anyone had ever seen, and beaming, and holding little Christabel by the hand, who was, in her own flouncy white dress, toddling along on her own two feet.

'Bloody hell, that is *so* annoying,' said Flora.

Olivia's simple gown and plain white lilies were every bit as lovely among the Highland colours of the kilt-wearing crowd, as she slowly advanced on Malcy's arm towards Anthony, who had somehow borrowed a kilt several sizes too big for him in a ridiculous purple colour, but was grinning from ear to ear. Joel and Flora embraced them, then moved to the side as the second ceremony took place and everybody clapped and Flora, looking around the crowd, was amazed to see Jacinth, who must have arrived under her own steam, in the crowd. She wouldn't even get paid. She was there as a friend. No Mrs Forbes – but Lucy was there. There must be hope if someone from the family was there, Flora thought.

And then – as the kisses were traded, and the applause sounded – then there was a sight to see. From inside the kitchen of the Rock, out poured a line of Jan and Charlie's boys, Charlie at one end and Gaspard at the other, led by little Luke Hoyer, each carrying a small plate of canapés.

There were miniature pork pies, tiny sandwiches, pâté with crackers and endless cake. It was the most gluten-heavy food Gaspard could think of, and he had an extremely satisfied look on his face.

Not only this, but being hastily set out by Isla and Konstantin now that it looked like there wasn't going to be an imminent downpour, at least not in the next twenty minutes, were bottles and bottles of the pre-ordered Champagne – the ones that Gaspard had planned on purloining – sold on a no-return basis, and now set to be enjoyed by everyone.

There was no fancy food. There were no fancy table settings or matching crockery or thrones or ice sculptures. There was an excellent buffet, and your two drinks' choices were posh Champagne or squash.

The band played, and Mrs Kennedy's school performed a sensational and only slightly wobbly *Seann Triubhas*, and then Tripp followed it up with a special cowboy dance which hadn't been specifically requested, but everyone clapped anyway, and the sun shone and Joel and Flora stumbled around everyone, hugging, laughing, kissing and as happy as they'd been in their lives, as indeed were Olivia and Anthony, although every time one of the older farmers attempted to sell Anthony a house, Olivia smiled and kept him marching swiftly on.

'I see,' said Eck, when they had a little hush for the speeches, in his old-fashioned, quiet way, 'that this is a day that the Lord has blessed, when he keeps us and holds us in the palm of his hand.

'Flora is the flower of our family, the flower of our island to us, and although our hearts broke all thegither when we lost our Annie there, I give thanks every day that the Lord saw fit to send my Flora home to me, and she would be just as proud today as I am.'

This was the longest speech anyone had ever heard Eck give, and even the very least religious of them bowed their heads, just a little. Anthony's best man had an incomprehensible speech about various rituals they'd got up to at school, but everyone smiled politely and listened nicely to the English person. Then Mark stood up.

'This place,' he said, looking happily at Marsha, 'has, from the moment we arrived here, been welcoming to us. It's a place for everyone. You can come, you can leave, or live here every day of your life, but it will always live in your heart, for long periods or short. You will carry Mure with you and I hope you will all carry the joy and happiness of this day with you all the years of your lives.'

Lorna caught Saif's eye, and was taken aback by the naked yearning she saw in his face.

And at the speeches' end, only Flora heard the noise from far out at sea, and she squeezed Joel's hand and he looked at her for a second and did not hear – did he? – the sound of the whales, gently singing to the bright sky.

Chapter Forty-seven

Lorna couldn't look at him again. Saif wouldn't have come if he could have helped it, but he couldn't deny Ash such a happy day, wouldn't dream of it. Indeed, even now, Ash and Agot were ruining the ceilidh for everyone, and nobody minded in the slightest.

Saif would like to have found a quiet place to have a word, but it was impossible. Word had got out – he supposed it would have eventually – and people were coming up to tell him how much they would miss him, and how much the island had benefited from him. He was touched, but he could not speak to the one person he truly wanted to.

Flora realised the situation and pulled Joel aside from the dancing. He couldn't stop beaming; it looked strange on him, that closed-up man she had known who had never smiled. He was watching Mark throw Marsha around the ceilidh with joyous abandon, and slight concern, given that Marsha wasn't getting any younger and was as petite as a bird. A broken ankle was all they needed right now.

She explained her plan to Joel, who smiled again and said he was looking forward to every night for the rest of his life so he didn't think one was going to mess it up too much, then to Innes, who was beyond relieved, as the pestering was getting too much even for him, and then took Charlie aside for a quiet word. Charlie being Charlie didn't ask questions, just nodded. Jan marched up.

'Can't leave him alone even today?' she observed, and Flora stared at her, having completely forgotten their animosity. On the other hand, Jan being Jan was one good sign that things were returning to normal.

'I'm so, so glad you and Olivia have managed to make it up again,' she tried.

Jan couldn't help it – she smiled rather smugly.

'Ah, wasn't quite so grand in the end, was she? Had to get off her high horse. Brought her down a peg or two.'

She beamed with satisfaction.

'Such a shame Douglas couldn't walk you down the aisle.'

'I must just get on,' said Flora quickly, glad Jan had redis-covered equilibrium, at least. She glanced over at Olivia and Anthony, who were swaying alone, completely wrapped up in one another. 'But thank you,' she said in a low voice. 'For not dobbing in Lorna.'

Jan snorted.

'What kind of a person do you think I am?'

Flora smiled as she moved through the room – you could move quite fast as a bride, she had found: everyone assumed you were terribly busy, and nobody was asking where the sugar was or could they have a sea view or why was there a dog in the kitchen – and she grabbed Lorna by the arm and took her out to the quiet reception hall.

'What?' said Lorna, who looked so distraught Flora could barely believe she was still standing. 'I'm going home.'

'No, no, hang on. You're not super-pissed, are you?' said Flora. That probably wouldn't work with her plan. Lorna shook her head.

The terror, the absolute terror of getting tipsy, out of control, bursting out crying, telling everyone, throwing herself at him, all the awful, awful things she could do – Lorna hadn't been completely drunk for years. Even at the hen night, she'd only had a couple of glasses.

'Good,' said Flora, hugging her. 'Here.'

And she handed over the key to the suite at the top of the hotel.

'What's this?' said Lorna.

'It's ... Joel and I were going to stay there tonight. But we're not now. Innes is taking Ash for a sleepover with Agot, do you understand?' Lorna blinked, trying to focus through her misery on what Flora was telling her. 'And Teàrlach and Jan are taking Ib. They're camping out in the garden.'

Lorna looked at her.

'So. It's for you. It's just for you. You could ... you could have one more night. Talk. Or be together. Or something. Something, Lorna. Otherwise ... if you don't ... he's going to go. For definite.'

'I know,' said Lorna, her voice tremulous.

Flora glanced over.

'Be quick; he's trying to prise Agot and Ash apart.'

Of course, Lorna knew where he was. She always did.

'But I can't ... I don't ... '

'It might be your last chance,' said Flora.

'But does he ... ?'

'Go,' said Flora. 'I mean it. Please.'

Back in the main dancing area, the noise and hubbub were immense, the heat rising with the dancing and yelling and laughing.

Lorna could read immediately, as Innes approached Saif, that the situation was being made clear to him. His face looked drawn and confused. Oh God. What if he rejected her? What if he said no for the very last time, to draw the last line under everything?

Thank God, she saw, as Flora approached him full of confidence and beneficence in beauty, a bride in full, sharing her joy, radiating her gift. Nobody could say no to Flora today.

Lorna had never been in the top room at the Rock, and as she mounted the last of the steps up towards it – there was a side staircase that led to the tiny attic rooms where the seasonal staff stayed, but this was a large suite at the front of the building, with a grey stone balcony out the front with thick carpets that muffled the sounds of the revelry two storeys below – she saw a double wooden door which opened with the ornate key.

Inside, she drew her breath. It was a huge room, the width of the dining room, softly done out not in the loud tartans of below, but the palest creams and eau de Nils, calm and soft and lovely.

The bathroom was as large as another bedroom, with a circular jacuzzi right next to the window where all you could see were the circling gulls in front of the dimming sun.

A bottle of Champagne and a plate of strawberries were waiting on ice, and the staff had put balloons everywhere, presumably for the happy couple. Lorna felt the pain grip her again, turning her inside out at Flora's happiness; at her having absolutely everything she ever wanted, while she, Lorna, was left with nothing. She didn't begrudge her friend, of course; how could she? But this was . . . this was a mockery. A bad idea, she realised, going out to the balcony to look out over the empty sea, the bobbing waves, faint noises of joy and dancing coming up from down below, while she had never felt more empty and alone in her entire life.

This had been stupid, accepting it. When Flora had suggested it, it had sounded like a good idea. But now she could see it for what it was: a cold travesty of something that could never be hers; a stage set, a fakery. It made everything worse, not better.

The knock on the door was quiet, reserved.

Chapter Forty-eight

He stood there, rangy and tall as ever, but without the cheerful look he normally got when he saw her when he turned up at the flat, or when he saw her on the street and there was nobody else there, so he could smile as widely as he wanted to.

Now, oddly, he looked a little as he had when he had arrived on Mure for the first time, before the welcome and the people and the good food and the safety and beauty of the island, and his children returning had mended the broken man; fixed him up. To send him on to fight another day, thought Lorna ruefully.

But now there was a haunted expression on his face, even in his suit, the smart shoes. He stole a glance behind him but there was nobody else on the entire floor.

'I don't know if this is a good idea,' said Lorna, and he nodded silently. But he couldn't stay out on the landing, and so she let him in. He looked around the room, smiling gently.

'It's nice,' he said, touching the sofa carefully. It was the nicest room he'd been in since Edinburgh. He looked at her and they both read the other's mind immediately; in other circumstances, this would be a miraculous gift, a wonderful thing.

He still stayed away, didn't go near her.

'Are you ready?' she said, hating herself for saying it. 'Packed?'

'Not quite yet,' said Saif. 'Ash is still very, very worried we won't be able to get Pokémon Go.'

'Will you?'

'I don't know,' said Saif.

'Do you want a drink?'

'Tea?' he said somewhat weakly. Lorna nodded, happy for her hands to have something to do. They were still miles away from one another in their huge room, moving in the same space but further apart than they had ever been. She fiddled around, finding a kettle, leafing through the six different types of fruit teas and artisanal shortbread biscuits. Her hands were shaking. When Flora had suggested this, she had clutched at straws, desperate for anything, for one more moment spent with him. Now, though, now she was here it felt like everything was worse. That this was a stupid idea. She couldn't . . . she couldn't cry any more.

She didn't hear him cross the room. Only felt, suddenly, his presence behind her, and the next second, he was simply standing beside her, his large hand resting on her back, a warm comforting presence, and she felt the tears well up regardless.

'I don't . . . want . . . you to go . . . ' she choked out, no longer furious or argumentative or in denial or trying to change the facts. It was just a cry, a truth, from the deepest, tiniest core of herself. 'I don't want you to go!'

'I don't want to leave you, Lorenah,' he said.

'But you're going to.'

He nodded, and she straightened so her face was looking up at his, into those huge, serious brown eyes.

'I must,' he said softly.

She swallowed.

'It's not fair.'

'It is not.'

She shook her head.

'My nan. She used to like this old TV show called *The Winds of War*.'

Saif didn't say anything, waiting for her to finish.

'I never knew what that meant, *The Winds of War*.'

She swallowed hard.

'And now I do,' she said. 'It means, when there's a war, everything gets tossed about, and you don't get to choose where you land.'

He nodded.

'And . . . and you're just at the mercy of it. Of something else. That's what it means, isn't it?'

'I think so.'

'And there's no point . . . there's no point saying it isn't fair. Because even if it's not fair to me to lose you . . . it would be less fair to Ash and Ib to lose their mum. There's always someone worse off.'

'There are no good choices,' he said.

The kettle boiled and clicked off, and they ignored it.

Saif sat down on the bed, then sprang up again, holding up his hands.

'I didn't mean to assume . . . '

'God, I know,' she said, and came over and sat down beside him, a tight smile on her face. 'Honeymoon suite, that's a joke.'

'It is not a funny one,' said Saif, and he put his arm around

368

her as he had so many times – but never enough, never enough. She curled into him, let her tears soak through his white shirt, inhaled his scent with every breath, trying to let it calm her down even though it could not.

'Can you go and visit and come back?' she said, grasping at her last hope.

'I cannot,' said Saif. 'If I leave, I cannot return.'

He felt behind him on the bed suddenly and frowned, drawing up his hand.

'Oh,' said Lorna, opening her eyes and realising. There were rose petals sprinkled right across the counterpane. She sniffed and wiped her eyes to stop the tears.

'Remember when Struan Macintosh thought he'd steal some of Mrs Baillie's roses for Mother's Day?'

Saif smiled. 'I have never heard anyone make such a noise about one or two thorns. Everyone in the waiting room thought I was murdering him.'

'He did say "The new doctor tried to murder me" when he got back to school and everyone was very impressed. I think he said he fought you off with kung-fu.'

They laughed, then he lifted his arm and let one or two petals fall gently from his hand, coming to land in the heavy coils of her hair, her bare shoulders and the pale dress.

'You look like a bride,' he said gently.

'I know,' said Lorna, glancing down. 'It was quite the stramash.'

Saif didn't know what this meant, so he simply nodded.

'If . . . ' Lorna started, then didn't want to go on. And then she thought, Well, if not now, when?

'If I were a bride . . . '

He looked at her, the petals scattered in her pretty hair, the soft pale green of the dress so nearly white in the half-light of the half-night beyond the curtains.

He swallowed hard, and his tone was very soft and low.

'Yes?'

'What would it have been like?'

He smiled sadly.

'Well, there would have been a lot of food. But no dancing.'

'And no toasts?'

'No.'

'And would we have exchanged vows?'

He shook his head.

'Would I not have said anything?'

'You would,' he said. 'You would have said three times: *qabul*.'

'What does that mean?'

'"I accept",' said Saif.

Lorna blinked heavily.

'Three times?'

He nodded.

'To be sure.'

Lorna's face was very close to his.

'I accept,' she said very quietly.

He took her hand, traced the fingers with his own much larger ones, then brought the hand to his mouth and kissed it.

'I accept,' he said, but when he said it, he intoned it with much deeper meaning, with a great sadness at the way things were.

'I accept,' said Lorna again, straight into his eyes, and this time he gently kissed the space on her finger where a ring would have been and muttered the words once again: 'I accept.'

Lorna closed her eyes, then moved still closer to him. Her silky skirt rustled on the crisp fresh linen of the bed as she knelt

370

up to reach him. 'I accept,' she said, her head before his, her eyes still closed, and he leaned forward, pressed his forehead to hers, squeezed both of her hands in his own.

'I accept,' he said, his voice husky and low and so, so sad.

Eventually, Lorna pulled back, opened her eyes and looked up at his face.

'And what would happen now?' she said in a very quiet voice that nonetheless had a challenge in it. He looked straight at her.

'I would tell you not to be frightened,' said Saif steadily.

'I am frightened,' said Lorna.

'I know,' said Saif.

She glanced down at her beautiful dress.

'Please,' she said then.

And she stood up and turned around, and he followed, both of them trembling, as he attempted to work his fingers deftly enough to take down her zip, infinitely slowly, not wanting to miss a second. In all their time together, so often they had had to rush, to be back for work, or for the children, or before someone noticed they were both missing at the same time. Or simply because they had waited for too long; they were both pent up and frantic for one another.

But now, there was not a minute they would not have held back, prolonged if they could. Then she felt his soft beard and lips bend down to kiss along her shoulder blades, infinitely slowly, his hand coming round to caress the gentle curve of her stomach as she stepped lightly out of the dress, wearing only the high shoes, and turned around, and heard him take a sharp intake of breath and she felt suddenly beautiful, and smiled hopefully at him, and then it was as if something had changed. There was something in the room that shimmered and they were in this place, this hotel, that was not a home, that was not

371

his space or her space but somewhere between the spaces, on an island that was not a home but together something that they made between themselves. And that there was no such thing as a first time or a last time; that everything here was liminal; and this was an island wedding, neither on land nor sea.

And they made love gently and quietly and achingly, tortuously slowly, Lorna's tears turning gradually into the lowest of keening moans; and then again more urgently, and they dozed, and made love, and bathed and ate – for they both found themselves starving – every strawberry, every chocolate, every piece of heart-shaped shortbread that was strewn across the honeymoon suite; they drank the Champagne, which was a mistake for Lorna because it made her weepy, and they had to quickly run the jacuzzi bath and fill it up with far too much foam and Saif had to tell her funny stories about medical school until she got a hold of herself, then they tumbled onto the bed once again, and now it was ferocious and desperate and noisy and dirty and that time, after that time, Lorna found herself, raw, her mind jangled, on the end of the bed, with Saif as fast asleep as if someone had clubbed him. It was five a.m.; the sun was high, the mists burning off from the sea.

She turned round and looked at Saif, snuck a couple of photos of him sleeping – his chest, the dark hair on the golden skin, the fine lines of his eyelashes. It made her feel like a thief.

She kissed him full on the mouth, hard.

'Stay,' she whispered, feeling bold and exhausted and strong and different, as bright as the sun burning off the mist. He did not stir.

'Stay and I will tell you a story every night, and I will hold you in my arms and I will not let you go and you will stay,' she said, as if intoning a ritual. She took a sprig of hawthorn from the bouquet, discarded on the dresser, and tucked it under his hands as a binding spell and, as again he didn't move, Lorna held her head high, shimmied her beautiful dress down over her and strode out into the silent corridors.

The hotel was like Sleeping Beauty's castle: people were asleep where they lay. Joel and Flora were curled up on one of the sofas which looked out to sea; they had obviously been talking all night and were entangled, arm in arm, foot to foot, so it was impossible to tell where one of them ended and the other began. There were violins, shawls, empty glasses strewn and, carrying her shoes, Lorna walked lightly barefoot among the debris, her dress flowing behind her, her hair free, tangled, a cloud in the air as she carried on down the stone steps. She stepped into the perfect garden as the peacocks strutted and the mist curled above her ankles and drifted out to the sea dawn.

Chapter Forty-nine

Three Days Later

It was a high, clear, bright morning, and the entire village was out, it seemed. Quite the difference, Lorna thought, to the day he'd arrived, when it had just been her and Ewan Clark, the policeman. She looked for Ewan, over on the far end of the pier, almost involved in crowd control.

'But I cast a spell,' she had told Flora on the phone. 'I thought I could change his mind. Oh Flora. All the things I should have done. I should have let Jan tell everyone. Shout it from the rooftops. I should have forced his hand right from the beginning. Moved in. Taken the children, raised them. Insisted.'

Flora had sighed down the phone. 'Darling,' she said. 'Darling.'

'But what if?' Lorna had said, frantic. 'What if I could have changed things, Flora? What if I hadn't just waited like a ninny? What if I had made my move?'

'Darling. You couldn't, either of you. You wouldn't have been the decent, kind woman he fell in love with. He wouldn't have been the good man you know if he'd thrown his children's happiness to the winds like that. If you had both been selfish ... '

'We could have been together now,' said Lorna.

'You couldn't have been happy,' said Flora urgently. 'Believe it, Lorna. Believe it. You couldn't. Because you wouldn't have been the people you are.'

'And now I have to go down to the harbour ... '

'I know,' said Flora. 'I'll be there for you.'

Saif looked completely bemused and couldn't quite believe the fuss was all for him, but it was. The entire island had turned out to say goodbye. Few was the people he hadn't made feel better with careful diagnosis and a gentle manner. No one was ever made to feel they were wasting their time, or that, over the years, he didn't know them and care for them and their families. Any early suspicion had long faded into affection and fierce loyalty.

Lorna and Mrs Cook had all the children turned out from the school, of course. They had made a memory book for both the boys, and there were plans to organise a project with whatever school they attended, so they could set up a sister school. Mrs Cook was keen, Lorna less so and Ibrahim wasn't showing overt signs of desperation either.

There was a tear in the eye of some of the older ladies of the town, many of whom had felt strongly for the poor man who had lost his wife, as the pile of lasagnes that regularly accrued outside his house attested. The RNLI men all came down and hoisted their lifejackets in the air. There were more bags of tablet stuffed into the boys' pockets, and more tins of shortbread than could ever possibly be piled on top of the luggage they already had, but Saif did his best and thanked and shook hands with everyone. He was not terribly comfortable having to go around crowds of people, but it was expected and he was grateful at least to have something to occupy his thoughts.

Flora came down from the Seaside Kitchen, which was doing an absolutely roaring trade for eight a.m., just to be close to Lorna, who had absolutely no choice in the matter, and was staring out to sea as stoically as she could manage. Flora squeezed her hand gently. It was the hardest thing Lorna had ever had to do, to stand there, her throat choked up, and pretend to the children that this was all completely normal.

Saif was still shaking everyone's hand and thanking them deeply, meaning it, and when he got to Lorna he did exactly the same thing – offered the hand she knew as well as her own, clasped it briefly, but neither could look at the other, and she dropped it very quickly, which led Mrs Cook to believe that, in fact, she had been right, and the pair never had got on.

'Thank you,' he said humbly. 'For everything.'

Lorna wanted to speak, but found then that she couldn't. She managed only a tight nod and even that took everything that was in her.

There was a very long moment where she thought he was going to say something more, that he was going to throw everything in the air, turn around, change his mind, take her in his arms in front of the entire island – and so did he, and they stood, horrified, but then the ferry blew its horn and she gazed at him, stricken, and the moment had gone.

That's it then, thought Lorna as he moved on, terrified she

was about to let out a choking sob, and Flora gave him the biggest cuddle and a squeeze as if she could make up for it on Lorna's behalf, even though the squeeze had a crossness in it, which they both recognised.

'We're getting that gormless girl locum,' Flora said to him, annoyed. 'The one who keeps stitching her own hand together.'

'I'm sure she'll be very good,' said Saif in his gentle way.

'You've condemned us all to painful unnecessary deaths,' said Flora. 'I hope you're proud of yourself.'

Saif blinked and stood back.

'I am not proud of myself,' he said very quietly, and passed on.

'Here,' said Flora, handing coffee to Lorna, lending her an arm to keep her standing upright. 'Once he's gone, I am getting you good and drunk.'

Lorna still fixed her eyes on the horizon, refusing to watch him walk away.

'It's eight a.m. and I'm teaching school,' she finally managed with difficulty, still part convinced that at any second he was going to turn back – turn back, she urged with her mind. Turn back. It's not too late. Turn back. I made the spell. I bound you. Turn back!

'Yeah, just get them to put their heads down on their desks,' said Flora, trying to keep things cheerful, to hold up her friend as best she could as she watched his dark head move to the end of the line. Then there came a commotion and rather a lot of shouting.

'Agot,' she said grimly.

The ferry had started up its engines. Everyone else who was travelling that day was already on board. The ferry captain knew and liked Saif a great deal and was happy to let him say his goodbyes, but the tide was turning.

Agot was standing there, the wind whipping in her white hair.

'NO!' she was shouting, 'You are not going yet! *Chan eil thu a'dol fhathast!*'

And clinging to her was her best friend in all the world, Ash.

Saif stood at the foot of the gangplank, heart in his mouth, not knowing what to do.

'I don't want to go any more, *Abba*!' Ash was saying.

'He'll stay with us,' said Agot. 'You can come visit him. If you like. You don't have to.'

Saif's face was pained. He had not expected this and was in no mood for a scene and to have to prise the boy away in front of the entire island. Ib tutted loudly.

Saif came forwards and knelt down.

'But I would miss you so very much,' he said to Ash, whose eyes were enormous.

'I SAID you can come and visit him,' said Agot. 'We'll all be right here.'

'Every night I would think, where is Ash, and every day when Ib comes in from school and you won't be there and when we go ...' He had been about to say 'visit Mama' but couldn't, because the child looked so stricken. '... visit the gardens and the river I will spend all the time saying "Ash would love this".'

Ash looked up at his father, who held out his hand.

'And perhaps Agot can come visit us sometimes?'

'Have you got an ice rink?' said Agot rudely. 'If not, then no, I can't.'

'And you know you can speak to Agot and play Roblox and chat whenever you like. You can call every day.' At this Ash perked up.

'Every day? Can I play more than I play now?'

'Absolutely,' said Saif.

'Every day,' said Agot fiercely. 'It has to be every day because otherwise we couldn't be best friends. I am not saying this as a threat.'

The ferry blew its horn once more. People had trains to catch on the mainland; there were things to be done, produce to get to the expensive bars and restaurants of Edinburgh and London; the world to keep on turning.

'Every day,' said Ash, and they hugged fiercely, and Agot stood back with her arms folded, a gimlet look in her eye. One or two of the other children came forward to give Ash a last hug as well, but she wouldn't let them anywhere near him.

Saif led them towards the little gangway to the ship, Ib still looking uncomfortable and embarrassed even as, pushed by Mrs Cook, his classmates approached him and handed over something in a bag.

He eyed it carefully, then pulled it out, gasping. It was a ball signed by the players of his beloved Hibernian football team.

Ungiven to emotional outbursts, he couldn't help the broad grin spreading across his face, and his classmates all cheered and gave him high fives as he headed for the ship, and a particularly daring Lynette McGhie ran forwards and kissed him full on the mouth even though she said later she only did it for a dare, and everyone cheered and Ib got on the boat, clutching the ball to his chest, a smile lingering on his features.

Ash turned around at the last minute, as if realising something. Then he broke free of his father's hand and ran to Lorna – his teacher, the person who had taken him in, who had learned enough Arabic to help him, who had sat with him, day after day, teaching him the strange English sounds, and the strange shapes of the letters, who had never lost patience, had always been there for him, had been there, kind, patient, warm, day after difficult day.

Of course, there were many others – Neda, Flora in the café, Jan on the Outward Adventures, Agot's mother Eilidh who welcomed him in her home as her own, Mrs Laird – who had all stood in one way or another for the person he missed the most.

But it was Lorna he ran to.

'Bye, Miss Lorna!' he said. And she did the one thing she had never done; was not allowed to do with a single pupil in the school. She took him in her arms and hugged the breath out of him.

People waved for a long time at the figures on the top deck as they receded into the great blue breadth of the sea, unable to see Saif's face, which was staring ahead over the heads of the boys, who were holding his hands very, very tightly. Saif's jaw was set; he felt astounded.

He could not believe what he had just done. It took everything in him not to throw himself off the back of the boat, swim back to her, beg forgiveness, promise to never leave her again, not for a second, no, not once, to bury himself in the sweet scent of her hair, tell her he loved her, over and over again.

He picked up Ash to protect himself, let the boy sob into his neck; kept a strong grip on Ib who would not let his feelings show, but they ran so deep nonetheless. He clung on to them both for dear life, because if he could not do this for them, and for a woman who had lost her children, he could not do it at all.

Back at the harbour, the people on the beach turned round again and headed up to the Seaside Kitchen for perhaps just a little smattering of something before lunch. Flora looked at her friend, but Lorna had to take the children back to school, had to carry on, through this day, then another, then another. Until she could escape, grab Milou and walk herself up and down the Endless Beach, where she had first got to know him, when he was waiting for a boat to come in, a boat that had never come. Because she had thought he might turn around. Even as he got on the boat, she thought he might turn around. That the boat would turn around. That he would return.

Even though she knew that all that would happen was that the cold winds would blow, and the years would come and go, and the tides would come and go, from shore to distant shore.

Epilogue

September

It was a beautiful evening and as it was a Monday, so Flora was hosting a get-together, Monday being the chef's night off and their quietest night in the hotel especially after the entire summer had been crazy, absolutely bananas. It had been wildly busy on sunny days; it had been wildly busy on rainy days. They had had so many enquiries for weddings next year, Flora couldn't even look at them yet but she was feeling so happy nonetheless. And the pod had gone, back to their winter hunting grounds, without a single beaching or any more incidents, which was surely cause to celebrate.

Joel had his shoes off in the grass, still trying to persuade a very indolent-looking Douglas to walk. All the child's uncles were stationed carefully to catch him but he did not seem very interested.

'I think perhaps he's an idiot,' said Flora.

'Bad luck,' said Fintan. 'Mind you, hardly surprising.'

'No, it's good he's an idiot,' said Joel. 'Might mean he stays on the island.'

'OI!' they all shouted and pelted him with grass and napkins and whatever came to hand.

'Yes, yes, here it's so awful,' said Flora, leaning back and enjoying the rays of the early September sun. August had had its ups and downs but now the schools were back and most people had taken their summer holidays, you could rest assured the weather would turn absolutely perfect.

Gaspard turned up with something he wouldn't tell them until after they'd tried them were duck hearts, even as Flora told him to take time off and he frowned and said *évidemment* duck hearts were time off, and nuzzled Fintan on the top of the head, who smiled lazily and grabbed his arm. They appeared to be still together, Flora noted, more seriously than ever. Well. Konstantin and Isla were lying in the long grass; they had worked so hard this summer, they could do very little when they were off except collapse, which suited Isla very well, but the hotel was due to shut for a month and they were off to tour the fjords. Isla wasn't exactly sure what one wore to a fjord, but was looking forward to it nonetheless.

Lorna joined them for the first time in a very long while. Flora invited her to everything, but it had been so hard to get her out of the house, and she was monosyllabic in it. She wouldn't talk about anything; Flora was profoundly worried about her.

There had been no news from the Middle East, apart from occasional garbled messages back from Agot who was equally likely to announce that Ash was her friend, not theirs and it was none of their business. Ash had, though, seen his mother, that much she knew. Though how or in what circumstances, she had absolutely no idea. Lorna would not discuss it at all; would not even say his name.

'Come help me in the kitchen,' said Flora. She didn't know what was up, but she could feel her friend, enervated, slightly breathless beside her. Presumably she was after a large glass of wine.

'How are you?' she said. 'It's so good to see you out ...'

'What do you mean?' said Lorna.

'You've been lying with your face turned to the wall for three months and not answering the phone. Now you've turned up and you sound weird and, my darling, I am so worried about you and please, please, please tell me you're okay. We've all been so worried.'

This came out in a bit of a rush and Lorna looked at her, concerned that people had been so upset. She swallowed hard.

'I ... I think,' she said. 'I think ... something's happened.'

They looked at one another, and instinctively Lorna put a hand to her stomach.

'You aren't!'

'I don't know,' said Lorna. 'I can't bear to take the test. But ... I've skipped three periods, and ...'

She pulled a test out of her bag.

'Oh my God. Oh my God, Lorna. Are you going to tell him?'

Lorna shook her head fiercely.

'Of course not. He's been through enough ... and I don't even know yet ...'

Flora looked her up and down with a practised eye.

'Oh my God, your bangers are gigantic.'

Lorna blushed.

'Oh for God's sake.'

'I'm just saying, those are pregnancy barrage balloons if ever

I saw them. Look at those thick blue veins! I don't think we even have to do this.'

'Can we though?' said Lorna, clearly in agony.

Flora poured them each a glass of water.

'Yup! Neck this! It's going to take about nine seconds.'

It did not. It took what seemed like about an hour before Lorna finally emerged from the loo, her face so wan and broken Flora couldn't interpret the result at all until she wrested the stick out of her hand.

'Oh my God, Lorna. Oh my *God*!'

She hugged Lorna, who was in shock.

'Oh my God. You're pregnant! But ... you're not in touch at all?'

Lorna shook her head shortly as Flora sat her own and waited till her breathing calmed.

'It's not ... He has ... It's not right,' she said. 'He has a life there. And a wife. And a lot to do. He was ... he was only ever borrowed. And I can't ... I can't torture myself, every day thinking what he's doing now, what time it is there, thinking how he's living. I've done that, Flora. I did it for years. I did it from the moment he first set foot here. And I can't do it any more. And it's not good for him either. If Am— if his wife is there ... Then ... he has to sort that out. I can't ... '

'Yes, but,' said Flora, pointing to her – now you looked at it, obviously protruding – stomach. 'I mean, he deserves to know about this, doesn't he?'

Lorna swallowed.

'I ... We were always so careful.'

'Mmhmm ... '

'But then that last ... the night of your wedding?'

Flora's eyebrows shot up.

'A honeymoon baby!' she said, delighted.

Lorna half smiled. Then she shook her head.

'He can't have known. I can't, Flora. The man has already sacrificed everything for his children. He deserves ...' She sighed. '... to find some peace, I think. If he can.'

She looked at Flora.

'Do you think it's a bad idea?' she said.

'I gave up trying to predict what I thought about anything after Colton died,' said Flora. 'I think the only thing that matters is right now, because the future is absolutely bloody impossible, and you never get to the end anyway. I think maybe the only thing that matters is, are you happy?'

'I don't know,' said Lorna, 'if I am ever going to be happy. But this is ... as close to it as I can be. Right now.'

She caressed her stomach carefully.

Flora hugged her again, and they shared a moment of silence and deep understanding. Then Flora popped her head up.

'Oh my God,' she said. 'All those years of keeping it a secret and in ...' She counted up on her fingers. '... six months' time, you're going to have ... *please* let it be a tiny Saif. *Please*. OMG. Come on. Admit it. This is going to be a tiny bit *hilarious*.'

'Shut up,' said Lorna, but she was almost – *almost* – smiling.

'I mean it. I want him or her to be born with a full beard.'

'Shut up!'

'OMG, how Mrs Cook is going to gossip! She always fancied him, you know!'

'Stop it!'

'No wonder she always cast his children in the school plays.'

'Oh my God!'

Weirdly, Flora's teasing had the best of all effects on Lorna. After all the thinking, the pondering, the worrying, the heartache, hearing her best friend joke about it just as if she was a normal person, just as if everything would be fine, would be manageable, would be a laugh, even lifted some of the grave heaviness from deep inside her, made her heart blossom just a little.

'And you know,' said Flora quietly, 'it's not necessarily the end of everything. This child ... this child will be British. It might not be anything. But it might be something. One day.'

Lorna nodded, swallowing hard.

They took their cups of tea back towards the lawn, hearing cheering, because it looked like Douglas had finally, tentatively, taken his first few steps, straight into his father's arms, and, roused by the applause, was making plans to do it again to a loud '*Allez, allez!*' from Gaspard and a 'Gaun yerself, wee man!' from Innes and a 'Flora! *Flora!*' from Joel.

'Full beard. Severe aversion to prescribing antibiotics. Wears a tie ... OH MY GOD, IS MY CHILD WALKING?'

Flora tore down the steps to coax Douglas towards her arms.

'Oh my God! Look at you! You genius!'

'I think,' Joel was saying, 'we may have to put him in training for the Olympics.'

'Caber throwing,' said Innes. 'He's going to be a big 'un.'

'They don't have caber throwing at the Olympics, you divot,' said Fintan. 'I can't believe you don't know the difference between the Olympics and the Highland Games. OMG, you are *such* a farmer.'

'Shut up, cheese fiend! Also, *you're* the sports expert now? That'll be the day.'

'And,' added Flora, turning to Lorna in a low voice, 'you know how they say it takes a village to raise a child? Well, I'm afraid this is going to be it. The full village of morons all around you.'

Douglas wobbled on his tiny feet on the grass, and Lorna blinked back tears looking at them.

And, smiling, the girls – and Douglas – sat down on the grass in the golden evening under the bright washed sky of their tiny island.

Acknowledgements

Huge, huge thanks to Darcy Nicholson, Rosanna Forte, Joanna Kramer, Rachel Kahan, Deborah Schneider and Jo Unwin, all of whom read and turned this book around at lightning speed so we could get it into as many early reader hands as possible.

Again thanks as always – at Little, Brown: Lucy Malagoni, Charlie King, David Shelley, Hannah Wood, Gemma Shelley and Stephanie Melrose; at JULA, Donna Greaves, Milly Reilly, Nisha Bailey; at Curtis Brown, Jake Bosanquet-Smith, Kate Burton, Alexander Cochran and Matilda Ayris.

Scots Gaelic (pronounced *gah-lick*, and a different language from Irish Gaelic, pronounced *gay-lick*) carries on its struggle to stay alive and kicking in our Highlands and Islands; it is a language with the most elegant grammar imaginable, and vocabulary stickier than a treacle-covered beaver.

If you would like to learn a little more, the Duolingo Scots Gaelic course is excellent, particularly if you would like to learn how to say 'the Loch Ness monster is eating the haggis' (*Tha Niseag ag ithe an taigeis*).

And BBC nan Gàidheal, which you can tune into from anywhere in the world via the BBC Sounds app, plays the most beautiful traditional music, and that works in every language.

Once again, my dear friend's nephew, Luke Hoyer, age fifteen, killed in the Parkland school shooting of 2018, walks on Mure, with kind permission of his parents, Tom and Gena Hoyer.

Escape with
JENNY COLGAN

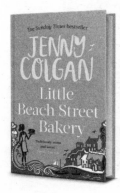

In a quaint seaside resort, where the air is rich with the smell of fresh buns and bread, a charming bakery holds the key to another world…

'Deliciously warm and sweet'
SOPHIE KINSELLA

Escape with
JENNY COLGAN

Escape to a remote little Scottish island and meet the charmingly eccentric residents of Mure…

'Charming, made me long to escape to Mure. Total joy'
SOPHIE KINSELLA

Escape with
JENNY COLGAN

Nestled amidst the gorgeous Scottish Highlands lies
a magical world of books and romance…

**'Gorgeous location, dancing dialogue and
characters you'll fall in love with. Irresistible!'**
JILL MANSELL

Escape with
JENNY COLGAN

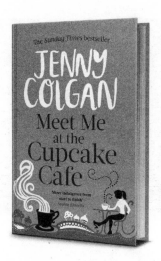
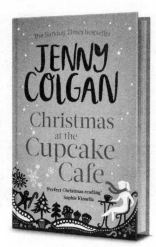

Meet Issy Randall, proud owner of the most enchanting café the world has ever seen, who is about to discover that running her own business isn't as easy as she thought…

'Sheer indulgence from start to finish'
SOPHIE KINSELLA

Escape with
JENNY COLGAN

In a delightful little sweet shop, pocket money jangles, paper bags rustle and, behind the many rows of jars, secret dreams lie in wait…

'An evocative sweet treat'
JOJO MOYES